ZEBRA BOOKS
KENSINGTON PUBLISHING CORP.

ZEBRA BOOKS

are published by

Kensington Publishing Corp.
475 Park Avenue South
New York, NY 10016

Copyright © 1985 by Karen Harper

All rights reserved. No part of this book may be reproduced in any form or by any means without the prior written consent of the Publisher, excepting brief quotes used in reviews.

First printing: October 1985

Printed in the United States of America

The fiery brilliance of the Zebra Hologram Heart which you see on the cover is created by "laser holography." This is the revolutionary process in which a powerful laser beam records light waves in diamond-like facets so tiny that 9,000,000 fit in a square inch. No print or photograph can match the vibrant colors and radiant glow of a hologram.

So look for the Zebra Hologram Heart whenever you buy a historical romance. It is a shimmering reflection of our guarantee that you'll find consistent quality between the covers!

"WHERE IS HOME?"

"Where the heart is," she shot back at him so flippantly, she instantly regretted her words.

"But since I met you, my dear little nameless betrothed, the question of where my heart is, is really becoming most difficult. Is it back at Moll King's, or in my carriage—or warm in that bed right there?"

She froze. In flickering firelight, his loose, tousled hair made his head look cast from bronze while his eyes gleamed glinting emerald. They stared silently across the narrow space from his chair to the bed until little flames leapt alive in his gaze, and she forced herself to look away. "Please take me home now," she thought she said, her words the merest satin whisper in her own ears, despite the alert readiness of all of her senses.

He stood. She watched his feet, his legs, and his hands as he came right up to the bed. "Too late for that, my sweet. Fate has thrown us together, and we both feel the impact of that." His voice vibrated through her as though he had already touched her as skillfully as she desired him to. "We both share this feeling, my sweet little mystery lady. Your topaz eyes have bewitched my very soul—"

She gasped a tiny, timeless breath as their lips met, hers as curious, as awed, and then as eager as his. Everything spiralled in to focus on him; everything was new. Never had she imagined a man, a stranger, could mesmerize her brain and body so. . . .

THE BESTSELLING ECSTASY SERIES
by Janelle Taylor

SAVAGE ECSTASY (824, $3.50)
It was like lightning striking, the first time the Indian brave Gray Eagle looked into the eyes of the beautiful young settler Alisha. And from the moment he saw her, he knew that he must possess her—and make her his slave!

DEFIANT ECSTASY (931, $3.50)
When Gray Eagle returned to Fort Pierre's gate with his hundred warriors behind him, Alisha's heart skipped a beat: Would Gray Eagle destroy her—or make his destiny her own?

FORBIDDEN ECSTASY (1014, $3.50)
Gray Eagle had promised Alisha his heart forever—nothing could keep him from her. But when Alisha woke to find her red-skinned lover gone, she felt abandoned and alone. Lost between two worlds, desperate and fearful of betrayal, Alisha, hungered for the return of her FORBIDDEN ECSTASY.

BRAZEN ECSTASY (1133, $3.50)
When Alisha is swept down a raging river and out of her savage brave's life, Gray Eagle must rescue his love again. But Alisha has no memory of him at all. And as she fights to recall a past love, another white slave woman in their camp is fighting for Gray Eagle.

TENDER ECSTACY (1212, $3.75)
Bright Arrow is committed to kill every white he sees—until he sets his eyes on ravishing Rebecca. And fate demands that he capture her, torment . . . and soar with her to the dizzying heights of TENDER ECSTASY.

STOLEN ECSTASY (1621, $3.95)
In this long-awaited sixth volume of the SAVAGE ECSTASY series, lovely Rebecca Kenny defies all for her true love, Bright Arrow. She fights with all her passion to be his lover—never his slave. Share in Rebecca and Bright Arrow's savage pleasure as they entwine in moments of STOLEN ECSTASY.

Available wherever paperbacks are sold, or order direct from the Publisher. Send cover price plus 50¢ per copy for mailing and handling to Zebra Books, Dept. 1717, 475 Park Avenue South, New York, N.Y. 10016. DO NOT SEND CASH.

To Anne,
who found Susannah Cibber
and helped me with her
elaborate costuming

How hard is the condition of our sex,
Through ev'ry state of life the slaves of men!
In all the dear, delightful days of youth
A rigid father dictates to our will,
And deals out pleasure with a scanty hand.
To his, the tyrant husband's reign succeeds,
Proud with opinion of superior reason
He holds domestic business and devotion
All we are capable to know, and shuts us,
Like cloistered idiots, from the world's acquaintance
And all the joys of freedom. Wherefore are we
Born with high souls but to assert ourselves,
Shake off this vile obedience they exact
And claim an equal empire o'er the world.

Susannah's lines as Calista
from *The Fair Penitent*
by Nicholas Rowe,
Act III, scene i.

Part One

"A single intrigue in love is as dull as a single plot in a play."

line from *Love Makes A Man*
by Colley Cibber

Chapter One

As the sound of silvered applause from the theater audience swept over and through her, sheer excitement shivered along Susannah Arne's spine and feathered deep into her very core. The wives of London's petty tradesmen and their broad-faced husbands clapped and cheered from their inexpensive middle gallery seats. Ladies, elegantly attired in the most stylish fashions of King George II's 1734 England, nodded their staid approval from the three tiers of elevated, luxurious boxes. The brocaded and bewigged dandies in the pit and those fops who had purchased seats along the sides of the stage winked or leered and roared their raucous praises at their "sweetest Susannah's" song. Even the ten musicians seated at her feet in the pit amidst the dandies tapped their string bows on their fiddles in encouragement, while her brother Tom simply gloated from his clavichord before charging into her exit music.

A smile of pure pleasure touched her soft lips, and the applause rose again like a rippling sea in response as she curtsied pertly and started off the stage. One portly fop who had paid a guinea extra for his stage seat to flaunt himself and his new chartreuse garb smelled so stiflingly of wig powder and snuff that she almost sneezed. He darted a lace-cuffed hand at her skirts as she made for the wings. "A bit of dinner later, pretty little thrush?" his clipped voice floated to her when she brushed past him. "You sent my filigreed bracelet back, lovey, and I meant for you to wear it on that satin arm, I daresay . . ." She did not even look back, and fortunately he was not brazen or sober enough to lurch to his feet and follow her offstage.

Susannah's father, Thomas Arne, stood in the wings watching her, sharp-faced and narrow-eyed as always, one thin shoulder barely pressed into a muslin-painted flat that awaited its turn to slide onstage along the floor and ceiling grooves to become part of the Forest of Arden.

"They love you, dearest, love you," her father said and his hands lifted jerkily to his new wig to be sure it was in place. "We've got London's theater folk where we want them now, all of us Arnes, I tell you." His taut mouth almost smiled. Under a long nose, pale blue eyes looked lit by wavering inner fires.

"I'm only doing little songs between acts, father, but at least it feels closer to acting than just singing in oratorios and Tom's little operettas," she responded as she glanced quickly at herself in the long mirror the tiring boy mechanically held up for any lady who darted offstage. She sent the lad away with a flick of her wrist and he went gladly, cradling the heavy framed mirror under one thin arm. She took a deep breath and broached her usual topic of late to her father.

"I'm happy they like my songs of course, father, but you know I still want to act. Did Mr Cibber say anything about it? Did you ask him if I could attend the rehearsals as you promised?"

She peered out across the stage now alive with sliding, olive-hued flats and green-coated stage attendants positioning paint bushes and wooden benches. More chandeliers descended over the forestage, and the whole forest scene glowed green and golden in her eyes.

"Susannah—" her father's voice came harshly to her. His thin hands on her silken shoulders, he turned her around. "I told you, my fine little lady—told you more 'n once—the key to Mr. Theo Cibber's heart and to his favors is up to you. He likes you, watches you all the time, and you give him naught but those infernal, pert little snubs of yours."

"That's not true. I work hard and well here for him and his company and I am kind to him, so—"

"Kind? Kind! A pretty word for what a man like that wants—a man who happens to be an influential theater manager on the rise in London and would like to take all us Arnes with him if you'd but unfrost a bit and bend those stiff, infernal whalebone stays of yours."

She pivoted her graceful auburn head, and her topaz eyes sought the stage again despite how firmly her father held her shoulders. "I don't wear whalebone stays, father, especially not when I sing. But I'd as soon wear them clear up to my ears as get close to Theo Cibber despite the fact his father's the great and lofty Colley Cibber of Drury Lane Theater fame and King George's poet laureate. I'm sure," she said more beseechingly as she turned her head back to her father and gently shrugged his hands off her shoulders, "that Theo Cibber and the London theater world will recognize my acting talents and Tom's musical genius too if we but get a chance to show them, and then you'll have two children to make the Arne family proud and well-to-do again."

Her father looked as if he would give her another lecture on the dire necessity of throwing herself at the bow-legged knees of the pompous Theo Cibber, but he only shook his head so sharply that his wig bobbed. Then he frowned and darted off into the dim canyon of muslin scene flats to one of his myriad self-imposed tasks.

Another between-the-acts performance—this time four

apparently boneless French acrobats—filled the stage while the change of scenery was completed. The audience shifted and talked, but applauded only sporadically now. They were much more restless than when she'd sung her two pastoral songs, both composed by her brother Tom Arne, a budding composer and self-taught musician whom Theo Cibber had also taken into his infamous group of actors defecting from the Drury Lane Theater Royal. The little rebellion had made all the important London papers—how Theo Cibber and his band of some of England's finest theatrical personalities had started their own theater company in protest of wretched treatment at Drury Lane. She admired the rebellion, if not the man. She ought to rebel too. Singing was fine and she loved it, the approval and adulation of the crowds being the only ecstasy she'd ever known. But she wanted to be out there on the boards with the great actresses, amusing the vibrant crowds with clever repartee in a sophisticated comedy or emoting in some great tragic role as real as life.

She jumped at the touch of another hand, this time on the small of her back. "My sweeting, Miss Susannah Maria Arne, standing in the wings watching the actresses again, eh? Egads, I wish you'd watch the theater manager only half as much as you stare at the actors. I would wager you know all their parts *par excellence* by now," the rough, high-pitched voice of Theophilus Cibber came to her ears to drown out the opening lines of dialogue.

"Mr. Cibber, you startled me," she said and forced a little smile. What had he just asked her, she thought. His ogling always annoyed her so she often had to force herself to focus on his words. "My father was just here and I really must go join him in the Green Room," she added in a rush.

"Not so quick," he shrilled, but when she glanced over her shoulder at the unfolding fourth act of Shakespeare's *As You Like It*, he lowered his voice. "Your father walked off a good five minutes afore and you've been standing here just dreaming again, I'd say, though for love of a bawd, I don't know how you manage to keep all the sparks and gallants swarming you at bay."

He took a step closer in the dimness of the wings and she could smell both snuff and whiskey on his heavy breath. Suddenly, there was nowhere to go but to push by him in these close quarters or dart back out onto the stage. Rampant chandelier light from the stage threw itself in distorted patterns across the man's face. Her narrowed eyes took in his squinting leer; his pointed, pitted face; his skewed nose; his full mouth. Looking at Theo Cibber she sometimes wondered how any woman could desire any man. Although she'd managed to keep her distance these past months while he'd pursued her, his small, darting frame had seemed to block out any other suitors. However rich or handsome the tiring room gallants, she wanted adoration from none of them; she passionately desired only to be allowed to act out there before the adoring audiences on the glowing stages of London.

"Susannah." His breath so close stirred the auburn curls tumbling along her slender throat.

"What?" she faltered, unsure of what he'd asked again. "Excuse me. I must go home. I'm to visit my aunt in Camden Town until Monday."

"Nonsense! It's barely seven now, and it won't be dark until nine. I said, I don't see how you keep the gallants at the tiring room doors and from the pit away. You see, sweeting, when you give me that lovely, elegant cold shoulder—it's your *métier*, my dear—it only spurs me on; but then I am no ordinary mortal to be put off with fluttering whims or chilled receptions—not I," he finished grandly as though he stood center stage and not in the dim wings.

"You see, Mr. Cibber—"

"Theo. Your father calls me Theo, and he and I are

best of friends. You know, when I take my little acting company home in triumph to the Drury Lane as I've been asked to do, I intend to benefit all the Arnes. Your father Thomas shall have some sweet sinecure like gatekeeper or seat numberer. Your ambitious brother Tom shall compose set pieces and maybe a masque or two—just songs for you to warble, of course."

"My brother Tom has wonderful talent, Mr.—Theo. He's worked with Handel—King George II's great composer—so surely Tom's genius will soon be recognized far and wide."

"Ah, to have such a lovely and loyal woman on his side *ad infinitum*," Theo intoned dramatically while his mouth grimaced in that characteristically disdainful way of his, topped by a quick eye squint for effect. "My dear, everyone knows the German genius Handel was quite seduced by your lovely, low voice and smitten by your slender, innocent beauty as was that audience out there tonight and, alas, even as I. Admit it, sweeting, your part in George Frideric Handel's oratorio *Deborah* last year, when you were but nineteen, and all those private voice lessons he so charitably gave you had naught to do with Tom Arne's fiddling or composing. For love of a bawd, I'd wager old Handel's fed up with Tom's silly claiming to be 'The Proprietor of English Opera' when he doesn't have so much as a published song to his credit. It was your voice Handel wanted and your voice he got."

"I don't appreciate your implications, Mr. Cibber. Let me pass, please. Good evening to you."

For once Theo Cibber didn't budge when she attempted to snub him. Her pulse began to beat low in annoyance and anger. Although her impoverished family profited handsomely from the bounty of his influence and favor, she'd brushed this gawking man off for months with not much more trouble than it took to keep the theater door lapwings away.

Then too, simply everyone believed the rumors to be true about Theo Cibber. His squints, grimaces, pock-marked face, and volatile fits of temper were but thin veneer over an inwardly profligate and libertine personality. His all-night wild forays into the bagnios and brothels of the nearby infamous Seven Dials and Covent Garden haunts were common knowledge among theater folk, and stamped Theo Cibber's daily lewd expressions and his swaying gait just as they did now.

His grip moved to her upper arms, taut fingers pressing through her short, ruffled yellow satin sleeves and pulling her deep-cut bodice so awry that his eyes nearly popped out as they lowered to survey the cleft between her high, firm breasts exposed by his movements.

"Let me say this very, very plain, my sweeting—then you just listen and think on it. I've tried to court you honorably and aboveboard like the gentleman I am. Oh yes, I know you've heard I started as a mere actor's apprentice years ago and that I am a widower some ten years older than you. Still, you can't claim social status or wealth either *per se*, my dear—not since old Tom Arne ruined his fame and fortune before I rescued him from this cockamamie attempt at staging your brother's operas. So, the Cibbers and Arnes are birds of a feather, you see Susannah, and like to be a good deal closer yet if you'd but unbend a bit."

Unbend a bit . . . the words rattled in her brain. Unfrost a bit and bend those stiff whalebone stays, her father had warned her. He'd been pushing her for months to be kind to Theo Cibber, even allow the man a few liberties—she, whom her parents had initially reared to be such a lady with her careful tutor's lessons in French, Latin, drawing, and music before the wolf of bankruptcy had knocked at the Arne household door.

"Well, my sweeting?" Theo was asking, his sharp brown eyes jumping from her annoyed face to her breasts once more before she dared to lift her hands to his blue-gray frock coat to shove him away.

"I thank you for your kindnesses and concern for the Arnes' benefit," she managed. "We are all, of course, grateful. Excuse me please, before something passes between us we shall regret."

He winked broadly and his hands hooked nervously on his waistcoat lapels while behind them on the stage the popular actress Mrs. Heron, dressed in boy's garb, played the lovely Rosalind. It was a part Susannah knew line by line in this act where Shakespeare's heroine traipsed after her lover in the Forest of Arden.

"I cannot possibly fathom, my dearest Susannah, that I could regret anything that passes between us," Theo retorted and snickered.

Although her brother said she had ice in her veins for anything but her passion to get on the stage, so that she never blushed, Susannah felt her face and neck go prickly hot. Drat this pushy, pompous little wretch! He and her father must be in league. Her salary was good for what she did—very good—and Theo would probably flaunt that at her too. Worse, he'd complain to father and she'd never hear the end of it. Thomas Arne would likely rescind his agreement to let her go by coach and visit her Aunt Emma for two days in nearby Camden Town. She'd never escape any of them and would stand eternally longing in the theater wings between her brief little songs, just waiting for a chance to try her hand at acting! But as badly as she wanted that chance, being intimate with Theo Cibber was too steep a price to pay.

He pressed hard against her as she tried to edge quickly by him. He seemed stronger than she'd imagined. They were exactly the same height at five feet four inches. His avid face shut out the theater; his hot breath stifled her; his tense body smothered her as he pressed against her breasts and belly.

"Loose me or I'll scream, Mr. Cibber!"

"I'm master here, my sweeting. I'll be incensed if you scream. Your father, bless his avaricious soul, would probably let me turn you over my knee *in loco parentis*," he added smugly.

"Loose me!" she hissed in a voice no one could term a stage whisper.

Surprised, he stepped back, but blocked her in so tightly with raised palms on the muslin flat behind that the whole slanted stack of scenery swayed and shifted.

"So lovely, so tempting Susannah, just barely out of reach. All right, I'll pay your price. I'm a businessman too and, holy hell, a damn good one to be sitting pretty here with this illegal theater group and be asked back to Drury Lane to boot."

"I want no price for anything. You pay me well for the little interlude songs I sing."

"I do know what you want. Who wouldn't, watching you mooning over the plays and actresses' parts as you do? I'll take you on Susannah, train you, put you in some small parts back at Drury Lane when we all return, plays I'm reviving to star in and can watch you closely in."

Although she detested the man, her heart thudded at his words. "You could speak to my father, as he manages our whole family," she heard herself say in a much too breathless voice. Her pride almost crumbled until his hands dropped to her waist and he spoke his next words so ludicrously low in her ear she almost laughed.

"No father, no family. I swear to you, my sweeting, I'll get you on the stage, make a great actress of you, but you will in return show me proper gratitude—*vis-à-vis*, alone—while we work together toward our common goal."

His face blurred and shifted close to hers before she could startle, laugh, or scream. His mouth descended, trapping hers; his wet tongue darted out to separate her lips. Furious, she raised both arms. An elbow struck his chin. He grunted and stepped back, half bouncing off the flat behind.

"Vixen!" he shot out low, fingering his chin where she'd hit him. In the candlelight his jeweled ring winked at her startled face. "Your father is convinced I'm such a fine match for you, naughty little girl, so we'll just see then."

"I'm sorry. You surprised me," she managed, taking two steps farther away into the depths of the wings. "I value my reputation greatly—I thought you knew—"

She turned and fled, grateful that she'd at least chosen a vantage point where no one would come upon them in their varied exits and entrances to the stage; but giving Theo private access to her in the dimness had been her mistake, after all.

She hurried past the Green Room with its cozy fire where the actors and actresses awaited their summons on stage by the darting callboys. She'd heard the others say it was not as grand a room as that at their Drury Lane Theater Royal, but they would make do for now. Soon they would all be heading back to Drury Lane since the feud had been settled and a new owner named Charles Fleetwood held the royal charter. Though the play on stage this evening would not be ended for a good hour, fashionable if bored young men who had paid an extra half guinea at the stage door were already clustering about the tiring rooms. Unfortunately, she recognized several who had tried to induce her to share a private dinner with them last week.

"Reg, look! Our own little songbird, Miss Arne!" One tall blond spark chortled and fell into quick step beside her. "Adored your shepherdess songs earlier this evening, Miss Arne, simply adored, and your eyes slayed me! Slayed me! I'd be your good, obedient sheep anytime you but crook your little finger, golden-eyed, sweet-throated songbird."

She shot him a quick look at the door to the stairs. She didn't need him traipsing after her, for she intended to wait in her brother Tom's small practice room until he came upstairs for his break. Susannah had already learned her lesson well today not to go off alone with avid, leering wretches.

She paused, one satin shoe poised on the first step, one hand lifted prettily to the door frame as if to playfully block the cad's way. Unfortunately, several other young faces she vaguely recognized pressed in behind this blond fop whose name she could not even recall.

"I'm so pleased you enjoyed my singing, gentlemen. I certainly hope I shall see your faces in the front row of the pit when I sing again a bit later. I can count on that, I dare hope."

"Indeed! Oh yes, Miss Arne, and then we'll come backstage after. Laws, but didn't know you sang later. I came last week and thought only the Frenchies that twist and turn their bodies like a bawd in love performed as the afterpiece!"

She smiled at the little group of vapid, half-glazed faces pressing close. How easy it was to pretend, she marvelled, to act something she did not feel: a fiction or a lie. Drat Theo Cibber, but that's another reason she just knew she could be a great actress if but given a chance!

"But if I do sing at the last tonight, I'd expect you all there in the audience," she said, pleased her gentle drawl sounded so much like the great actress Nancy Oldfield whom she had heard only once years ago at Bartholomew's Fair. "I really must run upstairs to see my father now just for a moment, then I'll be back, and when I sing again, I want to see you all there." She finished off the brief scene with an intentionally winsome smile, appealing gaze, and slight tilt of her head for effect.

She even allowed the one they called Reg to kiss her hand as they backed away with a flourish of plumed, tricorn hats and a chorus of "we'll be there" and "see you afterwards." They watched apparently awed as she turned away.

She went a short distance up the enclosed stairs and leaned against the wall for a moment. Another curtain down on another wholly imaginary scene. Such shenanigans, as her mother termed them, but that was the magic of the theater, a magic mere singing could never hope to conjure up. Here, she'd dispensed with those underfoot tiring room dandies and she had not the slightest chance of singing again tonight or the slightest whim to see them afterwards.

On the landing of the stairs, she nearly fell over Old Sam the candlesnuffer, sprawled out either asleep or stone-drunk. They'd need him downstairs soon enough at the play's close to gut the candles and urge everyone out, and if Theo Cibber knew he didn't show up again like last week, there'd be the piper to pay.

She leaned down and shook Sam's shoulder. Drunk! He stank of gin or cheap whiskey. "Sam! Sam, get up! The last act's almost begun. Get up and go on down in the wings."

"Mm! Pox on you! Cuss it! Lotsa time left!"

"No," she persisted gently. "Go down nor or Mr. Cibber will be furious. You can't always expect the musicians to wake you when they come up after they're done."

One slit eye opened in the wrinkled face half covered with a wig shoved away. "Oh, Miss Arne. Oh. Didn't know it was you, a real ladylike or I wouldn't a cussed." He half sat up, reminding her of a nearly shapeless sack of turnips tossed aside at Covent Garden market. "Mm, I'll go on down if'n you say so. You're not like them others, not like your nasty brother neither what pushed me down the steps to get me up an' broke my last pipe."

"Tom did that? I'm certain he didn't mean to. Best go on down then. You know Mr. Cibber won't take you along back to Drury Lane if you don't work hard here."

"Mm," he moaned as turnip sack rose to become a crooked, boney scare-the-crows. "Theo Cibber nor his sire never did nothing for nobody what they didn't have their own good interests in mind. I know'd 'em a long time, both of 'em. I don't plan to be taken along to no Drury Lane, no way. Theo Cibber'll leave me here to rot with this place and not give a tinker's damn 'bout no one."

He went slowly and unsteadily down the narrow stairs, leaning heavily first on one wall and then the other as if he strode the decks of a vessel pitching in gale-force winds. Strangely, it was then that the plan to rid herself of Theo Cibber's attentions popped full blown into her head.

On the stage below two actresses masqueraded in boy's clothes and cleverly got what they most desired that way. This wretch, Old Sam, was in desperate straights as she, but he had no recourse to protect himself against Theo Cibber's whims. After all, she'd grown up on King Street, a mere stone's throw from the places Theo was rumored to haunt every night—all night. Disguised as a boy whom no one would bother, she'd find her way there long enough to spy on Theo and then tell her father where to inquire about the reputation of the man he so admired.

It was crazy and dangerous, but surely she could make it work. Hadn't she easily tricked those fops downstairs into doing exactly what she wanted? If Susannah were ever to prove herself the actress she knew she could be, this evening's venture would be a mere lark. When Tom came up she'd simply ask him for his advice to discern if there were any other way. If not, she could pull it off and laugh about it later when she finally had her evidence to make Theo Cibber's lecherous advances and her father's proddings a thing of the past.

Men! Her sharp, single laugh echoed briefly in the empty candle-lit upstairs hallway as she went into her brother's little practice room to await the end of the play.

When the steward went to answer the door of the great Sloper mansion on St. James's Square in London, several other servants dashed along in his wake. The persistent, frenzied rapping permeated this vast, silent house in one of the city's most staid, stylish neighborhoods. From his spacious suite of rooms upstairs, Will Sloper, the twenty-seven-year-old son of the old master of the house rose from his brandy and book and went to the top of the curved oaken staircase in his dressing gown over breeches and shirt. When he heard a woman's pleading, shrill voice below, he hurried down.

"Temple, is there a problem?" he asked.

Martin Temple, who was the dour-faced head steward of Sloper House, three other servants, and the cloaked female visitor all turned at once to gaze up at the tall, imposing young master as he came down the staircase. The fashionable world of London knew Will Sloper by the sobriquet "Tenn" because a major part of his considerable reputation in town was that of the premier tennis champion of landed gentility, which was the backbone of German-born King George II's Whig power base in the land. His height of just over six feet, powerful athlete's body, striking coppery hair, handsome chiselled features, and deep voice seemed to freeze the five people crowded near the open door for an instant.

"Ah, no sir, no problem," Temple's voice rose at last and one of the maids shuffled her feet. "A lady insists on seeing you, sir, a lady from near your home at Berkshire, I take it. May I present from Berks, Lady Amanda Newbury."

The woman who had stood silent and staring from beneath the dim cavern of her ruffled hood, swept it back and stepped forward suddenly. The servants fell away; one gasped. Amanda Newbury was strikingly lovely, and tears streamed down her painted pink cheeks from her brimming eyes.

"Tenn—Squire Sloper, please may I speak with you in private? I am in dire need of help, you see—"

In great long-legged strides, Tenn Sloper almost reached her across the shiny black and white tile of the foyer when she lifted a lace handkerchief to her flushed face and swayed forward. She seemed to pull away from Temple's stabilizing touch on her elbow and fell perfectly against Tenn Sloper's broad chest.

"Shall we send for the master's physician, sir?" Temple shot out.

"Oh, she's all right, isn't she then?" a woman's voice came to Tenn.

"But who is she, Squire? She came all the way from Berks alone?" someone else asked

"Calm down, everyone. It seems she's just fainted." Tenn lifted her, fully aware the apparently helpless damsel he held so easily in his arms had not really fainted. One of her slender kid-gloved hands curled possessively around his forearm; the other rested across the small of his back to help steady herself. Her curly blond head nestled snugly against the hard muscles of his shoulder.

Temple hurried ahead to open the drawing room door, light candelabra about the elegantly appointed room, and start a coal fire in the grate while Tenn followed and carefully deposited his armful upon the blue-upholstered settee.

"Is she having an attack of the vapors then, sir?" Temple was back, bending over her. "I really must inform Master Sloper, don't you think?"

At that, Amanda Newbury managed to open both eyes and dab at them. "No, thank you. That's not necessary, really. I'm better now—just a bit weak after the journey and all the worry. I must speak with you, Tenn Sloper, not your father, and privily, if you please."

Tenn towered over her now without them touching. She had to lie back nearly full-length on the settee to take him all in. He was even better than she remembered—tall, angular, and powerfully built with a raw, masculine impact neither genteel manners, elegant clothes, nor a mysterious past could disguise. His green eyes always burned right through her even when he seemed not to really see her. She wet her pink lips with the tip of her tongue as Tenn dismissed his man named Temple and the others still hovering at the door.

"Amanda," he said so low it sent shivers up her backbone, "I thought you understood what I said at West Woodhay when I left, and then you turn up suddenly and mysteriously like this."

"Heavens, I expected more of a gentlemanly welcome for a lady in distress," she began in a whisper and fluttered a hand across her eyes. It annoyed her that he evidently felt no need to further comfort her, but rather leaned his narrow hips against a heavy wooden table at the foot of the settee and folded his arms almost ominously.

"I've seen you in distress before, Amanda," he said slowly, "and I believe since I made myself very clear about your forays to see me at West Woodhay . . ."

"But this isn't West Woodhay—it's London! And I only came to see you because I'm desperate for help and absolutely couldn't think whom else to ask, so don't pride yourself I'm really here to see you." She sat up with her back against the brocaded arm of the settee and smoothed her ruffled skirts over her knees.

Damn this handsome devil, she fumed silently. Did he indeed have ice water in his veins? He hardly batted a jade-green eye at her carefully selected cloak she let fall away from her low-cut shrimp-pink gown, her silk-stockinged trim ankles he'd obviously just seen, or her apparent discomposure!

"I'm sorry I acted so brusque then, Amanda," he told her quietly. "I shall summon my father and together the Slopers are at your service to aid you in whatever desperate plight you face."

She darted off the settee at that, a little too adeptly, he mused. Then she came closer. She really had been crying and he felt a twinge at his own callous behavior, but he thought he had stopped the spoiled if lovely Lady Amanda Newbury's disconcerting habit of throwing herself at his feet in dramatic attempts to seduce him. He decided that she looked like some cheap actress as his eyes swept her face noting each feature highlighted by skillfully applied cosmetics. Her delicate pink-ruffled gown and cape, her dishevelled stance, and her delicate posture were all magically arranged like the few times someone had dragged him to see the talented actresses on London's varied, garish stages.

"No, Tenn, please don't summon Squire Sloper," she went on. "This—well, this is embarrassing and I can trust you. Besides, everyone knows he's awfully busy with everything."

"And I'm not?" he queried as one copper eyebrow lifted in that terribly disturbing way of his.

Damn this villain, but it was impossible to read his thoughts, unlike most of the men she'd desired since her dear old husband had left her a rich Berkshire widow over two years ago.

"Of course, I didn't mean that, but I must say West Woodhay could use you this March with lamb shearing coming up and all," she ventured.

"I'll be back in a few weeks, Amanda. I always divide myself between the Sloper concerns in London and the estates in spring and summer. Now tell me your desperate plight if I might be of service."

"My young cousin Amanda—you know, the one you met last autumn at the ball—the one named for me . . ."

"I remember her vaguely."

"I swear, Tenn Sloper, you remember all women only vaguely. She's missing."

"Missing? Meaning what? My dear Amanda, how can I possibly aid you? Let's hear it bluntly now before we have the servants all atwitter over the mysterious lady who fell into my arms in the front hall and then asked to see me privily behind a closed door."

"I didn't think gossip would faze you one little bit."

"It doesn't if I think there's some basis of fact to it."

"What?"

"Amanda, what about your cousin? Missing how?"

"I'm sure she's either run off or been abducted, and I believe she's come here to London. She could be in dreadful peril, held prisoner or worse; heavens, I don't know."

His jade eyes studied her face so thoroughly that she shuddered with a sensual desire to brazenly disrobe for him, but his square chin and high cheekbones, his straight nose and taut lips made her feel deliciously afraid. Still, she dared a step closer so that her shrimp pink satin skirt hems rustled against his feet and ankles.

He had obviously been at leisure, for he wore a brocaded dressing gown over his breeches and a stark white silk shirt. The shirt was enticingly open slightly at the neck with no cravat to reveal an abundance of copper curly chest hair, which complemented the strikingly deep bronze color of the dishevelled full head of hair he had pulled back in a short black tie at the base of his strong neck.

"I'll tell you the rest of it about Amanda, but it's not pretty. Still, Tenn, I know the Newbury family's reputation will be safe with you. Amanda was—ah—compromised by a man she met last month at the Greenwood's house—a man who's a cheap spark, a rake, and a gambler, and is said to inhabit some of those wretched bagnios and hummums of Covent Gardens here in London!" she finished in a rush.

"His name?"

"I swear, how can you be so calm, Tenn Sloper? He called himself Jackson Milner. Don't you see, she's probably come to London with him and perhaps been deserted or worse! She was such an innocent, you see, and I'd just perish to think of what could happen to her if he takes her to any of those terrible places he inhabits." Her blue eyes filled with tears and she bit her full lower lip.

"He told you he inhabited such places?"

"No, Amanda did—before I knew she was seeing him in private. Tenn, please, I would be forever grateful if you could just inquire at those places to see if she's there."

"I don't know how much you know about 'those places,' Amanda, but straightforward inquiry would do no good. Hellholes such as The Rose Tavern or Tavistock Row are hardly going to admit they have a certain country girl servicing customers, willing or not."

"Willing? Oh, but she wouldn't be—not willing! And everyone knows if I just told those watchmen they call Charleys around the area, it would never help to find her as they have enough to do just keeping order in the streets."

She folded her hands in a beseeching pose and stepped even closer. "Please, Tenn, I know I can trust you to find out if she's there somewhere. I've come to stay with a friend just two streets away from here. You could call on me there—Squire Epworth's on Charles Street. I know you Slopers have good connections. I'm sorry I came here so distraught, but on the way over in the Epworths' carriage, I just kept thinking what I'd heard about the terrible practices and all the aberrations that go on in London's worst haunts in Covent Gardens, and poor Amanda—"

She dared to lean against him, her face carefully turned

away to rest on the left lapel of his green brocade dressing gown, one hand raised to dab her eyes. She held her breath for one moment as he moved toward her, against her. His hard thighs pressed into her skirts; his huge hands that all West Woodhay knew could ride a horse, design a building, shear a sheep, or hold a tennis racquet with equal skill went firmly against her pliant back. But he stood her away, then sat her back on the settee and strode to the door.

"I will inquire after your cousin Amanda and send you word if I find out aught," he told her almost grimly with his hand on the door. "And I shall send a maid in here with tea while you compose yourself. Our carriage will deliver you to Charles Street should Squire Epworth's driver have misunderstood and driven off to leave you here as it sounded earlier."

"Oh, yes. I thank you. I shall be most anxious to have you visit or I can call here to hear what you've learned."

"No. I said, I shall see to it." He paused at the door and turned back to take in her all too obviously disappointed expression at his controlled desertion of her when she'd done her best for an appealing performance.

"Amanda Brompton, was that not her whole name?" he asked. "Auburn hair, freckles across the bridge of her slender nose, light brown eyes. She was an inch or two taller than you, about as fully built." He saw Amanda Newbury's jaw drop but he plunged on. "Her voice was low—quite musical—and she was appealingly shy and modest; I remember I appreciated that. I will send a carriage for you after tea, Amanda. Try not to worry."

He quietly closed the door on an expression he would have to term somewhere between surprise and rage and went quickly upstairs to his father's rooms. He knew Amanda had not concocted the whole thing like some fancy stage drama; even she was not fully capable of that. But how much the minx worried over her poor runaway cousin, or anyone except herself for that matter, was a wager he'd be willing to take.

He knocked once on his father's carved oaken door and opened it. The tall white-haired man sat at his desk literally up to his brocaded elbows in stacked books and loose papers.

"Tenn, come in. What the hell was all that ruckus? I would have gone down, but I heard your voice below and knew all was well."

"A lady apparently in distress, Father, in need of an errant knight, and evidently I'm errant enough to fit her needs."

"Hell's gates, a lady?" Will Sloper, Senior said as he looked over a stack of maps at his son. "Someone to make you forget the sad past at last, my boy?" Their green eyes held, and the inheritance of the son from the father was evident not only in the unusual hue of emerald eyes, but in the set of square, determined jaw, the high cheekbones, and the straight nose. If Will Sloper's hair had still been burnished bronze, each would indeed be the physical replica of the other.

"Hardly, Father," Tenn said. "I told you, I don't ever look for that. No, the lady downstairs is poor dead Squire Newbury's *femme fatale* on the loose."

"Oh, her again," Will Sloper said brusquely and removed his wire-rimmed reading spectacles to study his son. "What in the whole realm of the king's England does *she* want?"

"She thinks a cousin of hers may be here held unwillingly in town in a place not healthy for ladies to be so I told her I would check for her."

"I see."

"No Father, I'm not sure you do. I could hardly turn down a plea like that from one of our neighbors at home in Berks. I do not intend to get entangled with Amanda Newbury or any other woman. One female disaster is enough for a lifetime. I just wanted to tell you I'll be going out soon and not to worry."

"Worry? About you? At age twenty-seven, you've been taking care of yourself for longer than I'd like to remember. Anyone who can teach our foul-mouthed, fat Prime Minister Walpole to play tennis one day, and get appointed the youngest member of The Commission of Trade and Plantation for the American Colonies the next by Walpole's enemies in Parliament, is certainly able to recover a lost wench in London."

Tenn marvelled with pride at the admiration and trust between them, spoken and unspoken, that was always there. Through the best of times, when they'd worked side by side to make West Woodhay a model rural village and manor and in their mutually loved sporting, their iron-clad respect endured. Even through his catastrophic marriage to Catherine, whom he'd wed to fulfill his mother's deathbed wish almost ten years ago, his father's love was the one steadying constant in his life. Real love with a woman was something Tenn Sloper could not even fathom anymore. Women were for assuaging one's needs, and not for loving. They were temporarily amusing at times, but more often a strain on one's reputation and even temper, just like Amanda Newbury and her stupid lost little cousin.

Tenn's big head jerked up to find his father still studying him. He'd been staring into a candle and sitting like a dolt; who knew how long since his father had said those last words? He stood, suddenly self-conscious as his father had read his most private thoughts of loneliness.

"See you tomorrow then, Father."

"Tenn, you will take George along in case you have to go someplace a little awkward, won't you?"

The taut corners of Tenn's mouth quirked up in a wry, boyish grin. "Of course. I'm taking George and the carriage. The men will probably like where I'm headed."

He closed the door quietly and went down the long, carpeted hall. Trust and mutual admiration—why was that so impossible for a woman and so possible between men? At least this little venture would be an education, as he didn't usually visit the lewd haunts of Covent Gardens where so many of the more jaded young men he knew spent money and time in riotous debauchery. Nothing worthy could ever come of those places. Just give him his work on the manor or in London, his friends, his race horses and sports, and a good, uncomplicated night's sleep.

Women! His rumbling deep laugh echoed briefly in the portrait-studded upstairs hallway as he went to the back stairs to summon his coach driver George.

Chapter Two

Susannah heard her brother in the hall singing one of his own tunes. The door swung inward. His agile fingertips drummed the beat of the melody on the wooden fiddle carried under his arm. The lofty forehead over his long nose lifted even higher when he saw Susannah standing in her stage dress silhouetted by the single narrow window of his cluttered practice room. One arched brow shot up, and he did not smile.

"Susannah, I thought father had probably packed you off for Aunt Emma's when I didn't see you in the Green Room. There are some baby-faced sparks down there looking for you."

"Oh, them," she said. There was a little pause while his hazel eyes studied her. "About father," she changed the subject adeptly, "he said earlier you could drop me by sedan chair at the inn to get the coach. My things are ready downstairs."

Tom placed his bow on his music stand and, still cradling his fiddle, slumped in the single straight-backed chair. "Can't help you unless you hurry, Susannah, or else His Majesty, Thomas Arne, Senior, will have to take care of you. I'm headed to a little concert at Cecilia Young's house on Villiers Street, then probably to make the rounds with my friends Festig and Lamp."

"The rounds?" Susannah repeated. "I don't mean to pry, Tommy, but have you ever been somewhere like the places you said Theo Cibber goes—you know, somewhere around Covent Gardens?"

His intent expression crushed to a fleeting frown. His right foot lightly thumped the floor to echo one of the mental melodies he always carried about in his fertile brain. "Theo?" he drawled and laughed in counterpoint to his foot rhythm. "Well, lookee here, the pert Miss Susannah does care and she's going to please His Majesty by going soft on Theo Cibber after all!"

"I am not! And stop calling father 'His Majesty' all the time."

"When you stop calling me Tommy," he shot at her, and his bemused expression turned boyishly taunting as she had often seen it over the years. "Tommy this, Tommy that," he gibed. "A pox on it, Susannah. You talk to me like I'm mother's little boy yet, and I haven't been that—well, ever since you were born and she got suddenly so damn busy."

Susannah stared agape at his strangely contorted face. Her brother was so dear to her, but when he turned all tense and bitter like this, he frightened and annoyed her. She regretted coming here for help, for any sort of comfort or advice.

"I'm sorry, Tom. I didn't know it upset you so much. And you surely realize mother has not been too busy for you. Why, even now she loves to hear your tunes played and says—"

"I don't want to talk about it. She's busy, all right—too busy with going here and there at all hours to care for other people's children as well as her dear little Henry Peter, our own baby brother."

"Drat it, Tom, you're twenty-three, and with the family's financial problems, it's fortunate for us she can still be a midwife to help people and earn money!"

"I said, we won't discuss it. Now, what about Theo? Has father sugared you up on him and you're conducting a little survey about his reputation before you take the plunge in the vast, rough sea of love?"

"That's hardly humorous. Actually, I thought if father knew for certain what Theo Cibber was really like, he'd forgo his insistence I be kinder to him. I thought maybe you could help. The rumors about Theo's nightly excursions and the way he looks in the mornings at rehearsals and such—I thought you could tell father or at least tell me what you know about places he might have been."

The tall, lanky man jumped to his feet and began to pace around his music stand and chair while his restless fingers beat a feverish tattoo on his brocaded arm. He alternately glared at her, then darted swift looks away as he spoke.

"Pure foolishness, Susannah. I'm a paid musician and composer here and hardly enough of the latter. In short, I'm retained to write music for Theo Cibber, not to spy on him."

"I didn't mean to imply that."

"Besides if I attest to any sinister places the man inhabits, where does that put me with our employer of His Majesty Tom Arne, Senior? Oh, no. As I said, I'm heading for Cecilia's and then to a reputable coffeehouse with my friends, but first I'll put you in a sedan chair. Come on. Let's go down and get your valise. It's a poxy miracle you obtained royal permission to get out from under His Gracious Majesty's nose clear to Camden Town for two whole days."

Susannah held her ground, hands on hips. "Tom, please, I detest Theo Cibber. I've told you that before, but I don't want to make him angry either. It's not at all like how you really feel for Cecilia Young."

"Oh ho," he chortled and came toward her to beat his

finger on the back of his wooden chair. "Do enlighten me, Susannah; how do I really feel about Cecilia Young?"

"You loved her at first sight, of course."

"Of course, of course." His voice dripped sarcasm now, and she had the nearly overwhelming urge to throw the flute perched on the rickety table under the window at him.

"Tom, what ails you tonight? You told me even last year that you wanted Cecilia the minute you saw her."

"*Wanted*, silly goose girl, not loved! This world is not one of your foolish, romantic stage comedies or ludicrous melodramas, and you'd best learn that fast. Pox on it, you're twenty now and had better recognize the difference between love, whatever that is, and merely wanting. I love music, I want Cecilia—at least I want that golden voice of hers that Handel covets as much as I do. Just like Handel covets your voice, speaking of which . . . you know, sister, perhaps that's what Theo really wants from you. Still, considering the fact his eyes tend to cling to other places on your sweet person besides your throat and lips, I doubt it, that's all."

"I detest you sometimes. You're worse than the rakes in the pit, Tom, I vow you are."

"Look, my girl, it's late. It will be dark soon. A pox on the rakes in the pit, on Theo's dubious habits, on your scolding me, and a pox on your trying to make me feel guilty like mother does. Now, I'm either going to put you in a sedan chair or let father do it."

"All right, I'll go. There's no reasoning with you. I should have known you'd get on your high horse over it. I just want all of us Arnes to be friends—and happy."

His sharp features softened and he actually threw a careless arm around her shoulders as he pulled her gently toward the door. "I know, I know. Poor little Susannah, the family peacemaker who always wants everything in the world to be goodness and light. But I know you're ambitious too; after all, our bandy-legged friend Cibber could give you the chance you want to act and help us all to further ourselves even more than we already have under him." He cleared his throat awkwardly at his last choice of words.

"I know," she said and then sighed.

He shrugged his narrow shoulders as though she had argued with him further, and his eyes drifted back to the half-finished music he evidently had been composing on the stand. "Why not Theo for you?" he added suddenly. "He's even promised to put Henry Peter on the stage in children's parts. Then mother and father would have their precious little thirteen-year-old earning a living on the boards too. Think about it, my dear, that's all. You're the family's good mentor, our angel—always have been. Just think about it."

She had thought about it, and Tom's sudden honeyed and wheedling tone aside, she decided what she must do. She must rid herself of Theo, not capitulate to him whatever anyone advised.

In twenty minutes she had let Tom send her off in a sedan chair and allowed her chairmen to carry her a few streets away before she had bid them take her back. It was already graying dusk, and she had little time to waste. The evening audience and performers had mostly scattered; the alley door to the theater creaked ominously after she paid the chair bearers and slipped back into the theater. The invigorating scent of sawdust, painted muslin, and a thousand other mingled aromas made her nostrils flare with excitement as always.

The muted laughter of both men and women floated to her. Hefting her valise, she lifted the huge tallow candle by the door and went unhesitatingly down the steps to the common wardrobe room. The seamstress and tiring boys would now be finished for the night. She knew where everything was, even which court personality had originally donated which costume, and what actress had worn the garb before it was delegated to common usage from her sumptuous personal wardrobe locked in an upstairs private tiring room.

She secreted her valise behind a jumbled pile of dingy-looking Roman armor. She'd be back for it in an hour and would arrive at the inn with plenty of time to catch the last coach to Camden Town, a short first stop on the transportation lines due northward. She only needed to follow Theo when he strolled away with some of the rich patrons he cultivated. No one would note a mere boy tagging a distance behind for a little while and hurrying back before dark.

If she were clever and careful and acted her part well, she would be fully prepared to face her father, her brother, or anyone else who suggested Theo Cibber was a worthy suitor. She'd simply say one of the tiring room lapwings had mentioned Theo Cibber visited a certain lewd establishment on a certain street and let them check on it further to find the full extent of the man's all too obvious habits of debauchery.

The candle flickered shapes and shadows over the lines of solemn, musty wigs on wooden stands, and glinted dully on dented shields and blunted swords. The celebrated Elizabeth Bowman had worn this wrinkled deep-blue velvet gown in many parts, and these brown breeches had once been the touted property of Lavinia Fenton who'd been fortunate enough to catch the Duke of Bolton's eye early in her promising stage career. If only father wanted her to go on the boards to find someone rich and handsome like that instead of that wretch Theo Cibber, Susannah mused. She quickly stripped off and hid her blue cloak and yellow silk bodice and skirts and pulled on the breeches over a man's pale blue linen shirt entirely too large for her.

"It's fine," she whispered aloud as if to buck herself up.

"You've got to act the part of low-class lad, so no footpads will be foolish enough to demand your purse."

Her long, luxuriant chestnut tresses bound up under her low-brimmed hat, her feet thrust in old buckle shoes and moth-eaten gartered trunk hose, she was out the back alley door in ten minutes. She lingered in the shadows between the theater and the next door millinery shop, strangely exhilarated, just the way she knew she would feel before she stepped out boldly on the stage to seize her fabulous future.

It seemed barely a moment before Theo Cibber emerged from the front door of the Little Haymarket Theater with just one other man. Despite the thickening dusk, Susannah instantly recognized Theo's portly companion Charles Fleetwood, the new Drury Lane Theater owner who had invited Theo and his defected "Comedians of His Majesty's Revels" home. Charles was a man with little stage experience but a great deal of money and, therefore, exactly the sort of partner Theo Cibber needed.

Susannah's pulse quickened as the men set off at a good pace toward Covent Garden. Everything was perfect, she gloated silently, as the two dandies started up St. Martin's Lane and cut down New Row. Surely, they would turn on King Street and go directly by her family's house. It was not yet dark. She knew the area, she had a plan, and everything was carefully plotted as if it were a play she had written. In her excitement and the damp March chill, gooseflesh caressed her skin and her nipples pointed taut against her silk camisole under the thin man's shirt and loose linen vest.

Too near the narrow, three-storied brick Arne house on King Street, the two men shared a laugh and a drink from a small hip flask. Susannah stepped into the deeper shadows, but they appeared not to glance back. Perhaps, she thought, Theo was telling Fleetwood the house was hers for she caught the words "a sweet little filly all ready for the trot" before they started on again. Though she'd heard Fleetwood kept racehorses, their ribald laugh hardly suggested Theo referred to that.

Yes, that was something both ludicrous and degrading like Theo would say. She darted a look at the only home she had ever known on this street of tradesmen, a neighborhood gone more ragged each year since Queen Anne's reign. Two second-story windows shed wan light over the frayed and faded "Two Crowns and Cushions" sign which still advertised the now defunct upholsterer and undertaker's trade her father had run before bankruptcy crushed the family's hopes that Tom would be a university-trained barrister and she a fine lady. If mother or young Henry Peter should glance out to see the slim boy hurrying by their house in the deepening evening, they would never realize it was their own proper and prim Susannah.

The air became alive with movement as she hastened to keep up with her quarry at the fringes of the big market square called Covent Garden. Because it was Saturday and the shops stayed open longer, the vegetable merchants were just closing their stalls or trundling off what they had not sold in carts or barrows; only now the square began to burgeon with drifters and the after-theater crowds of rakes, beggars, bawds, and fops.

The taverns, coffeehouses, inns, the disreputable whorehouses masquerading as the bathhouses called bagnios and hummums, pressed into the market square on all sides as if to squelch the once elegant grandeur of home and church of an earlier era. St. Paul's Church, with its vast portico and heavy columns, hunkered over the southwest end of the square, its roof gilded an eerie red by the last rays of setting sun behind it. From the fine neighborhoods of London, from outlying rural areas, and from the stews of the infamous Seven Dials District to the immediate north, myriad bustling Londoners converged on Covent

Garden.

Susannah, her tricorn hat pulled low across her face, hurried closer to Theo and Charles Fleetwood. Market porters with tall, mostly empty piles of wicker baskets balanced on their heads darted erratically through the throng after closing their cluttered shops and stalls in the various arcades. The Punch and Judy shows, the auctioneers on boxes, were stilled now; but in the gray passage from day to night, the scene quickened like the awesome shift of new settings behind some great, unlifting curtain.

Theo and Fleetwood seemed to be arguing about which establishment to visit, for their voices were raised in the cacophony, and each man pointed his silver walking stick at a different place. They moved away again, and Susannah edged even closer. She needed to actually see them enter somewhere besides just one of the numerous coffeehouses—a bagnio or a tavern she'd heard rumors about, at least. She ducked back behind a man standing on a wooden box as the two men halted for snuff.

"Get them here, my fine dandies, my Adonises," a sharp voice nearly over her head separated itself from the jumble of vendors' cries. "Dr. Rock's turpentine pills here for protection from the French pox. Here it is, take a peek before you buy—for your doxy or your favorite bawd at Moll King's across the way—the newest in the leather device. Come on, come on. Protect yourself, protect your purse and fortune from unwanted bawds with babes in arms they says is yours. You boy, get out of the way or put up!"

The rapid patter of words tumbled right over Susannah until she saw the man who called himself Dr. Rock pointing at her. She darted back only to bump into a gaunt flower girl who had violets and daisies as well as a frayed basket stuffed with torn cabbage, limp turnips, and a green cauliflower. Susannah bounced off her and hurried away. It was only then she realized she was hungry as well as chilled, and that Theo and Fleetwood had disappeared.

"Drat!" she spit out as a sedan chair with brawny carriers shoved past her. For the first time she felt the prickle of regret and fear along the nape of her bared neck under the hat brim. She hesitated in the bustling, raucous crowd, suddenly knowing what it must be like to be out on the stage and forget one's lines.

Think. Think! She had to reason it out or else hurry back, take the coach to Camden Town, and try this some other time. But it had gone so well, so perfectly until now. Dr. Rock back there on his precarious wooden box had indicated that building straight ahead was Moll King's place. She'd heard of that: a tavern and sort of bagnio opposite St. Paul's run by Tom King and his wild wife Moll. It was a terrible place despite—or perhaps because of—its aristocratic patrons. Surely, Theo and Fleetwood had vanished because they'd simply stepped in there.

"Early daisies, me boy? Vi'lets fer a penny?" the same thin girl she had bumped into screeched in Susannah's ear. Her birdlike hand perched on Susannah's arm. "Aye, but ye're a pretty enough lad fer the likes a me. . . ."

Susannah pulled away and darted toward the lighted entry to the building clearly marked by a crudely painted sign with two crowns and the word 'Kings.' She would go to the door and when someone entered or left, she'd merely look in. After all, it seemed busy and in numbers there was no doubt safety. Light glowed from behind the curtained windows of the establishment; it was probably too noisy and crowded to worry that Theo would notice her peering inward.

She took a deep breath and pressed back into the narrow archway at the right of the raised doorstep. From here, she could use the lights and her costume to step forward when her cue came. If only her grand entrance could be warmed by the presence of an awesomely handsome actor of similar charisma and charm, she mused.

"Stand back then, lad, you're hardly going in here," a gruff voice told her, and a hard arm elbowed her back.

Annoyed, she leaned back farther against the wooden entryway. As the ruffian opened the door for his corpulent, foppish, bewigged master, Susannah's view into the King Tavern was blocked by the door and the burly arm of the lout. But as the door stood open, it briefly illumined in warmest gold another man with a companion who came up behind the rude pair of fashionable lord and rough lackey. A tall man, his hair gilded almost to burnished bronze, was caught in the square of light from the tavern door.

Susanah gasped, pressed back to steady her quaking legs. Though she stood in darkness, her gaze collided in stunning impact with a pair of green-gold, devouring eyes. He was garbed plainly but expensively in brown and russet to match his striking hair, but the eyes—the unfathomable eyes—were green as forests and drowning as the seas. The gaze burned into her very core as if he knew her, but then went hooded in dimming light until the man behind him moved ahead to open the door for them.

Again, the open door bathed in light the proud angles and lines of the face; the shift and pull of velvet, leather, bone, muscle, and tawny flesh of the man's magnificent form. His body was huge, tapered from broad shoulders to the slant of ribs and lean hips. The muscled thighs in fawn-colored breeches stretched taut as he stepped up toward her one leg, then two. The cheekbones were high and chiselled; the mouth firm but sensual. Instinctively, as if she had been physically caressed along her breasts, stomach, and thighs, Susannah pressed her palms to her chest, crossed her legs, and swayed forward. The green-eyed, copper-haired man's voice resonated through her when he spoke to his companion. "Damn, George, but if our little Amanda isn't here, I'm afraid there are plenty of other dives to search. This could be one long night, so I hope to hell it's worth it."

She was stunned he hadn't seen her, hadn't noted her at all. The door behind them thudded shut in her face.

She stood for a moment, dazed, warmed from within by a flowing, pulling tide so deep and swift it was irresistible. One group after another entered before her inner voice began to chatter at her again.

This was pure lunacy; her plan had fallen into pieces. She could hardly elbow men and their burly servants aside to peer in; nor did she dare to enter. Yet, when the next little pack of visitors swept by her, she shocked herself by unhesitatingly stepping in after them.

She hung along the stretch of wall almost behind the continually opening and closing door. A bluish-silver haze of tobacco smoke hovered in the air above the heads of drinking, laughing patrons. Sharp guffaws occasionally drowned the clink of money or pewter mugs. And it wasn't just men, though the deep buzz of their voices swarmed to her ears. Women in various low-cut, high-slit garb were draped everywhere, their shrill or musical laughter punctuating the resonant rumble.

Across the bobbing sea of wigged or hatted heads, she saw Theo and gasped so loudly, several nearby turned to eye her. One very painted slattern tipped her frowsy head as if to peer under the cocked brim of her hat. Susannah scooted farther along the wall, grateful the woman moved quickly away across the floor.

Yes, that was Theo, arm around a blond doxy brazenly gowned in lime-green across the blue haze of the room. He had his arm around the woman's nearly naked shoulders and Charles Fleetwood, two steps above Theo as the four of them mounted the stairs, dared to dip his black head on his doxy's low-cut bodice to drop a kiss or flick his tongue there.

That is enough, Susannah's inner voice shouted at her

through the dim and pounding rush of her own blood in her ears. Enough! Theo caught and at the infamous Moll King's: justice and a perfect finale.

She meant to flee, but as she turned, she saw the stunning green-eyed man again, this time in profile across several clusters of people. His hair was indeed burnished copper and so distinctive it was obviously his own in this room of wigs and layered curls. He, too, had evidently been surveying the crowded, smoky room, and it was as his lofty head swivelled above others, she fancied he now looked at her.

Susannah had only pulled herself away a few steps when she came face to face with the painted slattern who had eyed her earlier. This time, to her dismay, the woman leaned so close that the scent of cloying perfume drowned the acrid tobacco smell in the room.

"Eh, I knew it! See, Moll! With them eyes and mouth—a skirt, sure as I'm living'."

"Please, let me pass. I was just leaving," Susannah managed, desperate to keep her voice low and not attract undue attention.

The painted younger face was replaced by that of a frowsy, florid older woman's, which shut out the busy room. "Indeed a skirt, an' a young one at that. Steppin' out tonight, my little hussy, or lookin' for work at Moll's?"

"No. I apologize for this garb. It's only—I was looking for someone."

"Saints alive, how fine! You've found someone, hussy, and glad to see the likes a you too."

The faces pressed in. The scene tilted wildly. Susannah grabbed for the brim of her hat fearing one of the women would seize it to free her hair, but she was mistaken. Instead, from behind a big hand covered her mouth and an iron arm slapped around her middle to half lift, half drag her backward while her two female tormentors shoved close.

"Here, in here," the older woman hissed. "Good work, Herbert, as she didn't get out a peep, and I wager no one really noticed. On our property, trespassin' she was, if anyone inquires. Here, let's have a good look at the baggage."

The pressure of the crushing arm across Susannah's stomach lessened, but her hands were pulled sharply behind her back and the painted slattern adeptly tied a bright piece of silk around her head and cheeks to gag her. The old woman named Moll—oh, heavens, not Moll King, the owner of this place, Susannah prayed—yanked off the cockeyed hat and plucked at her previously hidden ribbons to tumble her long chestnut curls loose.

"A real looker, I'll say. Sally, I swear, you can spot 'em, and this one's got breeding too. I heard how fancy she talked and all, no street accent here. Saints alive, the auburn-haired little hussy will fetch a pretty price one way or t'other."

To Susannah's abject horror, the woman dared to reach both hands out to tug her linen vest down her imprisoned arms and to unlace the huge shirt she wore while the man pulled her arms so tautly back she didn't dare kick. The painted slattern pressed close, her eyes wide, and for the first time Susannah saw her captor's burly head as he leaned his chin forward on her shoulder to take a look too. She tried to jerk back from the woman's prying fingers, but the struggle was fruitless.

Susannah thought she would retch against her silk gag as old Moll slipped her shirt and chemise aside to expose and finger one naked breast. Her fingers flicked one nipple to life, then pinched it cruelly. "Fine and firm—wager the rest is too. Now you just stop slatherin', Herbert. This little chicken's for the pluckin' by someone who'll pay real pretty for the privilege of wallowin' between these sweet thighs—virgin, too, if we're lucky. Sally, who's worth bleedin' in the house right now? She'll be easier to reason with later if'n we take care of her right proper first."

"Well," Sally drawled and winked lewdly at Susannah's enraged glare over the silk gag, "there's a few well-heeled friends of King George, only they's with Annie and Mary upstairs already. Then there's that copper-headed, tall one what's never been in before, but he's dressed so fine thought I'd board him myself. Besides, he's lookin' for someone special, that's certain. If we hold her here a few minutes, fresh fish'll be in, I know it."

Susannah's sharp gasp through the gag during Sally's recital of men had hardly been noted. The copper-headed one, her mind screamed, perhaps to be brought into her as if she were a breed mare or a slave or a whore like these foul, painted creatures. She tried to protest, to spit out garbled words, to beg them to release her, but she halted frozen at the slattern Sally's next words.

"Moll, I just thought of it!" the woman crowed and grinned, as if she were enjoying all this immensely. "That lecherous spendthrift Theo Cibber come in with another gent'man in tow. They already just started upstairs, but for this piece a fluff, who knows. He'd pay dear for this, maybe both of 'em would and that room's free upstairs with the velvet on the walls to muffle sounds an' all."

For the first time since they had dragged her into this dim, small room off the main chamber, Susannah began to tremble uncontrollably. Her knees shook, her stomach churned, her teeth chattered futilely against the cruel gag. Theo! It would probably mean salvation from this shame, but another degradation begun. Surely, he wouldn't dare to go along with this plan to take her, but if not, he would have her right where he wanted her in more ways than one, at the expense of her pride, reputation, and precious, damned innocence these beasts would barter so eagerly.

She closed her eyes to stop the spinning of their avid,

cruel faces, to halt the whirling of the small room. Theo's face, her father's, her mother's, spun by. She would be sick. She would faint. She must, must awake now from this blackest nightmare of utter despair.

The room jumped and resounded dragging her back from her dizziness. Theo—oh heavens, no—he couldn't be at the door already. She was doomed by her own mistake and fate, like some helpless actress in a tragedy who wanted only to die.

"Who the hell is that?" the older woman's voice hissed. "Sally, see to it, an' Herbert and I will hold this one steady."

They pulled her into a corner and pressed her close against the wall. The sharp repeated rapping on the door rattled its very hinges.

"May I help you, sir? Here, I'll just step out an' speak with you." Sally's voice floated to Susannah through a fog of fear and fury.

"No, but I'll step in. My man George will wait here at the door. You see, I'm very interested in the lady you brought in here."

The voice slid like deep velvet over Susannah's quaking flesh, yet it alarmed her in its tone of intense authority.

"What?" the slattern Sally protested. "Now, wait! There's no lady here that—"

Susannah's head snapped up as her captor swung her hard around to face the intruder. Moll darted out to block her view of him, but he was so tall that Susannah's wild eyes met his hard green gaze over the woman's frowsy head with a jarring impact more devastating than this mere physical captivity. He looked surprised for a moment when he saw her face, then almost pleased.

"I thank all of you for holding her for me," he said, his eyes still unwavering on Susannah's topaz stare. "She's run away from me, you see, from a betrothal, and I'll pay a handsome price for your troubles now that you'll just hand her over."

"Hand her over? Just one lily-white minute, my man, but this ragamuffin's just one a my little skirts what's actin' up and we brung in here to straighten out a bit," Moll protested in a shrill squawk.

"She's a runaway young lady from a poor but upstanding family in Berkshire, and I've come to take her home," he went on as though Moll King had not even spoken. "You see, she's my intended, but she most foolishly bolted. Release that gag and loose her, and she'll admit it all now I've found her at last."

Moll King snorted while Sally kept eyeing the brazen stranger up and down. To Susannah's amazement, when the big lout who held her hesitated, the tall man stepped around Moll and dropped huge linen-cuffed hands onto her captor's restraining burly forearms.

"You'll loose my betrothed now, at once," the deep, caressing voice said low, but no one in the dim room could mistake the barely leashed threat of violence beneath the surface of the suave demeanor.

Tenn Sloper's eyes went thoroughly over the captive woman. She blushed hot from the roots of her tumbled hair to where he could see the sweet cleft between her firm, high bosom carelessly displayed beneath the dishevelled man's shirt she wore. Despite the worn, oversized garments pulled awry in these people's rough handling of her, the girl was obviously a natural beauty. Her topaz eyes snapped with an unquenchable incandescence of rage and the great promise of fiery love.

Her face was a perfect oval; her hair thick, curly, and deep chestnut with burnished tips of tendrils even the dull light of this tawdry room could not dim. The nose was pert and fine; the teeth white, small, and even where the cloth gag had forced her smooth lips apart. Her body looked firm, but beseechingly soft with graceful limbs and a narrow waist he could span easily with two hands. But it was the spirit, the fierce pride of this captive woman, which smote him like a deep-set, iron-tipped lure.

This ravishing, disguised female was not the woman he had sought, but she needed him almost as much, perhaps, as he instinctively longed to protect and possess her. He had watched her but a few minutes after she came inside, and he had known she was not Amanda Brompton; she was too slender, too satin-faced with no freckles, and her eyes of shimmering topax outshone any maid's of the palest brown or other ordinary, earthly hues.

"What's her name then if she's your betrothed?" Moll King broke into the tense silence. "She don't seem so glad to see you, my good sir. And who might you be then, bargin' in like this?"

Moll's long-fingered hand seized the man's brown brocaded arm when she saw her hired henchman Herbert had decided not to protest. The tall man shook off Moll, pushed Herbert's arm away, then loosed Susannah's gag all in one swift chain of movements.

"I'm a squire from Berks come to claim my lost beloved," he said, more to Susannah than the three who stared agape at his bold daring. "This woman is Lady Amanda Brompton of Newbury Manor in Berkshire. Ask her. She'll tell you," he nearly whispered as his eyes went smoothly over Susannah again and his big, warm hands rubbed her freed wrists where Herbert had held her.

Her gratitude flowed out to him, but her knees went watery at his magnetic caress of her chafed arms. She felt blood flow back into her wrists, and she swayed ever so slightly against him before she regained her composure. This man was a miracle sent for her salvation. If he could just get her away from these fiends, out into the darkened streets, she would escape back to her life, her plans, her once untrespassed dreams.

They all stared at her as if she stood on the most

forward thrust of stage. They waited for her speech, her carefully rehearsed gestures, to convince them her part was real. She lifted her head and straightened her shoulders, pulling her gaping shirt back together with a haughty grandeur.

"Yes, I admit it. I am Amanda Brompton, though I thought I'd never see you again, squire."

She caught the quick relief in the man's watchful eyes. How, she thought erratically, could any man's eyes be that sinfully silken green?

"Well, what's his name then?" Moll King hissed, her voice gone rough and furious.

Susannah warmed to the part now. Surely, he wouldn't betray her if he'd come this far. "I'm not certain he wishes to tell you, though it's branded in my memory forever. I ran away, you know, squire, because I felt you really favored Rosalind over me."

One corner of his firm mouth quirked up in apparent admiration or amusement before he caught himself. And, as though they stood the fondest of familiar lovers in some sunny garden spot, she slowly slid his warm fingers up along her forearm and elbow to intimately press the tender inside of her bare upper arm, and graze the curve of breast though thin linen shirt with brief caress of thumb.

"Never, my sweetheart," he rasped. "How could you ever believe I desired Rosalind or any other woman over you?"

She gasped aloud at the brazenness of his next ploy: He moved swiftly forward and swept her hard into his arm while, before the trio of lawless captors, he took her lips.

The touch of him against her staggered her senses. Astounded, she leaned full-length against his strength; his arms, one around her waist, one across her back, cradled her. His thighs were iron against her quaking limbs, and his lips drowned her in an ecstasy she had never imagined.

Mindlessly, she parted her soft lips for him, even as he deepened the devouring kiss and explored the silken cavern of her mouth with his sure tongue. This wretched room and these threatening demons were no more. It was the grandest stage, the most exquisite garden, the soaring sky, that wrapped and sheltered them from all but each other. It was sheer madness that she clung to him before he released her gently.

She struggled to seize control of her legs, her pounding heart, the treacherous trembling clear down between her thighs. Then the cold reality he must surely be playacting as well as she, slowly sobered her.

"I will be taking Lady Brompton with me now," he told the fish-eyed Moll King. "As I mentioned, I shall donate a suitable reward for your finding and not harming my betrothed."

"No, no. 'Course we weren't harmin' her, but when she come all disguised here like this in boy's trappin's, what was we to think? I've got a fine clientele here to protect from louts and spotters, a course; gentlemen like yourself, of generous means and equipage, squire. Now if you'll just tell me where you're visitin' here in London, my good man—"

"No. I'm taking the lady back to Berks in the morning so I will settle with you now. My man is right outside within easy summons. George!"

The burly brown-haired man appeared instantly, almost as expensively dressed, it seemed to Susannah. Her rescuer's hand tightened on her arm. He moved her away, and her feet went gladly. "My man George will pay you a generous price for your services," he threw back over his shoulder.

They left through the smoky, noisy outer room and went beyond to the door. The dark evening air was sweet and good; she wanted to laugh and dance and run with him across the square.

"I can never thank you enough," she told him, purposely avoiding the gaze which continued to study her so intimately. "However did you know I needed help?"

"You're hard to miss even in those ridiculous, oversized boy's togs," he told her as he moved her off at a good clip down the square toward St. Paul's Church.

She strode happily along for a moment, then pulled back. "It's all right," he said down at her. He was a good six inches taller, and in the enveloping darkness, the slash of white silk cravat at his neck and green lodestar eyes shone radiantly.

"Squire, I—I don't even know your name, but I'll try to pay you for your efforts. Just tell me your name, and I'll find a way. I'll be fine from here, truly, so if you'll just loose my arm."

"No," he said flatly. "My carriage is over here. I'll at least see you home. Then too, you see, I was looking for a runaway Amanda Brompton, and you gave such a convincing performance back there, I swear you could be she."

His hand tightened on her arm. His gently forced pace quickened. A tall, elegant carriage with four grays and two waiting footmen emerged from the tall-pillared gloom before St. Paul's portico.

She didn't even know his name, and thank heavens he hadn't learned hers. Yet his words of praise at her convincing performance warmed her even as his very touch.

"Up you go, my sweet betrothed Amanda," he said, and despite her growing alarm at the surprising turn of events, she almost smiled at the suddenly bemused tone of his teasing voice in the darkness.

"I cannot," she protested even as two large hands clasped her waist and hoisted her up into the dim, enclosed coach richly aromatic with soft leather and the faint masculine odor of sweet tobacco. She heard some-one running, men's voices outside then above, on the driver's seat and roof.

He snapped the door shut behind them, and they jolted off immediately into the darkness of the mazelike London streets.

Chapter Three

Susannah could hear him breathing beside her on the fine soft leather seat of the carriage; she could feel the aura of warmth and power he emanated with such apparent ease. The rattle of carriage wheels over cobbles and rough bricks mingled with the thudding of her heart against her ribs.

"Here," he said in the gray velvet darkness, "I'm going to put my frock coat around you. You must be chilled."

"I'm warm enough—really," she heard her own voice amazingly calm and assured. "I need to get out here anyway."

"Here?" he asked, a new note of surprised amusement in his voice, as his warm russet brocade coat she had admired earlier nestled around her shoulders. "And pray tell me, my beloved runaway betrothed, where is 'here'?"

"Anywhere is all right as I know my way," she faltered while in the darkness his sure hands dared to gently lift her long strands of hair free from where they were captured under the coat collar. "Besides, shouldn't you go back for your man George?"

"George is driving," he said, "and he's probably feeling one hell of a lot better than a young woman I know who almost was abducted and worse from prancing around in lad's garb in one of the foulest dives in Covent Garden."

"It wasn't something I wanted to do," she shot out, suddenly furious at the ludicrous and dangerous situation in which she found herself. "It was necessary, that's all, and it's necessary you let me out now, this instant."

He laughed—a loud, almost rough sound. One big hand closed warmly over her wrist. She could see him in the near darkness now as her eyes adjusted, as he could obviously see her to place his coat so perfectly around her and touch her wrist like this with no fumbling.

"I do not laugh at your obvious discomfiture, my dear, only marvel at how easily you slip from mood to mood almost as if you were different people. I tremendously admired your performance back there at Moll King's—and before such a hostile audience. You see, you almost have me believing now that you are my little errant betrothed whom I've rescued just in the nick of time."

"I said I do thank you, and I would be willing to help restore whatever your man George bribed them with back there."

"I would accept that offer but, you see, dear Amanda, the mere experience of meeting you was worth the price, and I don't think you have that sort of wealth despite your elegant accent. No, that sort of repayment would hardly be fair."

She bit her lip and slid her hips encased in the worn, thin breeches back away from him on the leather seat. He did not move closer but patiently extended his arm and hand that still held her wrist as if to give her a little slack.

She had to get out of here, without his knowing her name. He had rescued her, even paid for her, and although she was so drawn to him, she had to get away now. He was taking her out into the black night of London streets, and her family would not know until Monday afternoon she had never been to Aunt Emma's. The tiring boys would find her untouched valise and discarded clothes in the cellar of the theater. Her path would be untracked; they would never know. This man had said he was a squire from Berks. Was she to be his captive clear to Berks?

She twisted her wrist loose and he let her, but he moved closer on the seat. She wrapped his frock coat more tightly about her; the heady masculine scent of mingled leather, tobacco, and an undefined lemony aroma made her nostrils flare and her stomach flutter.

"Don't be afraid, sweet," he said low, "but I can hardly let you out on London's dark streets—not a naive beauty who manages to almost get herself ravished. Even the disguise and that foolish boyish swagger couldn't hide a woman's body like yours. You're slender enough for the breeches, but not on top."

"You're saying I wasn't convincing?" she challenged him, desperate for something argumentative to ward off his intimate tone.

"Only when you said you were my betrothed and kissed me back—like this."

He moved against her gently, surely. Her hands were trapped in the folds of his coat against his hard chest as his firm mouth covered hers.

Protest, scream, fight, she told herself, but she did none of those things. Warmed and cradled, she savored the caress of his lips on hers as he tasted first one corner then the other of her pouted mouth. His thigh pressed hers; his arms were enveloping bands of undeniable strength. He settled her back farther in his embrace as her wild tresses spilled across his shoulder and arm. He seemed to hesitate at her stunned, curious acquiescence for one staggering moment before the kiss deepened.

His mouth slanted across hers now, enticing a response from her she had never dreamed possible, never learned to give. He lifted his big head slightly and began again, eliciting from her a willing, then bold reaction. Her inner voice of panic halted, drowned in a rush of sweet, sensuous feeling that cascaded through every fiber of her body.

His tongue slid, darted, and she welcomed it. Her silken tongue met his, tasting, then challenging before utterly submitting beneath the sweeping power of his devouring kiss. A raw hunger she had only known in her desperate desire to become an actress drained her, swamped her senses, as he began to move his hands over her slender, arched back through the crisp feel of his own brocade frock coat wrapped around her like an elegant cocoon.

Her response, he told himself through the roar of his swelling passion, was untutored, strangely trusting. She was no street girl and yet not quite a real lady; more like a beautiful butterfly or many-colored chameleon who would change shape or hue at the blink of an eye. She beguiled him unwittingly, seduced him so effortlessly. This was foolish, insane. It was not at all what he'd planned whether he found the real runaway Amanda or not, but now he felt so deliciously ensnared. He had to woo her, discover her, possess her.

"Squire, is it to be home now, sir? We're almost to Westminster, squire." His driver George's voice from outside and above halted his flow of jumbled thought and feeling. Reluctantly, he lifted his head from her and held her to him for a moment while he breathed raggedly against her silken cheek.

"No, George," he called up, his decision suddenly made. "Go south to Chelsea."

She sat up stiffly away from him, and he released her slowly. His words to his coachman came at her like the slap of cold reality. Chelsea! Chelsea was miles away from home, from that last coach north to Aunt Emma's. And this powerful man obviously meant to keep her with him now that she'd made such a fool of herself returning his kisses like some slattern back at Moll King's. She might have well stayed in Covent Garden if she wanted a man to have her so easily. Drat it all, he was a deceitful, seducing brigand, a thousand times the villain Theo Cibber would ever be!

"Please, squire, I'm so thirsty and rather faint," she told him in her most beseeching voice. "Would you have anything here in the carriage to drink?"

He loosed her completely and bent away to fumble with something on the floor. "Of course," he told her, his voice muffled now. His slight distance helped; the sheer madness his touch invoked dissipated. Her fingers groped for the cold metal carriage door handle nearly at her elbow. They had slowed for a minute, perhaps to turn.

"We'll go to an inn I know, and I'll get you dinner. I was thoughtless not to realize you were hungry," his words came at her. "Here's a sip of brandy. This foolishness of not even exchanging names has gone on long enough. I'm William Sloper, but everyone calls me Tenn since—"

She hit out at his extended wrist and yanked the door handle downward as the brandy splashed in his face. She half fell, half flew out into the vastness behind her and tried to break her fall by clinging to the swinging door. The metal carriage step grazed her knee; the hard dirt roadbed smacked against the soles of her buckled shoes. His frock coat whipped away. It was not so dark out here. A man's voice above called out, and from the depths of the carriage behind, her one-time rescuer, now her captor, foolishly shouted, "Amanda!"

She fell to her hands and knees in the gritty road, leapt up, and scrambled on. Grass was underfoot, and the slender, leafless limbs of the weeping willow trees ahead were like dangling whips against her face and upraised hands. She heard him running behind her, thrashing through the trees.

"Stop! Wait! The river's there—"

His words made sense only when there was nothing under her feet. She vaulted into chill emptiness, futilely lit by a bright, blurred half-moon overhead. She wanted to hide from her failed plans, from her own shame, from his unbridled magnetism. She must hide, then run home to the theater.

Cold water whacked her clear along her thighs and stomach, her hands and face. It grabbed her, pulled her down. She tried to scream and sucked in a great gasp of river. She turned over, upended, then fought to right herself. Her sopping shirt encased her body. Fizzing bubbles hissed at her, lifted her. She surfaced, her thick hair a slick, smothering curtain thrown forward over her face. She hated water, feared it, had never learned to swim. She thrashed wildly and screamed for air.

"Here! She's down here, squire. I hear her!"

Her shirt ballooned out on the surface of the water to press against her face and neck. She kicked wildly and felt both shoes tugged away by the pull of inky river. Her mouth and nose went under when she tried to shove her hair away, then she surfaced kicking and splashing again. She swallowed a huge mouthful and choked her throat clear again before she went down a third time.

She heard the splash, the men's panicked voices, even caught a desperate glimmer of lantern or cavorting moon. A light—she must not be afraid. She must get to that light, a calm voice told her, which surely did not know she was drowning. A stage light, distant and clear for the end of the play. A terrible tragedy, another voice prated at her in her terror.

Hands, hands on her, a man's voice yelling very close. No, not father, not Tom or Theo—a wonderful voice, but too close again, too loud. She'd let him kiss her again, let him do anything and wanted him to touch her anywhere like this. She was so frightened, so exhausted, and his hard arm felt strong around her shoulder and across and under one armpit. He was all wet too—all wet.

"Relax! Stop that thrashing. I have you. Stop it! Don't

fight me!"

Her head no longer dipped under now, and in the icy black current he felt strangely warm against her. Don't fight me, he had yelled in her ear. But if she didn't fight him, she was lost, helpless at his mere touch, and that enraged her.

"No, no!" she choked out, but he was swimming hard against the current and he ignored her.

"Here, squire. Over here! A tree limb. See it in the lantern? We got it. Grab it or the current'll take you out again."

Running footsteps on the bank nearby. A splash. Her head cleared. He was really here. His big wrist holding her to him pressed hard against the cold, slick skin of a breast beneath her loosened shirt and floating camisole. She would not drown now if they could reach the limb in the flowing wet, only drown from his touch as in this swift-flowing river everywhere.

He swirled them in the cold current as they hit into a tree limb. His free hand grabbed for it; he nearly lifted her onto its rough, wet bark.

"He's got it, he's got it. Drag it in!" a man nearby shouted.

Hands lifted her, pulled her from the strangling waters. Instantly, she collapsed to her knees retching on slick grass. She began to tremble uncontrollably as the cold night air washed over her as surely as the river had. A coat covered her, then something else warm. Two men lifted her between them, carried her back into the carriage, and laid her on a seat.

Where was he? He had to be all right! He had told her his name when she had jumped out—something with numbers. One man bent over her, then two, then three, blessedly his face. Tenn—his name was Tenn.

"Tenn," she thought she said. She was so dizzy, so weak, she was floating—no, not in the river again!

"Let me have your coat too and drive on, George."

"Still to Chelsea, squire?"

"Yes, The Blue Rose Inn at Ranelagh Gardens, and hurry or she'll die of chill."

Tenn sat on the same seat she lay on, settling against her legs to give himself room. His face was just a white blur so close, and his hair dripped water on her forehead when he bent over her.

"You little fool," she heard him say low. She could feel his warm breath caress her quivering lips. He was wrapping her soaked hair in something like the turbaned actors always wore when they played the Turkish sultans in melodramas—played their parts so charismatically that even proper English ladies wanted to be ravished by them in their harems or seduced in distant palaces. . . .

Exhaustion descended like a heavy black curtain and she slept.

Within a half hour, Tenn Sloper had stripped the boy's wet garments from Susannah's chilled body, and he and the upstairs servant girl of The Blue Rose Inn at Ranelagh Gardens had lowered her into a hot bath. Her lips, still in that irresistible pout, were bluish, and her fingers and toes felt cold to his touch. But on the whole, he marvelled, unable to keep his gaze from roving her beautiful body, she radiated life and spirit even half unconscious like this.

His eyes skimmed the delicious twin swell of her breasts above the bath water, which turned her ivory skin a rosy hue. Pink-budded nipples thrust out impudently just below the gentle ripples, and her elegantly tapered rib cage and soft belly were caressed by the shifting water. Her graceful hands with buffed, oval nails rested on her exposed knees that were separated ever so slightly, as if to tempt his hand to touch that sweet chestnut triangle of hair he had glimpsed. He felt hot all over despite the shaky discomfort of his own wet, cold clothes. As soon as he had her safe and warm in bed, he'd steam himself dry on the hearth, or perhaps use that enticing bath water.

"But however did your wife fall in the Thames, my lord, and in them clothes?" the raven-haired servant girl asked for the second time. "Clear along Grosvenor Road, there's all them willow trees before the banks."

"Thank you for your help, my girl," he said, ignoring her questions and curious eyes. "You can see the lady is warming up now, so I'd appreciate your helping your mistress downstairs get the hot food I've ordered ready. Tell my coachman and footmen we're both fine and to bed down the horses."

Bed down the horses—the words drifted to Susannah's stunned brain. Her limbs floated, heavy, torpid, so hot and so deliciously warm in this water. . . .

Water! Drowning water! Her eyes flew open. Steam wafted upward from the bath around her naked knees, which peeked above the top of the waterline in a wooden tub. Naked—she was naked like this and here, somewhere, with his voice in this room. . . .

"Oh!" was all she managed as her eyes locked with his green gaze. Thank heavens he was clear across the room, turned halfway in a chair with a linen towel lifted to his wet, coppery hair; but still, someone had carried her in and disrobed her like this.

"Are you all right?" he asked, calmly solicitous as though she must surely be used to waking naked in a room with a strange man. "Hot food for us both will be here in a moment," he added and went pointedly back to drying his hair.

She slid down even lower into the hot water until she realized a heavy towel was wrapped around her hair and she was soaking its lower edge. "I remember you pulled me out," she said, hoping she sounded both sincerely grateful yet somewhat nonchalant. "Where are we?"

"At The Blue Rose Inn. You could have drowned. The servant girl who was bathing you will be back momentarily."

He seemed suddenly nervous too, she thought, or perhaps afraid she would bolt again. Her mind raced: The Blue Rose Inn, in Chelsea he had said earlier, and surely no servant girl alone had lifted her in here. But he had saved her again, though it was his fault she had fled and nearly drowned in the first place. Her terror of the dark, devouring waters shot through her, and she became all gooseflesh even in the warm bath.

"Could you ask the girl to fetch a dressing gown or towel or something?" she asked. "I'm just fine now. I want to get out. Could you leave, please, and send back the girl?"

To her dismay, he stood and gave a final flourish to his thick head of wild hair that glistened all bronzed in the dancing flames of the fireplace. "I believe she's downstairs so we'll have to make do," he said. "Besides, if that water's still warm, I think it would be sensible for me to get in too."

Sensible! Too! Alarmed, she shrieked much louder than she had meant to. "Just leave, please! Go out or turn away or something."

"Frankly, I prefer the something." The lazy, wicked tone of his voice floated to her, and he dared to chuckle. But, just as she considered screaming this Blue Rose Inn down about their ears, he turned his back and zealously began to towel his head again. "There's another cloth and a woolen dressing gown on a stool beside the tub." His words came muffled to her now. "I won't look. Sorry I can't offer you my frock coat like the first time I rescued you this evening, but it was evidently lost back on the road somewhere when you jumped out. You could have broken your neck at that point and never had the chance to drown, of course."

Drat the villain, doing all this to her and then making her feel guilty, she fumed. Yes, there was a towel on the stool, and she had no choice but to move quickly and hope he didn't turn. And how did he know these items were right here?

She pulled herself up and snaked a quick wet arm out for the towel. The room tilted and whirled, dizzily spinning down into the drowning river again. She fell back into the bath, sloshing a great wave onto the floor.

"Sweetheart, here, you're just dizzy and a bit hungry." No! No, he was right over the tub; so close, touching her, and she was naked. A towel flapped open. He lifted and covered her as she leaned into him. Her knees went limp. He carried her, still damp, wrapped in dressing gown and towel to the bed and flipped heavy quilt and coverlet over her.

She blessed the sweet protection of the covers, but cursed the fact that she lay here giddy and languid in a bed at his mercy. She tried to picture what a scene she had just made for him, half spilled nude from the tub, but she was too light-headed to think.

When he bent over her to finish towelling her hair dry, she did not protest. She had neither the strength nor the desire to resist. Why, with this stranger, this man so uniquely named Tenn, did she not want to resist at all? He had rescued her from peril and yet he was the greatest peril she had ever known; still she desired him more than feared . . . His hands still in her hair, she slept.

Sweet aromas tugged at her brain as she nestled closer into her warm feather bed. This was not her own narrow bed, she mused, nor Aunt Emma's yet, because she had missed the coach to Camden Town.

Her eyes shot open as reality crashed back. She was here with him after the humiliating debacle at Covent Garden and the accident in the river. She had almost drowned, but she smelled food, pungent and rich: a hot gravy dish or partridge with sweet sauce like mother used to fix on Sundays. She uncurled her limbs and sat up carefully, cocooning the covers to her. She was not as dizzy now but rather floaty, and so toasty warm.

"I was about to wake you for the food, but I thought you might need your sleep more," said the deep velvet voice she must have concocted from her dreams.

"Didn't the maid ever come back?" she asked sharply, unsure why that demand had come to mind.

"Certainly, my sweet, came and went with this fine repast. Now prop yourself up against a pillow, and I'll bring you a plate. I can hardly chance another dizzy tumble from you into bagnios, out of moving carriages, or from bathtubs, as it's getting to be an awful bother chasing you about like some love-struck rural lout. Here," he said, one russet eyebrow lifted in apparent amusement at her annoyed expression, "partridge pie, toast and strawberry jam, and some tea laced with a jog of rum."

He placed a small, crowded wooden tray across her knees, and kept a hand on it so she wouldn't spill it all onto the bed. Ravenous, despite his jade-eyed scrutiny, she downed the succulent poultry and vegetables in pastry and sipped the tea, cradling the pottery mug in both hands.

"Thank you," she said at last between final mouthfuls. "You needn't stand there, you know. I assure you, I can manage. This is exactly what I needed, and I'll soon be on my feet so we can head back."

"So we have progressed to the point you would at least consider riding with me in the same carriage," he murmured low, as if talking to himself.

"Only back home," she said and took a sweet, crunchy last bit of jam-laden toast.

"And where is home?" he countered, drawing up a chair and lounging back in it, apparently at ease.

"Where the heart is," she shot back at him so flippantly, she instantly regretted her words.

"But since I met you, my dear little nameless betrothed, the question of where my heart is, is really becoming most difficult. Is it back at Moll King's, or in my carriage—or warm in that bed right there?"

She froze with the toast still in her mouth. In flickering firelight, his loose, tousled hair made his head look cast from bronze while his eyes gleamed glinting emerald. He wore a linen shirt carelessly laced at the neck and someone's dark-blue velvet waistcoat, entirely too small for him, under a rough woolen dressing gown much like the one she wore. A towel was draped around his neck as if to keep him warm. The impact of his haphazard, dishevelled look was entirely disarming and appealing.

They stared silently across the narrow space from his chair to the bed until little flames leapt alive in his gaze, and she forced herself to look away. Now, right now, she had to insist he take her back to central London. She must summon every actress's skill she had ever beheld on stage to make him agree to let her dress and take her home. The room, the bed were too warm. The rum in the tea was dangerously heating her blood, causing the oddest sensation she could not control.

"You'll please take me home now," she thought she said, her words the merest satin whisper in her own ears, despite the alert readiness of all her senses.

He stood. She watched his feet, his legs, and his hands as he came right up to the bed. He lifted her tray away. "Too late for that, my sweet. Fate has thrown us together, and we both feel the impact of that." His voice vibrated through her as though he had already touched her as skillfully as she desired him to. "We both share this feeling, my sweet little mystery lady. Your topaz eyes have bewitched my very soul—"

His gaze of sheerest green swam closer before deep chestnut lashes flickered down along his high cheekbones. She gasped a tiny, timeless breath as their lips met, hers as curious, as awed, then as eager as his. Entranced, they clung together, soft mouth to firm one until the reaching out began: His hands encircled her slender back where the coverlet split; her arms lifted to embrace his neck. His powerful thigh pressed heavily against hers, branding her skin through cover, sheet, and robe.

Her senses bombarded her brain with vibrant images. Though her eyes were tightly closed, she could picture their room: the oaken table, the braided rug, the peach-hued glowing hearth. The fire crackled and the sweet scent of hawthorn branches wafted on the air. And the touch—the pure, raw feel of him against her, pressing her down like this—was indescribable. It must be a fantasy, a dream of desire more potent than those that paraded so often across the stage of her mind.

Now everything spiralled in to focus on him; everything was new. Never had she imagined a man, a stranger, could mesmerize her brain and body so.

He cradled her supple form to move her farther into the depths of the feather bed. Her chestnut hair polished to golden gilt by firelight fanned out across her pillow. He rained flurries of gentle, then wild kisses along her forehead and temples, down her jawline to her throat. One arm supported her shoulders; one hand slid down to squeeze her slender waist until she gasped aloud and tossed her tresses at the combined sweet assault of his skilled mouth and hands.

She was burning—so hot. How could she have ever been cold in the waters tonight when he came like this to save her? Her arms lifted again to tighten around his neck and draw his head down. In eager response, he moaned deep in his throat and plundered her willing mouth.

He moved to lie against her full length, though the constricting coverlet still separated them. His insistent tongue skimmed her teeth, darted in to taste the slick skin of her inner cheeks, challenged her wet tongue to a delicious duel she mindlessly fought before utterly surrendering.

She felt as if she drifted; one instant serene and fulfilled, the next hungry for more of what his caresses promised. Again, some new tactic she could not have imagined pulled her careening down a crashing wave and swept her upward to new cresting joys.

"You're so perfect, my sweet, so beguiling, my little runaway love I've found." He breathed against her small ear as his hands raced along the length of her, through the coverlet that clung to her seductive curves. This woman cartwheeled his usual orderly thoughts to shambles. The moment he'd beheld her, even though he knew she could not be the woman he had sought at Covent Garden, he had to have her, protect her, even—curse his total lack of all rational self-control—love her.

Carefully holding his weight off her on his forearms and knees, he moved atop to press her down. She seemed eager yet naive, sensual yet unpracticed. Surely, she was an impoverished greengrocer's daughter or schoolmaster's girl run away, even a governess some cruel master had cast off or an innocent maid merely turned rebellious in the disappointment of first love. Perhaps she was no virgin, but either way, he intended to stroke and feed this instinctive fire that sprang to hot red-gold between them.

When he reached over to swiftly snuff the bedside candle with the open palm of his hand and stood to remove his garments, Susannah knew she would not protest. Wild pulsations raged through every fiber of her being; fear went down with clinging sanity in the flow of desire.

A breath of chill air licked at her limbs when he lifted the coverlets to climb in. She had twisted the rough blue wool dressing gown and wrinkled linen towel awry, and she marvelled how the avid look on his face glazed with passion as he glimpsed an ivory slash of thigh. Jolted back, she tried to tug the material closed.

"No, sweetheart, don't. Let me take care of it," he rasped. "Trust me, and I swear to you all will be forever well. Let me take care of everything . . ."

He trailed molten kisses down her throat while his unruly hair etched by firelight rubbed along her chin. His whole body hovered closer beneath the heated tent of coverlet. His lips and tongue traced lower, kissing and nipping across one shoulder and fluted collarbone, down to the beginning swell of silken breast.

"We can't, we can't," she said, almost startled by her own denial.

"We can, we will," he murmured as his head dropped lower to capture a taut, pointed nipple between firm, insistent lips.

"Oh—oh, Tenn—no."

"Tenn—yes. I'm crazy for you. Trust me; no more dangers or cold nights ever, I swear it!"

His lips pulled tenderly at one nipple while his treacherous tip of tongue flicked it wetter, hotter. His free hand lifted now to separate her robe and bare her to his delicious assaults from the waist up. The hand moved to circle her other breast, trailing taunting fingers. Swept along in a rush of sensual delight, she tried to grasp at rational thought. The circles went smaller like a little rushing whirlpool, spiralling in until they raced around the sensitive aureole of the other pert, pink nub. His thumb and finger touched, teased, and gently rolled the peak until she thought she would beg him to go on.

He changed tactics again, even as she began to kiss and bite his earlobe in her sweet abandonment. He pulled her robe free from all contact with her body; the warm, damp linen towel about her hips went with a flurry as his leisurely constraint turned to taut desire.

"Only so far I can go to act the gentleman," his words came at her, but she paid no heed to their real meaning.

Act he'd said, but she was not acting now. He stroked a hand along the outside of her bare hip, then slid it smoothly to her inner thighs where she pressed their warmth together. His mouth took hers repeatedly, demanding, giving, promising a higher climb to what wonderful heights she could not fathom. She'd been a mere foolish child all these years to believe the only passion in her life could be coming alive on the stage. His swift, sure fingers brazened upward and inward to the fiery core of her womanhood, evoking rapture with no name.

No name! They were doing all this together and he did not know her name. "Susannah. My name's Susannah," she tried to tell him, but his lips insistently covered hers again as he nudged a knee between her thighs.

Her eyes shot open, staring wildly into his dark face. His second knee spread her legs wider, and she gasped at the sheer impact of her complete vulnerability beneath him. His eyes grew green as forests or the raging sea, the drowning sea. This was a dream, a devouring dream like that tumultuous river!

"Lie still. Just trust me, my sweet."

"Tenn, please . . ."

Whatever she had meant to say or ask was gone in a crashing cascade of their own making. He moved gently, slowly, deeply into her. A sharp pain between her legs jabbed her fully awake, but he covered her little gasp with a searing kiss and the pain ebbed to a slow-building, satiny pull and push she thought would make her faint with its piercing sensation. He was part of her, and she revelled in it all, entirely entranced and unabashed. This woman kissing him, clinging to him, lifting her knees along his powerful ribs as he bid—she must surely be some wild wanton not even a part of that fond and lonely daydreamer Susannah Arne!

It went on, upward; at times, he stilled his rhythmic plunge until he could control himself no more. His motions turned frenzied, rampant, sweeping them both along in the careening current of their passions. But this time he did not rescue her, for they were drowned until at last they lay on the calm shore beyond the reaching realms of deepest seas.

Sometime, she knew not when in spite of the faintest hint of gray light in their chamber, she wakened. She lay, leaden-limbed, listening to him breathe evenly and deeply beside her, this intimate stranger who had possessed her body as a lover and her mind as a magician. She remembered every tender gesture, every spoken line so very clearly; it still shattered her sense of self. Yet she had been this woman who had fallen asleep in Tenn Sloper's arms while he promised her the world: a town house near St. James' Square, a carriage, clothes, servants, and himself as adoring if demanding lover in her life and bed every night.

She almost laughed aloud. It was insanely impossible to think of her, the properly reared Susannah Arne, who only yesterday desired to be rid of Theo Cibber and have a great acting career, as a rich man's mistress royally ensconced in common shame and scandal.

She lifted her head, then froze as she realized her long tresses were caught under his shoulder. But his velvet breathing was steady; his fine profile silvered by predawn light did not turn. Carefully, she slipped one naked leg from the warm bed, then edged out, smoothly pulling her hair free.

Stealthily, she padded across the room where the fire glowed scarlet coals upon the cooling hearth. She gasped as if to sneeze, but pressed her finger under her nose to halt the tickling sensation. Yes, the boy's clothes from the theater were spread out here where they had been dried, though of course her shoes were long gone in the swift Thames. She tugged on socks, breeches, and hose, and hurriedly donned the dark blue waistcoat and hat Tenn had worn. On second thought, she pulled his stockings up over hers in case she had to run far before she could beg a ride back to London. She had no choice. The scene of love had ended; the curtain must come down to hide her before he took this further.

Just as she turned to go, the bed creaked. She stood stock-still. But nothing, nothing. Surely, he had been as exhausted as she. His open, ticking pocket watch glinted dully in the crimson ember glow as she took another step and halted. Her tapered, trembling fingers caressed its cold gold cover, and she picked up the watch stooping low near the fire to read the time: six-thirty and five—and here on the inside of the cover something engraved, perhaps his name.

Susannah squinted, then tilted the watch until the wan light glinted the finely etched script alive: "To William, my beloved husband. Always, Catherine."

Susannah blinked, stared again. Husband! No wonder he crooned words of a man to a well-kept mistress. A rage that turned her hot then cold shot through her and energized her languid limbs. Her once chill flesh flushed with anger; she dropped the watch onto his shirt like a burning brand. Her fists clenched, and she clasped her fingers so tightly together they went prickly numb.

A wife! She'd not only been seduced by a stranger, but a married one who'd abducted her and played her for the fondest fool there ever was. She knew his name, William "Tenn" Sloper, knew he lived near elegant St. James', knew he must be wealthy, but now she knew all there really was to ever know of him. Deceiver and villain! When she became famous and powerful, she'd have her own ending to this comic tragedy. They'd all see, the whole wild audience of London, what revenge could be!

She was out into the hall and down the back servants' staircase, while her rampant thoughts raced as swiftly as her feet. Lavender-rose dawn fingered the eastern sky, and the thick grass behind the inn was dewy wet on her stockinged feet. She tore down Ebury Road until she thought her lungs would burst. Gravel scraped her stockings, and a pain grabbed her side. She sat behind a barely leafed-out thorny thicket to catch her breath and think.

Susannah reasoned that even walking, she could be back to the theater by mid-morn and easily sneak in, as it was Sunday and the sweepers would be the only ones about. With the coins father had given her in her valise, she could hire a sedan chair and then catch the coach to Camden Town. Then perhaps Aunt Emma would never know she was to have arrived a whole day before.

Susannah's ear was intent for the thunder of pursuing carriage or horses behind her as she emerged from her cover and strode briskly along the road. It was as if, between her legs and along her breasts, she still felt the touch of that seducing demon. But she would survive and flourish—on the stage, too—and someday would have her revenge.

Her thoughts matched the steady rhythm of her stockinged feet; her mind concocted little scenes of justice and revenge. Finally, a drover's cart piled with turnips creaked along beside her, and the cloddish cart man gave her clever version of an impoverished apprentice a cheerful ride all the way back to the everyday normal city.

Chapter Four

It's been an entire year this very month, Susannah thought, as her tiring woman Anne Hopson adjusted at her hips the wide wicker paniers over which her skirt would drape . . . an entire year since that wild, mythic night she'd spent with a villainous magician named Tenn Sloper in the fairy-tale world of The Blue Rose Inn.

Tonight she was singing the part of Venus, goddess of love, in her brother's new opera *Love and Honor* at the magnificent Drury Lane Theater where her family, except for mother, was now employed with Theo Cibber's entourage of actors. Theo had given her father a sinecure as the numberer who counts the house to keep the ticket men honest. Tom's composing was being subsidized by the wealthy theater owner, Charles Fleetwood, and under Theo's tutelege, she had risen to be Drury Lane's highest paid singer at two hundred pounds yearly. Even the youngest Arne, Henry Peter, was on salary as a child singer. Yet the Arnes' rise in importance and salary, as well as all Susannah's frenzied activities in their new theater home, had not wiped the memories of Tenn Sloper's touch and words—and his deceit—from her heart.

"Here now, my fine goddess, I think you're star gazing again, I do." Anne Hopson's lively voice halted her reverie. "Arms up, please, for this criardes skirt to go over your head, and we'll have to give a care to that ornate coiffure. Laws, but it's a heap of foolishness actresses wear this heavy, stiff, cracklin' material when the real fashion is all softer satins."

"It's stage tradition, Anne, that's all." Susannah's voice came muffled from under the huge golden and cream skirt as it dropped into place over the paniers. "Besides, I'm only a singer and hardly an actress."

"You're paid as much as some of 'em and that's what matters in my book," the sprightly, sandy-haired Anne told her and clucked her tongue as her quick hands fussed over the folds of skirt material, then darted upward to fluff the tiers of ruffled bodice lace exposed by the deep cut of the pointed neckline.

Susannah eyed Anne's suddenly stern face. Though she hadn't asked her, she judged Anne to be about ten years older than she, at perhaps thirty and one. "I know my wages are good, Anne, but it's not really what I want. You've told me a hundred times you wanted to leave mantua-making to be a fine lady's maid, and now you've taken a step toward that here at the theater, if any of us ever gets enough to hire you and turn into a fine lady to boot," she added wryly. "But, drat it, I've been on the boards over two years and everyone sees me as just a singer."

Anne Hopson's sharp brown eyes focused on Susannah's serious face before she returned to her task, this time carefully positioning the tops of the lace-edged sleeves on the curves of Susannah's almost bare shoulders. "And you're too proud to beg Mr. Cibber for it like he wants you to even with the pushin' of your father and brother. I admire you for that, I do," Anne clipped out.

"Is it so obvious to everyone then?" Susannah asked. She pirouetted slowly for Anne while the gold-threaded gossamer overskirt was tied on and draped back by rosettes to display the gold and creamy skirt underneath.

"Obvious enough, I guess, at least to Anne Hopson, but then she is grateful you treat her like a friend, a friend unlike some of the rakes and theater types what are always hangin' about I've seen. And then you can't trust those silly jakes what's been writing nasty rumors in the London papers about a certain lovely singer, Miss A of Drury Lane Theater, and all the hearts she's been breaking."

"I appreciate your worrying, Anne, but I can handle that. I detest those rabble-rousing, gossiping papers that breed on hints of scandal, as I've never done one thing to warrant such lewd tidbits," Susannah protested, and then blushed when she thought of Tenn Sloper.

She could just imagine the foul black-printed words now. "Young virgin," it would read, "a certain singer Miss A of Drury Lane Theater nearly ravished at notorious Moll King's is rescued by man who saves her from suicide plunge in River Thames and then seduces her at Chelsea Blue Rose Inn while she revels in his very touch. . . ."

"You're not feelin' faint, Miss Susannah?" Anne broke into her impassioned thoughts.

"Oh, no. I'm fine, thank you. You're a wonder," she told her and grasped the woman's hand for a moment as she moved to fasten the single high, stylish neck ruffle nearly up under Susannah's chin. Besides the mirror-like spangles and gilded feathers in her hair, a glittering gold half face mask completed her costume as Venus for this fantasy performance where she appeared descending from Mount Olympus to cause and then solve all the romantic dilemmas of the opera.

Susannah surveyed herself in the narrow mirror of the small tiring room Theo had wrested for her from the Drury Lane actresses. There was hardly room to turn about, as gowns belonging to the middle-billing actresses hung along one wall. Then too, she had to share Anne's services with several others, but it was better than attempting to gown oneself crowded in among a group of shoving, gossiping women with avid admirers hanging on.

Actually, she admitted to herself, Theo had probably given her this spare, private room only to get her off alone, but she had managed to still hold him and that rich reprobate Charles Fleetwood at bay. Anyhow, after her dramatic experience with Tenn Sloper, no one else could ever really—

"Arne! Arne, is that lead-footed tiring woman Hopson in there again?" a female voice shrilled on the other side of the door.

"Laws," Anne moaned, cradling Susannah's lip rouge pot in her hands, "I don't need another of Kitty Clive's scoldings, not tonight, I don't."

"Don't fuss. I'll just finish up myself and you can go help the others," Susannah told her and took the rouge pot. "You just keep smiling like I do, Anne, and someday we'll both get what we want, you'll see."

Even as she opened the door, the distinctive voice on the other side started in again. "Arne, I don't intend to stand out here on this drafty landing to be ignored by the likes of a mere young, snippy little upstart like you!"

Susannah yanked the door open wide before the tirade could go any further. "Good evening, Mrs. Clive," she crooned, her voice intentionally sugary. Kitty Clive, the theater's most popular and volatile singer-actress, stood in her dressing gown with arms akimbo on her voluptuous hips. "I really did hear your first request, you know. Anne is going right down now."

Anne brushed by them both and shot Kitty Clive a mocking curtsy that Susannah caught before Kitty could turn to see it. Kitty whirled back to Susannah, a frown on her florid face. Susannah regretted the instinctive bad blood that seemed to flourish between them, for she admired Kitty Clive's work as the darling of the stage in ballad opera and comedies. Everyone knew Kitty Clive had climbed out of the slums to get where she was, and though Susannah rose readily to Kitty's ribald or subtle taunts, she was at a loss to understand their cause.

"I dare say, Miss Arne, elegant as ever and got the tiring maid first while the rest of us mere street wenches twiddle our damn thumbs waiting for her grand arrival."

"I'm sorry if I detained her, Mrs. Clive, and for the fact you felt you had to traipse clear up into this little garret chamber from your large, private second floor tiring room, but I do have an entry before you this evening. I shall have Anne dress me earlier tomorrow so you won't be kept waiting and merely twiddling your poor thumbs."

"Forget it, Miss Arne. You golden goddesses out of fine families born with silver spoons in your mouths wouldn't have the vaguest of half of what I say, let alone been through."

Susannah studied the impassioned woman with the snapping dark eyes, rosy complexion, big, carelessly flaunted breasts, and tiny waist. Kitty was always demonstrative, blunt, and bawdy in rehearsals but there was a new tone here, a hint at what was underlying her frequent snubs.

"Mrs. Clive, I don't want to argue with you—I never did. I know you think I've lived in a palace or some such, but do you really think my whole family except my mother, who is a hard working midwife, would labor here for the wages Mr. Cibber pays if we were wealthy? Really, I think—"

"You think, you think! Don't lecture me, Miss Golden-throated Arne. I've seen your breed before sweeping in here, capturing the audience not as much for your talent but because you're respectable and acceptable. Pox on it! That's why!"

"That's not fair! My education and background have nothing to do with why Mr. Cibber hired me!"

"Saints' blood! Now we have it! Mr. Cibber, always Mr.

Cibber, is it? I've seen that randy goat slathering over you, and I swear snubbing him's the only smart thing you've done so far, only I know you're just leading him on for now to get that fine salary—a far sight more than I started out with around here in this poxy hole. Piss on it, maybe you deserve that slimy toad after what I know about him, but I don't wish him even on you, and that's the kindest I can say. Hell fires, I'll be late standing in this drafty hall jawing with the likes of you!"

She whirled and ran down the steps in a flurry of skirts and rattle of her wooden-heeled slippers. Susannah leaned over the railing, careful not to disarrange her voluminous skirts draped over the wide paniers. "Mrs. Clive—Kitty, wait! What do you know about Theo Cibber?" she called foolishly down after the woman.

A door slammed below, and she almost dropped the lip rouge pot over the balustrade. Drat, but no wonder they all hated her, maybe hated her whole family, she fumed. They envied her hefty salary and her lack of coming up from the bottom, as some of them had. There was also some sort of jealousy over Theo's blatant attentions, though anyone else was welcome enough to that.

When she had a chance she would talk to Kitty about Theo. After the catastrophe of her ruined plan to spy on him last year at Covent Garden, she had given up any plot to expose his obvious debauched reputation. Instead, she just consumed her energies in her work and refused to speak about Theo, although her father or Tom brought him up almost daily. Besides, after experiencing a man like Tenn Sloper, immoral wretch that he was, she had no intentions of ever letting Theo Cibber have his lewd way with her.

Curse Tenn Sloper, she thought, as she rushed back into her tiring room and carefully colored her lips, then stroked the faintest blush on her cheeks with what was left on her finger. She looked about for the powder shaker, but didn't see it. Pox on it, as Kitty always said, what did it matter anyway, as she was to be hidden behind her mask except for the cast call after the finale. What did anything matter, when the most heartfelt desires of her whole life were perpetually out of reach and tarnished by the haunting memories of one night last year that could not be obliterated, however hard she tried?

She heard the orchestra's familiar, lilting overture as she entered the wide wings of the theater. She could picture her brother Tom without even peeking out as she often did. Proud, in ecstasy, directing his own music at King George's Theater Royal, Tom had arrived while she still stood in the shadows waiting only to sing.

Theo materialized immediately behind her and draped a quick arm across her bare shoulders.

"Theo, with that loud music I didn't hear you," she mouthed.

"You're a bit late, sweeting. I was about a send a callboy upstairs for you. I hear Clive gave you a tongue lashing," he added as his eyes darted to her low decolletage and he blatantly wet his thick lips.

"It was nothing. Just a hearty discussion. I didn't realize this place had spies."

"It's my job, my care, for all of you as I'm actor-manager *ad perpetuam*, I hope. And your care, Susannah, I especially crave," he told her, leaning much too close to her ear.

She shrugged her shoulders and fussed to tug her bodice up. "I've got to go now before they winch that cloud up without me. Excuse me, Theo."

"Wait!" he told her a little too loudly as the overture ended and his hands seized her waist. "My beautiful Susannah, Venus, goddess of love—this foolish pretense between us cannot go on as it has for over a year. The more unreachable you are, the more I—I burn for you!"

"Miss Arne—cloud's ready," a callboy hissed from behind them. With a grimace and a twitch of his mouth, Theo loosed her waist. Her approaching entrance, which even Theo could not halt, saved her. She moved quickly to her position on the small, cloud-shaped platform, and the stage men winched it up.

She forced herself to breathe easily, to concentrate on the music. Her self-discipline always sustained her when she was onstage, for that was all that mattered then. It became her total reality no matter what her problems or memories or dreams.

She tied her mask in place when her gold and gossamer cloud had been lifted and swung over the central stage, still out of the audience's view. On the stage below her the poor, foolish folk whose lives the goddess Venus was about to render pure chaos sang their lyrical duet.

She turned forward, her hands on the golden ropes of the cloud to await her swaying descent. She stared down under her half mask at pieces of the expensive, gilded French paper which would cascade as a glittering shower beneath her as she came down from Mount Olympus. Theo and Charles Fleetwood had spared no expense for this production, and Tom and her father had been jubilant. Besides these ornate costumes and machinery effects like clouds and gilt rain, there were new chandeliers, new green carpet on the stage, ornately painted scenery, and a half keg of brandy ignited each time her young brother, Henry Peter, leapt out on stage as a half-clad Cupid to help Venus invoke her romantic spells.

The song below ended; the ropes jerked, creaked, and slowly lowered her. The magnificence of her entrance had been met with gasps of awe and wild applause the past four nights *Love and Honor* had played, so she had learned not to begin her first song until it was quiet. With Theo's blessing and her father's boasting, she and Henry Peter had begun to take a sort of grand promenade along the edge of the stage before she even sang a note.

The music swelled below her as she came into the view of the crowded, three-tiered theater. Without tilting her head downward she noted that the pit was full to bursting, and—drat Fleetwood—there were several fops in chairs on the stage who had evidently been allowed to put out the guinea bribe for the privilege of making fools of themselves and getting in her way. Besides, it was ludicrous that the theater management spent all this money and effort to make Venus seem believable, and then let half-drunken sparks ruin it all by draping their extravagantly clad bodies along the fringes of the stage on chairs where everyone could see!

Her cloud thudded barely as she landed. The hushed murmurs thundered to applause. Cupid vaulted in from left stage, above magic flames, to appear at her side. Her little brother winked his upstage eye at her; he always did, though father had seen it once and threatened to beat him if he ever did it again. In the warm adulation of the crowd and in pride and love for her brothers, Susannah Arne smiled, and the sea roar of the theater's approval crashed over her in thrilling waves.

She felt exhilarated, vibrantly reborn as always when she took the stage even to sing; after all, opera was only a step away from acting. If she could but walk out here to act, she thought, how much more wonderful then, to become those heroines who faced all problems, who conquered every love or rage . . . .

She halted in half stride. Stiff skirts over paniers swayed and swished jerkily. Henry Peter, two steps back, hissed, "Go on!"

In the green and white and gilt royal box sat some guests the king had obviously let use his facilities tonight. It was common; it was expected. But she moved forward another step and stopped again as she dared to dart another look upward through the slits of her mask. In the flesh, not six yards away, Tenn Sloper sat in the royal box leaning forward and talking to a beautiful flame-haired woman at his side.

Susannah's heart thudded so loudly beneath her lace and golden bodice she was terrified it could be heard over the now dying applause. Her insides cartwheeled over; she bit her tongue between her teeth to keep from screaming his name. His hair shone coppery and he turned his head to stare down at her, though he still commented to the woman hovering nearly on his shoulder. He sees me, he knows me, a little voice in her head shrieked; but no, she was masked, her hair gilded and piled atop her head. He'd never think to find her here; but, with a striking wife like that, he had never intended to find her anywhere.

Henry Peter's fingers grabbed her waist, and he tugged once to pull her on. Smoothly, as if it had all been part of her practiced entrances, she pirouetted once and moved to the center of the apron stage which thrust boldly out into the audience.

She thought that the watching crowd—and he, Tenn—quieted sooner than usual when she had jerked to a stop. They were waiting for her to sing. Her eyes caught Tom's sharp, sobering stare from the musicians' pit at her feet. He lifted his slender baton, frowned, and nodded to her. Her musical cue began.

The words and the melody flowed smoothly as her low, plaintive voice came amazingly to her own ears. She was fine now, in control of everything, her voice one with Tom's lilting melody. She hated that man who watched her from the king's box, daring to come here with a beautiful wife he had been so disloyal to last year, at the mere whim of his own masculine pride. Her voice caught in a near sob on a high note, but she recovered and went on.

She moved, she gestured, she sang, she listened, not really hearing, as her innocent-faced little brother sang his brief song about the darts of love. Then blessedly, neither daring to look both ways nor curtsy to the royal box as she had been taught, she stepped onto her cloud to disappear heavenward.

Both Theo and Charles Fleetwood came at her when her platform was winched over and down into the wings. "For love of a bawd, Susannah, what ails you out there?" Theo's shrill voice scolded.

"Now, Theo, back off from our little thrush," Fleetwood's rich voice comforted. "She recovered beautifully." He patted her arm and his portly form pushed Theo slightly away. Fleetwood's face, which Susannah always thought of as flat, pushed close to her, framed in the wig of shiny, black hair he pomaded into stylish curls. His eyebrows seemed painted on over brown eyes that always darted in his florid face. "What was it, Susannah? I thought you didn't ever allow the comments of the pit asses out there to disturb you, but you halted during the best beginning entry applause you've ever had."

"It was just," she faltered, "I—for one moment—I thought maybe the Prince of Wales was in the royal box."

"Egads, girl, we would have told you that," Theo said and elbowed Fleetwood back a step. "Usually your concentration is good, *par excellence*. I'm only grateful your little imp of a brother pushed you on!"

"Susannah, my dear," Fleetwood said, turning her to him with hands on her forearms under the tiers of ruffles and lace, "no one from the royal family is in the royal box. Those are friends of the king. If there's to be a command performance, even if the king's family just drops in unannounced, we'll tell you. It's only a racing friend of mine who's a close advisor of His Majesty's Prime Minister in the box tonight. His name's Tenn Sloper, and he has his father and current mistress or some such with him, so don't think a thing of it."

His words pierced her, and she sucked in a ragged breath to keep from falling over. Current mistress! Damn the cad, but she had been taken for a fool, and willingly too! And yet, if he had meant what he'd whispered to her that night at the Inn when she had fallen asleep naked in his arms, could not that bejeweled, laughing woman at his side up there be her? She actually felt sick, shaky, hot, and so enraged she'd like to shoot the green-eyed Satan dead with one of Henry Peter's Cupid arrows!

When she did not answer, Fleetwood loosed her, patted her shoulder, and darted off. Theo stepped closer and both hands went to her wrist as he had held her earlier. Numb, she hardly noticed and did not protest.

"That's the first *faux pas* I've ever seen you make on stage, my sweeting," he told her. "Mistakes like that and you'll need more private tutoring to ever have a chance to become the fine actress you long to be."

"Long to be," she echoed. Her brain threw explicit, tormenting scenes at her: She was in Tenn Sloper's arms in the carriage, drowning in the river, swept away in the deep, dark bed where he pretended to value her, care for her, while inwardly he laughed. . . .

She retied her mask on her face as she felt her eyes fill with blinding tears. "I do long to be an actress, Theo," she said very low. "Quite honestly I desire it so fervently, I believe I would be willing to strike a bargain with you to attain that—as it's all I really care about now."

"Sweeting, do you mean it? A bargain *vis-à-vis*, a bargain, of course. Listen—that's your next cue. Are you certain you will be all right? Only two more songs and that silly repartee with your little imp of a brother."

"Yes," she said and turned woodenly away. "Don't worry. I'll make everyone happy. Father's probably ready to throw a snit over my stopping out there too."

She stepped back on the platform and stared through her mask at Theo. She forced a still, half smile that felt more like a sneer. "I will get through this act, Theo, but I must go home before the unmasked finale. I—feel too ill to make that. If you wish to discuss my wanting to become an actress, I am certain the Arnes would be pleased to receive a visit from you tomorrow early afternoon on King Street. You know where we live, I believe. . . ."

She stopped her words when she realized she was calling too loudly down to him as her cloud platform lifted toward the high ceiling again. The painted scenery, the stage, the audience—and Tenn Sloper—lay beneath her now. All that remained was her other dream, her childhood fantasy, her maidenhood desire to be a famous and accomplished actress to set all London agog. Surely, no price was too great to pay for that goal, as it would make her father and brother Tom so happy and blot out everything else.

She forced a smile to her crimson lips beneath the gilded mask, and went back to being the goddess of love, a superior being immune from what she herself would only inflame in others.

Three weeks later, on her wedding day, April 21, 1734, Susannah Arne sat stiff-backed on the worn settee in the only drawing room of the house her parents now kept open. Other rooms in the once prosperous Queen Anne style home were hired out to impoverished gentlemen or simply kept closed. The downstairs room, where an upholstery business and undertaker's establishment had once flourished, went now untouched except when Tom used them for practice rooms or parties when father was not home. She remembered and smiled inwardly at the thought of how stubborn Tommy used to employ coffins as his practice stands before father allowed him to spend hours rehearsing his music. She would use funeral garments that were rented to mourners to play actress and stage her imaginary dramas when father was not about. And now—now father pushed both her and Tommy to do that which he had once forbidden.

"My dear, dear daughter, you look wonderful," her father said bending over her to pat her hand as if her memories had summoned him. He sat stiffly down beside her.

"Thank you, Father. Everyone will look nice, I am certain."

"But you, my dear, a raving beauty even with that sour face you've sported for weeks. Buck up. Theo will be here soon and he'll want a sweet look from the lady he's just bought that pretty gown and gold wedding band and leased a new house for."

"I suppose," she sighed. "But he may need to watch a sour face of his own when he hears I insist he sign the agreement before I go to the Sardinian Chapel to wed him. He wasn't too happy when I finally convinced him I actually meant for him to sign prenuptial articles to protect my present salary and increases I might make later. He's a spendthrift on the most wretched things, Father, and I will not be left destitute as mother was when her family inheritance was lost."

"Was lost, is it? Your mother destitute!" His high voice poured from between sunken cheeks and pouted lips. "Fire and brimstone, I should have known it was your mother who helped you concoct this silly scheme to have a husband—one whose benefits the Arnes value too—forced to sign his rightful and lawful control of his wife's funds away to her 'sole and separate use.' What silly feminine poppycock!"

"Please don't shout, Father. Mother's upset enough today."

"Mother? Mother! How dare she bend your ear about how I saw fit to handle her infernal family trust, and I'll speak my mind on it to both of you when the time's ripe." He halted, gasped, then began to breathe quickly as if he were out of wind from having run a long distance. His silver wig seemed to shudder as he quieted.

"Father, please don't work yourself up to be so distraught," she told him and rested a hand on his thin brocaded arm. "Be happy today, for you've wanted me to be kind to Theo Cibber ever since you heard who his father was. And, if we're lucky, perhaps his father will come with him to the wedding and we can make definite plans."

"Eh? Plans? What plans? Theo told me his father hasn't come around to the idea of his only son wedding a tradesman's daughter. Though I can't see Theo's the romantic sort to catch a duke's heiress or some such, his father is one of the most influential men of the London theater these past years as well as King George's poet laureate, so I suppose he thought Theo'd fetch more of an heiress."

Susannah sighed again and rose to go into her parents' bedchamber where her friend Anne Hopson had come for the day to attend the wedding and help Susannah and her mother dress. Anne had obviously not approved of this union with Theo Cibber, but she had defended Susannah to Kitty Clive who had thrown a raving fit when she heard. From then on, Susannah had judged Anne a true friend and had vowed to hire her for her personal maid as soon as she and Theo could afford it. She still had no clear idea of Theo's financial holdings, but everyone knew his father had become affluent over the years, and Theo was following in the footsteps of his career.

"Nanna, we're almost done here," her mother greeted her when she knocked and entered. Musically talented and sweet-voiced like her daughter, Katarine Shore Arne was still pleasant-tempered and lovely-faced, and her heritage to her daughter was remarked on by all who knew her. Yet, she was buxom where Susannah was slender and had brown eyes instead of golden. Even now she had a habit of humming to herself no particular melody when she was not speaking, but her eyes had looked haunted and sad for as long as Susannah could remember.

"Mother, you look marvelous. I told you Anne's a great talent as a lady's maid. Come on out now. Tommy's late, father's a bear, and your Nanna needs you."

Susannah and her mother embraced while Anne beamed. The older woman's brown eyes misted but she blinked away the tears. Ever since this precious child came into our lives, she thought, ever since she tried to speak her own name and could only babble Nanna, she has been my joy. And now her day of ruination has surely come, for she weds a pompous, eccentric little man she does not love to attain a dream that may be unreachable. She blinked again and hugged the slender girl tightly before she stood her back to look at her again.

"I say, Nanna, but we're a fine pair. Almost the same hue of pale water-green gowns for both of us, eh? I can't say I feel a bride, though."

"I can't say I do either, Mother," Susannah said and went over to the table under the window to lift the carefully worded document before her eyes to study it again. It named her uncle, Aunt Emma's husband Charles Wheeler, executor of a trust under which he would draw Susannah Cibber's salary, invest some one hundred pounds of it in government securities, and turn over what was left to her sole and separate use. It was daring and unheard of, but then so was marrying someone only to become an actress, Susannah told herself. She was ruined anyway, besmirched in the wretched gossip-mongering press who hinted at imaginary liaisons to sell their cheap papers, ruined by being used then thrown away by Tenn Sloper. Drat, nothing mattered now, nothing but building a career with which to consume her dangerous energies and errant thoughts over the years to come.

The minutes tumbled by after that firm resolution. Theo came, decked to the hilt, with only his sister Charlotte Charke, whom Susannah had never met, on his arm.

"So lovely, my sweeting, a veritable goddess *par excellence*, isn't she, Charlotte?" he gushed. When Charlotte insisted on shaking hands and winking, he scolded. "Charlotte, I asked you a direct and civil question!"

"I was going to say hell yes, if you'd but give me a chance, brother," the petite girl with saucy, huge blue eyes retorted and glared at Theo. Her gown was brick-pink with a yellow underskirt, but men's boots protruded from under the ruffled hem, and she sported a curly coal-black man's wig to frame her small face. Impudently, Charlotte thrust out her hand to Susannah again, who took it with a smile while Theo fumed.

"Glad to meet you," the girl went on. "Anyone brave enough to wed with Theo is fine by me. Sorry about the boots, but Theo made me change and men's things are so much better," she announced with a smile and proceeded to pump everyone else's hand too.

"I told you, Charlotte, lady's manners and hold your peace," he glowered before old Thomas Arne spirited him off into the corner to whisper, and Susannah brazenly produced the prenuptial agreement. She felt reckless now, headstrong and heedless. Let him sign it or, if not, she wouldn't wed him. Let his sister romp in here completely dressed as a man and the two of them could go off to all sorts of wild adventures together without Theo; but no, she had already tried wild adventures garbed as a boy, and had both revelled and suffered from what happened as a result.

Amazingly cheerful, Theo signed. Quite smoothly, they were wed. Too soon, everyone left her alone with him, in the lovely small house he had leased at Twelve Little Wild Court, not far from the theater. At least, Susannah told herself as he latched the front door firmly behind their families' departure, Theo Cibber obviously did have money. Surely her other hopes would now fall in place as readily.

"It's a lovely house, Theo, lovely," she told him sincerely.

"Better be as it cost a pretty penny and has made me *persona non grata* a place or two, but we'll handle that another day."

Her brothers had earlier delivered her few possessions and meager wardrobe by hackney, and she stared at her small valise with the precious signed agreement on top of the pile of her things in the small tiled entryway. "I will enjoy decorating the rooms here, Theo. My mother and Charlotte really liked the house."

He snorted rather inelegantly and proceeded to empty his pockets of snuff box, coins, and watch on a chain. "Charlotte would live in a pigsty and be happy. The chit's been looney ever since she refused to dress like a girl when she was four. She used to galavant about the grounds at Hillingdon shooting, from a donkey's back, at neighbors' chimney with father's pistols. 'An ass upon an asss' father called her once. He's disowned her since."

A cold wave of foreboding raced through Susannah. "Your father has disowned his own daughter? But I rather liked her."

"Enough on Charlotte, my love—my wife. I'd rather give you my full attention, and it's high time you learned exactly what that means. You've held me off, led me on much, much too long."

"I'll need just a few of my things," she protested meekly.

"No. You need me as husband, lover, lord, and master, that so-called prenuptial contract notwithstanding. I signed nothing, I believe, that states I cannot bed my own wife when the whim takes me. Come into the bedroom now and show me all of the beauty that is fully mine, Susannah—Mrs. Cibber. I've waited much too long. Now and *ad perpetuam*."

Emotional exhaustion swept her under, or was it only total resignation to pay the fee for what she'd done? She deserved Theo Cibber. She would try to make the best of a fruitless life so far, of a ruined passion she had once felt for only one powerful, magnetic man, which was all over now.

"Yes, Theo, all right. I want us to be happy."

He led her into the ground-floor bedroom she had barely glanced into when the others had traipsed through the newly leased house upon their return after the wedding. The bed stretched out against the wall, yet much too narrow before her gaze. It was poorly made, but that would not hinder what Theo had in mind. He said that three servants, including her dear Anne Hopson as her maid, had been hired starting tomorrow.

His hands were hurried as he fumbled to untie the eight yellow satin bows that closed her pale water-green silk bodice in front. She stood stiffly, her mind a blank as she stared at the top of his bent head. Even when he roughly tugged at the bodice and attached sleeves back over her shoulders and peeled it down her arms to strip her to thin chemise and corset, she didn't budge. He loosed her corset stays and discarded the garment.

"Goddess of love—Venus, ice goddess too, eh?" he murmured as his mouth went immediately to her breasts through the linen chemise, but he soon tired of that and pulled it down so that her full, high breasts popped free.

"Exquisite! Exquisite, my sweeting, my shy little virgin," he mumbled brokenly as he suckled hard on first one pink nipple and then the other. His motions became almost frenzied as he untied her skirts and petticoats and yanked them down her hips until she stood stark naked before him with a pool of ruffles and crumpled satin about her ankles and on the floor.

His hands darted everywhere as if he were a man possessed. His mouth and hands ran riotously across her soft flesh until her ivory skin glowed pinkish where his beard stubble grazed her.

So different, so alien, so unnatural compared to—to him, her inner voice taunted as Theo tipped her back on the bed and pulled her legs apart. He stood over her, his knees between her legs where she lay spread across the bed, staring down, his brown eyes raking her while he tore off his garments. She gazed at him as one mesmerized, afraid to close her eyes for fear she'd see that other handsome, austere green-eyed face. It was Theo Cibber now for her—and a great, awaiting career as an actress, just hovering in the wings of life.

An actress—that was the answer. She had to please him; she owed Theo Cibber that at least. Tonight she must be an actress.

Naked, he came down hard against her, knocking her breath away. She forced herself to lift her arms around his neck as he spread her legs farther to press against her.

It was so different, for she was not ready for this as she had been with Tenn. Damn you, Tenn Sloper. Betrayer, liar, I hate you. These frenzied thoughts tumbled through her brain.

Theo pushed in hard. The pain was terrible, or was that all in her head and not her body?

"You sweet, icy little virgin bitch, all those months keeping me in heat," he ground out as he rocked brutally against her. "Tight little virgin, I'll teach you the love of a real man now."

She closed her eyes as heedless tears crept out and slanted down her temples. The words taunted her, and she could not check her crying. A real man now. A real—man—now.

Chapter Five

Susannah lifted her skirts to free her flying feet and darted through the roaring, jostling crowd in her sister-in-law Charlotte's wake. The two slender maids squeezed through some narrow gaps in the crowd and made others. Charlotte's curly coal-black head under a jaunty man's tricorn hat twisted back for a moment.

"The devil take it, Susannah, come on. The royal carriages will go right by a great place along the Mall I know we can see from. Damn your skirts! Come on!"

Although her newly purchased high-heeled buckled shoes hurt, Susannah managed to keep up with her hoydenish sister-in-law. Unlike her brother Theo, Charlotte was always exciting to be with, even if she was a brazen eccentric, Susannah thought as they cut onto the grassy margin that stretched along the crowded Mall. Granted, Charlotte's own family found her a flagrant embarrassment, but to Susannah that was part of her charm. After an entire year of marriage to Theo Cibber, during which she had only met his eminent, pretentious father twice and his mother not at all, she felt a real camaraderie with anyone who could rock the pious, pompous Cibber ship.

"Devil take them," Charlotte clipped out, hands on her hips clad all too noticeably in boy's breeches. "Those damn little brats are in our spot, but I'll handle that!"

Susannah halted, panting from their run, and her eyes tried to follow Charlotte's snapping blue gaze. People were everywhere along the Mall awaiting the ornate parade which was to present to the wild, cavorting Londoners the newly arrived foreign Princess Augusta of Saxe-Gotha, who later today would wed Frederick, Prince of Wales. Fops, merchants, urchins, thieves, and parliamentarians—simply everyone had turned out on this warm April day to welcome their new Princess of Wales.

But Susannah's fancies of viewing a romantic, royal parade were jolted by Charlotte's obvious intent: Bandy-legged, almost as if in imitation of her brother Theo's distinctive swagger, the feisty woman walked to a tree crowded with little boys.

"Down, down, all of you. Better run closer as I hear the prince himself is scattering coins from the carriage, maybe the king too," Charlotte shouted.

"Naw!" one lad yelled down. "Not German George. He hates Frederick whether he got hisself a princess or not. No coins from German George."

"Be stupid dolts then," Charlotte screeched undaunted. "But see, over on the other street real near St. James' where the parade started out, they were throwing these—see?" She flipped a gold guinea toward a tree and caught it without looking, while small lads dropped like bouncing apples from the tree and darted off shrieking.

"Really, Char," Susannah scolded, mock serious, "how you do lie. They'll come back and beat the stuffings out of you. And you can't be serious we're going up that tree. I don't care how low that one big branch looks. I am not dressed like a lad, this gown is new, and I do not climb trees!"

"Pox on all this preachy, proper talk of yours, Susannah. I swear to heaven, but Theo will turn you into a prissy one yet if you let him. The trouble with the world is it sets up all sorts of silly rules no ass in his sane mind would heed if he were honest. Look, we're really close to the Mall here and I thought you weren't the gushy type, but a risk taker like me. Married Theo, didn't you?"

"Don't start all that again or we'll have another of our sisterly arguments about your rudeness to everyone including me, my dear Char. Go on up if you must, and I'll watch from here."

"Devil take you, goose, you can't see worth a damn from here," Charlotte ground out and darted behind Susannah to lift her up.

"Stop it! Char, you're a lunatic fit for Bedlam," Susannah protested, but the idea suddenly appealed to her when several people nearby laughed and applauded. One big lad even came over to offer both women his interlocked hands to step up. Charlotte squealed delightedly and clambered up. Then she helped to steady Susannah who joined Charlotte with her legs hanging down from the big limb, which leaned out almost over the edge of the bricked Mall. Charlotte laughed again and flipped the lad her guinea that she had flaunted earlier.

"Theo would just die!" Susannah groaned, but she liked the view, the way she could peer down over the crowd, and the way some nearby still waved and cheered their daring location.

"Theo would just die," Charlotte echoed, "and I wouldn't mind a bit."

"Really, Char, you mustn't say such things," Susannah said low, and she stared out over the noisy crowd at the scarlet-coated soldiers riding along to clear the edges of the streets.

"Ever the loyal wife," Charlotte goaded. Then she added hastily, "I didn't mean it like that, Susannah, swear to heaven, because I know you really are, only I think you're not really happy and the wretch hasn't made good on all his high-flying promises. Men never do, you know, not brothers, not fathers—especially not husbands. That's why I left Richard, and that's why I do what I want and show them all I'm free and as good as any man. And, of course, that's why father has disowned me."

"Because you left your husband?" Susannah prodded, fascinated. Before this, Charlotte had been tight-lipped about her past, and Theo had refused to discuss his sister's antics at all. He had even forbidden Susannah to see Charlotte, but in that, she thought, I'll choose whom I will to associate with.

"It's nothing," Charlotte said so low that Susannah could barely hear her over the growing ruckus of the people. "Supposedly just men leave their wives and that's all fair and fine, so remember we women can do what we damn desire too, only at great cost. Just you remember that, my friend Susannah."

They peered under elm leaves to see down the Mall. White and silver matched pairs of huge tufted and tasseled horses pulled massive gilt carriages in fantastic shapes toward their vantage point. Despite the double red slash of soldier sentinels dotting the way, people darted out, strewing the long length of ramrod straight roadway with branches and flowers.

Some of the prince's personal entourage and members of the powerful Whig governmental party, all bedecked in opulent brocades and satins or sporting military uniforms with blazing medals and vibrant sashes, rode by on horseback, so tall they gazed eye to eye with Charlotte and Susannah on their tree limb.

Hoofbeats in staccato rhythm clattered and crunched on brick or gravel; people screamed and shouted as the royal coach approached. Huge golden wheels rotated around on hubs painted black and crimson. A quick glimpse into the glass window of the royal carriage, as if at a swift scene on the stage, showed the Princess Augusta tall, white-faced and quite nice looking as she waved, her eyes as glassy as the pane that separated her from the Londoners.

After all, she was but seventeen, Susannah thought, and it was said that she was marked somewhat by pox, stood very tall, and knew not a bit of English because her mother had been certain all England would speak fluent German since the Hanovers had ruled the land for twenty-one years now. If only she, Susannah Arne Cibber, could be so stared at, so admired, Susannah marvelled, her mind adrift in a dazzling daydream—if she could only be so studied and applauded.

"I said, Susannah," Charlotte hissed, "who is that handsome devil staring at us like that? I swear I don't know him as I'd have remembered those green eyes. Some randy friend of the prince who's seen your ankles, I suppose."

Susannah's heart thudded as she scanned the crowd below, but all faces were raptly swivelled toward the back of the passing royal carriage. "Where?" she asked as her gaze jolted into a devouring green scrutiny through suddenly faded leaves. The entire parade seemed to have come to a grinding halt, but of course that could not be.

In Persian-blue breeches and fine coat, Tenn Sloper sat astride a huge dappled gray stallion. Unlike the others more gaudily clad, his broad shoulders sported simple fringed epaulets, and a single bronze medal glittered on his chest. His big hands on the reins and his feet in the brass stirrups were encased in the finest supple black leather. A white ruffled shirt and stark cravat made his neck and face look more bronzed than she had remembered. When she dared to assess the shocking reality of his presence, she realized he was as stunned as she.

He said something to another rider at his side, an older man, stern-browed and elegantly attired, whose face bore hints of a common heritage. Tenn Sloper—her rattled brain shrieked the alarm that froze her where she sat so foolishly displayed on the branch of a tree—Tenn Sloper and his father. Tenn Sloper, urging his horse over here notwithstanding the crowd between them.

"Come on, Char! I've got to run now. Come on if you want."

"Who is he? Damn, he's coming over and he's wild looking!"

Susannah half slid, half fell to the ground despite her undignified exit and the distinct rip of her lace undersleeve on a protruding branch. She darted off into clusters of people southwest along the edge of the park, while a furious Charlotte yelled behind her, "Is he one of Theo's damn creditors or what, Susannah?"

Susannah felt instantly out of breath, instantly panicked. Last time she had fled from him it had almost led to drowning, then to drowning indeed in his arms. And when she had seen him at the theater, she had lost herself again—lost her poise, her sanity, her heart!

"Jupiter, lady, slow down!" someone shouted and put hands out as if to restrain her, but she shoved on.

She had already lost Charlotte in the shifting mass of noisy crowd, but when she paused, wracked by gasping breaths, she felt safer. There was no tall, copper-haired, blue-garbed mounted man chasing her anywhere among the stretch of thinning people along the Mall. She couldn't bear it, this obsessive fear that she would always see him anywhere she went. Worst of all, she could not bear the fact she desperately wanted him to find her, to touch her again, and to love her as no one ever had.

Their paths had crossed only twice in the two years since that single night they had spent together, she thought, scanning clusters of crowd, and she had been saved from discovery both times. She must keep her head just as she had that night he was at the theater with that beautiful woman, the night she had recklessly decided to wed Theo. Theo—she'd have to head home now to Theo and the little world she'd made for herself of keeping their home and singing in Tom's operas at Drury Lane. Susannah had been married to Theo for a year now. It might be another year before fate would let her glimpse Tenn Sloper again, a year no closer to her dream of being a great actress on London's stages than to finding some way to avenge what he had so effortlessly done to her beleaguered heart.

She doubled back along the fringe of St. James' Park with yet another quick, guilty glance over one shoulder. Char would be in a snit and Theo in a rage if she didn't get home soon after everyone else drifted back from the parade. In spite of the pain from her new shoes, which seemed to increase in direct proportion to her mental anguish, she hurried north past Marlborough Road that fronted St. James' Palace where the parade had ended.

She ignored the gingerbread and oyster hawkers screeching their wares as people headed homeward from the parade route. She glanced back once, then plunged into a little alley which connected with Pall Mall. There, there on the same horse ahead—no, it could not be—Tenn Sloper!

She turned to run, but not before the big gray mount exploded toward her, knocking a strawberry cart awry. Hoofbeats, beats of her heart, her own frenzied wooden heels, and her breathing—then his voice.

"Wait! Wait, please. Don't run!"

Two years of memories and dreams of longing, all steeped in shame and anger at what they had done and shared, energized her. But one high-heeled shoe twisted, and she stumbled. The man and mount blocked her within an apparently deserted, enclosed alley.

"Wait," his deep voice repeated, lancing through her as if he had actually thrown a sword. "I won't hurt you—hell, I've been looking for you for two years." He dismounted, closing out the rest of the sane world.

"Get away—you have no right!" she managed before she dared to look him straight in his emerald eyes again. Two years, he'd said—two years looking for her! He stepped very close, looming over her. No one was that much taller, she thought erratically, and Theo was barely her height. "I could hardly believe my eyes in the parade," he was saying as his voice shivered along her spine and shredded her poise. "I actually dashed off from a royal parade, and I'm expected at St. James' Palace even now, yet here I am chasing as always hither and yon after you. I swear, mistress, but you'll be the ruin of me yet!"

She almost accused him of ruining her performance on stage that day last year, of being the real reason she panicked enough to marry Theo Cibber, but she couldn't find her voice.

"You've had me at a great disadvantage," he went on, "for you have known my name and where I lived all this time, but I've never yet learned yours." Suddenly angry despite his irrational joy at finding her, he frowned. His hands tingled at the mere thought of touching her. He pictured how crazily he had scanned crowds in Covent Garden for her off and on these past two years; how his heart had pounded when there were unannounced visitors at the house on St. James' Square; even how he'd tried to put her out of his mind with an occasional other woman.

"Then I am grateful for something!" she threw at him, and her voice broke. But only one rakish russet eyebrow lowered at the insult as his eyes went thoroughly over her again.

"We will speak of such oversights later," he went on, apparently now unperturbed, "for we have much lost time to recapture. And since I discern a characteristically enraged tone, and evidently cannot immediately dare to hope you will give me your name and address so that I might call on you properly later, of necessity, you will have to accompany me now."

In one swift, astoundingly smooth motion, he reached behind for his horse's dangling reins and lifted her up high into his saddle.

"What? No, let me down! I can't—you—you're married and I am too!"

His face looked as if she'd kicked him for one dark instant; then he mounted quickly behind her as if she had not shouted that tirade. "You don't know what you're talking about," his voice cracked at her like a whip. "Whatever marriage I had once was over long ago and you—we'll see."

Susannah was stunned to muteness by his daring ploy of abducting her and then riding out onto busy Marlborough Road with her perched before him. She sat stiffly before him in the big saddle, desperate to hold herself away from the bounce of his hard thighs against her buttocks. She scanned the meager crowd near the gilded and black gates of the palace, hoping to see someone to call to, yet foolishly terrified there might be anyone she knew.

Then her thoughts settled and his impassioned words fell into place. He was riding directly into St. James' where the entire wedding procession had gone. He dared to take her into King George's London palace on the day of the Prince of Wales's wedding!

She turned her head sharply back to him as they clopped by the large contingent of guards with ceremonial pikes just inside the gates. "You're daft, Squire Sloper. Let me down this instant. You cannot take me in here!"

"So you at least recall my name," he shot back low. "I suggest you smile and nod a great deal once we are inside. Don't fret—the king's men will all have their ladies here. And, if you do one thing foolish before we can get away from these festivities later to talk, I promise you, you will be whisked back so fast to The Blue Rose Inn in charming Chelsea you won't know what happened. I've lost a good many nights' sleep over you, and I don't need all this furious fussing. I believe there were two very willing people in bed that night, if that's what all this outrage is over."

She jerked away from him even as he halted the horse next to a mounting block within the bricked and vaulted courtyard of St. James'. The man was insufferable, perhaps demented, but at least he had brought her to a public place simply awash with guards and proper people. Her eyes took in the fine, huge courtyard where so many rows of glittering windows gazed calmly down. The gilt and festooned carriages now empty of their passengers rolled off in a noisy line to the royal mews.

"You are indeed insane if you believe I'm going inside with you," she told him levelly as he lifted her down and his hands lingered overlong on her waist. "This is ludicrous, and I'll be heading home now."

" 'Home is where the heart is,' I believe you told me once," he said as he pulled her off the two-step mounting block and across the courtyard with him to a covered portico. "Don't worry. Stunning women are always welcome at the king's court, and despite the fact you've merely been tree-climbing and running about alleys for a change today instead of dangerous slums and rivers, you'll set the gossipmongers on their greedy ears even as you are."

She yanked back at that even though two liveried, white-wigged footmen evidently recognized Tenn Sloper and swept the wide portals open for them. Her heart crashed into her ribs in rhythmic pounding. Gossipmongers! What would Theo say—and her father? What would these noble and powerful people say when they saw some dishevelled, unknown woman dragged into a royal wedding on the arm of the married king's man, Tenn Sloper?

"Please, Squire Sloper, I must look a fright. Please, Tenn, I need a mirror and some water at least," she told him, and the frenzied pace at which he'd swept her along slowed.

"You hardly look a fright," he said very low, all too obviously moved by her sweet voice and her use of his Christian name, "though that's what you gave me today when I saw you. There's so much to say, to explain, but I'll get you the mirror and the moment's respite. Down this way. Over here."

He touched her now very properly on her elbow, and motioned her toward a side chamber in a long stretch of corridors. He opened the door. Mirrors and windows lined the large, lighted room that lay before them. Only two clavichords, a few chairs, and an indoor fountain broke the length of polished parquet wood floor.

"It's the Princesses Amelia and Caroline's music practice room," his voice assured her when she hesitated. "George Frideric Handel, no less, gives them weekly lessons here."

Susannah almost told him she had sung for Handel also, but that would have been giving entirely too much away. She still needed to get away from him and soon—preferably without his learning her name. She wondered what the outrageous Charlotte had told Theo when she returned from the parade alone today. How Theo always wished he could get royal patrons, attract royal or noble attention for his theatrical endeavors. Perhaps, he could even forgive her if she could invite someone she met here today to see one of his plays; but of course, with Tenn Sloper here, that was utterly impossible.

She smoothed her windblown coiffure under her plumed and ribboned bonnet, and tried to tuck in the lace inner sleeve torn in her quick descent from the tree. He watched her avidly for a moment, an almost stunned look on his face as if he could not believe they stood here alone together in this room of mirrors. She dared to glance at his moody reflection in the glass. Military lines of tall, copper-headed, blue-garbed Tenn Slopers went on forever in the double wall of opposite mirrors.

"Here, some water," he said at last and dipped his handkerchief for her in a large brass urn beyond the pair of polished clavichords. "This little fountain sometimes runs during their amateur concerts. I've had to sit through several lately and this fountain puts me to sleep as much as their wretched music does."

"Oh," she only said and took the proffered damp cloth. Then he hated music, she mused as she cleaned her cheeks, nose, and hands. How furious he'd be when he learned she was just an impoverished tradesman's daughter who sang for a living—when her husband let her—but how impossibly ludicrous this whole situation was anyway.

He moved closer to her, wiping his own big hands on the handkerchief she wordlessly returned to him. He was frowning slightly again as his eyes went over her. She felt undressed before him here in this maze of mirrors, utterly stripped and willing to have him touch her or whatever he would do. . . .

"No!" she got out as she tried to dart sideways, but he was too quick. His hand on her arm swung her back hard against him as their lips met in a jarring, vibrating kiss.

Only her thoughts protested as she went limp in his fierce embrace. He pressed her hard against him; no, she was actually clinging to him in a rapture she had forgotten could exist in the wild and swaying world. His mouth demanded, then softened almost beguilingly as his tongue darted to utterly possess her lips and mouth. Sharp, swirling colors assailed her as she met each caress and kiss with an unnameable hunger of her own.

He could feel his heart thudding against his blue coat and her soft breasts crushed to him. He shifted his weight to control her more, to encompass her alluring body in his grasp before she could recover and pull away. Perhaps, he dared to hope, the unfathomable depths of his longing had been her experience too; only she had not come to him and now she said she had married!

Even as they clung breathlessly, voices and trumpets exploded in the hall outside their private mirrored room. Reluctantly, he set her back, watching to be certain she was not tipsy.

"The procession where the bride is to be formally presented to the king and queen in the Banqueting Hall," he rasped low. "We've got to go out for that. My father and Prime Minister Walpole will have my head if I don't appear for some of this."

"Yes, I see," she managed, praying he could not tell she detested herself for wanting to stay here with him, for wanting him to hold and kiss her again.

In the hall, they followed the end of the long procession inward. They ascended a broad, curved flight of marble stairs festooned with bridal garlands, where several greeted Tenn Sloper and eyed her askance. She pulled back once in the returning rush of realization that she had no part in this, but he gently, firmly escorted her on.

A portly man with a long nose and large wig appeared by her side at the top of the steps and nearly bumped her into Tenn as he moved closer. His face was ruddy, his eyes sharp, and a huge gold watch chain dangled from maroon frock coat to his plump hand where he stared at an open-faced timepiece. "You're bloody late, Tenn, my man, and you know," he added lowering his voice almost conspiratorially, "His Majesty wants us all to be prompt. You know he's an absolute fanatic on that."

"It simply couldn't be helped, Sir Robert," Tenn replied calmly, then added quickly as if to change the subject, "but how are the Hanovers today? Any sign His Majesty will dare snub the new bride just because he can't abide the groom even if he is his own heir?"

Sir Robert snorted and shook his head as he pocketed his watch. "Can't tell, Tenn. They're not speaking as usual. The king's digestion is giving him fits though he won't admit it, and he's obviously longing to be back visiting Hanover and his little mistress Madame Walmoden."

Sir Robert leaned closer, pressing Susannah against Tenn's broad shoulder as if she were not there at all. "Frankly, Tenn, I've counseled the queen to accept little Walmoden. Let him bring her back here so he's not always dashing back to Germany. The people still call him German George, and damn me if this incorrigible Frederick, our illustrious bridegroom, isn't a far sight more popular. See you tomorrow at the Commission meeting then." His sharp brown eyes, apparently for the first time, alighted on Susannah and briefly studied her tense face. "A pleasure making your acquaintance, Madame," he clipped out and rolled off into the crowd preparing to enter the Banqueting Hall.

"But I didn't make his acquaintance," she observed, "and who is this Sir Robert who seems to counsel kings and queens?"

Tenn looked surprised. "The Prime Minister, though he hates that title, Sir Robert Walpole. If you would not guard your identity so zealously, I would have introduced you, but I never thought for a minute you wouldn't recognize him."

"Really, Squire Sloper?" she asked sarcastically, hoping her tone was as acidic as she intended. "Of course, he evidently took me for one of your many mistresses and thought he simply must have met me before, but don't you dare to make the same error!"

His fingers on her arm tightened and he pulled her back a step. "No more comments like that here or anywhere else. And, damn it, if you'd ever give me a name I would not feel such a fool to have to admit I don't know what to call the woman I'm with!"

Anger and hurt built within her, and she tried unsuccessfully to pull her arm back. "At any rate," she spat out, hardly caring whether or not anyone else in the noisy throng heard, "I'll surely recognize Sir Robert Walpole again. He's a crony of yours clearly enough and not for some Commission meeting either. Anyone who would counsel a king to bring a mistress back to flaunt before his wife is surely a friend of yours!"

His features turned to austere granite as they entered the vast Banqueting Hall. He led her firmly toward the front along the side wall heavy with gilt-framed portraits. "Look, sweet, we'll talk this all out later," he told her between grim frowns, "but you don't understand. Walpole's desire is to protect the king and his Whig party at any cost. The king's going to have the mistress anyway and he might as well see to duties here so that the Prince of Wales who can't abide his royal sire—and vice versa—doesn't win the masses to him and turn the power base of government pro-Tory."

Susannah had listened to all this rationale couched in other more abstract terms, she realized, overhearing frequent political discussions and arguments throughout the years. The English masses, as Tenn Sloper put it, loved to argue and to gossip, and the newspapers of the day pounced like vultures upon any hint of discord or scandal. But now, suddenly thrust in here with all these powerful forces who ran the British government, it was all so staggeringly real.

All she could see ahead of them was a bobbing sea of heads or wigs: the men's now bare of tricorn hats; the women's plumed or hatted, a few uncovered with glittering tiaras.

"On what sort of commission do you serve?" she whispered before she could tell herself she should not show him the slightest interest. Since he had said he hated music, why should she suddenly care a tinker's damn for his wretched politics that had always bored her so before?

"Trade and Plantation Board for the American Colonies," he whispered as he wedged them into the shifting crowd. Then, his mouth dipped close to her ear as he said low, "I know you can pick out the king, but let me tell you the others. Queen Caroline is there in emerald-green and diamonds. That's Anne, the Princess Royal who wed the Prince of Orange last year—the bored looking woman. The other two princesses on the far side are Amelia and Caroline. Then behind them is William; he's eighteen and the king and queen's favorite son."

Entranced and awed despite the alarming feel of Tenn Sloper's hands on her waist as he stood in back of her, Susannah peered around the tall coiffure before her to take it all in. If only she could tell mother, father, Tommy, Char, even Theo that she had seen all this and had really been to court, as if on some magical sultan's flying carpet.

Yet as she studied the scene, even with the pomp and glitter, the distant, lofty images she'd always had of England's royalty shrank to human size. The queen and her namesake, the Princess Caroline, looked terribly fat and dumpy, beautiful gowns and jewels notwithstanding. Princess Anne did look bored, even as Tenn had said, and Princess Amelia seemed sour-faced or almost waspish. They all waited for the obviously trembling bride to greet them.

Susannah saw the tall, attractive German bride's eyes lift to face her soon-to-be royal in-laws. Augusta of Saxe-Gotha jerkily halted directly before them as if skewered to that spot of floor by their piercing stares and sharp faces. Only Queen Caroline forced a smile and nodded. Augusta darted a quick look at her fiancé Frederick, Prince of Wales. It seemed she would curtsy, yet to everyone's amazement, the girl dove straight to the black-and-white floor tiles and prostrated herself before the king and queen.

The crowd murmured, whispered, tittered, then burst

into wild applause. Susannah saw Prime Minister Walpole across the way, beaming and clapping and nodding. Even the stern-faced king smiled now as he indicated his detested heir Frederick might help his properly humble betrothed up from the cold floor.

Astounded, Susannah turned back to Tenn who hadn't applauded one bit as his hands had never left her waist. "Is that—do they do that?" she mouthed at him in the tumult.

"No," his voice came warm and deep in her ear as he leaned forward to her, "but I wouldn't mind if you were a little more that way." When he saw the frosty look she shot him, he only grinned stiffly. "I'm sure there's worse to come among the Hanovers before the night is done—more abasements, more stern looks, and general discord. It's just the way it is for them, and I tire of it easily. And so, I'd like it not to be the same for us."

"There is no 'us,' " she told him as he wedged them into a crush of people moving suddenly forward in the hall.

"There hasn't been for two long years, but there will be now," he countered.

"You're daft. You're as terrible as they are," she vowed and tried to gesture toward the royal family with her hand, only to hit a man's arm in the press of people now funnelling into some sort of line. "The Prime Minister of this lunatic country may counsel for mistresses and you may flaunt them and expect women to throw themselves at your feet like that, but I'll have no part of it. I told you I'm wed and I heard you are too!" she hissed and a long-faced woman with three pink ostrich plumes nodding from her head turned to stare.

Tenn Sloper looked suddenly furious as he pulled her on. "That's not true, and you don't know a damn thing about it no matter what you heard. I clearly told you we will get to that later in private," he clipped out. Then he added, evidently before he could stop himself, "Are you happily wed then?"

"Of course!" she said, but she could not bear to meet those green, devouring eyes. Her voice merely halted at that, and she wished her face could convey the utter disdain she did not feel for what he did to her so close like this. She wanted to be the greatest actress in the land and she could not even manage this little charade with only Tenn Sloper as avid audience.

She turned swiftly away from his austere face; too late she realized why they were in a line. Several persons ahead, a gaily bedecked steward was calling out names and titles as people were presented to the king and royal family.

She whirled to face Tenn again. His stern, watchful expression had not changed. "Perhaps if you won't tell me your name," he said levelly, "you will be willing to tell King George II."

Color drained from her face, then she blushed hot from the tops of her rounded breasts to her forehead. "But I—I should not be here," she sputtered. "This isn't fair!"

"Nor is it fair what you—or lack of you—has done to me these last two years. That was not some silly, quick tumble I meant to give you, you know, and—"

"Hush up!" she hissed with a quick look around to see if anyone had heard. She began to tremble while he looked so dratted controlled now—almost despotic!

"What name shall I give the king's steward to announce, my dear?" he pursued. "And, I assure you, as soon as we get through this line, we'll leave as we have much to settle, and I'll be expected back here for the wedding in less than two hours."

Her brain raced with possible escapes: a dramatic gesture, a pretended act of illness here for them all in her first royal performance. She could faint, but then he'd pick her up and carry her away before them and that would cause a scene.

"The Duke and Duchess of Norfolk!" the steward's voice sang out, ever so close.

Susannah stared up into Tenn's glittering jade eyes and tried to ignore their devastating impact on what was left of her poise. "Tell them what you will, Squire Sloper," she managed. "Make up something appropriate or, I swear, I'll tell them all you abducted me today."

One corner of his firm mouth quirked upward, but he didn't smile. "This quibbling is useless, you know," he whispered. "We're inevitable. I know it and you do too."

"Lord and Lady Chesterfield!"

Trying to feign an aplomb she did not feel, Susannah grandly turned her back on Tenn Sloper to await their turn. Surely, she had him now and had regained control of the life that he had turned so topsy-turvy ever since she'd met him, even when they were apart and lost to each other for good. Drat the man! It was greatly his fault that she had married Theo Cibber, and certainly because of him that she'd never been in love with her husband or anyone else. But if he thought for one instant that his charms and aggressive attempts at flattery and possession would ever make her tell him who she was, so he could continue to taunt her and ruin her calm, safe world, he had much to learn!

The steward sang out the last names and titles before they halted before him, but the words blurred right by Susannah. The blond steward's eyes actually lighted when he saw her, but before he could ask their names, close behind her Tenn said, "Squire William Sloper, the younger, from Berks, and my cousin Aman—"

"Miss Arne is your cousin?" the steward interrupted. Tenn's jaw dropped, and Susannah gasped. "Miss Susannah Arne, I've heard you sing both at the Haymarket and now Drury Lane," the steward went on. "I admire your songs so much, especially the sweet love songs your brother, Master Arne, composed."

"Ah, oh, thank you," Susannah faltered, terrified to meet Tenn's eyes. "But I'm married now," she blurted out before she realized she should have held her peace. Oh, damn—what did it matter now anyway? "Mrs. Cibber," she murmured low even as Tenn leaned forward. "It's Mrs. Cibber now."

"Indeed, the poet laureate's family," the wretched steward blundered on. "I believe he's here today too, probably has composed something suitably poetic for the occasion."

Susannah lifted her hand to her face to halt the sudden roaring rush in the room. Maybe she would faint or be carried off for dead. Tenn knew her name; there was no hiding now. Her father-in-law, who probably detested her, would know she was here with another man, and King George would know she was some upstart swept into his royal receiving line from the very streets of common London.

"Squire William Sloper, the younger, and Mrs. Cibber!"

Woodenly, she moved forward with Tenn Sloper's too possessive, maddening hand at the back of her waist urging her on.

It is only like being at center stage, Susannah, she told herself, just what you've wanted, and with a handsome supporting man to boot, damn him. She curtsied low as she had seen the others do, as she herself had done so often during wild applause at the theater.

A pink hand seized hers and lifted her. She gazed directly into the pale blue eyes of George II of Hanover, King of England. His nose was long, his forehead high, his lips full and somehow pouted. But before he could address her, his daughter Caroline bent forward, her chin wobbling as she spoke.

"Your Majesty, I saw Miss Arne in Herr Handel's lovely oratorio *Deborah* two years ago—you know, when I went without your permission and you scolded me for weeks. I went *incognito*, you see," she ended and smiled directly at Tenn Sloper and offered him her hand to bow over.

"I believe, Your Grace, Miss Arne would appreciate that as she often goes out *incognito* herself," Tenn dared to say. Susannah caught the barely controlled edge of his voice, and blushed even pinker.

"A singer, one of Herr Handel's singers?" the king was asking, his voice heavy with an amazingly thick German accent. "Then I shall appreciate your talents someday, though I fear my son, the Prince of Wales, would not as he detests my Handel and favors only those vile Italian operas."

"But he only does that to spite you, Your Majesty," the plump princess insisted as the next name rolled off the steward's all-knowing tongue, and they moved quickly past the queen and affianced couple with nods and bows.

Tenn's hand tightened perceptibly on her arm as they moved away from the royal receiving line. She felt stunned, numb, as though the whole day had been a dream: The king himself had spoken to her, and Tenn Sloper had stepped out from her smothered fantasies into flesh and blood existence.

He spoke first as they approached the back of the vast hall. "Miss Susannah Arne, now Mrs. Cibber, and the poet laureate's daughter-in-law. And," he added, "the king shall appreciate your talents someday."

She spun to face him, tears inexplicably blurring her view of him. "Do not dare to mock me. So now you know. I'm a singer, Squire Sloper, and I'm sure quite beneath your concern. Did you think I was some country heiress off on a spree or some homeless orphan you could dazzle? The closest I've ever come to the king or likely shall again, you see, is that my brother mockingly calls my father 'His Majesty,' so I would be eternally grateful to you if you'd just set me free now and stay out of my life, as I'm sure all of this is a huge jest to you now anyway—"

"Stop it, Susannah." She quieted at his unexpected use of her first name and the soft, caressing way he said it. He took her arm and led her out from the entry of the Banqueting Hall where they had halted under the huge painted and carved doorway. He walked her quickly to the curved staircase they had climbed earlier, and she descended with him, thankful he was letting her go away, yet loathe to have this all end. The ornate balustrade swept by like a sinuous snake; a parade of portraits heavy in gilt frames stared down at their retreat.

But in the long, nearly deserted hall through which they had originally entered St. James', he finally pulled her to a stop and turned her to face him. "Susannah Arne—Cibber," he said slowly as his green-gold gaze swept her. "Susannah fits you—very graceful and lovely, but full of Biblical fury. You know, Susannah, if you would have told me who you were earlier, I would have sent you home."

Her heart fell to her feet. Then he had believed she was someone worthy, someone perhaps even noble because of the way she spoke, since father had once had the dream to educate her as a fine lady before he lost everything. Tears crowded to her thick lashes again. "Oh, of course," she brazened, "a mere theater singer and you can't even abide music—"

Both of his big hands lifted to her upper arms, and he shook her once. "I assure you that's not it at all. I only needed to know where to find you, who you were. And now that I know these things, I will send you home and we will meet another time very soon without all these people and these demands on my time and, no doubt, yours too."

She could feel her pulse beat wildly at his words, and she detested her own foolish weakness after all the times she'd cursed him and plotted her vague revenge against him should they ever meet again. "No," she told him.

"Stay away. I'm very happily married and I never want to—to see you again."

"But my sweet Susannah, I believe anyone who will buy a seat is welcome at London's theaters—even Princess Caroline *incognito* or the king's chief protocol steward. Even the king searching for pleasure or Tenn Sloper looking for his."

She yanked free of his touch and darted back two steps. She'd never be free of him now. He'd be there in her mind's eye each time she sang, out there green-eyed and magnetic to ruin her poise in any crowded audience. She faced him squarely, her head high.

"I am certain, Squire William Sloper, the younger, you will not wish to involve yourself in the life of a tradesman's daughter who earns her way by singing and desires desperately to be an actress—nothing else from life but that. And now, as my family and husband are no doubt worried for my whereabouts, I shall bid you farewell."

She pivoted smoothly about and started away, praying he would at least allow her a dignified exit, but his long strides easily brought him beside her.

"Susannah—Mrs. Cibber, I apologize for detaining you, but at least your day was not a complete loss since you met the king. And I must insist on sending you home in a carriage."

"No thank you, Squire Sloper. I'm hardly used to carriages, and I am quite capable of walking or hiring a sedan chair. It was, I admit, of interest to see the king's family, but I need no more surprises from you—ever. Goodbye."

Amazingly, he let her go. She strained her ears for his big booted feet running after her across the bricks of the central courtyard as she hurried toward the gate, but there was nothing except the sounds of guards' voices and the increasing noise from the street as she approached it.

He had let her go at least enlightened, sobered by the

knowledge of whom and what she really was and hardly fit to chase for a rich squire who knew the king—hardly fit to bed. Now, she could finally put the haunting dreams of their one rapturous night aside to go on with her sane and reasonable life.

She glanced up and down Marlborough Road. Shadows stretched across the street to snuff out the day. Under the huge painted royal coat of arms above the still open palace gates, she raised her trembling hand to summon a sedan chair.

Chapter Six

The next afternoon after Susannah's tumultuous visit to King George's court with Tenn Sloper, she sat in an empty box seat at Drury Lane and watched rehearsal for the revival of a play written years ago by her famous and aloof father-in-law, Colley Cibber. She had already sung her new songs to the apparent satisfaction of Charles Fleetwood, the theater owner, and her own husband Theo, the manager, and she only hoped they would leave her alone now to sit here and watch. She leaned her elbows forward on the carved and painted edge of the box rail and studied the clever actress-comedienne Kitty Clive at work.

"If I've told you once, I've told you a hundred times *ad infinitum*," Theo was telling Kitty as, playbook in hand, he strutted to the edge of the protruding stage, "this comedy is not entitled *The Fool in Fashion* because the actors foolishly forget their lines, Kitty, my dear."

"Mrs. Clive to you, Mr. Cibber!" the robust, rosy-faced Kitty clipped out as her balled up fists shot to her hips. "Piss on it, if I have to take smart-ass orders from this banty rooster, Fleetwood, I'd rather perish. He killed his poor wife Janey—my dearest and best friend—with overwork, but I swear on my mother's grave, he'll never do the same to me!"

"Now, Kitty, dearest," Charles Fleetwood soothed as he pulled his portly frame slowly out of his chair in the nearly empty pit inhabited by only a few paying patrons who had come to watch rehearsals today.

Susannah's daydream that she was out there on the stage evaporated; she leaned even farther forward. So Kitty Clive had been friends with Theo's first wife, Janey, and blamed him for her death, Susannah mused. No wonder Kitty spit cruel, insulting words at her whenever their paths crossed. And now Theo, evidently aware Susannah was perched in a theater seat all too eagerly imbibing the many actresses' parts she coveted, glanced nervously up toward the box before glowering at Kitty and turning back to Fleetwood.

"Now, Charles, stay seated," Theo intoned. "It's nothing Mrs. Clive and I can't solve *de facto*, at least *ex tempora*."

"Pox on you, Theo Cibber," Kitty clipped out and threw her playbook on the table center stage. "If you'd ever just talk king's English instead of all that silly foreign jabbering to try to put us street wenches in our place, then maybe—just maybe—you could do the job directing these damned plays your illustrious father wrote. *He* was great here once, Theo Cibber, but you can't so much as lick his bootstraps!"

Kitty stalked offstage, canary-yellow skirts swishing so loudly that Susannah could hear them even where she sat. She sighed as she watched Kitty's flagrant exit and the way Theo and Charles Fleetwood huddled over what to do next. Both actors who had been onstage with Kitty—the venerable, mammoth James Quin, and the swarthy, impulsive 'Mac' Macklin everyone called 'the mad Irishman'—simply stood and stared.

Suddenly Macklin, who flirted with Susannah whenever he got the chance and pinched her if he ever got her alone in the wings, caught her worried eye and flashed a smile. "Mrs. Cibber, Theo's own little angelic colleen watching from the heavens. Come on down then and read Kitty's part for us 'til she cools off a bit today. My own love scenes with her part of Amanda are coming up next, sure as we're livin'."

"Mac, really!" Theo looked up long enough from his conversation with Charles Fleetwood to frown at Macklin and then up at Susannah. "Mrs. Cibber is a singer. She does not act and certainly not love scenes with you!"

Susannah leaned even farther forward. "But it would help rehearsals if I just read Kitty's part until she comes back, Theo. I mean, it's holding up Mr. Macklin and Mr. Quin, and there are several here who have paid to see a rehearsal," she called down beseechingly. Her voice sounded almost woeful in her own ears for she already knew Theo would still say no.

Below her on the stage surrounded by the other three men, Theo turned his face upward again and squinted to see her better. His voice seemed especially shrill, his eyes sharp as he dashed her hopes again. "Susannah, please! If you're going to fret so, go on home. I believe you and I have had this discussion *sub rosa* more than once before."

"But never with me as official arbiter, I believe, Theo," a booming voice from the back of the theater interrupted.

Theo's jaw dropped while Fleetwood, Macklin, and Quin just stared. Susannah gripped the side of the box at the sight of her father-in-law, Colley Cibber, charging down the far side aisle.

"Father!" Theo stammered, all too obviously shocked at this rare appearance. "You—did you come then to see how I'm directing your old play?"

"Let us just say I came to see a lot of things, my boy. Fleetwood, good day. James Quin, you cut as imposing a swath as ever; glad Fleetwood has managed to net you for our beloved Drury and paying a pretty penny for the honor, isn't he?" Colley Cibber addressed everyone as though he were beginning a formal speech. He wore a vibrant peacock-green frock coat and gestured grandly with a gold-headed walking stick to punctuate every line.

The huge Quin and much shorter Colley Cibber shared a laugh while Theo fidgeted from one foot to the other.

"And so, this is Charles Macklin—Black Mac—named for your temper and not your hair, I reckon," Colley Cibber went on, occasionally with a broad sweep on his arm. "Ah, sometimes I realize I have been retired to king's service as mere poet laureate far, far too long. But to the order of the day. Theo, I came to see your little song thrush of a wife, Susan."

Susannah gasped so loudly that the four men turned to stare up at her, and the sparse audience in the pit whispered. Her eyes met her father-in-law's shrewd, assessing gaze. It was the first time since the two previous occasions they had briefly met that she was certain he had ever really looked at her. Her heart thudded and she wet her lips with the tip of her pink tongue. He had seen her yesterday at St. James' Palace with Tenn Sloper and he'd come to tell Theo. Drat him! She had managed to convince Theo she'd had the opportunity to observe the royal ceremony only because some random Londoners in the streets were invited in on the spur of the moment, and she had dared to go, but now she would be ruined!

"Ah, there you are, dear Susan," Colley Cibber intoned.

"Her name's Susannah, father," Theo put in sharply, "and what, pray tell, do you want with her?"

"Ah, dear Theo, I only regret you have let me down, let all of us down by not thinking of this in the months you have been wed to her. It came to me in a flash, you see. Her voice—have you not all heard her voice, gentlemen—so full and sweet?"

"Like the little colleen herself," Macklin put in, and from behind the others threw her a grin and a leer she totally ignored. She stood slowly in the box taking in the little scenario below her and nervously brushing off her pale pink skirts.

"You came to—you wish to hear me sing, Mr. Cibber?" she asked, not daring to believe he could mean more.

"There, gentlemen, the dulcet, plaintive tones of a natural born actress. Come down and read for me, my dear; after all, it is my play they were working on here, I take it."

She dashed down the back stairs as Theo's protest and Macklin's laughter floated to her disbelieving ears. It was a miracle, a prayed-for miracle! The famous playwright, comic actor, theater manager, and king's poet laureate here to see her act! The only man, praise God, who could probably handle Fleetwood and Theo too, if they balked.

She felt suddenly shy this close to him and, as she walked toward the men, she could hear her wooden-heeled shoes clomping forlornly on the stage currently denuded of its green carpet. At first Colley Cibber looked too much like Theo close up: middle height with a thin face, full mouth, and darting hands. But his long nose turned up at the end and the face was dwarfed by a fashionable, full-bottomed flaxen periwig. His complexion was sandy pale in contrast to the flash of his peacock-green brocade frock coat and winking jeweled buttons. He even smiled at her; perhaps, she prayed, he had not been at St. James' at all yesterday to see her make a fool of herself with Tenn Sloper.

"I would be pleased to read for you, sir," she told him. "Mrs. Clive was here a moment ago, but she's gone off, and I am very familiar with both the roles of Amanda and Narcissa in this play."

Colley deftly elbowed Theo back a step. "Are you, my dear? Both roles? You like my play then?"

"Oh, yes. You see, all I've ever been allowed—all I've done here, I mean, is sing, but I would so love to try my hand at acting."

"Susannah is trained solely as a singer, father, trained partly by Handel, you may have heard, but I believe when I asked you to hear her sing earlier you were too busy."

"Enough, Theo. I'm not too busy now. You know Susan—Susannah, several very important people have remarked to me how they adore your voice and, well, since I absolutely made Mrs. Oldfield's marvelous career years ago from nothing and she was dumpy with a crooked nose, who knows what I might make of a beauty like you, eh? Geniuses need challenges now and again, and Theo," he added, his treble voice gone hard and flat, "it is obvious to me you have overlooked possibilities here."

Theo's dark eyes glittered dangerously, a look Susannah knew often preceded a tantrum. But, blessedly, Colley Cibber ignored his son entirely from then on and ushered her over to the wings for a private word.

"Now, my dear Susannah, I'm going to give you a little section to read for me. Your voice is so alluring, so—shall we term it—plaintive. Something by Amanda will be good, I think, as she has her sorrows as well as joys, h'm?"

"Yes, that's fine. Someone told you they liked my singing and you thought to see if I could act?"

The light brown eyes over the *retroussé* nose met her gaze. "Quite right. I said that, did I not? I hope to heavens with that voice, face, and figure you turn out to be a quick study, that's all. Perish the thought and all we have planned for you if not."

"We? Who has planned, Mr. Cibber?"

"We—those of us here who appreciate your obvious talents, my dear. You may call me Father Cibber, you know, now that you've been Theo's wife a while and even my silly jade of a daughter Charlotte evidently dotes on you. Go on, now, just fetch that playbook on the table and we shall try a little dialogue here."

Despite her curiosity as to whether the Princess Caroline, who said she had heard her sing, or perhaps the king himself had recommended her voice to her previously aloof father-in-law and their royal poet laureate, Susannah fetched the book under Theo's glare.

"It's Kitty Clive's book, Father Cibber," she told him low as he flipped through it. "She was reading her part as Amanda but she went off."

"Doesn't matter, it is my play. I created it and brought it to life just as I shall you."

She swallowed hard. It was impossible to believe. He had suddenly descended like a magical wizard and had evidently decided to believe in her before she even read for him.

He thrust the open playbook at her and pointed to a paragraph of speech. "Go on now, my dear. Take the stage as if it belongs to you. Just read—maybe with a fillip of a brief gesture or two. Mr. Macklin," he called out louder, "if you are so eager to help, read Loveless's words there on page fifty-one, if you please."

With that final pronouncement, Colley Cibber strutted down into the first row of the gallery and sat, arms folded across his green chest. Behind her, the kindly James Quin, who had always been polite to her, although apparently detesting Theo, mumbled something encouraging and strolled off with Fleetwood to watch from the left wings. Macklin winked at her, and Theo, his face a veritable thundercloud, stalked off a few yards and glared.

As if for the first time ever, Susannah lifted her eyes to gaze out over the rim of stage to the pit, gallery, upper gallery, and boxes. How beautiful the theater looked with its upholstered seats of green baize padded with tow, its curved rows of benches rising one over the other toward the paint and gilt ceiling. It was all waiting for her as Colley Cibber had said, to make it belong to her. She heard her own voice—Amanda's voice—fill the waiting theater:

" 'Bring me word immediately if my apartment's ready, as I ordered it. Oh, I am charmed I have found the man to please me now, one that can, and dares maintain a noble rapture of a lawless love. I own myself a libertine, a mortal foe to that dull thing called virtue . . .' "

She glanced down once or twice, familiar with the words, aware of how jauntily Kitty would deliver the lines, but that was not her style. The Lady Amanda had been hurt by a husband who did not love her. The speech was from a comedy but such a sad speech too. She half turned and, in a rustle of skirts, faced the satyr-eyed Charles Macklin who shot her a fiery look hardly called for in the play. Curse the man, but he'd better not ruin this for her, Susannah thought fleetingly as she went on.

" 'Speak freely then. Does my face invite you, sir? May I, from what you see of me, propose a pleasure to myself in pleasing you?' "

" 'By heaven you may,' " Macklin's marvelous baritone voice swirled around her. " 'I have seen all the beauties that the sun shines on, but never saw the sun outshined before.' "

" 'Spoken like the man I wish might love me—pray heaven his words prove true,' " she added aside and stared right through the furious Theo as if he were not standing close at all. " 'But while we chance to meet, still let it be with raging fire. No matter how soon it dies, provided the small time it lasts, it burns the fiercer.' "

"Marvelous—all I had dared to hope!" Colley Cibber's voice broke into her next words and several others clapped loudly. "Theo, come down here with Susannah, if you please."

Susannah held Kitty Clive's playbook tightly to her breasts, and hurried down the right side steps while Theo swaggered down those on the other side.

"You realize what a find she is, do you not, Theo?"

Colley Cibber said pointing at his son as if to punctuate each word.

"Susannah's a singer, father. She has no theatrical training, and we've plenty of actresses. She is my wife and—"

"—and, perish the thought, but I believe you have never balked at that before!" Colley Cibber interjected.

Susannah's wide eyes collided with Theo's fierce stare, and he frowned at his father's obvious reference to his first wife whom Kitty Clive had accused him of working too hard. "Susannah's different," Theo said low. "Her father reared her as an educated lady, and I won't have her on the common stage with the like of Clive and various and sundry other wenches for the rabble and nobility alike to ogle."

"That's what's wrong with you, Theo, damn me if it isn't," Colley Cibber lectured him as he stood and pulled his lace cuffs down at the wrists from his green brocade sleeves. "If you make your livelihood from the theater, don't regard it as some street strumpet. 'For the love of a bawd' you're always saying. Damn it, Theo, the king's Theater Royal is not a bawd or an embarrassment, and I won't have any son of mine regard it as such. Your elegant wife will be as safe treading theater boards as she wants to be. You only care for what will bring in ticket prices, I daresay. Besides, Susannah on the stage will do that, do you not agree Macklin?" Colley Cibber added with a quick flourish of lace-edged wrist and gold-headed walking stick.

Macklin had ambled up to casually lean his hips against a green-painted gallery divider. "Indeed, sir. I'd pay a good price to see the lady any day."

"There, Theo," Colley concluded grandly. "That cinches it. She will need some months of training, I grant you that, and I shall arrange it. I was speaking to Aaron Hill just the other day, and he is searching for a bright, young talent to take the lead in a new play he is writing, so perhaps he and I shall see to her instruction."

"Father, she is my wife and, if she's such a *rara avis*, as you claim, I'll see to it."

"I think not, Theo. You are busy enough here, and I believe her credibility would be greater were I to mentor her, no offense, my boy, perish the thought. Besides, we all know tragedy was hardly your style, Theo, and with her voice and eyes, it may well be Susannah's final pinnacle. I'll call soon at Wild Court, my dear Susannah, and don't let Theo browbeat you or he shall answer to me. Fleetwood, Macklin, good day."

Susannah stared speechless, her heart pounding wildly. So easily, so perfectly accomplished after all the years of longing to have even the slightest chance, she marvelled, watching her father-in-law depart up the aisle, then hearing his treble voice again as he evidently stopped to talk to someone just outside. Weak-kneed, she sat in the seat he had vacated while Macklin and Theo still stood over her.

"We'll see about all this later, Susannah," Theo ground out. "And if anyone's to oversee it, I will, *au contraire* whatever my despotic father says. Mac, let's get back to this rehearsal as enough time's been wasted here. Oh, for love of a bawd, I'll fetch Clive myself if I have to drag her out by her hairlocks!" He grabbed Kitty's playbook from Susannah's hands and marched off.

Susannah jerked her gaze up at Charles Macklin's avid, dark-eyed perusal. "Well, Mr. Macklin?" she said low, but her voice was much softer than she had intended.

"Well, indeed, pretty little song thrush," he chortled as his eyes went deliberately over her again and lingered blatantly on her bosom. "May I only say you were smashing, but then you've always affected me that way. Anytime you tire of that sour banty rooster you're fettered to, then maybe I can help. The offer's always open."

She shot him a withering look. "Is it, Mr. Macklin? Then I believe I understand at last why they call you 'The

Mad Irishman.' The only offer I will ever accept from you, you see, is as nice a job as you did in reading with me—and that is all!"

"So tempestuous, like the Irish Sea off the green coasts of fair Dublin, beautiful Susannah—and for the likes of Theo? What a bloody shame your ripe body is wasted for—"

She flounced up and pushed past him toward the back of the theater before she could hear more. The man was crude and rude and he only twisted each insult to suit him, so she wouldn't even listen. He was ruining her moment of glory, her ecstatic mood. How dare he leer at her the way he always did and mention her body like that, for she legally belonged to Theo. But when she thought of Tenn Sloper, things became so confused.

She shoved through the partially open door into the small, deserted foyer and sat on a green carpeted step of the stairs leading to the upper gallery. Her body and her mind and her heart: They were the great betrayers that turned totally traitorous at the mere presence or thought of Tenn Sloper. Those words of the Lady Amanda she'd just read a few minutes ago from *The Fool in Fashion* about finding a man to please her now and 'a noble rapture of a lawless love' had been only too real. Amanda—that had even been the name Tenn had used for her the day they first met, when he had gone to Moll King's looking for his supposed runaway betrothed, Amanda Brompton. To her dismay, Susannah felt her nipples point to hard peaks against her corset as a wave of erotic memories of Tenn's kiss yesterday and their wild lovemaking two years ago feathered the feel of rough velvet along her thighs.

"Susannah," the deep voice came low, but she didn't budge at first. It was her vivid thoughts of him perhaps, or Macklin was calling her back inside the theater, and her foolish brain merely turned his magnificent stage voice to her own longing for Tenn Sloper.

"Susannah, are you all right?"

She jumped, turned, and gazed up. Above her on the narrow steps stood Tenn Sloper, hat in hand. She heard herself gasp as she leapt to her feet and moved two quick steps away.

"What are you doing here? You are not welcome here!" she managed and backed up step for step as he descended to her.

"My dear Susannah, I believe we have had this discussion before. And did you really think I would not call on you now that I know your true identity after all this time? I would never have even let you go yesterday had I not learned who you were."

"Please keep your voice down. And you'll have to leave. My husband is here and my father-in-law just left."

"I know. I saw Colley Cibber and heard from out here the little scene you read. Well chosen, I'd say—'Let us chance to meet in raging fire that burns the fiercer' or something like that. I would have gone in to sit down, but I feared I might break your concentration."

She stared up at him with slightly parted lips. The man was entirely dangerous: a mind reader, a magician of her moods. The little velvet brushing along her thighs which alarmed her so began again.

"I must go back inside," she said, her voice a whisper. Her gaze locked with his drowning green-gold stare before she looked away.

"Fine. I'll just go along. That was my original plan anyway. I came hoping to see you sing as I've only been to this theater once over a year ago. I've gotten in the habit, I'm afraid, of giving private dinner parties at home and seldom going out in the evenings unless I'm at court for social functions with all the other watchful Whigs. I still have the Berkshire habit of rising with the dawn, only," he said, his voice gone raspy, "I overslept one time in Chelsea and have regretted that ever since."

Susannah almost swayed toward him before she caught herself. Drat this powerful, ruggedly alluring tempter. He looked so elegant today in his midnight-black breeches and frock coat and his stark white cravat and shirt, which set off his teeth and eyes against his tawny face. His copper hair in this muted foyer light looked all burnished or brazen, and she simply couldn't let him go inside.

"My husband's directing a play inside," she said, sounding blessedly sane to herself again. "I don't think you would especially enjoy it since you're hardly much of a theatergoer."

"But I do intend to be now," he retorted and shot her a swift smile. "Your husband—is he the tall one with the unruly black hair who read the scene with you?"

She turned back to face him. "No. That's Charles Macklin, the Irish actor who's new here. I just—well, Theo's the shorter man."

"The little Caesar? I had no idea. I see."

She frowned at him suddenly almost embarrassed. She knew others commented on how mismatched she and Theo seemed in looks, temperament, and character, but she could not bear to think Tenn Sloper thought she had married for anything but love or that she was not wildly happy.

"I doubt if you see at all, Squire Sloper. My husband and I are very happy, and now I have the chance I've always wanted. I was reading a part this morning for my father-in-law, and he intends to train me to be an actress; that's what I've always wanted desperately anyway."

To her amazement, he smiled and nodded. "To want something desperately makes one so alive in all the senses. It gives life a fiery, burning purpose," he told her.

She nodded too, astounded he understood. She startled, but did not protest when he took her right hand in both his and lifted it for a brief kiss to his warm lips. "I'm glad you're happy, Susannah. I swear to you that's what I want for you, only we're both going to have to be very truthful about what will really make you—and us—happy."

She tugged her hand back and put it behind her. "I told you yesterday, there is no 'us.' There was once a long time ago only for a moment, I suppose, but I was pretending to be someone else then, and it was all a mistake."

"Really? And yesterday when you responded so warmly in the music practice room of the palace? And now?"

He dared to pull her back several steps into the entrance to the stairs and move her against him. She shoved hard once against his broad brocade chest, but did not really fight or cry out as she could have before his masterful mouth covered hers. Curse you, Susannah, she told herself as she felt her soft body press full-length to his hard one, you want him to touch you all over like this.

Thoughts stopped. She swam in feelings so deep she could not surface, could not resist the rapturous currents that swept through her. His fierce lips slanted sideways across her open mouth pulling a raging response from her that she gave him mindlessly. His solid thighs rustled her skirts; his hands stroked her supple back and narrow waist to bring her closer—closer.

His hot tongue invaded her mouth in a welcome intrusion. They were surely back in that warm soft bed in Chelsea, all safe against the world. They were once again only one powerful, alluring man and one eager, innocent woman who did not belong legally to anyone named Theo Cibber.

She jerked her head away and stared up into his dazed face inches from hers. She could see the glittering depths of his eyes and each separate dark brown eyelash tipped coppery at the ends, even in this dim light. His sweet breath wafted at her, all enveloping and embracing.

"What is it, sweet? Get your bonnet and cloak and

come out with me. We have to talk."

She pulled back and he released her, steadying her elbow for a moment with one hand. Still, even away from him like this, her head spun and her lips felt sweetly rasped and tingling.

"You must know I will not—cannot—go out with you. I want you to, please, go away and stay away." To her chagrin, he reached out to tuck back a stray curl at her temple. "Don't!"

"I told you I'm willing to to inside. I'd be interested even to meet people. I do know Charles Fleetwood distantly anyway as we have both raced our horses against the king's stock several times."

She stared aghast at him expecting to see a tease or challenge in his eyes, but he looked utterly sincere. "You're daft, Tenn Sloper," she managed and fixed the curl that he had just tampered with.

He laughed now. "Look, Susannah, I'd rather not go in and watch a rehearsal or talk to Macklin, Fleetwood, or Theo Cibber either. It's a lovely April day. I believe your husband tried to send you home a while ago. At least let me walk you partway there."

Her brain raced. Then he had indeed sat up in the gallery watching for a long time, but she hadn't seen him when she'd been on stage. Was he bluffing about being willing to meet everyone inside? And had it been he whom Colley Cibber had perhaps spoken with as he left the theater? He might already know where she lived, but if he didn't she would be certain he would never get near her house. She had no intention of letting him go anyplace with her where she would have to face him alone.

"I am going to see my mother to tell her my good fortune," she said. "If you wish to stroll a little way, that's your business, but I really must be off."

Susannah went back inside to the Green Room to retrieve her straw-ribboned bonnet and pink cloak, hoping her exit looked disdainful. She thought of going out another way, but he would probably be brazen enough to go inside to look for her; besides, it was obvious he would come back another time unless she managed to dispatch him thoroughly today. Yes, she assured herself, that's why she had said he might walk along with her. On the public streets of London, he would not touch her nor would she so foolishly lose her head again. As she left she waved to Theo, who barely glanced up now that Kitty Clive had returned to rehearsal.

They strolled, not speaking at first, along Floral Lane where he bought her a nosegay of violets and daisies, which she refused to accept. Apparently unabashed, he carried the fragrant little bouquet while she pretended to gaze in shop windows to avoid his eyes.

"My mother lives just south of here, and I'll go on now alone," she said at last.

"No other questions? I said we have to talk."

She glanced at him in the reflection of a shop window that displayed parasols, the new fashion rage, like vibrant, open flowers. "Then talk, for I have nothing to say."

"Will you not take a carriage ride with me so we can speak privately, or at least walk a few more blocks?" he asked.

"A carriage ride with you? Never again, and we've walked quite far enough. I have to hurry home as my father-in-law will be coming over so we can plan for my acting instruction."

He frowned slightly and she dared to face him rather than his big, dark reflection in the window glass. "You said you were going to your mother's, Susannah. Damn, I admit you rattle me too, but that's just it, sweetheart. I don't know why you married Theo Cibber, though I have a pretty good idea; only I found you first."

"You certainly did not!"

"My dear lady, a man can well enough tell when he had

a maiden in his bed her first time."

She swirled away and set off at a good clip down the busy lane with him beside her. "You really are despicable, squire. How dare you bring that up—and out in public?"

"Don't you shout then. And I only brought it up in public because you won't see me in private."

"You are so right I won't. Not ever again, you blackguard."

He grinned tautly as his huge strides easily kept up with her steps. "Susannah, I found you first—at least the way that matters. And damn Theo Cibber whom I have nothing against right now except he somehow coerced you to marry him, but I loved you first—if he loves you."

She jolted stock-still while people hurried by on their own sane, reasonable business. They stood alone on a vast stage, and there was no audience but her own enraptured heart. "What? You can't mean that, it was over two years ago."

"And yesterday and today, and there are so many tomorrows."

"Impossible. I don't—I couldn't do that sort of thing."

"I made an unfortunate marriage when I was young, Susannah," he told her as they began to walk again. "I was seventeen and my mother arranged it on her deathbed with an older friend of hers."

"Older?"

"She was twenty-four when I married her. And then in two brief years I grew up and grasped the bleakness of it all."

"You didn't love her ever?"

"No—I don't think I had it in me to even try. Perhaps it was wrong of me, but my father and a lot of money managed to get the marriage finally annulled after many years. It's the only thing we ever fought over, he and I, and unfortunately, Catherine's powerful family and many countryfolk back at West Woodhay still think it a scandal and consider me a wedded man though I hardly ever see her."

He halted under a tall chestnut tree and turned to face her. "You see, Susannah, I'm a rebel at heart and I could not fathom living a lie. I chose to take the scandal first and I've never regretted that."

She took in his words and the almost defiant, impassioned look on his rugged face, but her thoughts turned inward: marriage with Theo—the bleakness of it all, he had said. Dazed, she accepted the little nosegay which he pressed into her hands.

"Please think on what I've said, Susannah, and why I said it all. It's a painful subject I'm usually loath to discuss with anyone, only it had to be said here. I'm considered somewhat of a loner, a dark-mooded eccentric, I suppose, but I really am not that way at heart."

"But, I saw you once—the one time you came to the theater, I guess—and with a beautiful woman. Charles Fleetwood said, I recall, 'that's just his latest mistress.' "

He looked surprised for a moment. "You were there that night? But I didn't see you."

She started to walk on at a good pace again. "Drat you, but you're caught on that one, aren't you, Squire Sloper? I was the goddess Venus that night, but of course you don't remember a thing about it as you hate music and the theater and couldn't take your eyes off that woman!"

To her surprise, he grabbed her arm to swing her around. His rakish brows crashed down to hide his narrowed eyes. "She was a friend of a friend—Prime Minister Walpole's to be exact—and not my mistress," he growled. "And if she was, so what? I'm no monk in a cloister any more than you're some nun with the likes of Theo Cibber, that beady-eyed Macklin, and whoever else you've had stashed about these past two years. I swear, I will get us a hackney and you will listen there where half the folk of London can't be an audience to your theatrical carping!"

"Get your hands off me!" she hissed. "This walk—all this soul-baring—was strictly your idea. Have your private dinner or annulled marriages, your mistresses or whatever, but stay out of my life!"

She thought he would grab her, but he suddenly looked like a granite statue along the bustling street. Too late she noticed that several people stared. She looked up and down the street, made a broad half circle around Tenn Sloper, and hurriedly crossed the cobbled roadway.

She almost ran down the little alley connecting Floral to King Street, where her mother lived. It had been only yesterday Tenn had cornered her in such a place to take her with him into St. James' Palace—only yesterday and yet so long ago. But there were no hoofbeats now, no big boots running behind. In a fierce rage at him and at herself for letting all this happen, she threw her nosegay against the wall where it slid to the hard, rutted mud of the unpaved ground. Tears blinded her, and she bit her lower lip hard to stop them.

On this most fortunate day of her life, when at last it seemed her cherished dream of becoming an actress had come true, Tenn Sloper had crashed into her life again to set everything on end.

She leaned against the brick wall oblivious to the smudge it made on her pink shoulder. She had been happy enough in her marriage to Theo before yesterday—hadn't she?

She sniffed hard and carefully wiped the tears from under her eyes with the back of a finger. But before she went on to her mother's house to tell her the news of Colley Cibber's miraculous visit, she went back and rescued the bruised flowers from the mud.

Chapter Seven

Tenn Sloper dove at the tennis ball and missed. He'd never played worse, he told himself; but then his form, ever since he'd parted from Susannah two weeks ago, had been wretched in all pursuits. He couldn't concentrate at Commission meetings, stared right through acquaintances he met on the street, was short with his father and his servants. He lofted his next serve and whacked it soundly. Damn the little witch, but she even ruined his sleep at night. It simply had to end!

The crowd lining the enclosed tennis alley in the elevated, protected seats murmured, then broke into applause as the next sustained set of volleys went on and on. Tenn threw his big body this way then that, returning smash after smash of the leather ball. He felt burning hot although the sweat of physical exertion always energized him even more. Was this what it was like for Susannah on the stage, he mused, this physical sweep of emotion urged on by the roaring adulation of wild approval?

The ball whisked inches past the end of his extended racquet. The game was over, and he'd lost the entire last set.

His man George held out his familiar black tennis frock coat as he walked off the walled court and sat to drink his usual mug of ale. His heart was pounding. He had lost today, had looked ludicrous out there for one of London't best tennis players, and it was all her fault. He stood and shook the hand of his opponent, the young Earl of Chester, but hardly saw the man's beaming face. It was seldom anyone beat "Tennis Tenn" Sloper at this game, but let the lad have his moment in the sun. As for him, he had to do something and soon to rid his mind of Susannah; then he'd be back into all his endeavors full strength.

Others came down to talk to him, but he moved quickly away through the crowd, pointedly ignoring someone he would have ordinarily trounced for shouting he lost some wagered money because Tenn must have intentionally thrown the match. He had to think of something to clear his addled brain of Susannah and make his powerful, traitorous body stop this unquenchable longing for her. He even considered calling on the pliant Amanda Newbury with the excuse of wanting to see if she'd ever located her lost cousin, but then he'd have her underfoot later after he tumbled her. No, all he needed was a quick hour with someone to slake this raging lust he had for Susannah Cibber, and that would set him at rest again.

He bathed more hurriedly than usual in the tiring room off the main court and dressed himself recklessly without a glance in the mirror George held. He refused his heavy frock coat and let George carry it. After all, it was the tenth of May and warm weather out. He was suddenly glad he and George had ridden mounts today rather than brought the carriage. He had half a notion to race his horse in St. James' Park and see what ladies had gone there for the afternoon to flaunt themselves.

He gazed back a moment over the tennis court where two other players were already well into a set. Suddenly, it was hard to believe he had actually lost a tennis match a few minutes ago on his favorite court in front of a familiar crowd who had no doubt lost some good wagers from his defeat. He shrugged his shoulders and went out into the May sunlight.

In the little courtyard where a stable boy held their horses, he heard a woman call him by name. His heart thudded, but no. This voice was higher than Susannah's, shriller too.

"Tenn—Squire Sloper, over here!"

The carriage with the delicate arm and waving handkerchief extended from it was a fine shiny black landau with four matched grays. It registered on him that he had seen that flashy equipage somewhere before, but he couldn't place it.

"Wait here, George. I'll be right back," he told his big, brawny companion and went across the courtyard.

He recognized the woman instantly: Prime Minister Walpole's promiscuous, extravagant wife, Lady Catherine.

"Hello. I greatly admired your form today," the raven-haired, round-faced woman told him and pointedly licked her red lips.

"Are you certain you saw my match, Lady Catherine? I was terrible today."

"I know you lost, but then I've watched you numerous other times," she told him as her blue eyes set in her milk-white face framed by coal-black hair flickered over him. He judged her to be at least forty, but she managed to look and act a good deal younger. Perhaps it was her wild reputation that accounted for that aura.

"I've watched you at the king's court too, and from the Strangers' Gallery in the House of Lords giving them all those reports on the American colonies," she went on while he only studied her. "It's so wonderful to know my dear Robert has such loyal Whigs at all levels of the government bolstering his efforts. I was just wondering if perhaps I could give you a ride wherever you're going. Don't worry, I won't tell my husband I've been gambling on tennis games or whatever. I won't breathe a word if you won't."

There it is, Tenn thought to himself—a blatant if cleverly couched invitation to tumble the prime minister's wife, though why she'd targeted him was a mystery. Perhaps, he thought and grinned before he could stop himself, considering what he'd heard about her, she was just working her way down the vast list of her husband's supporters and she'd finally come to the *S*'s in the alphabet.

"Tenn," she said, her blue eyes gone wide and innocent, "did I say aught amusing?"

"No, my lady," he said as his eyes went curiously over her. "It's only that I am surprised at so charming an invitation out of the blue as it were." And, he told himself, he was surprised at how a way to rid his mind and body of this foolish need for a married woman he could not have had fallen effortlessly into his lap from one he obviously could have.

"George," he called across the courtyard, "take the horses home, and I'll be back later."

He climbed up into the carriage on the opposite seat, while Catherine Walpole sighed in a suddenly annoying way. Her footman closed the curtained door and they started off.

"I want you to know," she told him, her voice gone silky, "that I don't make a habit of this, but I find you so terribly appealing and obviously unattached, though you were with that charming girl the day the prince married his German Augusta."

He frowned at the mention of Susannah. He didn't need that from her if she was going to help him forget the little actress-witch who had thrown all his deep confessions and protestations of love right back in his face on a public street corner two weeks ago.

"I don't mean to pry, of course," she went on smoothly and smiled, obviously deciding to change the subject.

"You know, it's such a lovely May day, would you like to ride anywhere special—a little spin in the country perhaps?"

"Perhaps," he heard himself tell her. "But if you want to enjoy the day, shouldn't we turn up these window flaps?"

She laughed sharply, and her long ear bobs jangled. "But I do favor privacy too, don't you, Tenn? There are other things hereabouts to appreciate besides the lovely day, you know."

She ran her tongue over her red lips as her hands lifted provocatively to pull the neckline of her moss-green gown lightly off each shoulder, just enough to have it gape away from her breasts. "I do hope you're not too tired or sleepy after that grueling tennis match today, Tenn. You're so big that I can't imagine that, but if so, you could just sit back and relax, you see. My driver knows to go about and leave me undisturbed."

He felt his muscles tense as she brazenly unlaced the mauve ribbons up the front of her bodice and lifted two voluptuous breasts free. The huge nipples looked so pink, he thought, she must have actually roughed them. His jaw muscles tightened as he stared. This was what he thought he needed, but now it annoyed and angered him. He had wanted Susannah in the carriage that first night he had rescued her, wanted her two weeks ago to do just this for him, but this was not Susannah and not for him.

"My lady, please—you misunderstand—"

"Do I, my lovely stallion? That's the way I think of you on the tennis court or the time I saw you at the races. Your body is just like a fine, eager stallion's. Hush now. You know, several people saw us leave. My husband trusts you, trusts your father, and I should hate to have to tell him otherwise."

"Then don't, my lady. And pray don't go any further here. I should not have come with you."

"But the point is you have now, and you're so handsome, my dear. I cannot believe those rumors your wife let you get away—the utter fool."

She separated her knees and ruffled up her skirts while she scooted her hips toward him on her opposite seat. Furious, he moved forward to cover, with her own skirts, the thighs she skillfully bared above her silk stockings. She moaned and seized his shoulders.

"Yes, Tenn, we can go slower if you'd like—"

"I want you to cover yourself. I'm getting out."

"Out? No, you can't. Wait, they'll know if you just get out."

"They? Your driver and footmen? Fine, because I don't want them telling the prime minister, whom I happen to admire, any different." He tried to pull her bodice over her bared breasts, but she pressed her soft flesh to his hand and held his wrist.

"Your touch, my Tenn—it's wonderful. I knew it could be like this when I watched you out there sweating, stretching those big muscles."

"Tell the driver to halt or I shall. Now!"

"But my husband knows all this. He doesn't care—really. You do know, of course, he encouraged me to lie with King George when he was but Prince of Wales."

"So you actually have done this all these years?" he asked dumbfounded and yanked his hand back. "Driver! Driver," he bellowed, "stop here!"

"You'll regret this," she shrilled. "You will regret this."

"I regret this already, Lady Walpole, but I assure you I am angry at myself and not at you. Your behavior is your own affair. Say whatever of this you will, but I believe you are clever enough to say nothing at all."

He opened the door himself before the footman could climb down to look in. Without a backward glance, he closed the door quietly and walked off with huge strides in the direction the carriage had come. He saw they had gone quite a ways up along the river almost to The Tower, but that suited him well enough. He'd eat somewhere along the docks, if he could stomach any food after what he had almost let happen. Then he would walk off more energy going home, and change and go to the Drury Lane Theater.

The six o'clock performance would be well underway by then, but she would hardly be acting in anything yet. At least his talk with Colley Cibber at the Prince of Wales's wedding had worked: The old man had a new discovery and Susannah was happy. But he wanted to be happy too and she owed him at least a little kindness since it would be greatly his funding that would finance her debut at the theater.

He had tried doing without Susannah for two weeks now, and it was destroying him. Nothing would do but to see her and have it out once and for all. He wanted no one else—no other woman's body however freely it was offered. He only wanted and needed Susannah Cibber.

Tenn Sloper quickened his steps along the Thames as wild river winds whipped his hair.

Susannah, gowned in brightest emerald brocade with a pale pink underbodice and sleeve ruffles, stood watching the performance of the tragedy *Cato* from the crowded wings of the Drury Lane Theater Royal. The huge actor James Quin, whose kindness and politeness Susannah greatly admired in this theater world full of fops and flirts, declared speech after marvelous speech in this Joseph Addison play. It greatly annoyed her that the rakes and sparks Theo and Charles Fleetwood allowed backstage for a half guinea were talking and joking so loudly behind her she could barely hear Quin's booming voice.

"Mrs. Cibber," one very blond man who looked vaguely familiar whispered in her ear and edged so close to her she could smell heavy brandy on his breath, "Theo says you might be accompanying him and me for dinner after the performance if I but ask nicely, I assure you, I shall select an elegant place and pay the fare too."

She turned her head momentarily to study the elongated, pinched face of the yellow-brocaded dandy who reminded her of a canary except for his ludicrously raspy voice. "Mr. Cibber must have misunderstood or misinformed you, sir. My little brother Henry Peter is in the farcical afterpiece *Trick for Trick* tonight and I intend to leave with him and my father directly after that. I am certain Theo meant you were going only with him, especially if you're covering the bill. Excuse me, please, but I am listening to this speech by Mr. Quin."

She stepped closer to the stage even as she thought of the man's name: Foster Calaway, one of London's numerous footloose young fops intent only on spending their wealthy fathers' fortunes on fashions, gambling, and general debauchery. At least, she thought before she could check herself, Tenn Sloper was obviously not that sort and he and his wealthy father evidently got on famously, except for their disagreement over the annulment of Tenn's marriage.

Drat it, Susannah, she scolded herself silently as she had so often these last two weeks since she had rejected Tenn's fervent explanations on Floral Lane and run to her mother's home. She was certain that she ought to be glad to have gotten rid of the man, but she wasn't. She felt sure that she should be proud of herself for spurning him so completely, but she was only miserable.

To wild applause, James Quin exited the stage directly at her, breaking her reverie. "Susannah!" he beamed, ignoring the others who swarmed around him in the wings, though he took the cup of stout offered by the callboy. "For the life of me, if I were Theo Cibber, I wouldn't let my lady watch from the wings amidst all these rambunctious gadflies. Tell me if anyone's been a whit rude, and I'll trounce him soundly for you."

She smiled up gratefully at the huge Quin. The traditional flaring coat of tragic heroes and Roman armor encased his massive body; his full wig and plumed helmet, called a toor, towered toward the rafters. "No, I'm fine, James. It's just Fleetwood and Theo's usual rabble of hangers-on, and I've had several years practice in how to handle them."

"And Black Mac isn't lurking about, I see. Saints preserve us all, perhaps you are safe then. And how are the histrionic lessons going with Theo's eminent father, my dear? Oh, blast it, there's my cue—"

The bulk of the armored, bewigged man rotated away as he grandly strode back out onstage in the flood of lights to the traditional trumpet and slow drum that accompanied a tragic hero. Again, at his mere booming entry line, applause rose and swelled clear back to drench the wings in its richness. After she learned the nuances of acting, Susannah told herself, perhaps someday she too might command such respect and fervent love on this very stage.

"The windy old boy's in usual form today, isn't he, Susannah?" A rich baritone voice she placed instantly came so close behind her it stirred the curls over her left ear.

"Mr. Macklin," she said and looked pointedly back out on stage to watch Quin. "I thought that about now you'd be tiring yourself to become the rogue Sancho for the coming little farce."

"So," the treacherous tones lapped over her, "you're at least thinking of me. I think of you all the time, my pretty colleen."

"Leave off!" she hissed more loudly than she meant to as she noticed the avid canary Foster Calaway move closer as if to eavesdrop. "Just leave me in peace to watch a fine actor, please, Mr. Macklin."

To her dismay, he stepped against her from behind

pressing her almost out into view of the audience where he knew she dare not budge or make a fuss. If only Theo weren't sitting up in the royal box tonight playing host to Sir Robert Walpole, she thought, he'd stop this rakehell Irishman from his increasingly blatant ploys.

"Now," his voice came low, "let's just watch old Quin together if that's what you want. No, pretty, don't fret or we'll both be out there and what would the great Roman Cato say then, h'm? You do know Cato was quite willing to lease his wife out to another man for a fee? For the love of St. Patrick, if only Theo were of that set o' mind, eh?"

She elbowed him as hard as she could, but his big hands only tightened on her waist to hold her still. "Sh, now, or cannonball Quin will have our heads. Rolling cannonballs in a trough like the kind we use backstage to simulate thunder—that's old Quin, eternally declaiming and sawing the air with the same classic, overused gestures."

"Loose me. You're just jealous of his talents," she whispered.

"Jealous perhaps of how you waste your smiles on the old *roué* and that milksop husband of yours when Charles Macklin's yours for the merest word, my little colleen."

"No. Stop it." She tried to push him back from the very edge of curtain where he held her, but he gave ground only a step and captured her waist again to hold her when she spun to move past him.

"Listen to me, you starchy little songbird," he clipped out, fully angry at last. "Quin's getting old and his acting's dated. He's one of the last holdovers from Restoration style—he's a fossil. If these acting lessons of yours with Colley Cibber ever end and when you get on the boards, I will be Drury Lane's premier actor and you're going to need me then. You've a natural way about you, a plaintive, seductive voice, so don't let them turn you into a mechanical declaimer like Quin. And work on being a damn sight more natural and sweeter to me, Susannah, as you're going to need me very badly to help you then."

The swarthy satyr's face grinned down at her as he leered and winked. Like a stroke of lightning, he lifted one quick hand upward and firmly caressed her heaving breast, then loosed her. Astounded, she hit out at his hand and fled. He let her push past him. She ignored the eager-eyed canary Calaway, who had evidently hovered near to hang on their every word, and hurried out of the wings toward the Green Room where she knew she'd find her father and her fifteen-year-old brother, Henry Peter. Quin's booming voice faded behind her. How dare the renegade Macklin deride the most respected actor in London to her, and how dare he make the wings of her theater a treacherous place to inhabit when she could so easily handle all the others Fleetwood and Theo let in there!

The green-coated stage attendants, who would soon remove the Roman set for *Cato* to prepare for the short afterpiece chosen to please the tastes of the sixpenny audience let in at half rates after the third act of the tragedy, played cards on a rickety hall table. Besides the din and confusion in this hall, reverberating clearly from the front foyer of the theater she could hear the voices of the noisy lackeys of rich patrons who, after holding choice seats for their masters all afternoon, had to wait for them during the play until time to go home. No wonder Quin's voice had to boom so loud to gain attention, she told herself, and no wonder actresses like Kitty Clive were forced to clown, emote, and posture to keep everyone's interest.

The Green Room was fairly crowded but at least it was quieter here with no fops, callboys, prompters, or stage attendants—and, blessedly, neither Theo, Fleetwood, nor the wild Irishman Macklin. She nodded to her drowsy father who had evidently just come from counting the house and reporting his numbers to keep the ticket takers honest, but she sat by Henry Peter, on a bench near the low burning fire where she'd left her cloak earlier.

"Susannah, I'm sure glad to see you," the boy told her and smiled radiantly. "You always bring me good luck 'fore I go on. Anyhow, I hate all this garb Theo's always making me wear—like Cupid and now these girl's things for Estifania in this farce. Can't wait 'til I get older like Black Mac to do real men's parts."

She frowned at his mention of Macklin's familiar sobriquet. "I know, my dear, but your voice is only starting to change now and you're simply marvelous out there. And someday, we're going to both act in the same play together, and then we'll just look back and laugh over all we've been through to be successful—you'll see. Henry Peter, you haven't been hanging about Charles Macklin, have you?"

"I think he's fine. He's going to be first actor here soon, I'll bet, and then he's going to ask for me to be in some of his plays—and not in wench's parts neither. He's going to come over to the house sometime to talk about it."

"Sometime when I'm there, I suppose," she groused under her breath as she grasped handfuls of green skirt in her frustration. She'd tell Theo or father that Macklin was using Henry Peter like this, or else tell Macklin off in public where he dare not try his usual tricks of pinching her bottom, touching her waist, or stroking her breast.

As if her anger had summoned the villain, Macklin came in behind another actor, Thomas Hallam, who was to be in the farce too. Both men looked furious as though they'd been arguing. With his feet nearly in the fire, Hallam sat on their bench on the other side of Henry Peter, and Macklin sat directly across from them where he could obviously eye Susannah.

"Good evening, my dear Miss Estifania," Macklin told Henry Peter and winked.

"Hello, Mac," the boy grinned.

"Really, Henry Peter," Susannah said and shot her

brother a sharp glance she refused to bestow even on Macklin, "if, as everyone says, this Irishman is to be such a great actor here someday, you really must address him by his proper name at least."

"*Is* presently a great actor here, songthrush," Macklin's voice said dangerously low.

"Really?" she dared before she could contain her anger. "And is that why James Quin's out there declaiming Cato and you're here waiting, wig in hand, to play someone called Sancho in a little farce to the sixpence pitlings?"

Henry Peter gasped and, across the room, their drowsing father stirred himself at her strident tone. "Damn, but you need a lesson, Susannah," Macklin threatened and sat forward, elbows on knees, his big hands rotating his large, curled wig. "I swear, a mere half hour with just you and me and you'd learn a few sweet manners—and more."

Thomas Hallam, on Henry Peter's far side, leaned forward too. "Come on now, Mac, none of your usual temper, at least right before we go on. Look—don't you and I have our wigs switched?" Hallam said all too obviously, hoping to soothe the tension. "That one in your hands looks more like my character Guzman's—"

"Damn you for a rogue, Hallam, keep your own greasy wigs and greasy opinions! This is strictly between Mrs. Cibber and me, and as there is a good ten minutes until we go on, I would like to speak to you in private—now, Mrs. Cibber!"

"Just a minute here, Mac—" Susannah's father's voice sounded weak and shaky from across the room.

"*Now,* Susannah, damn it!" Macklin repeated as he stood and reached for her.

She hit out hard at his arms, and chaos erupted. Henry Peter shrieked and, amazingly, Thomas Hallam threw himself at the tall Macklin to pummel his back. His swarthy face furious, his black eyes luminous in near madness, Macklin grabbed Susannah about the arms and waist to still her and shoved Hallam off.

"No, Mac, no!" Henry Peter screeched very close as he too hit at Macklin's big form. Susannah felt the shoulder of her gown tear down; her father came into view, his mouth moving distortedly, his eyes wide. Macklin held her so tightly against him now she could hardly breathe.

Then, again, the wiry Thomas Hallam sprang toward them with a sharp stick from the fire. "Damn you, Macklin! Damn you, you're no better than the rest of us!" someone shouted.

Macklin shoved or dropped her into Henry Peter's arms. A woman nearby screamed. Macklin grunted once and swore. When Susannah righted herself to look, Thomas Hallam was on the floor with blood streaming from his face. Macklin, his legs spread, stared down at the bloodied, charred stick in his hand, then threw it into the fire in a shower of sparks. Hallam held his eye and screamed. Someone pounded on the door. Macklin's black gaze raked Susannah, then he turned and shoved his way out of the room and disappeared.

She stood dazed, holding Henry Peter to her while her father bent over Hallam. Suddenly Fleetwood was there, then Theo, then—impossible! Her knees gave way and she crumbled back on the bench as Tenn Sloper pushed in behind the others.

"Tom Arne, what happened here for love of a bawd?" Theo shouted and bent over the writhing Hallam. "Shut that damned door and send the others back out, Fleetwood!"

Susannah's teary eyes met Tenn's green glance as he shoved farther in before Fleetwood closed the door on the crowd in the hall. She blinked back stunned tears. Tenn's big form doubled then blurred in the candlelight of the chaotic scene.

"Macklin went all crazed at nothing—infernal hell-bent he was on bothering Susannah and Hallam," old Arne told Theo.

"Susannah?" Theo said. "This looks bad—his left eye, maybe deeper, I don't know. Send for the theater surgeon. Mr. Coldham, Fleetwood, and stay with Hallam. And send Susannah home somehow. There's a play to go on here, so I've got to find Macklin. Hallam's part I can handle myself."

Theo bustled out while the portly Fleetwood tried not to look at Hallam. "All right now, we've had a bit of a problem here, but we must protect the theater from this sort of scandal at all costs. The prime minister's in the audience and we don't need a lot of loud fussing. Mr. Arne, please take the boy out into the wings until his call, and I shall send Susannah home. Then—Tenn, what the hell are you doing here?"

Tenn moved aside as Thomas Arne hustled Henry Peter through the crowded hallway, then he closed the door on the rows of curious onlookers. "I came to meet a friend and heard the tumult when going by in the hall, Charles. Hardly a night to talk ponies now, is it? Might I be of help to you by dropping Mrs. Cibber at her home?"

"Damn me, yes! Tenn, my thanks!" Fleetwood said over Susannah's shaky gasp of protest. She tried to avert her eyes, from both Hallam's crumpled form and Tenn's gaze, so there was only Fleetwood to look at.

"I'll be fine," she told him and stood. "Thomas Hallam—I will stay. He was only trying to help when Macklin became very rude."

She knew Tenn looked furious without even glancing his way. She couldn't—just couldn't—be handed over to him like this.

"You heard Theo, Susannah," Fleetwood told her and took out his snuffbox. "The surgeon's sent for and everyone will be busy with the afterpiece soon. We've got nearly a full house out there, and we don't need rumors flying about Macklin, you, or anyone else. I'm beholden to you for this, Tenn," he got out before he was wracked with sneezes.

Her legs felt wooden as Tenn rescued her discarded cloak. He bent briefly over to comfort Hallam, wrapped Susannah in the cloak, and claimed her. Strangely, she felt better and safer as soon as he touched her, after all this sudden shocking tumult and poor Hallam's pain. Tenn opened the door and, dazedly, she was out into the hall with his strong arm around her shoulders. Instantly, dozens of faces pressed in and dozens of voices shouted frightening questions.

"Did Black Mac hurt you? We heard a woman scream. Was that you, Mrs. Cibber?"

"Mrs. Cibber, is someone dead or what?"

"Is it true? Foster Calaway says Macklin accosted you earlier?"

She turned her face into Tenn's big, welcome shoulder as he swept her onward. The lights went dimmer. It was cool here in the back courtyard outside the theater. Susannah heard Tenn's voice to his driver. There was a carriage step; he helped her up.

She huddled in the far corner of the dim carriage holding her cloak tightly around her. He sat beside her, very close as the door snapped shut and they rolled away. Wheels rattled on cobbles then brick as they rounded a corner.

"Are you all right, Susannah?" his words came low, his tone edged with an emotion she could not place.

"Yes. I had no idea you were here—there, I mean."

"I came to see you, apparently a moment too late."

He had only touched her shoulders to pull her within his embrace when she amazed him by leaning trustingly, perfectly against his chest. His heart thudded wildly as he cradled her in the circle of his arms. Her voice came to him muffled, nearly drowned in the rustle of her brocade cloak as she nestled even closer. He bent lower to catch her words as the jasmine scent in her hair assaulted his senses.

"It was dreadful," she murmured. "Thank you for not accusing me. I didn't—nothing happened to call for all that."

"I'm not angry with you, only at what could have happened. Last time I was at the Drury, I saw how that lunatic Macklin looked at you even on the stage."

She lifted her head. Her perfect oval face looked pale in the wan carriage lantern and the jagged path of a single tear glittered on her cheek. "Please don't talk about him or any of them. Just take me home."

The carriage slowed and halted almost immediately. So he did know where she lived, Susannah thought; he had whispered it to his driver when they had climbed in. She wondered if she dare ask him in for a moment; but no, of course not. Theo would no doubt be home very late, but she felt so glad to see Tenn—so feathery and shaky that she dare not let herself be alone with him. Ordinarily, her maid Anne Hopson would be there or even have gone to the theater with her, but this was her one day a week free. She should offer a sincere word of thanks; perhaps a veiled promise that she would see him some other time, or a single, fond kiss.

Holding Tenn's warm hand, she stepped down onto a smooth flagstone walk. Flaring lanterns lit a vast, tall town house like sentinels to gild the night. A pillared, porticoed doorway beckoned. It was hardly the narrow little house on Wild Court that she had expected to see.

"Oh! Where are we?"

"My house on St. James' Square, sweet. My father's gone to the country. Come in now."

Her lips formed the words "I can't" but no sound emanated from her throat. Her feet walked. Her heart pounded. The door swept open; soft lights displayed a stylish vestibule.

As if she were in a dream where something alluring and unseen beckoned her on, she walked with him step for step, then stair for stair as they mounted a curving staircase, onward and upward.

At last she dared to dart him a sideways glance through her wet lashes. His burnished copper hair was uncovered now, and she swam in his eyes green as turbulent sea channels. In the long, silent upstairs hall lined with watchful portraits, he lifted her in his iron arms at last and strode on.

She clung to him, her face pressed to his warm neck above the elegant twist of ivory cravat. She was safe and happy and cherished here; nothing else outside existed. It was as mystic as that stolen night in Chelsea eons ago—a rare jewel to be adored and treasured for all time.

He stood her by a low burning fireplace on a thick, moss-green hearth rug. His handsome, craggy face nearly blocked out the distinctly masculine room behind. His eyes became the entire universe. . . .

They came together, standing in a mutual raging embrace. His mouth was fiercely demanding, yet so tender; his arms were iron and stone, yet so gentle. Her wet eyelashes blurred little streaks of tears along his high cheekbones. A tiny sigh of utter ecstasy escaped deep in her throat. The room was spinning faster than the planet. She clung to him so hard and kissed him back so intensely that she could hardly breathe.

"I missed you terribly, terribly," he rasped out as he rained hot kisses down her jawline to her throat arched back away from him as if to offer him complete compliance. "These two weeks were hell, worse than the two years but never—never again—"

When Tenn lifted her cloak away and let it drop, she remembered too late that Macklin had torn her dress; but what did that matter now? Tenn's lips dipped to her collarbone, touching her soft flesh where the gown was ripped; his skillful hands lifted to her supple back, untying her bodice lacings.

"I thought of you all the time, Tenn. I felt—I'm sorry for what I said that day and how I just ran off."

"It's all right now. It doesn't matter. Only this matters," he whispered, his deep voice gone completely husky.

He peeled her bodice, corset, and chemise away with flurries of wild kisses. She let him. She helped him. She—wanted him. While he unlaced her green skirts, she even lifted her hands to help him shrug off his russet frock coat.

Even as he divested himself of his own garments where they stood in rampant, darting firelight, his kisses burned the curve of her sleek shoulders and rasped along her high, pointed breasts. At that, she lost control of her thought, of her breathing. She felt her nipples point to taut nubs of blatant invitation that he eagerly ravished.

She stood completely nude before him, her shed pink and green gown in a silken pool about her ankles. His right hand cupped then lifted each pert breast to his lips, while his left hand wandered her back and buttocks to mold her to him. Her knees went weak as water, and she clung to his powerful neck with linked arms until he lifted her and strode to the huge, canopied bed.

She jolted at first from the cool caress of silk sheets along her back, derriere, and legs. She tried to sit, to pull up a coverlet, but he quickly discarded his black breeches and was tight against her again.

"Susannah, I love you so desperately—from afar and then like this—every way. From now on, we'll be together!"

Whatever sane answer she could find to give him was inundated by the coursing pulse of mutual passion. He rolled them over into the middle of the vast bed; her limbs got all tangled with his strong ones as he positioned her perfectly under him. He balanced himself over her; her topaz eyes locked with his green-gold gaze. Then, even as they stared raptly, she felt between her long legs the masterful nudge she trembled for so eagerly and then the deep, sliding push of full possession.

Once deeply in, he held still to begin a new assault of licking, biting kisses until she moaned and writhed under him. Only then did he lift his head from ravishing her mouth and breasts to stare fixedly into her eyes while he began his deliberately slow rise and fall against her quaking flesh.

Wild impulses and vibrant visions bombarded her brain and shook her body alert and alive. Such a perfect joining had not happened to her since that first time with this man; what Theo Cibber tried to do to her body at night was not even the same kind of thing. For no one, no one but Tenn Sloper, had she ever felt like this or ever could again.

"Yes, yes, my sweet love, yes, move like that," he moaned. "Damn, you can't know how you've done this to me from the very first. Susannah, but I want you so desperately!"

The bed, the room, the world, exploded for her in shattering sparks of shimmering wonder. Frenzied with joy, she clung to his big body by wrapping her arms and legs fiercely around him. Then she went sleepily, silkily calm in utter contentment.

He pulled them side by side, still pressed tightly together, still gently inside her, and yanked the coverlet up over their damp, entwined bodies. She felt one of his hands around her shoulders and one resting possessively on her hip. She nestled her tousled head closer under the angle of his chin and jaw, realizing that her once carefully piled and curled coiffure dear Anne had labored over was now spread wildly over the pillows.

"My hair," she murmured.

"A beautiful auburn curtain of silk," he whispered. "Sh.

We'll care for it later."

She shifted her hips slightly and felt him start to grow within her in instant response. "Oh," she said and turned her head to stare at his rugged, happy face. "But we can't again. I have to go."

"Later. We've only been gone a little over an hour, and I haven't yet begun to show you how much I need you."

"But twice—I can't. This is all impossible."

"Is it? Not if you want it the way I do. And as soon as the time is ripe, we'll get you away from him."

"But that's—I said, it's impossible."

He frowned. "Are you going to tell me you really care for him?" he said, his voice gone hard. "After all this?"

"I—well, I don't love him, but of course I care for him."

"Hell's gates, Susannah, let's not fence here. Do you care for the man or only the chance to act at the Drury Lane Theater Royal he manages? Do you care for living with the man—bedding with him—or for the acting instructions his influential father and Aaron Hill are giving you?"

She pushed at his chest, but he didn't budge except to roll her under him. He pinned her down even while he so sweetly pierced her still. "I don't need your accusations," she raged. "And how, pray tell, did you know about Aaron Hill? Let me up!"

He dipped his mouth to tease a soft earlobe so she wouldn't see his face to know he'd made a slip. He had had no intention of telling her, when she was getting all argumentative, that he had arranged and greatly financed her acting lessons and the play she would debut in next January.

"What Colley Cibber does is common knowledge in theater circles, and I do know Charles Fleetwood, remember," he murmured against her neck as he began to brazenly rock against her. He just knew she would feel guilt for this night, maybe even throw one of her temper tantrums tomorrow. Then too, there was bound to be a lot of trouble over this Macklin stabbing affair at the theater tonight. She might be smack in the middle of that and he couldn't bear another two weeks away from her, not to see her or touch her like this. He moved faster, lost in his wild longing for her preciously beautiful body and spirit.

A hundred protests darted through her reeling brain, but none made it to her sweetly bruised lips as he moved against her, in her so wonderfully. Each thrust was sweet torment for the marvelous futility of it all. But, she told herself, sane and sensible Susannah Cibber, who only desired to be an actress, now desired something else as much as that: love and rage for the theater; a love and rage for this one man, like this—here or anywhere.

Again, the sensual assault of his skillful touch swept her to quivering submission, and then to a wild, frenzied aggression she had never known. His words, his powerful body against hers and in hers, pushed and pulled her swiftly onward until there was nothing else but blinding rapture and a blazing release from all things but this man.

Chapter Eight

Susannah sat in her small but fashionably appointed parlor with her lady's maid, Anne Hopson, awaiting Tenn Sloper's arrival. Theo had left again at dawn after a late night return where he smelled of rum and tobacco and mumbled in his fitful sleep about damned Fleetwood and money. She could understand that, of course, Susannah told herself, for Theo had been obsessed these last three weeks since poor Thomas Hallam had died from Macklin's attack on him. But Theo was distressed not for the actor's cruel death nor for the Drury Lane's reputation: Theo had had a tremendous falling out with Charles Fleetwood over who was to select and direct the theater's plays. And now that Fleetwood was laid up at his home with a debilitating attack of gout, Theo was running the theater with a frenzied, iron hand—and no available revenue for salaries, as all receipts went legally to Fleetwood.

"Laws, Miss Susannah, such a dreary day out there and us heading out into it when your friend comes for us."

Susannah glanced up from the newspaper cuttings she had been rereading on the table. "I saw it, Anne, a chilly, drifting fog so thick in spots one could cut it with a knife."

She hoped her voice sounded normal to the often too observant Anne, her friend and companion as well as her maid, whom Theo had allowed her to hire from her own funds when they were married. It was the only money from her precious prenuptial agreement she ever used, as the rest of her two hundred-pound yearly salary was cared for by Theo's prompt delivery of it to her uncle, who invested it. Soon, she'd visit her Uncle Charles and inquire what amounts had accumulated with all the interest.

But her excitement she hoped to hide from Anne Hopson today was entirely for another cause: Unbeknownst to Anne, Susannah had seen Tenn Sloper daily in the three weeks since Hallam had been killed, but today was the first day she had allowed him to call on her here. Even though Anne would be present for appearance's sake and the events of the afternoon promised to be somewhat unsettling, Susannah was thrilled to have him here in the little refuge she had made for herself as Mrs. Theo Cibber. Now there would be no place left for her to hide from memories of Tenn's magnetic presence.

"Melinda fixed apricot tarts to go with the coffee, I said, Miss Susannah," Anne interrupted her reverie. "Shall I fetch 'em now then?"

"Fine—yes. Squire Sloper should be here soon."

She glanced down again at the little pile of newspaper cuttings she had saved to try to decipher what was really happening in the complicated Macklin-Hallam affair, which went to trial at the Old Bailey law court today. Macklin had finally come back from hiding to stand trial for murdering the poor minor actor Thomas Hallam, who had died of his wound the night after the stabbing.

Anne was back again, her stiff grisette skirts rustling. "Sit and rest, Anne. You've been darting about all morning now, and you know Mr. Cibber has a fit when you take on duties other than those of a personal maid."

"Laws, but the household's small and things need tending to that neither Melinda nor Mr. Cibber's cocky valet Rogers will touch. I'm just glad to be going out today with you and the squire, fog or not. This Squire Sloper—he's the first gentleman you ever met at the theater you've let within a mile of you, so he must be something special," Anne said smugly. "And, if he's rich—and rich he must be—I wager even Mr. Cibber won't mind his fetching us to the trial seeing he's so set on controlling the theater while Mr. Fleetwood's off ill 'n such."

"Mr. Cibber is just worried that without Fleetwood there the salaries of players will be affected, Anne. And I'm just worried without Fleetwood to testify in court to tell them what a hothead Charles Macklin is, father's and James Quinn's testimonies won't be believed. At least I wasn't called in to testify, so Theo must have seen to that."

Anne only snorted as she did too often when Theo was mentioned, then she dashed instantly up the minute the door knocker sounded in the front hall. "The squire's on time indeed," Anne mumbled. "Laws, a quarter hour early, he is."

Susannah stood in the small parlor and nervously smoothed her pale blue skirts over her narrow paniers. This gown sported a dark blue fitted riding jacket over the bodice, from which rows of stiff Irish lace spilled slightly over the lapels. It was both feminine and tailored, she told herself, and in spite of how she had been forced to argue with her dressmaker to have it put on Theo's running tab, she was now glad that she had ordered it.

"Susannah, you look marvelous," Tenn told her as he followed the beaming Anne in from the small, tiled entryway. He bent over her extended hand to kiss it. Behind him, Anne Hopson's eyes nearly popped as she gave Susannah a silent mock applause to show she approved of the tall Squire Sloper, elegantly attired in rich blue, which echoed Susannah's new ensemble. Susannah blushed even hotter to think that the sharp-eyed Anne might ever guess her secret that she had not just met Tenn for the first time at the theater three weeks ago.

"Thank you, Anne. That will be all for a few moments," Susannah managed as she indicated Tenn should sit in the rose-hued velvet upholstered chair that matched her own, on the other side of the parquet table with the carefully arranged coffee, tarts, and paper clippings.

As soon as the parlor door snapped shut, he jumped to his feet and pulled her up into his arms.

"Tenn, really. We mustn't here."

"Just a single, sweet kiss then. It doesn't help me to see you at the theater or for a brief stroll everyday if I can't hold you even a little. It just makes me hungry for you, sweet."

"You said you were pleased I agreed to see you everyday," she pouted as she felt her soft body instantly mold itself to the hard planes and angles of his muscles.

"I am, but it's a heavenly torment. You've got to agree to see me somewhere private, and without your maid."

His lips took hers gently, beseechingly. All protests, all resistance fled, just as she had feared. She knew it would be like this any moment they would be alone and so, after their passionate night at his house when he had rescued her from the theater, she had made him promise at least temporary restraint. Only, when he held her like this and his mouth slanted sideways across hers, there was no such thing as restraint.

"Tenn, please, I—"

"All right, I know. This damned Macklin business today and then your maid may be back soon." Reluctantly he loosed her, stood her back as if to study her face for a moment, then sat her back in her chair and moved away to peer out a crack through the heavy brocade draperies. "A whole damned army could get lost in these floating patches of fog today, but it's an appropriate setting for this trial," he murmured, half to himself.

Susannah pushed her hips back in her chair and tried to quiet her trembling knees. She attempted to ignore the treacherous velvety feel low in her stomach that made her go all weak whenever he kissed her. "Why, Tenn? Because of these wretched news stories being so confused?"

"No, love. Susannah—you *do* realize Fleetwood has hired a very expensive, clever lawyer for his drinking comrade Macklin, don't you? I suppose you've never seen the work of such a lawyer, but I have. Just be prepared to hear a much different story today from what really happened the night Hallam was stabbed in the Green Room, that's all. And keep quiet about it and be glad for it as it's probably the only real way to keep your name from being dragged into this public, scandalous mess where you might be further harassed or have to testify. Remember how crazy it was the night we walked out of the theater. I couldn't bear it if they put you in the witness box, so whatever your father and Quin come up with today, we will just sit in the back of the court and accept quietly and gratefully."

"Whatever they come up with?" she repeated and sat forward again. "Do you mean they intend to lie to keep me out of it?"

"Something like that, but mostly to clear Macklin. The Theater Royal wants no scandal among its actors, as the king is the theater's patron despite the fact he hardly ever attends and is enough a perpetrator of scandal himself."

Her low voice rose louder than she had meant it to, and she flipped the plate of tarts over on the table as she reached for the newspaper cuttings to wave in his all too-knowing face.

"And how do you know all about this, Tenn Sloper? If that's true, no one told me—Theo, Fleetwood, father, no one! I read the papers, you know. Here, *The Craftsman* says Macklin 'made his escape over the London roofs,' then this one tells how he came back to stand trial; at least

Theo told me Fleetwood talked him into that, and secured his bail so he never had to spend a night in prison, the rakehell. And now father and Quin are both testifying—are you saying they will lie?"

"Hush, sweetheart, or you'll have the servants in here. Sit down, won't you, and pour me some of that coffee I can smell? I brought you some imported strawberries from Virginia, if your maid ever gets back in here with them."

She did as he said, shakily replacing the upset tarts and pouring two cups of coffee. He sat again, apparently studying the room. "Tenn, I know for a fact," she said quietly as she handed him his coffee, "that James Quin and Charles Macklin have almost come to blows numerous times and Macklin even tried to choke him once. Quin detests Macklin, and I don't think he'll lie."

"But actors are a close breed when they are attacked from without and tend to protect their own, I've heard. Just don't be surprised or disillusioned if you hear things told a way you don't recall them."

"And you have learned all this from your usual source of Fleetwood, of course, despite the fact he's been incapacitated almost two weeks with gout?" she queried disbelievingly.

His green eyes met hers over the little space of the parquet tabletop. "Why?" he asked. "Did you believe I had some other source? And may we not drop your maid here after the trial and go off ourselves for a little while? I haven't really touched you for three weeks."

"Tenn, I just want us to be friends right now until I can sort out my feelings. You agreed to that if I'd just see you and I have, so—"

"I know, I know, damn it. But do you really think we can just be friends after the way we feel for each other—the way we"—he lowered his voice so that she leaned sideways to hear his next words—"are when we're really alone together?"

Susannah breathed a sigh of relief as Anne knocked and came back in with a large porcelain plate laden with huge crimson strawberries. But their sweet, luscious taste was the last palatable thing she had that day.

Tenn Sloper, devil take him, was prophetic about the trial, she told herself later. Quin vouched for Macklin's "peaceable disposition," shattering her idealization of her protector. Her own feeble, aging father said Hallam, a mere minor actor, had simply started a row after he had stolen one of Macklin's wigs. Tenn Sloper again cautioned her to sit still in the crowded court and be grateful her name was not being mentioned. Worst of all, the mad murdering Irishman, who Susannah believed as treacherous and guilty as Judas Iscariot, was merely charged with justifiable manslaughter and freed after a token branding on his hand with a cool iron, while eleven other defendants at the Old Bailey were hardly so fortunate that day. All the others were sentenced to death, one for theft of a velvet hood, another of a horse, and another of a single coin.

Susannah insisted Tenn take her directly home after the despicable trial she had so desperately wanted to see. Before she went early to bed, she anonymously sent by carrier the rest of the beautiful Virginia strawberries and a purse with all her extra coins in the house to Thomas Hallam's young, pregnant widow over on Shoe Lane.

Noises pulled Susannah from the misty realms of heavy sleep. She had been dreaming of Tenn as he reached for her in his big green bed, his green eyes undressing her.

"Oh," she murmured and sat up heavily to lean her head in her hands. Then she heard the noises again. Yes, that was what had awakened her. In the black bedroom, a crack of light crept under the door. Theo must have come in, she thought, as she threw back the coverlet and fumbled in the dark for her velvet mules and silk wrapper.

The glow in the parlor made her squint at first. "Theo? Is that you?"

His voice came muffled, whether with exhaustion or drink she was not certain. "Of course, it's I, Susannah. Were you expecting another?"

"What is it? Aren't you coming to bed?"

When Theo spun to face her across the space of the dim parlor, she gasped. His hair was dishevelled, his cravat and waistcoat soiled and awry, but worst of all, his eyes looked glassy—almost demonically lit from within.

"Go back to bed, Susannah. I need that little coin purse for tomorrow, that's all."

"My household money?"

"Our household money—ours!" he told her shrilly and rummaged loudly through the little drawer in the parquet table.

"It's not there, Theo. It wasn't that much and I've used it."

His brows crashed down to obscure his wild eyes. "On what, pray tell? I swear, if you've been buying copies of plays or newspapers again to sit about and wile away your time *ad perpetuam*, I'll have your pretty little head on a platter!"

"No, I spent it for a good cause. Poor Thomas Hallam's widow is pregnant and she obviously needs money more than everyone's clever fabrications in court yesterday."

"What?" he screeched and came at her. "What? There must have been a good ten pounds in there! Oh hell, for love of a bawd!" he cursed as he hit his shin on a chair and threw himself heavily in it.

"There was ten pounds and if you're so uncharitable about it after what happened to poor Hallam in all this, I'll ask to have it replaced for you from my next salary payment from the theater before you deliver it to Uncle Charles."

"Ah, well, let's not quibble over that. A mere ten pounds then, only I swear, it pains me to have my own wife on that turncoat Fleetwood's side. Fleetwood grandly paid off Hallam's widow too, I don't wonder."

"I wasn't paying her off. I grieved for her loss. And I sent the money anonymously."

"So. And what else, pray tell, has my little wife done of late behind my back?"

Her heart thudded, and she pulled her silk wrapper closer about her slender body. Tenn's face—the dream—taunted her and made her nipples point erect and her knees tremble. "Just what is that supposed to mean," she brazened, but her voice shook.

"Now, now, I'm just on edge from these terrible weeks at the theater trying to make ends meet without fat Fleetwood. I swear, I sometimes think the wretch is lying about the gout to just leave me there on my own while he undermines my authority and tries to make me look the fool from afar."

"But you two used to get on so well," she added quickly, grateful for the change of topic. "And surely he knows the actors will be fully loyal to you while he's gone."

"Fully loyal—a pretty phrase *obiter dictum*. Fully loyal as you have been to me by allowing my father to literally abscond with your talents."

"I am still singing at the Drury for you, and that's all you ever believed I could do anyway."

"You'll not lecture me, Susannah! It's late and I need not this woman's bickering. Besides, he hasn't asked us to underwrite any of the cost and that's all that matters now."

"Theo, are we—you've seemed so worried about money lately. The problems with funding are just at the theater because of Fleetwood's holding the purse strings, are they not?"

"H'm? Yes, damn the cad. I said so, didn't I? You'd best get back in bed then, and I shall be in shortly."

"What time is it anyway? You surely weren't at the theater this late. You know Theo, everyone including you assured me when we wed that your late nights at Covent Garden were a thing of the past."

He jumped up and advanced on her. Susannah saw clearly now his haggard look and bloodshot eyes, and realized she had overstepped badly. "I'm sick and tired of your carping, wife. 'Everyone assured you,' did they? Such stalwarts, I suppose, as your dear debauched brother Tom—or was it your beloved James Quin? Or perhaps one of the theater gallants who moan and sigh at the mere glimpse of their little song thrush, Mrs. Cibber. For love of a bawd, but I'll have a pretty problem *ad infinitum* keeping the jackals away if the illustrious, self-serving Colley Cibber ever does make an actress of you!"

She backed against the wall where he blocked her in, but now she was angry too. "You've done little or nothing, Theo, to keep the fops away before, have you—or foxes like Macklin? Was it so hard to keep them off your first wife Janey when she was an actress? Is that why you're so dead set against giving me a chance to act?"

"Janey! Ah, how dare you throw thoughts of that poor wretch at me. Next I suppose you'll ask again to have my two little daughters here that poor Janey left to rear. Well, I tell you, I don't need them underfoot and they're fine at the home of my sister Catherine! Egads, you sound like you've been listening to that street harpy, Kitty Clive, if you want to talk of Janey."

"Hardly to Kitty, Theo, as she won't give me a civil word since I married you."

"Get to bed, Susannah, before I use my husbandly prerogative to physically chastise you for your shrewish mouth. If I didn't have an important task for you in the morning, I swear, I'd settle you down in a trice!"

She pushed him gently back from where his wiry frame pinned her heavily to the wall. His breath smelled of rum and garlic; stale smoke clung to his clothes and hair. He budged a step back, then two, and slumped heavily in the chair. "Come on, dear wife," his mumbled words carried to her laden with mockery. "Do you think I'd let anything get by me? I'm referring to Tenn Sloper, of course."

She gasped and jerked so hard against the wall she knocked her head and numbed one elbow. No, Theo couldn't have said Tenn's name, couldn't know! But he sat there so calmly—he could not know!

"What about him?" she asked, her voice a fleeting ghost of a sound.

"It's obvious to me, my dear, the man has taken a liking to you *par excellence*, and for once, at least, you haven't handled it poorly by being completely standoffish, as I might have expected after the way you've treated others with fortunes to throw away."

She almost collapsed on the floor, whether in shocked horror or mirthful hysteria she wasn't certain. "What do you mean?" she managed, then held her breath.

"You do know he's rich, I suppose. The family owns rural estates hither and yon and keeps a huge town house here in London. Both he and his father are very influential in the king's government to boot."

His weary voice drifted off and he swivelled his body to study her. "Now, don't start a tirade. I can just tell that bleached white look you get when you're distraught. I'm not asking you to beg him money to tide the theater payroll over, though that's what I need, but if he's smitten enough to haul you to Macklin's trial, you can surely ask him for a little advice."

This conversation was ludicrous, she told herself, sheer madness; yet he evidently knew nothing more of her and Tenn. "I do not understand exactly what you're asking,

Theo, only—you do know he's an acquaintance of Fleetwood's."

"At least fat Fleetwood did that for us then when he had Sloper take you home the night of the trouble with Hallam, but that's it, Susannah, precisely it."

"What's precisely it?"

"I want you to get prettied up in the morning and call on Sloper, that's all, so don't fuss." He took her hands in his cold one. "Susannah, I need desperately to know if Fleetwood's in danger of going bankrupt or just holding out to cause a riot against me by players I can't legally pay. If there is any proof of his insolvency, I can use that to foment distrust against him and win them all over to my side, although I don't know where I'd ever raise enough money to buy the royal patent myself. Squire Sloper's evidently a racetrack crony of Fleetwood's, and you could entice at least some information from him."

She laughed once at the irony of it, her own voice strident in her ears. Her brain sought words to tread the way carefully. Theo was surely not above setting a trap, but lately he had been so obsessed with losing control of the theater that she believed his ploy was sincere.

"But Theo, you know how I feel about men I meet at the theater. I simply couldn't just drop in and ask him—"

"Use your head, Susannah. For love of a bawd, where is your loyalty anyway? I need this favor and, by Jupiter, as my wife you will comply!"

"It seems too forward, Theo."

"Ah, but you want to be an actress—always an actress. That's your passionate dream, your *metier*, is it not? Then act for me, wife, act for me with this rich squire, or I swear I'll take a whip to your icy little backside."

She yanked her hand from his and slid away from where he had imprisoned her against the wall again. Contempt all mingled with pity—that was what she felt for Theo Cibber, but if he wanted acting from her, so be it.

"I'm going to bed now, Theo. I think the plan is foolish, but if it eases your mind tonight, I shall ask Squire Sloper for you. Why don't you just come with me when I go?"

He dropped into the chair again and put his head down on his arms atop the table. "I've got too much to do—too damned much at the theater to keep the jackals all at bay like Fleetwood and those viper creditors. Besides, you alone, all dressed up for Sloper—that's the effect I want. I've got to write letters to the newspapers *ad infinitum*—"

His words slurred; his voice drifted off. Fine, she thought. Let him sleep his debauch off out here where he wouldn't snore and mumble and paw her in bed. He was incoherent, and his thoughts obviously jumbled newspaper articles on Macklin's trial with his own doings. The poor, selfish fool. Let him force her to visit Sloper as she was about at her breaking point anyway, holding Tenn off in her dreams and in reality. Now, tomorrow, even with her husband's unexpected blessing, the dreams and reality would merge.

She blew out the single big candle and felt her way in the dark back to bed alone.

Susannah's heart knocked as hard as the massive brass door handle at the elegant house on St. James' Square late the next morning. She was grateful the street looked fairly deserted. Her hand shook as she knocked again. At the last moment she had intentionally sent Anne Hopson on another errand rather than bringing her along, as she knew she should have, for the sake of propriety and sanity. And she had dressed much more carefully and stylishly than she usually would. Her brocade gown was a peach hue that set off her topaz eyes and complemented her rich chestnut hair. She wore no paniers, only extra petticoats in the newest style. Her bodice and neck ruff were edged with palest gold lace, which also dripped from her elbow length sleeves. Her tresses, swept up in an elegant peach silk bow, spilled from her forehead and temples in carefully tended curls. The day was warm so she needed no cloak, although the ensemble was hardly what she would ordinarily venture out in. Still, Theo himself had urged her to get "prettied up," and she had merely obeyed.

She heard crisp footsteps inside the door and braced herself. She had decided to face Tenn alone on his own territory: Retreat now was as impossible as not spinning to the clouds anytime he even looked her way.

The eyes of the dour, black-garbed steward who answered the door swept her in a curious if hooded way. "Please enter, madame. And may I not give the master a name?"

"Yes. I'm sorry this is unannounced, but I need a word with Squire Tenn Sloper. I'm a friend of a friend. Mrs. Cibber is the name."

"Won't you step into the drawing room directly off the foyer, Mrs. Cibber," the steward intoned. "Fortunately, I believe you have caught the young master before he went out today."

Her eyes swept the graceful drawing room as he ushered her in, bowed stiffly, and left. The carpet with its fruit basket and flower pattern, the lovely carved sideboard with silver wine cooler, the pink upholstered settee, delicate ceiling plasterwork, and moss-green draperies all bespoke elegance and cultured wealth. She sighed. How hard she had labored to make her rooms in the narrow house on Little Wild Court gracious, and yet they were eons from this muted magnificence.

"Susannah! Is anything amiss? I couldn't believe it when Temple announced you were here," Tenn told her the minute he closed the door behind himself.

His deep tones awed her; the comforting, yet arousing sight of him stirred her so that instantly the tiny velvet strokes fluttered along her thighs and lower belly. Standing very close, he took her offered hand and kissed it.

"No, I am fine. Actually, believe it or not, Theo sent me."

His russet eyebrows lifted over the fathomless green eyes fringed by thick lashes. "What? I don't dare to hope that means you've left him for me already."

She startled, then laughed shyly. "No, of course not, you rogue, and what do you mean 'already' as if you're so certain?"

"I am, sweet, for one way or the other, whatever it takes I mean to have you. Here, don't scold; sit down on the settee and explain while I call for some coffee to keep this all proper."

Her eyes went lingeringly over his casual attire as he led her to the settee, then moved away to pull the servants' bell cord. The steward's eyes were more disciplined, she noted before she went back to studying Tenn more thoroughly as he gave Temple brief orders.

Burgundy breeches, which stretched tautly over lean hips and full thighs, were accented by the crispness of white shirt and cravat and white stockings. Dressed informally, perhaps in haste to see her, she marvelled, he wore no frock coat, and his full hair was held simply back by a black velvet tie. When he strode over to sit an appropriate distance from her on the settee, she took in the high cheekbones and chiselled mouth through a swift, sideward glance, but she hesitated to dare the impact of the eyes.

"Tell me about it, Susannah," he said low. "It will take Temple a few minutes to send the butler with the coffee. Obviously, Theo knows nothing of us or he would not have sent you. He isn't after money, is he?"

"Of course, not," she said more vehemently than she had intended, and she swivelled her carefully coiffured head to him. "What have you heard to ask that right away?"

"Calm down. I only asked because word is that the Drury Lane is needful of funds to meet actors' salaries now that Charles Fleetwood's been off the premises. And those letters against Fleetwood that Theo has been inundating the newspapers with suggest he's getting a bit desperate."

"Letters?" she faltered, feeling a complete fool even as she had two days ago when he had warned her that Quin and her own father would lie at Macklin's trial. Even though she had agreed to meet him these last weeks behind Theo's back, she didn't want him to believe her husband thought nothing of her and never told her one dratted thing! Letters—Theo had mumbled something about letters when he'd drifted off to sleep in the parlor last night, and she'd thought he was alluding to Macklin's trial publicity in the papers. She knew what letters he must mean, but like an idiot, she had never thought Theo would be the one to publicly attack a man he had worked with for months and whose good will they both needed for continued success at the theater.

"Susannah? Just a minute now, and then we'll talk," he told her low, his voice like a firm physical caress as the butler carried in a heavy silver service, poured coffee, and departed.

She was glad for the coffee to hold; peering over the fluted china rim made her feel safe from that jade stare that could so effortlessly undress her thoughts as well as her body.

"I know the letters you mean," she told him after the heavy oak door quietly closed behind the butler, "but I never believed Theo would stoop—that they were his, at least. 'Well wisher' and others signed 'Y' and 'Z' bemoaning the situation and the Theater Royal where 'free men of genius must work to fatten the purse of a profligate, incompetent' patent holder. I just didn't think it could possibly be Theo, and when we've discussed them he never let on, drat him!"

"I hadn't really intended to bring them up," he said. He put his coffee down and turned toward her, lifting one big knee casually onto the settee seat between them. His hand along the tufted back of the piece gently stroked the slant of her cheek until she too put her coffee down.

"He sent me—he wants me to inquire of you if your horse racing crony Fleetwood had said aught of his finances being in ruin or given any hint of his plans for the Drury. And he said he's glad I have treated you better than most of the rich men who hang about backstage. Damn him, Tenn," she said in a rush as her usually low voice rose and quivered, "I just detest how he carries on sometimes."

He moved closer on the already shrinking settee to pull her to his chest with his long arms locked around her. She stiffened against him for a moment, then sighed and leaned her head on his shoulder. "I suppose he's desperate at the handwriting on the wall, sweetheart," he said. "And I'm afraid neither this break with Fleetwood nor the fact you're working closely with his father will settle his own financial problems."

"That's not so bad," she murmured, detesting herself for how easily she nestled closer in his warm embrace. "We both earn decent salaries though mine's mostly in trust, and next winter I'll earn even more when I begin acting—if I do well."

"Fear not, my Susannah. You will do well. No one will resist your charms on stage or off. I know I cannot."

"You tease," she said and lifted her head to smile up at him before she could halt her step into his magnetic web. She was so close that she could see the tiny pulse beat frantically at the base of his throat, and each separate russet eyelash, so sinfully long for a man.

He kissed her once, such a brief touch of his firm, warm mouth she almost cried out in disappointment.

"Hold that beautiful look," he rasped as he set her back. "I'm going to latch the door just in the event the servants come back before they're summoned."

Susannah said nothing, though she knew she should protest. As if mesmerized, she watched his broad shoulders, which tapered to narrow waist and hips above the powerful thighs, while he moved away, then came back.

"That gown is pure elegance," he said low, "but then anything you wear is—even boy's garb soaking from a swim in the Thames. I will try not to muss that peach brocade."

He sat beside her and lifted her onto his lap in one fluid motion. She clung to his shoulders then his neck, as kiss answered searing kiss. Surely, it could only be this much here, she thought wildly—a few, impassioned kisses, caresses, and the whispered words of more later; but she wanted more now!

In tormentingly slow adoration, his hot lips were skimming the ruffled neckline of her gown. She rained tiny kisses along his jaw and temples where his coppery hair brushed back. How, she marvelled, had she ever thought she needed to hold these feelings and even his passion back?

He tipped her head onto his arm and slid one ivory shoulder free of sleeve while her hands ran riot in his hair. "Sweet little witch," he groaned deep in his throat, and pulled her against him to take her mouth again. He too was breathless when he whispered low against her flushed cheek, " 'Friends,' the lady told me, 'we've got to be just friends.' " He deftly loosened the tight laces along the back of her taut bodice to allow her to breathe more freely—and to caress her heaving breasts more completely.

"Tenn—we can't love here like this—mid-morning and in the drawing room. I didn't mean to come here for this."

"I know, I know, but it pleases me you call it loving. It is loving with you, for you, Susannah. Just trust me. I'll keep my head, I swear it, though there's nothing I'd like more than to use this little couch now for our deep bed at the Blue Rose Inn."

I'll keep my head, he'd whispered, but she wasn't certain she really could. The engulfing sensual impact of the man devastated her poise and all notions of propriety. An actress—she knew she was a good actress, but with him there was never pretense, only the sweeping love and rage of mingled passion.

His big right hand ruffled up her stockinged leg under the petticoat and silk chemise. Her soft buttocks across his hard lap wiggled and shifted in little movements the greatest actress in all England could not have controlled, as he stroked her bare thighs now high above the last ribboned garter.

She felt dazzled, both sharply alive in her senses and yet floating outside herself in his fierce embrace, but he was merely holding her, caressing her. Her huge topaz eyes opened to link with his glittering emerald ones, so close she could see her own reflection in their vast depths. In that shattering moment, she knew she loved him, needed him so desperately despite Theo, despite theater, despite a sane world out there somewhere.

"I adore you, Susannah, adore you," he was saying. "I'd do anything for you. You've only to ask." Already, his inner voice, which usually spoke only words of reason, told him he had done too much for her: urged her aloof father-in-law to direct her acting, offered to finance the play she would debut in, planned to woo her away from that vapid, pompous husband of hers whatever the cost. From the moment he saw her in that dive in tawdry Covent Garden, where she had sparkled like an uncut gem, he would have risked anything to have her, and it was still true.

She always drove him so easily to the brink of sanity and control like this that he'd need a thousand nights to ever love her slowly, properly, thoroughly, as she deserved. Now his pulse pounded; his heart thudded in the nearly overwhelming need to have her here, not only in his arms, but under him and part of him, despite any crazy vows of self-control he had made. But his steely discipline that had served him well numerous times on tennis courts, in royal courts, running horses, or running vast estates saved him: With a heartfelt sigh he set her back on the settee beside him.

He kissed her again, then again, and watched her while she smoothed her skirts. He could have had her here, settee and midmorning be damned he knew, and that realization filled him with a sense of heady power as nothing else ever had. She evidently sensed his thought. She blushed fiercely and lowered her thick eyelashes to stare at her tightly clasped hands on her peach satin knees.

"Come spend the rest of the day with me, Susannah, and we'll go out in the carriage."

"Out where?"

"To the country for the afternoon. Chelsea, if you'd like."

"I do recall Chelsea, and I do recall your carriage," she said and smiled faintly at last as if she had settled back to earth. "But no doubt you have somewhere to go, and I do too, an acting lesson at Father Cibber's on Russell Street."

"I should have known. I do have a tennis match and a meeting, but for you, I'd cancel both."

She stood unsteadily and shook out her skirts as he stood behind her to lace her loosened bodice. "If you're unhappy with Theo, and I think you are, you should think about alternatives," he told her.

"I believe we are using alternatives now," she said low, "one I never believed I'd ever want."

"But there are others. I don't expect you to do anything to upset your January debut at the Drury, but as soon as you're established there, I expect some sort of decision. There are other theaters in town, you know."

She pirouetted slowly to face him as he smoothed his thick hair that she had so thoroughly dishevelled. "I don't think so. Such things aren't done."

"They are," he levelled at her. "I did and I don't mean change theaters. I'm not pressing you now. And what if you should get with child, my child? We need to think and to plan. Despite the rakehell life some people think I've led since I separated from my wife, and despite how this must look now to you, I do believe in single, serious commitments."

She meant to give him some sort of answer, but the knock on the door settled that and she moved swiftly away to compose herself on the settee, while Tenn smoothly unlatched and pulled the door open in one noisy motion.

"Yes, Temple? We were just going on a short walking tour of the gardens in back," she heard him say.

"Pardon, squire," the stage whisper came barely to her alert ears as Tenn stepped out into the foyer, "but Miss Amanda Newbury's come calling; says she's located her lost cousin back home in Berks, sir, and wanted to personally thank you for all you've done for her. I put her in the other drawing room under the circumstances, squire."

Susannah's heart plummeted; she felt her face freeze. A Miss Amanda from home in Berks! But that was the name of a supposedly fictional betrothed he'd used when they had first met. Then that Amanda was real and here now. She would never have stumbled on the truth if she hadn't come here and stayed to—to desire to lie with him at midday in this drawing room, one of his many drawing rooms, damn the seducer! Tenn Sloper was no better than Theo—a flirt like Macklin, a liar like Quin and the rest of them. And worse, she'd made a complete fool of herself wanting, longing for him to tumble her here like a treat with his wretched coffee!

Other words were being spoken somewhere. A woman's high tones and laughter floated to her. If he brought the woman in here, she would simply die; if he didn't, she would know he intended to continue his myths, his dramatic stage lines of loving her!

"Susannah, that was a friend, but I sent her away," he told her smoothly as he hurried in.

She stood, her face impassive. Colley Cibber was always telling her that stance and head positioning were everything, so she held her chin up. "But I don't mind, as I really must be off now, Tenn. It does seem 'she' friends just drop in on you every hour or so, doesn't it? I declare, it must be terribly taxing."

He studied her face, tipping his head slightly to the side. "If you insist on leaving, I shall at least drop you home or at the theater if you'll just wait a moment," he said, his voice wary. "Shall we talk about my caller?"

"No, sorry. I can't wait a moment, as I'm leaving now," she said, and lifted one hand in a careless attitude.

"Susannah, what is it? Something I said? Is it my other visitor? Is it the fact we've been so hurried here today of necessity?"

"Of necessity, I'm off. Thank you for the information, though it won't content Theo, I suppose. I've just got to—work harder to help him, I guess now with—all I know."

She skirted around him in a little circle while he frowned, then shrugged helplessly. His hand properly on her elbow under Temple's sharp eye, he saw her to the huge, carved door in the spacious black-and-white tiled foyer, then stood briefly outside with her in the gentle wash of May sunlight. Carriages rattled by; a dove cooed from the eaves above.

"When will I see you, Susannah?" he asked low. "I could pick you up around the corner on Russell Street after your lesson this afternoon."

"No, please don't," she said and forced a smile though she did not meet his dangerous eyes. "No more dissembling, I think. I love acting, but only on the stage. Good day."

She exited at a fast clip, cursing herself silently. Fool, coward, you do love him and want him no matter how many Theos, Amandas, acting careers, or potential scandals are in the way, she told herself.

She felt so shamed by doing what Theo wanted here today and by letting Tenn know he could have had her in broad daylight like some Covent Garden hussy; she felt terrified to have found something—someone—with more strength and self-control than she. Her passion for the theater—surely she could survive that, but this? And he was probably back there chasing after Amanda Newbury since she had turned down his invitation for later. How she hated him—or herself!

Her head slumped and her knees went shaky as she turned the corner of the Square east into Charles Street. Here she was piously lecturing Tenn about hating acting off the stage when she was acting to the hilt by even walking away like this. From now on, she vowed reasonably, all her energies, her passions, her very life, were for her career alone, or nothing at all—nothing else at all.

Part Two

"While frantic passions talk so wild and loud, the voice of reason is of little force."

line from *Xerxes*
by Colley Cibber

Chapter Nine

The October day was crisp and clear, and rehearsals for Susannah Cibber's Drury Lane debut in *Zara* had finally begun. For three hours now, the cast had been reciting lines from Act I, pushed here and there on the stage as the playwright, Aaron Hill, began to block in movements for the intricate tragedy. Finally taking a short break before returning to rehearsal, Susannah munched an apple, leaned her hips on a watering trough in the sun-washed alley behind the theater, and thought of Tenn.

She understood why he had been away all summer to oversee his estates at West Woodhay in Berkshire. True, the crops and livestock necessitated supervision, and the Slopers' model rural village there needed tending. But Susannah knew he had also stayed away because she had refused to see him alone after that day she had foolishly thrown herself at him in the drawing room of his father's house—the day Amanda Newbury had also come calling. And, despite the imploring letters he sent, which she had not answered and which had now finally stopped coming, only she knew how truly bereft she was without him. Whereas once she had been so certain this chance to have a title role in an admirable and highly touted play under Colley Cibber's aegis would fill her life, she found it amazingly empty without Tenn Sloper. Every day now, her smothered love for him turned to panicked rage at herself that she had lost him for good.

The theater door behind her snapped open. "Egads, Susannah, Aaron Hill's ready to start and you're mooning out here," her husband's voice shattered her thoughts. "I swear, but if you're to be an actress in *my* theater and work in a play *I* am in, you will report on time for rehearsals and appreciate them too."

She threw her apple core far down the alley. "I was on time today, Theo, and Aaron gave me and everyone a little respite. And I appreciate the fact Fleetwood agreed to allow the play at the Drury and cast you in it too after all the earlier trouble you had with him. He's very forgiving to overlook those low, anonymous letters you sent to the papers, I'd say."

"You'll not lecture me, wife. I believe it was such pressure I applied that has made Fleetwood and me *en rapport* again. That, and the fact your little visit to Tenn Sloper you so downplayed to me must have been a smashing success after all."

Her playbook slipped from her hands, and her notes and the last letter from Tenn that she carried in it sprawled on the cobbles. "What do you mean by that?" she managed as she bent to scoop up the strewn papers.

Theo jauntily put one silver buckled foot up on the end of the horse trough and gave her a ludicrous wink as she straightened. "Just musings on my part, but I'd say our country squire must have put in a good word for us. Fleetwood let slip that Sloper's invested in some recent theatric ventures *sub rosa,* and I can't help but wonder which ones."

Her mind raced; her heart fluttered, and she went

weak-kneed. "Such as what?"

"I don't rightly know, but then Fleetwood and Hill did come up with funds for extravagant rehearsals and a grand January debut for this play in a trice, didn't they, my dear? Fleetwood won't say boo on it, but *ab initio,* I've felt he would never have financed the Cibbers himself, not even for you, so who knows? Perhaps your little call on Squire Sloper was much more of a *coup* than you thought." He laughed shrilly. "For love of a bawd, I'd like to get that rich rascal back to London from wherever he's gone to luxuriate on his massive estates."

Susannah stared unspeaking at his crass implication. What if Tenn had financed all this? What if he had even arranged for her earlier lessons from Colley Cibber, who had suddenly appeared like a knight errant in her life? No, it was pure mania to believe such. Tenn had never said that, never alluded to investing in the theater or her career. Her eyes focused on her husband's pinched face, and she jolted back to reality.

"I'm going in, Theo. As you said, Aaron's probably ready to start." She swept past him with her playbook held tightly to her breasts.

"Calling him Aaron, are you now?" Theo mocked behind her and clucked his tongue as he followed her in.

On the barren stage not yet readied for the evening's regular performance, the white-haired, thin-faced playwright, Aaron Hill, stood talking to Colley Cibber and Susannah's old mentor, George Frederick Handel.

"Father Cibber! Maestro Handel, I had no idea you were planning to drop by or, I assure you, Theo and I would not be outside for a breath of air," she told them as each older man bowed in turn over her hand.

"As lovely as ever, our Susannah," Colley Cibber trilled and condescended a nod to Theo.

"*Ja,* My songbird becomes a great actress soon and James Quin told to me you sparkle on stage like a diamond," the white-wigged, portly Handel told her. "Quin's Cato always puts me asleep, *ja,* but for your play, I shall stay awake and bring the royal family too, king and all!"

"Oh, Theo, wouldn't that be wonderful!" she said and turned to her husband only to have her wide eyes collide with his narrowed ones.

"The jury's not in on Susannah's histrionic endeavors, yet, gentleman," he clipped, "that is, on pulling off a tragedy realistically. Holy hell, if she manages that, she'll be the first Cibber to do it, won't she, father? Excuse me, but I've much to see to in my duties here now that our illustrious patentee Fleetwood's so seldom about and there are things to tend to *ad infinitum.*"

"Susannah," Colley Cibber told her as Theo stalked off, I find it best to ignore him when he's that way, but I suppose that's more difficult for you. You see, over the years, neither Theo nor I have had the resonant voices or ponderous gait for tragic heroes," he went on, now grandly addressing anyone in earshot. "I've accepted that as I have triumphed in so many other ways, but Theo never has, and he couldn't even come up to my standards in comic parts. I used to say, gentlemen, I never would have believed Theo was my son but that I knew his mother was too proud to be a whore!"

As if on cue, Colley Cibber and Aaron Hill guffawed while Handel frowned and Susannah just stared. How hard those early failures—and this father—must have been on Theo. No wonder her husband became so cruel and frenzied himself at times, she thought, for however kind his sire had been to her, the thin veneer of manners was so easy to scratch to reach the brutality of the man.

Blessedly, the cast assembled, the visitors departed, and rehearsal resumed again. Act I slid by in this play translated from the French, which detailed the pathetic story of a young noblewoman forced to choose between family duty and romantic love. Aaron Hill's nephew, Charles, whose singsong delivery annoyed Susannah as much as it pleased Theo, was cast as Osman, the hero; Theo had the bit part of the French officer, Nerestan; and clarion-voiced Hannah Pritchard, whom Susannah liked immensely even though she was a close friend of Kitty Clive's, played Susannah's dear companion, Selima.

Susannah walked as she had been taught; she gestured and declaimed in her sweet, plaintive tones, but her mind kept slipping away. Theo stood nearby in the wings glaring at her, hating her. Could it be that Tenn, so far away, really had loved—did love—her? Hannah Pritchard's next words jolted her.

"Alas! But Heaven!" Selima proclaimed, wringing her hands in pure distress. "Will it permit this marriage? Will not this grandeur, call'd a bliss, plant bitterness, and root it in your heart?"

"Ah me!" Susannah picked up her next line as the sultan's beautiful slave, Zara, spoke. "What hast thou said? Why would thou thus recall my wavering thoughts! How know I, what or whence I am?"

"Susannah!" Aaron Hill's sharp voice broke into the scene, "I'm afraid, my dear, that *your* thoughts are wavering today. What is it, dear? We've been over these exact emotions for this part, you and I, just last week."

"I'm sorry, Aaron. I—it's nothing. Perhaps I'm tired today, but that's no excuse as I'm certain everyone else is too."

"Quite right, quite right. A gentle reminder we have been at this for hours and the January debut is a good ways off yet, I know. And as our Zara here carries the heaviest burden of this play, I do believe I'll release you others and just keep Susannah for a few minutes longer."

"I'll stay too, uncle," young Hill piped up.

"No, my boy, Susannah only," Aaron said and dismissed them all with a flourish of playbook in hand.

"I'm sorry, Aaron. I guess I wasn't concentrating," she said low.

"Understandable with that husband of yours throwing fits and Colley's bitter comments, eh? But you must learn to put all else away but Zara's grief, Zara's tumult as she loves one man but sees her duty with another."

"Yes, Aaron. I do know."

"All right then. Stay but a moment, and I shall let you go for the day. Let me just review for you. You must be natural, yet each line, each gesture, is ordained here in the script. Now, Colley Cibber taught you the various stances and tones to evoke the ten expressible passions, so you merely summon up the one you need—stance, gesture, voice level, and there you are."

"It always sounds so easy, Aaron, but just as a real passion is always unexpected, I don't think it can be quite so—predictable and planned for."

The pale blue eyes over the thin nose narrowed. "Nonsense, my dear. On stage, as in life, one must create and control emotion. Oh, I don't mean to urge you to be a set declaimer or ranter like Herr Handel's friend Quin, but if you think the emotion, it will appear. Likewise, you can snuff it out at whim."

"On stage perhaps," she mused, half to herself, "but not in real life. Truly, Aaron, I mean not to argue. Tomorrow I will be fine—natural and in control and just fine."

He studied her intense face. "I'm certain you will,

my dear. You know, your father-in-law and I—others too, I vow—believe in your talent, charm, and natural charisma so much that, quite frankly, we're relying totally on you."

"That's warming but sobering, Aaron. And thank you for your tolerance today."

Susannah went up the backstage stairs to her old, tiny tiring room that she still used when she sang her popular pieces between and after performances. Someday soon, if she was good and justified everyone's belief in her, she would be given a larger chamber, would have Anne all to herself to help gown her every night, and would begin to accrue the large wardrobes that helped to make a great actress an admired one.

Suddenly, Kitty Clive's robust voice sliced through her thoughts, and she stopped at the little turn of landing partway up. "How can you abide it, Hannah!" Kitty's voice sounded distinctly. "You—one of the premiere actresses of the Drury stage playing bit parts to that blue-blooded, gold-tongued little Cibber chit?"

"Nonsense, Kit, my pet," Hannah Pritchard's voice replied to the more strident tones. "The girl's got raw talent, and I believe you know it too. It's just a freak she married your arch villain, Theo, so sheathe your claws toward her. I'm starting to think you're getting jealous of Susannah's opportunities here."

"Pox on it, she'd not be debuting in a big leading role if it wasn't for all her fine protectors—old Colley, Aaron Hill, the king's Handel, no less. That black-haired devil Macklin had the glint in his randy eye for her. Then there's that tennis stud Sloper who owns half the rural estates in Berks, I hear, throwing money into her damned career—"

Susannah gasped so loudly she lost the next words. Her hand seized the rail of bannister for support; the flow of angry sentences went on but nothing else sank in. How could Kitty Clive know that? Maybe it was true! Theo had hinted—and now Kitty Clive.

Her feet walked, as if she had no control over them, to the half open door of Kitty Clive's tiring room. Already, Susannah could glimpse Kitty and Hannah Pritchard within, hot chocolate saucers in hands, their feet propped up on the same tufted stool. Before she could stop herself, she had knocked on the door.

"Well, then, what is it?" Kitty shot out before she turned her head to see who was there. "Bless me, Hannah, if it isn't our Mrs. Cibber, alias tragic actress Zara, come to call and no doubt put her two pence in this little talk she's been eavesdropping on."

Susannah shoved the door inward but did not step over the threshold. "I couldn't help but hear your remarks, Mrs. Clive. I suppose anyone in the theater or this side of town might have too. I only want to ask where you get all this arcane knowledge of me—such as who does or doesn't help to finance my career."

"Susannah," Hannah Pritchard soothed and put her slippered feet down to the floor, "I'm certain Kitty didn't mean a thing by it."

"Of course not, dear Susannah," Kitty mocked as her florid face got even redder. "After all, 'a fool and his money are soon parted,' so it's Sloper's folly if he wants to sink time or money in a little songbird who has a pretty tail."

Susannah stood over her in two huge strides. "Cease your dratted carping, Mrs. Clive. Who told you? That's all I'm asking!"

"None of your poxy business, Cibber. And dare we to assume from this little display that you're sweet on the squire or not? I assure you, I don't care if you and Theo have a pot to piss in but if Theo is as insolvent as I think he is, no wonder he allows Squire Sloper to lay out his funds for you and—"

Susannah watched her open palm smack Kitty's cheek before she even knew she would move. Hannah screamed; Kitty cursed and flew out of her seat spilling chocolate on her ivory robe. The saucer shattered somewhere.

"You bitch!" Kitty shrieked at Susannah. "You fancy little lily-white bitch, I swear, I'll tear your golden eyes out!"

Susannah retreated, dragging Kitty's vacated chair in her wake. The woman looked possessed—hands like claws, eyes demonic. Susannah backed to the wall; Hannah Pritchard dashed out into the corridor screaming for help even as Kitty lunged at Susannah's tensed body.

Susannah shoved her away, but Kitty swung a fist wildly, like a man. Susannah ducked, then hit out at Kitty the same way. She turned to run, but Kitty's talons were in her hair and ripping at the shoulder of her gown.

Suddenly, Theo was there, then her brother Tom shouting things Susannah could not comprehend in her red rage. She didn't mean to do it—to hit Kitty again—but she did. Fiddle bow in hand, Tom tried to haul her away a few steps as Theo grabbed the flailing Kitty and attempted to disentangle her from Susannah's streaming auburn tresses.

"Stop it! Stop it! Alley cats, both of you! Susannah, whatever ails you?" Theo shrieked.

She hung limply in Tom's arms before he released her. Then she straightened and threw back her loosened hair. "Ask Mrs. Clive if you must know. It is only that I became suddenly very, very tired of being abused for whatever you must have done to this woman's dead friend—your first wife, Theo. She hates me—hates us both for whatever you did to Janey, that's clear. Ask her if you want to know."

Amazed at her own cold anger and aplomb, Susannah shoved past her astounded brother without another look at any of them and ran up the stairs to her room. Immediately, she heard footsteps behind and turned to see Hannah. Grateful it was no one else, Susannah sank wearily on the top of the stairs and rubbed her bruised knuckles. Hannah stopped several steps down.

"I'm sorry you saw all that, Hannah. I'm not proud of it, even though I think I actually got the best of her."

"I know, Susannah. That sort of row is hardly your style."

"I realize you're a good friend of Mrs. Clive's—and so I shall apologize to you only."

To Susannah's amazement, the elegant Hannah sat herself on a step and leaned back against the dingy wall.

"I am Kitty's friend. I admire her immensely, Susannah. That's why I want a word with you. You see, I'm learning to admire you too."

Susannah's gaze snagged with Hannah's. "You are?"

"Indeed. Despite the odds, I believe you'll beat them all—beat the system that categorizes singers as singers only, beat the way Theo Cibber has been afraid to let you act. I've seen you in the wings for years, in love with acting, learning all the lines, longing for your chance."

Tears crowded Susannah's eyes, and her voice was a mere whisper. "It's true."

"It was the same for Kitty, you see, only she had it harder. She was a street wench who climbed out of the slums, fought tooth and nail to get her first chance—singing too it was, just like you."

"I—I've heard that."

"She and her dearest friend Janey, who later married Theo, used to chase the dashing actor Robert Wilks through the streets until one day they wheedled him into hearing them sing. She and Janey broke in just like you through singing and had to fight for their chances. But that's not all."

"I don't detest her, Hannah. Actually, I look up to her for her work. But she hates me for being Theo's wife, when I didn't even know Janey Cibber!"

"Listen now. I just wanted to tell you the reason she thinks she detests you for all your men friend protectors."

Kitty's sharp words, especially the implied accusations about Tenn, flitted through Susannah's besieged mind again. "Why then?"

"Because," Hannah said, her usually clarion voice now dropped conspiratorially low, "she either hates men or fears them, I'm not certain which."

"But—not Kitty Clive! She teases them, leads them on, insults them."

"Exactly, and not one thing more, not since her disastrous marriage. She insults them to keep them utterly at bay, Susannah. I've known Kitty for over ten years now and I tell you there has been no man who has touched her since her short and tragic marriage to George Clive."

Susannah's eyes widened. "Really? But Kitty's so wild, so—raucous with men."

"It's all a front, a brick wall. She's never explained it, but something evidently happened on her wedding night. I guess perhaps the poor girl was so appalled by the consummation act itself when she got right to it; anyhow, she left George the next morning and that was that."

Susannah sighed. Her fierce fury at Kitty ebbed away in common sympathy. How often she had wanted to leave Theo like that, for the revolting sham he made when he touched her that way. And like Kitty, if it hadn't been for Tenn, she would have gone her whole wretched life thinking union with a man's body must always be that way.

"So she's thrown herself so frenzied into her acting," Susannah said, half to herself.

"And her remembered love for her once dearest friend, Janey Johnson, who married Theo."

"I see. Thank you for speaking to me, Hannah. I do see."

Hannah patted her hand, then stood to shake out her skirts.

"Hannah, what Kitty said about Squire Sloper financing *Zara*—had you heard that too?"

"Not exactly, though it's obvious there are funds from somewhere, as the long rehearsal schedule and elaborate sets and costumes they've planned mean something's afoot. I only heard someone in the king's good graces from among Robert Walpole's Whigs, but you know rumors backstage. Why don't you ask the man himself?"

"Walpole or the king?" Susannah said and grinned, amazing herself as much as the serious-faced Hannah at the tease.

Susannah felt immensely better now as Hannah bellowed a quick laugh and hurried back downstairs. After all, although Hannah was Kitty's friend, she obviously still liked her. Furthermore, Susannah had overheard Hannah say she had talent. Now she understood too that Kitty's hatred of her was not her fault. They even had dreadful marriages in common. But, most of all, she felt relieved inside about Tenn. Now she had the excuse to write to him, to see him again, and she wanted that chance very, very badly. She would send a brief note to Berks telling him she had heard some disturbing rumors; a comment she had received his letter; word that the play rehearsals were progressing well.

She stood and hurried up to her little crowded tiring room to write the letter.

A quick ten days later, Susannah found herself not only enmeshed in rehearsals for *Zara,* but also treading the boards at the Drury in the singing and speaking part of Chloe in Henry Fielding's farce, *The Lottery.* The play was only a brief afterpiece to follow James Quin's *tour de force* in *Cato,* but Theo had whimsically decided that she needed experience in at least one small speaking part before her debut two months hence in *Zara.* Besides, he himself was playing Jack Stock, Chloe's scoundrel husband in the farce, and the extra salaries were a deciding factor. But most of all, Susannah learned entirely too late, Theo had intentionally given the part of Chloe to her to put Kitty Clive in her place, as the playwright had originally written the role for Kitty.

"Laws! Least you got another new costume out of all this to add to your meager collection," Anne muttered as she fussed overlong with Susannah's pale green, flower-sprigged silk gown. Pink satin ruffles edged the low-cut, square neckline to reveal the dip of cleavage between her full, high breasts, and the same seashell-hued satin dripped in layers from her elbow-length sleeves. The gown was fitted in front, but fell free from the daringly low back in gathered folds clear to the floor as if she pulled a train. It was the famous French imported fashion called the Watteau, and the first costume of its kind in Susannah's limited collection.

"How you carry on, Anne Hopson. I've got six full gowns and pieces of others, and I'll soon have four more new ones for *Zara.* Not so meager for an actress whose debut is not until January."

"Piffle! Your debut is tonight in the silly thing Mr. Cibber insisted on to keep his creditors at bay and rattle Clive the cat. Stop flipping that fan! Just a few more satin roses pinned here in your hair, and we're done."

The high-heeled green satin shoes felt good on her feet, and the gown rustled in whispers when she moved. She could smell the scent of sweet perfume water and powder on herself. Once again she fluttered the fan Aaron Hill had given her as a good luck present and stared at the silk painted with a picture of two lovers, which stretched across its delicate, carved ivory ribs that she had learned to handle so adroitly. Everything was as ready as she was for tonight. If only she had heard from Tenn about when he was coming back to town, everything could be settled.

The callboy's shrill voice in the hall jolted them both. "Mrs. Cibber! Cato's dyin' out there. Five minutes 'til the afterpiece."

Anne opened the narrow door and kept two adept hands on Susannah's voluminous skirts draped over paniers as she sidled through. "Someday, Anne," she said back over her shoulder, "when and if I get famous, I'll change the styles on stage to gowns that will at least get through tiring room doors."

"Laws, don't toss your head that way 'less you want those expensive satin rosebuds flying off your locks! For the life of me, I don't know why Mr. Cibber had to insist you wear this fancy new gown to that dance he's arranging on stage after the performance, I don't. You'll have to hold this whole back piece up when you dance, so don't forget!"

They went downstairs and stood in the bustling wings. Indeed tonight, Susannah mused, the stage would serve to earn the theater even more money than the main bill and this afterpiece would fetch in, for

Theo had published far and wide that guests were welcome—for an extra fee—to meet the actors and actresses, even dance with them on the stage to the music to Tom Arne's Drury Lane Theater Royal orchestra.

Susannah waited calmly, ignoring Anne's last nervous ministrations to her flowing gown in back as the sprightly overture began. This part of Chloe was nothing—breezy songs, a few good speeches; only Kitty Clive had owned the part and everyone knew it was now war between her and the Cibbers. Theo was getting both desperate for funding and publicity with Fleetwood seldom on the premises these last ten months. Her thoughts drifted to Tenn. It was ten days since she had posted that carefully worded note to Tenn at West Woodhay in Berkshire.

"That's your cue, Susannah!" someone hissed, and she swept out onto the waiting stage. She moved, she spoke and sang; she enjoyed herself despite sharing the green carpet they had left down from the tragedy with the posturing, bawdy humor of husband Theo as husband Jack Stock. Soon it was over, and she curtsied and smiled radiantly at the applause and whistles of the warm and noisy audience.

Backstage, when they rang down the big single curtain at last, it was chaos: Theo shouted orders; green-coated stage attendants skittered about clearing furniture and props; actors, prompters, property men, and seamstresses were all under foot. Fops, sparks, some familiar faces, others new, pressed in to ask to dance with Susannah. Across the burgeoning sea of heads she spotted James Quin, still in Roman armor, and waved.

New flats slid in across the grooved floor to give the stage the aura of an elegant ballroom. Nearly gutted candles in the huge chandeliers overhead were lowered and replaced with tall tallow stems to burn for hours. Theo's voice was bellowing something about showing one's ticket or seeing the treasurer. At last, Anne Hopson found Susannah in the swarm of noisy admirers and handed her a cup of welcomed stout for her dry throat, then darted away.

Much confusion later, the curtain, usually employed only at the very beginning and end of the theater evening, lifted, and Tom's orchestra began with a lively minuet from their position in the pit. The crowded floor cleared somewhat in the center. Hannah Pritchard was out there dancing with someone but Susannah could not see whom. She noted Charlotte, her gamine sister-in-law, dressed in men's garb serving drinks from a silver tray. Next to Charlotte, she glimpsed Theo in his element: frenzied, busy, obviously thrilled at the thought of all this good coin his brainchild theater dance would bring in. Susannah sighed. Now they would have to put up with these fops and lapwings in a dance hall atmosphere as well as backstage.

"Susannah," James Quin's unmistakable stentorian tones jolted her, "damn, but you're hard to get to in this sardine barrel. Let's joint the others for a turn on the floor to please Theo, what say?"

She danced the mincing, gliding minuet steps, pirouetting easily in whirling satin under James Quin's lofty reach while he shuffled heavily at her side. The orchestra swept immediately into a quick gavotte, and she could tell Quin would hardly last another step. The room spun, the staring faces blurred multi-colored as she turned. They must stop now, for the heavy man could obviously take no more.

Her satin gown whispered to a stop around her slender body. As she halted, a pink satin flower from her hair shot free to the floor. A very long, elegantly brocaded black arm reached down to recover the lost satin bloom. Half fearful, half ecstatic, her eyes slowly traveled from bronze hand over white silk wrist up black brocaded arm to the powerful shoulders and coppery head. The whole noisy room seemed to crash to a jarring halt.

"Tenn," she breathed.

"Hello, Susannah." He held out the flower stiffly, and she took it, afraid to look in his eyes. Their fingers brushed and she jerked her hand back.

"I had no idea you were here, back in London."

"Just hours ago," the finely chiselled lips told her while she dared at last to stare up mesmerized into eyes far greener than she had remembered. "This seems to be a dance," he said, his voice almost gruff, "so let's dance."

She was certain for a moment that her feet would not move, but they did. Her pulse was pounding to drown out the melody; his hand was warm and sure when he touched her.

Many other couples danced now, some in their way. Why hadn't she noticed that? For one moment she had been sure no one else was here—no one but she and Tenn. He didn't look angry exactly, but maybe just intense. And his gaze possessed her utterly each time she dared to stare back.

Everyone applauded when the dance ended, and another one began. It was very warm here, and she could feel the heat from her scented body clear down to the pink ruffles, which displayed the taut swell of her breasts above the constricting corset where her nipples had leapt erect at the mere appearance of the tall, masterful Tenn Sloper.

"It's too crowded here. You wrote you wanted to talk," he said in her ear when the clapping quieted and the next music began. Even his voice, the rustle of his warm breath in her hair, sent icy shivers up and down her spine.

"Yes, but I'm expected to stay here for this," she answered. "Theo wants all of us here for it."

"He won't miss you for a moment on this jammed stage. He's no doubt counting money as he's been selling drinks. Come on."

His hand was firm on her arm above her left elbow, so she went with him off into the cool, dim wings and into the back hall. Indeed, as he said, she had glimpsed Theo overseeing others selling wine and stout in the pit of the theater behind the orchestra. Strollers and gawkers inhabited the hall by the Green Room, and several couples sat on the steps leading up, so they walked on.

"Where does this go?" he asked, indicating the down staircase at the very back of the theater, lit by lanterns placed periodically along the wall above the steps.

"To common storage and wardrobe," she said, "but it's musty and crowded with things."

"Better than with people. As we can hardly leave the building now, it will do."

Before she could protest, he led her down, going first with the same steady grip on her arm. She gathered her flowing back Watteau train so it would not drag. Anne would just roast her if she knew of her traipsing down here in this new, expensive costume. Her heart began to beat even faster when she realized this place would be totally private and deserted. Only seamstresses and tailors by day, and callboys sent down to replace items at night ever inhabited its cool, convoluted depths. Near the bottom of the steps, her knees became suddenly watery, and she stumbled into him.

His big hands went hard to her waist. He lifted her down the last two steps, then loosed her. His gaze travelled deliberately slow over her low-cut décolletage, her waist, her skirts, then back up to her nervous face. For one instant she was certain he would kiss her, but he indicated she should walk ahead of him farther into the depths of rows of costumes, wig stands, and armor.

"A real treasure house of the fantastic down here," he murmured low. She heard his feet halt, so she turned slowly to face him between two tall racks of old velvet and brocaded costumes.

"I guess you received my note," she said, annoyed the sure voice which had served her so well on stage tonight betrayed her now.

"Two days ago. And here I am the moment I could get free, just like some sort of little boy who's been without sweets too long—a much faster response, you must admit, than that of someone who receives a whole string of foolishly passionate letters and doesn't answer a one."

"I felt it—unwise."

"Did you? And now it is wise to see me? On your own territory only, of course, with hundreds of people hovering nearby so I don't abuse or insult you with my attentions—"

"Tenn, please don't be angry! You know our—being together is impossible!"

"I suggest, sweet, you keep that theater-trained voice down a bit even here among the ghosts. If I've only been summoned to appease your sense of curiosity about some rumors you mentioned then, let's hear it."

"You don't need to be so argumentative. I am glad to see you."

The strong, square jaw under the lean cheekbones etched by the wan lantern set hard, then moved. "Glad to see me because you believed I might have financed this play *Zara* you're working on?" he queried, his deep voice wary. "That was the implication of the letter."

"No, just glad to see you. Has—was Amanda Newbury in Berkshire these past weeks too?" she blurted out before she even realized she would ask such a blantantly presumptuous question.

His thick russet brows lifted in surprise to unshade the eyes now dancing with gold shards in lantern glow. "Amanda?" He grinned in her appalled face and shook his head once. "Do I dare to think you've heard rumors about that too and intend to torment me for weeks longer in jealous retribution?"

"Don't be ludicrous. I'm hardly jealous of her. I really don't give a rap if she just drops in at your various homes across England day and night to lie with you on drawing room settees or wherever—"

To her utter dismay he shouted a brief laugh, then sobered instantly. "Listen to me, Susannah, and very carefully because we have go to back up. I hope to hell the reason you've put me through this damned period of estrangement from you is not because your agile little brain has concocted some scenario about me and Amanda Newbury. Damn it, why didn't you ask that day at the house when I gave you the chance? I thought either you really wanted to be rid of me or had a temporary case of guilt—if not about Theo, at least because we've had to take our pleasure so swiftly as we've found the chance and place, and I know you're not the sort of woman to thrive on that as some others I could name."

"Such as Amanda, your long lost betrothed, I suppose," she shot at him.

Furious, he pulled her hard against him, one arm like an iron barrel hoop pinning her arms at her sides, crushing her voluminous Watteau folds to her back. His other big hand was clamped firmly over her mouth. "You will listen, I said, damn it, you little vixen. Amanda is not my betrothed, never was, and I've never once lain with her, although unlike you, she'd probably respond like a warm and loving woman afterwards if we had. But no, I'm smitten hard by a topaz-eyed tormentor who revels in making a man want her until he can't think straight, who makes a man take irrational, stupid risks like this in any nook or cubby-hole he can find to get her alone, damn you!"

His palm over her lips lifted away only to be replaced by a blazing, devouring kiss that ignited her senses. His mouth slanted fiercely sideways, tasting her; his tongue explored in a delicious little foray, then plundered deeper. She moaned and leaned forward, pressing to his angular stretch of hard muscles. So strong, so entrancing, so exciting was this man. He made love and rage combined go all wildly hot and mingled in every pulsating nerve and vein. He made all resistance impossible, any pretense at sanity a mere sham.

Her arms lifted around his big neck circled by an elegant white cravat. He was back with her now, and she could agree to see him in the afternoons for little rides or walks. If Theo liked him so well, she might even dare to have him with them for dinner some afternoon before the theater. She stepped even closer to him, her legs rustling satin skirts between his big spread thighs and knees. To her utter amazement, he groaned, then pushed her back, stood her stiffly at arm's length against the row of costumes, and loosed her completely.

"Hell's gates, no, woman! I will finish what I came to say and without losing my head to tumble you on a pile of theater armor in this musty cellar, so you can refuse to see me for the next few weeks rather than admit how you really liked it too."

She stared aghast at his vehemence and the tormented expression on his rugged, handsome face. "I love you, Susannah. I want you and not only in some tawdry, quick-hitting little affair. But if you won't give me a chance to show you how I'd like to really treat you as my beloved, my mistress, and maybe more if we can handle Theo, then we will have nothing. I cannot bear those accusing looks when we need to part so soon after we've loved—I won't have it!"

"Please, Tenn—"

"Listen, I said. Yes, I have financed this play *Zara,* seventy-five percent of it. Yes, I talked Colley Cibber into taking a good look at your talents and helped pay for your months of acting lessons. I did it because I wanted you happy, and wanted to see you have the means to escape Theo financially. Susannah, the man's beset with debts, and he'll take you down with him. It's common knowledge, his creditors are legion. And I did all that because I love you, and I'm not sorry for any of it. Besides, word is that people who have seen rehearsals think you're wonderful, so who says I know nothing about theater talent?"

Breathing hard, he stopped his torrent of words. They stared at each other for one tottering instant, three feet apart.

"I wish you had told me. I have some money saved and invested," she began.

"Stop it! I knew that would be next. Susannah, you can't pay me back, and I won't let you. If you ever really want to pay me back, just give me some time to convince you we should be together. Trust me enough to come away with me for a few days, a few hours even."

"But—days." she breathed astounded. "You know I couldn't even if I wanted to."

"Couldn't, or wouldn't, sweet? Don't worry, I won't grab you again. I won't lay one finger on you ever again unless you want me and ask. I want Susannah the woman, not the clever actress. I can't take the uncertainty and those hurt topaz eyes. I'm going back to West Woodhay at first light tomorrow, but I'll be back in London for Parliament and Commission business next month after harvest is over. I only came now to see you—to tell you all this. I'm yours, Susannah, but only if you'll have the love and courage to meet me halfway and be sure."

He turned sideways to her and looked away. "Don't worry, Susannah, not about me or your career. Both will keep a long while, I don't wonder. And I thought you were marvelous in *The Lottery* tonight. The plot amused me," his tone came sharp-edged again now. "Imagine a farce about a scoundrel husband who sells his wife to a wealthy man in return for settlement of his crushing debts—"

His voice broke and he turned away. His heavy footsteps thudded on two steps, then halted while she held her breath to think he might be coming back. She ached with longing; her gaze blurred with hot tears. "Don't send for me again, Susannah, unless you mean it. I'm better off exhausting myself in work than agonizing on the rack you put me on."

His feet echoed up the steps and then there was only silence. She touched her fingertips to her lips to savor the tingle where he had roughly kissed her. Along her waist and back, she fancied she still felt the imprint of his fierce embrace. She was drained, numb, and utterly exhausted.

She could run after him, go to his house tonight. She could say she was ill and wanted to visit her aunt, then take a coach to West Woodhay. But, of course, that would bring ruin and scandal to her name, her life, and her career, just when everything was looking so promising.

A huge sob wracked her and seemed to reverberate from the musty walls, archaic costumes, and tarnished armor. Promising? Nothing was promising! She loved a man she could never have and was bound to one she detested. And the start of her acting career had been a precious, parting gift from the only man who had ever made her feel so vibrantly alive.

Susannah sniffed hard and forced her shoulders back. Theo might notice she was gone; all those people were waiting. She had to go up and give a reasonable performance. She wiped her fingers carefully under her wet eyelashes and walked slowly to the dim, deserted stairs.

Chapter Ten

On the dazzling night she had waited for all her life, Susannah felt a deep inner calm while everything and everyone swirled about her. The voices of callboys outside her tiring room door had told her an hour, a half hour, now a quarter hour. Then the role, the play, the stage, the theater, and the audience would be all hers, and she was ready.

Granted, there were things to worry about and to regret. At the last minute Theo had insisted on adding a cloying prologue he would speak to present his wife's debut and his fervent wish she would be warmly—and monetarily—accepted. Then too, the male lead Osman, played by Aaron Hill's young nephew, had never yet outgrown his wretched singsong delivery. And, most unsettling, Tenn had finally come back to town and she had been terrified to communicate with him. Theo had grandly announced a few minutes ago that Squire Sloper had taken a whole box for his father and himself tonight. Worse, Tenn had sent her an emerald pendant, which Theo had seen and had actually gloated over, when she showed it to Anne. But nothing—nothing would ruin this night or cause her to become tongue-tied and stumble-footed as once before because of Tenn in the audience or Theo in her life.

"Sister, you look wonderful!" her brother Henry Peter's exuberant voice called through the half-open door. "Mother says to tell you we're sitting right behind Tom in the orchestra pit, but she won't let me stand in the wings for good luck."

Susannah turned her head to send him a radiant smile but did not budge from where Anne fussed for the hundredth time over her bouffant pink satin outer skirt draped over huge paniers. "My dear, you're always good luck to me wherever you are and, besides, with father ill at home, mother needs you to sit with her. Thank you for coming up though."

Anne patted Susannah's upswept locks one last time and rearranged the three spiral curls that dangled down her long, elegant neck. Susannah glanced quickly in the mirror. The two-tiered gown was exquisite, though it looked to her more a garb for a princess than the slave she played in *Zara*. The fitted bodice, elbow sleeves, and bouffant upper skirt that trailed an ivory-lined train were pink satin in a figured, swirling design. The undergown, which was displayed in front where the pink pulled away, was robin-egg-blue with ruffles and tiny swags of pink roses. To match the lining of the overskirt, her sleeves and bodice front boasted layers of satin ruffles, and the two tall feathers in her hair perfectly echoed the hues of pink and blue tiered skirts.

"Out, out, lad!" Theo's shrill voice sent Henry Peter away with a wave and caused Anne to curse under her breath.

"He was just wishing me good luck, Theo, and he wasn't in the way," Susannah told him.

"Nonsense. On stage we make our own luck, wife," Theo said and vehemently brushed the sleeves of his blue-braided French officer's uniform.

"How do I look, Theo? These paniers are so huge I

really think we should have rehearsed once at least in costume as Aaron suggested."

"Egads, and rip or soil something at the last minute? Let Aaron Hill pay for seamstresses and washerwomen if he knows so damned much about running a theater then. I swear, that's hardly his *metier*, or yours either. At least the house is full and with some influential individuals who can drag others in: Handel, my father, your admirer Sloper, and his father."

She chose to ignore the way he squinted his eyes accusingly at her. He hadn't said a word to encourage her tonight, hadn't even admired how she looked, and she refused to rise to his taunts just before she went on. "I sincerely hope all our efforts will be good enough tonight, Theo, that no one will have to *drag* anyone to see the play. Excuse me now, as I want to go down and Anne needs to help me get the skirts through these wretched doors and down the staircase."

"I swear, don't let me stand in your way, Mrs. Cibber. Oh, by the way, Fleetwood's here too and wanted to give you a gift of twenty pounds toward benefit money as we've filled the house tonight."

"Really? Twenty pounds? Theo, we can afford new draperies for the parlor then—"

"Not so fast. This is hardly part of your damned salary that silly prenuptial agreement purports to give you—money legally and morally in my care as your husband. I have taken charge of the twenty pounds, and I assure you it will go to good use. Well, enough for now. Time is fleeting, dear Zara."

Susannah could feel her pulse pounding in hurt and rage. For weeks Theo had taken every spare coin they had, yet creditors and billmen still came to the theater or house to see him. And worse, though her spending money for household goods had been sharply sliced, he still continued to be out dining or carousing at all hours with friends, and her questions about whether he paid for his own food, drink, and gambling bills too often turned to terrible tantrums from him.

Anne's gentle hands lifted to both Susannah's shoulders as she stared at the now empty door. "I'm really sorry he did all that right before you go on, I am," Anne soothed. "Laws, curse the rascal. You going to be all right?"

"Yes, Anne. I'm fine. You know, the worse things get for me with Theo, the more I feel the emotions I need for Zara, so torn to love where duty did not call—"

"What? You're mumbling, Miss Susannah."

"It's all right. Make sure that lovely emerald pendant is hidden under the ribbons in the lower drawer and let's go down."

The hum of the expectant audience warmed her, thrilled her, as she waited in the wings. She would finally be appearing in the main bill, which was a sweeping tragedy, and not as the little singer during a break or in farcical afterpieces. Whoever was out there watching would know her Zara. They would love with Zara, grieve with her, and suffer when she died, stabbed by the man she truly loved who didn't understand. She had waited all her life for this, and she would give them a Zara to cherish and to love.

"Best luck, Susannah!" backstage people whispered to her, and an intense Hannah Pritchard gave her a one-handed salute from the wings directly across where she awaited. Theo strode out and in his shrill, piping voice began the prologue she so detested:

> Tonight the greatest venture of my life,
> Is lost, or saved, as you receive—a wife.
> If time you think may ripen her to merit,
> With gentle smiles, support her wavering spirit.

"The slimy toad," Susannah heard James Quin's unmistakable deep tones behind her somewhere in the wings. One corner of her mouth quirked up in begrudging thanks that Quin and the others understood. How dare Theo rant and posture out there as though he had arranged all this, when he had actually fought and demeaned it every step of the way. She had Tenn to thank more than anyone. Drat it all, she loved him, and like Zara could not bear to be parted from her love another night!

If she conveys the pleasing passions right,
Guard and support her, this decisive night.
If she mistakes—or, finds her strength too small,
Let interposing pity break her fall.

My strength will not be too small, Susannah vowed, her lips moving so that Anne's kindly face peered around to see if she spoke. Not too small for the play, this career, or getting Tenn Sloper back—if it was the last thing she ever did.

In you it rests to save her or destroy,
If she draws tears from you, I weep for joy.

For joy and ticket prices, Susannah fumed silently. Her heart beat fast, faster as low applause answered Theo's poetic plea. The time was now, the curtain up. Zara and her slave friend Selima walked the halls of the Sultan Osman's Far Eastern palace, and Selima spoke.

The story unwrapped itself like a gilded, exotic flower. Beloved by the sultan, Zara nevertheless is devoted to her Christian brother and father. Beset by family loyalty, the beautiful slave Zara regrets how she has hurt the heart of her beloved Osman. At that very moment when the plaintive lines came almost melodically from her lips,

Zara looked up into the lights and saw her green-eyed beloved leaning forward from his balcony: "I have planted pain in Osman's bosom. He loves me, even to death—and I reward him with anguish and despair. How base! How cruel!" Zara bemoaned, and the audience murmured in a sympathy she could actually feel, even though the green-eyed lover's gaze harshly devoured her.

Between each tension-laden act other singers graced the stage with light songs of love, as she might once have done. "You're wonderful, Susannah," James Quin intoned between acts, in his version of a stage whisper. "Keep up that poignant energy."

She nodded, hardly aware of what he said.

"Osman's too damned nervous," Selima told her as they stood waiting for the last act. "That fiddle-faddle whine of his has got to go!"

Susannah's eyes only lifted to the box where Tenn sat like a sultan whose loving slave had dared to hurt the precious passions of his heart too long.

The last act began. The words came effortlessly, along with the motions and emotions: betrayal; Zara's own grief, so strongly felt and perfectly projected.

> This love, so powerful, this sole joy of life,
> This first, best hope of earthly happiness.
> There, there I sacrifice my bleeding passion.
> I pour before him every guilty tear.
> I beg him to efface the fond impression,
> And fill, with his own image, all my soul.

She was Zara. The low, melancholy tones evoked overwhelming loneliness and longing. She was Zara.

She waited expectantly in the wings of the palace where her beloved Osman spoke of her. Then she must step out to die for her love—to risk it all at any price. Osman—Tenn. Tonight she must be no longer blameless.

Yes, was I blameless—no, I was too rash,
And 'tis my duty to expiate
The transports of a rage,
Which still was love.

She stepped out to her fate unbowed and so swept away by love that she felt transported. Zara died for love; the audience applauded and cheered until they all took bows a second and third time before the spell fell away and the world of Drury Lane Theater Royal enmeshed Susannah again.

"Marvelous, Mrs. Cibber!"

"Susannah, they loved you out there—loved you!"

Loved you, she marvelled, and smiled to nods and handshakes, hug and kisses. Aaron Hill, Colley Cibber, and Maestro Handel kissed her hand and spoke warm words. But her eyes swept the stage for him, tall and copper-headed; only the emerald pendant earlier had said it all, and she knew he would not come. I'm yours, Susannah, but only if you'll have the love and courage to meet me halfway and be sure,' he had said. And now, like a gift more wonderful than this new adulation swirling about her, she had found the courage and love. Now, suddenly, she was sure.

Fleetwood kissed her hand as she made her way through congratulating swarms toward the stairs. "A miracle, Susannah," he gushed. "A new lead actress born at the Drury tonight."

"I appreciate your support, Mr. Fleetwood. And Theo and I thank you for the monetary gift."

"A mere pittance of your worth."

"Then, would you be so kind as to see that my salary is directed to my hands instead of to Theo's in the future? He and I do have an agreement to that effect, although he has always collected my money before."

The portly man frowned. "Sorry, but I don't want to get in the middle of that, whatever words I've had with Theo on other subjects. A wife's salary is her husband's free and legal in this civilized country, Susannah, and we hardly need to discuss such. Look—I know Theo's in debt, but aren't we all? Besides, he told me he'd have all his creditors off his back in a trice by merely selling some old family jewelry. Damn, almost forgot to tell you. He told me to let you know he had a dinner invitation to the Duke of Norfolk's or some such, but I couldn't go with this blasted gouty leg. Said to tell you to go home with your mother, I believe. Don't worry. It will be all men at Norfolk's, my dear."

Fleetwood bowed and limped off leaning on his silver-headed walking stick. Susannah stood frozen at the bottom of the steps, oblivious to the crowds, the noise, and Anne's voice urging her to hurry upstairs. Theo couldn't even face her after this triumph, couldn't say one good thing even for the money it would mean, which they obviously so desperately needed. Instead, he took any coins she had and turned bitter over tuppence; he squandered all they had on drunken living and sold their jewels.

Her head snapped up. Jewels! There were no old family jewels. She lifted her voluminous skirts and tore up the narrow steps, ignoring Anne's scolding to watch the dirty walls.

Her tiring room was a shambles: drawers dumped, garments thrown, a mirror shattered. "Damn him! Damn him!" she cursed aloud as she knelt to rake through the jumbled pile of ribbons and cheap paste jewelry.

"Oh, no. Oh, laws!" Anne shrieked as she breathlessly came in behind her. "A thief, oh, I told you we should have locked up that emerald, Miss Susannah!"

"It's gone, gone, and that's the last straw. It's all over

now," she mumbled, then bit her lower lip until she got control of herself. "Anne, stop that sniveling and help me change. Here—close the door before we attract a crowd. I have to go out."

"Out where? Not just straight home on your triumphant night and all?"

"Just do as I say. Then run down and tell my mother I won't be going with her, and don't breathe a word of this mess to anyone. We'll pick it up as best we can. I have to hurry."

Even as Anne's shaking fingers began to unlace the back of her bodice, she started to scoop up huge handfuls of her strewn and ravished possessions and toss them in the toppled drawers.

The two huge lanterns on either side of the great wooden doors gilded the crisp January night as Susannah's sedan chair halted before the Sloper's elegant town house in St. James' Square. She felt the carriers gently bump down the tall box on poles.

"This be the place then, mistress?" one of the men's voices asked.

"Yes. Here's a coin to take this note I mentioned up to the door."

Her hand shook as she extended the folded, scented square of vellum to the man. Sitting in the dark of her little enclosed cubicle, she waited, shivering slightly in the chill. It was daring and bold, this ploy of hers to win Tenn back—as if she had ever really had him in the first place. Despite her triumphant joy tonight of proving to herself and others she was an actress to be reckoned with, this great impassioned longing for Tenn had to be reckoned with too.

She watched the wide door of the classical style house swing open to bathe the burly sedan carrier in its warm interior light. The thin, curious steward reached out to accept the note. Temple, that had been the man's strange name, she remembered. The two men's words misted the frosty air as they spoke briefly to each other; then the door closed on the carrier.

She waited, breathing deeply, trying to calm herself at the mere thought of brazenly offering herself to Tenn like this. 'I'm yours, Susannah,' he had vowed, and now she was his for the merest loving word or touch.

She had written the note to him so carefully that she could see each word now if she but closed her eyes: a quote from her lines in *Zara* and a repetition of his own words—"Restraint was never made for those who love. I will meet you half way and I am sure."

But what if he didn't come, if he spurned her as completely as she had him—and more than once? What if she had waited too long or there was someone else—some Amanda—or he could never forgive her now?

Twisting sideways hurt her neck muscles, and she pressed her head back against the padded leather of the cab. This was sheer madness, dressing so seductively, putting perfume on the note, coming late at night on the public street before his house.

Quick footsteps on the walk. She leaned forward even as the sedan door was pulled open. Tenn, his face and voice so close!

"Susannah, I have waited so long. I'd almost lost hope, especially with your dazzling victory tonight," he said as he leaned so near she could scent sweet brandy on his breath.

"Tenn, I'm sorry, but I—love you and so I had to come," she chattered, soundly strangely inane to herself.

One big hand cradled the back of her elegantly coiffed head to pull her lips to his in a feverish kiss even as he still bent in from outside. She swam in desire, drowned in his touch, even though he pulled quickly back.

"I'll have the carriage brought around if you'll go with me to Chelsea tonight."

"Chelsea," she managed, thrilled and amazed by his decisive command of the situation. She had thought he would want to talk first to be certain of her; perhaps that at most he might ask her in. "Chelsea, yes, if you think so."

He closed the door and spoke to her carriers outside, then ran back up into the house. She sat stunned at the sweep of circumstance: this morning, despair she had lost him; tonight, her body already gone soft with desire at one kiss and the thought of a dark ride to Chelsea in his carriage, as they had done once before eons ago.

He came back out the front door coated and hatted; a carriage rumbled instantly close. He went around and pulled the streetside door of her sedan chair open, helped her out, and immediately up into the depths of the larger vehicle. As if in a daring, delicious dream, she rested within his arms as they lurched and swayed away.

She leaned back willingly in the warm circle of his embrace as streets, houses, and time went by. Theater, Theo—nothing else mattered or even existed but this need for Tenn, this sweeping ecstasy at his caresses.

"I've missed you so, missed you," she told him once between kisses.

"You little fool. We've wasted one hell of a lot of time, but the wait's worth it with your coming freely like this. We'll make up for every lost moment, I swear it, my sweetheart."

Slanted mouth and darting tongue became wild forays and little nips down her throat while she nibbled at his earlobe. Already she couldn't breathe, couldn't think. His sure hands slid fiercely over her back and slender waist to cup her soft buttocks through the folds of satin skirts and to hold her against him.

"You were so beautiful tonight on stage, my love, so

wonderful. I wanted you like this so desperately. . . ."

She slid up on his lap, feathering kisses down his square jaw to his strong neck above the cravat. One of his warm hands crept up her silk-stockinged leg, and then higher to gently grasp the warm, bare flesh of inner thigh.

"You drive me wild, my Susannah, always did. I can't ever reason when I touch you."

She gasped as his fingers explored higher and gently probed her ready warmth. "Oh!" she murmured against his ear, but other, saner words would not come. She only bit her lower lip to keep from crying out her excitement and let him stroke her. He made her want to seize him, beg him to take her now, again, and always. How had she ever forgotten he could so stir her to loving rage like this?

Too soon he sat her up gently beside him and ruffled her skirts down. "A few minutes, love," he rasped, so out of breath he sounded as if he'd run a far distance. "I see lights and I've got to be calm enough to at least get us upstairs to the room—our room."

She managed a shaky smile in the darkness as he squeezed her knee through the skirts and leaned over her to peer out the window.

He climbed down and helped her out into the dim yard of the inn, which was lit by two lanterns suspended from the same bent arm of the single, huge tree. She saw only the driver, George. If there had been two footmen, they were gone.

"Here, my sweet. We'll go in this back door and directly up the stairs."

"But what if someone is in the room?"

"Then my man will tell us, and we'll take another."

She obeyed, totally trusting, her slender hand in his big one as they ascended the narrow servants' steps. Upstairs, amazingly, the innkeeper was opening the door to the same room they had shared that one time before. A lamp was quickly lit, and tallow candles bathed the room in golden glow.

"Dinner, sir?" the innkeeper inquired. "Winter venison, bisquits, rabbit stew, wine?"

"Later. I'll send down," Susannah heard Tenn's low, resonant voice as she turned away to swiftly survey the room.

It was larger than she had remembered. The chamber was chilly, but the innkeeper was stoking a fire even now. A table and two chairs on a variegated rag rug graced the hearth. There was little other furniture but a tall, dark sideboard, the huge four-poster bed with red tester, and the same hip bath she had once used. She stood in the middle of the room and stared at Tenn dreamy-eyed, half unbelieving as he closed the door and latched it behind the retreating innkeeper. When he turned to her and smiled, it warmed her more than any rosy, flaring hearth fire ever could.

He came toward her, smiling now only with his green-gold eyes above the finely chiselled mouth. "A great triumph for my beloved woman tonight at the Drury," he murmured, "and a great triumph for me now. I love you, Susannah. I want to take you to bed and show you how much, but I don't mean to press or rush you."

"The note said I was sure, and so—I am."

He picked her up and whirled her once before he placed her on the huge bed. He stood over her looking down even as he doffed his frock coat, waistcoat, and untied his cravat. In two quick tugs he had opened his white silk shirt to reveal a deep V of curly, russet chest hair and bronzed skin.

"I'm afraid those bedsheets are probably cold," he said as his eyes swept from her toes to the bonnet she had begun to untie at last. "No matter. We'll find a way to get them warm—"

They both worked quickly at divesting her of her outer garments until she wore but lace petticoats, lace chemise, and stiff corset that mounded her ivory breasts up to his eager gaze. "Damn corsets," he muttered and sat at last beside her on the bed to unlace its back. "Don't think," he told her, "that I didn't appreciate the low-cut, elegant blue gown, but I find myself increasingly impatient."

The constricting garment gaped away and she drew in a shaky breath caused as much by his nearness as the sudden freedom and cool air. He lifted the corset from her, tossed it somewhere on the floor, and gazed at her proud breasts now covered only by a gauzy lace chemise.

He took her lips beseechingly while his skilled fingers flickered each pink nipple to even tauter fullness. Her graceful hands lifted to stroke his chest, then to part and push away his shirt and bare his upper body. His devouring mouth dropped lower to the arch of her throat, her fluted collarbone, still lower. His hand cupped and lifted a breast to meet his mouth; he licked and suckled the pert nub through the lace until her entire body quivered with desire.

"Oh, Tenn! It's so wonderful I can't think."

"Don't think, my love. Just trust me—just feel—"

He shifted the exquisite torment to the other breast. She could feel everyplace he touched, kissed, licked, looked. Even his hot breath against her bare flesh roused passions she had never imagined. When she could feel the slick vibrations of his tongue on her nipples race down between her legs, he stopped to peel the chemise away to completely bare her to the waist.

"So exquisite, so lovely, Susannah." He nuzzled her neck while she leaned into him, caressing the back of his neck where his full head of copper hair started. His hands were in her hair now, pulling pins, tumbling loose the glowing chestnut-hued bounty over her naked ivory shoulders.

"I love your hair down—down for me," he rasped. "Let me take your petticoats down—for me too."

Beyond reason, she helped him slide the ruffled layers from her small waist over her rounded hips. He stood one moment cradling her to him to yank the covers and lay her down. Then he had stripped away breeches and stockings and turned back to her. His huge male silhouette edged by rampant firelight behind blotted out the room—the entire world.

The cool caress of sheets felt fine along her heated skin. His hands under the coverlet grasped her waist and pulled her to him, then rolled them over so she lay suddenly atop his long, angular length.

"Tenn!" she gasped as she felt her breasts pressed to his resilient mat of chest hair and the way her knees instantly parted on either side of his muscular thighs. She felt herself go all hot at the feel of her impudent thrust of nipples against his own hard male nubs. And already she could feel his brazen readiness pressing against her soft thigh.

"My love, how long I have wanted this," he told her low. "I didn't dare to hope, but now it's true. This night, at least some hours of it, is ours, and so I don't want us to lose a minute."

She startled as she realized his intent. He lifted her hips slightly, settling her down on him full length while she pressed her hands to his chest and tried to kneel to take her weight.

"It's all right," he comforted. "There—see? You've got me all now. See how wonderful." He let her sit fully astride his hips and merely smiled languorously up at her and stroked her breasts until she thought she would burst with joy at the double caress. Then, slowly, he began to rock his powerful hips under her until any shred of poise and self-control shattered in the sensual onslaught. She'd never, never imagined it could be like this—so sweeping, so sweet, yet so piercingly fierce within her quaking, naked body. Her eyes locked with his and she willingly drowned in the deep emerald depths of pure passion she found there.

He rolled her suddenly under him and, lifting her hips up toward him with one big hand, increased the pace, plunging and pulling against her.

Her fingers grasped wildly, kneading at the taut muscles of his lower back, her legs lifting to hold him to her as he bid. It went onward, upward, and around, this making of one beautiful being, this perfect union of two bodies and hearts. A woman, very near, cried out in pure ecstasy, and he held her so hard she could not breathe as he surged wildly into her.

They clung together, breathing hard, not moving otherwise until he shifted his weight to lie beside her and cradle her to him. The warm little nest they had thrashed out in the deep bed was their bulwark against the outside world. Their breathing quieted slowly, almost in unison. She tried to move her head, but her loosed hair was all caught under him somehow.

"I hope you don't think you're going somewhere," his velvet voice came rough and teasing.

"I might," she murmured.

"Never! Well, maybe over to the table later if I order us some food."

"Are you hungry, Tenn?"

"Only for you, as you are about to learn all over again."

"Now?" she squeaked before she realized how silly she must sound.

His lips moved enticingly along her bare shoulder; then he turned her on her side facing away from him and traced her spine clear down to her waist with his slick tongue. She lay still for him, holding her breath at the sweet assault. His hand brazenly caressed the curve of hip, stroking first one soft, resilient cheek and then the other.

"You're going to be all mine, and I will be all yours when we bed together," his words flowed over her. "Every beautiful bare inch."

He turned her on her back and continued his little forays of hands and lips over both breasts gone shamelessly pointed for him again, then over the flat belly and slant of rib cage, down to the hips and thighs and velvety triangle where her legs joined.

"Oh, you can't—"

"Let me. Let me."

All denial, sanity itself, slipped over the sheer edge of rapture. He was in her again: She had pulled him to her, begged him to take her! She clung to him in a rage that was surely love, rocking to meet each powerful thrust, moaning and shifting and swept away in that wonderful flowing river.

She drifted somewhere in his arms, pulled from slumber by something he had said. She had gone under in the swift current, but he had saved her, and now she swam safely and eternally sure in his arms.

"Susannah. Sweetheart." His warm breath stirred her tumbled hair and tickled her ear.

"Mm, what?"

He chuckled low. "We've both been asleep, my love, and I'd better get up and see how long. I want us to have a little dinner here in front of the fire before we go back."

Back! She jolted instantly awake as the world crashed in. She was far from home in a little inn in Chelsea, but she felt terribly sure this was home now. She dreaded going back! A cold wave of disappointment sobered her, and she reluctantly disentangled her limbs from his as he got up and pulled on his breeches.

He fumbled for his watch, clicked it open, then padded near the fire to read it. "Barely eleven," he said. "We have a few hours yet."

A few hours, she thought. . . . an eternity before heading back! Time to talk and laugh and touch and perhaps even . . .

She felt herself blush hot at the wanton thought. What had become of her to turn all feverish and willing like this with him when the thought of a man in bed with her—Theo—always made her go so cold and stiff?

He ordered food and carried the heavy tray from the door so the innkeeper would not stare. They ate and drank in the fire's glow, laughingly toasting her debut tonight and their debut together here. They talked of acting lessons, crops at West Woodhay, tennis, horse racing, and gossip of the king's young mistress tucked away in German Hanover. They held hands and giggled about Theo's foolish prologue and how the elder Squire Sloper had fallen in love with Zara at first glance. They gazed deeply into each other's eyes in rampant firelight, and the little flames flickered alive between them again.

"You should have worn the emerald to grace that beautiful throat," he said suddenly.

She looked away. She had meant to tell him, but had almost forgotten it. Her voice was a mere whisper. "I can't. It—it's gone."

His fingers entwined with hers tightened slightly. "Gone where?"

"Tenn, I'm sorry. It was stolen from my tiring room during the performance. I guess I was careless. I hid it, but—"

His voice was like a whip. "Had Theo seen it?"

Her nervous eyes met his angry ones. "Damn the slippery bastard," he ground out. "I know he's hard up, but I didn't think he'd steal from his own wife. But, hell, after that sniveling prologue tonight, we shouldn't underestimate him at all."

"No—I guess we shouldn't. Tenn, he goes out with friends carousing almost nightly and comes in drunk so late, but—he can be so awful when he's crossed or desperate."

"I know. His creditors don't hound you, do they?"

"No, but they're always lurking somewhere about. Theo handles them."

"Obviously not, but don't fret for the emerald. One emerald was not enough for you anyway."

Tears crowded her eyes, and she squeezed his hand. "Thank you," she mouthed, but no voice came.

He moved around the table and picked her up in his strong arms again. The dark blue silk robe he had found for her in the room split from bare ankle to thigh of one slender leg. His eyes caressed the slash of flesh, then moved to her face again. Their lips met, tasted; his tongue invaded sweetly to part her soft lips and plunder deep within until she matched his every movement.

"Tenn, do we have just a little time yet?" she murmured and darted her pink tongue into his ear.

He chuckled so deep in his throat she felt the vibrations quiver her tingling breasts. She could hear the January wind moaning along the eaves; hear the crackle of fire and creak of soft bed where he put her down and leaned over her on one knee. His hands were on her waist, unknotting the single tie. He opened and spread the dark robe as if he were opening a precious package. His eyes raked her nude, languid body all stark white against the robe, and she revelled in his love. "Time for us, time for this, always," he told her.

Already the velvety rasp along her thighs that she always felt at his mere presence seduced her senses. Mindlessly, she arched her back ever so slightly to lift her rosy tips of nipples to his lowering lips.

This woman thrilled him utterly and completely, he

thought, as he moved to suckle her sweet nipples. How wildly passionate she was; yet paradoxically how innocent and untouched. All this—tonight—was more than he had dared to dream. And now, so easily and effortlessly, his body hungered to possess her again.

He moved over her, against her, long after he knew she was ready. How stunning she was tossing her auburn tresses back and forth, lifting her lovely knees for him. She ravished his brain, made him lose all pretense at sanity, made his blood go to hot rage of fierce desire. He would have her now, then again, later, soon, and always. Their melding muted all thought as the wild rhythms of love lured them on.

Chapter Eleven

Susannah stared at the lovely little scripted calendar on her Queen Anne writing desk and sighed: another monthly anniversary of the day she and her beloved Tenn had begun to share their love in earnest; eleven months of loving, eleven months of performing on the Drury's stage in a series of fine roles as her reputation and fame spread. She had come so far in so little time. But tonight her play was not on and she would be spending the evening with Tenn hidden away in their covert trysting place in Chelsea. Already she thrilled to think of it as if their love were fresh and new despite the numerous times they'd managed to slip away together. Increasingly now, her marriage to Theo was as much of a waking nightmare as her fleeting time with Tenn was a precious dream.

"Susannah, for love of a bawd, where's my best walking stick?" Theo's shrill voice startled her even though he was clear in the other room. "I can't find things worth a damn now that I've let Rogers go. You said you'd help with my things, and that pompous Hopson of yours is worthless!"

"It's behind the door, Theo, and pray leave Anne Hopson out of your imprecations. She already does yeoman's duty around here with Cook on half time, so don't start in again that I gave her the day free."

Garbed like the fanciest fop Susannah had ever beheld backstage, he stalked out of their bedroom with the walking stick. Usually she barely noticed what he wore now as he came and went at all hours, either to avoid his creditors or her, but she noted well this pale blue, figured brocade frock coat lined in buff satin, and the pale blue velvet breeches.

"Theo," she gasped, "you look dressed for court, I'd say, and that's all new! But aren't you just going to work?"

"Yes, of course, *ad perpetuam,* wife. I bought this on a loan from Usher Dangerford—and I got it to further your career, as that's really all I do lately. It's for your showy royal command performance tomorrow night, as we've both got to look *par excellence*. I've given up a lot for you, and I don't need your shrewish tongue on this."

"Loans eventually must be paid back, Theo," she said evenly.

"I knew you'd rant and rave! Egads, after all I've done to build your career so we can get a decent salary from it to augment my wages as Drury manager. I've given up the stage myself for you, denounced my *metier,* my *alter ego's* very life and soul."

"Then if you've given it up, Theo, you can omit the wild declaiming and the pretty speeches right now, at least for me. Save it for your friends—or for His Majesty tomorrow evening—or for those low newspaper stories you must spend hours composing."

He shook his silver-headed walking stick at her, and his bloodshot eyes looked as if they would pop from his grimacing face. "I swear, I'd never have wed you if I'd even fathomed what a sword-tongued little harpy you'd be! You're daft, Susannah! You insist on being friends with my nitwit sister Charlotte who believes she's a man half the time and shames the Cibber name by new eccentricities daily. You're even so addlebrained you fret when I try to settle that bitch Kitty Clive in her place, when she's out to get you—you, Susannah!"

Susannah stood to gain distance from the swinging stick. "She's not a bitch, Theo, never was. She's only a fine comic actress who's had to protect herself and her career from those who would harm her for their own ends."

"Here," she shouted at him before she could check her rising temper. "Look at this drivel you've written on her they have dared to print in their dreadful scandal sheets called newspapers!" She scooped up a handful of the latest printed journals she'd stacked on her desk top and waved them at him in imitation of his gesticulating stick. "Behold, some of your latest scurrilous attacks on her to get publicity for me and money for you. I don't need that sordid sort of fame, and I refuse to be a party to it anymore!"

"You?" he shrieked. "You?" He smacked the extended papers with the tip of his stick and they fluttered to the carpet. "It's all for you and you dare speak that way!"

"Please, Theo. Don't you realize we're the butt of laughter in London these days? The Lincoln's Inn Fields Theater is even getting rich on a burlesque of this whole thing where Kitty and I are mocked as Madame Squeak and Madame Squall. The papers are satirizing Polly Soft and Polly Smart, and I don't feel very soft about it! This sort of thing not only kept me from getting the part of Polly in Gay's *Beggar's Opera,* which has traditionally been Kitty's over the years, but it makes me look like a cheap grubber for parts."

She dared to advance on him another step as the pent-up frustrations poured from her. "Everyone snickers and dubs it the 'Polly Wars,' Theo. I have parts of my own, good ones I got because I can do them and the people want to see them. Even Mrs. Thurmond has of her own volition totally relinquished Desdemona to me. Theo, please, I can't bear this scrapping and alley fighting with Kitty any more and especially not made public by the Fleet Street presses. Fleetwood gave her the part to halt all this notoriety, and she'll have a fine opening tonight as Polly, so leave be."

Theo stretched himself up to his full height, holding his walking stick horizontally across his slightly protruding belly. "Are you finished with that histrionic speech now? No one—no one, Mrs. Cibber, ever bests Theo Cibber, so don't you forget it. Clive thinks she's won, Fleetwood thinks he's won, but they're both dead wrong, and I have to hurry to work now to revel in their most just and perfect comeuppance—my *magnum opus.*" He grinned at her, but his gaze was far above her as if for inspiration.

"What comeuppance? What *magnum opus*?" Susannah demanded. "What on earth are you talking about? Kitty's Polly will be magnificent as always and you know as well as I there will be a full house at the Drury for the opening tonight."

"True, my dear, only too true, and it cost me a pretty penny too, but she and Fleetwood have had this coming *ab initio*. Egads, I've got to go, or they'll scent a rat. Farewell, my little wife, and you know not to wait up as I'll be going to White's with some friends—some one at least who appreciates and understands me."

She darted after him across the parlor despite the walking stick he twirled so adroitly at her. "Theo, now you wait. What have you done? You're not going to sabotage something from backstage? What cost a pretty penny?" She held to his elegant, eggshell-blue brocaded sleeve. "Tell me, Theo!"

He plucked her restraining hand off, then pushed her against the papered entry wall with his walking stick pressed horizontally across her shoulders in front. He leaned close to look straight in her face as they were the same height; his breath smelled of gin and the anise candy he favored.

"As I and only I manage your budding career now, wife, I see no compelling need to tell you, but I believe I shall, just to amuse myself. You've heard of 'first night fun' in the old theater days, I believe, as your garrulous mentor, your dear Father Cibber, has no doubt told you how he had to lecture a rioting audience to silence when he opened in *Love in a Riddle* in 1729. Even the fact the future King George II was at the theater that night didn't stop the crude hecklers with their whistles, catcalls, and horselaughs; you have heard that little story from among the myriad other boring tales of his great triumphs he tells everyone, have you not?"

She stared at his grinning face so close as if she were seeing a grotesque mask, and the glimpse beneath the mask horrified her. "Theo, you didn't pack the house like that to ruin Kitty's opening—not at your own theater and not with our financial situation! How could you?" her voice rose toward a shriek. "And what if they get totally out of hand and rip the place up the night before my first command performance, or what if Kitty decides to get revenge tomorrow? Theo, you vile, stupid fool!"

He roared something at her even as she screamed her last words. He yanked her violently toward him. The walking stick clattered to the entryway tiles, but he shoved her away and bent to get it. Her wide eyes on him, her mind now on his words, she backed quickly away from him through the parlor.

"For the love of a bawd, Kitty's a bitch for defying me, but you're right there with her, Susannah. Egads! My own wife, my own scolding, icy bitch little wife. You promised me love and loyalty when we wed, and I have had precious little of either, damn you!"

"I've tried, Theo," she brazened back even though she knew his temper was at the snapping point. "And you promised me my own wages, which Uncle Charles says you've siphoned off most of before giving him the rest; and you promised to help build me a fine career, but all you've done is degrade and drag it through the mud!"

He swung the silver stick at her hips, but she darted back. He shrieked and came at her as she tore into the bedroom and tried to slam the door, but the carved end of the stick's silver handle intruded, then wedged the door farther open as he shoved it heavily inward.

"Theo, please—please just leave," she cried, but he threw himself at her and they toppled onto the bed. She screamed, but he turned her over to press her face down. No one else was in the house, no one, and he was so wild.

He whacked twice at her writhing, thrashing hips, but her skirts took most of the blow. He seized one arm and bent it up painfully behind her back until she lay still, gasping for breath.

"If it weren't for the king's need to see you in one pretty piece tomorrow, I swear, I'd beat you black-and-blue, Susannah. It's time you learned who's master in marriage, time you learned the law gives all rights of a woman's person and wealth into her husband's care!"

Even as he talked, he stroked her skirts up in back with his walking stick until she felt the cool air on her unstockinged calves and thighs. The stick shoved higher, baring her bottom to him. "Please, Theo, let me up. You said you have to go."

He snickered almost obscenely. "Now, my dear little wife begs me to go, begs me to leave, h'm? Time you learned a good lesson, beautiful Susannah. I own you legally, you see, like my new garments, like furniture, like this fancy wooden and silver stick. I don't think His

Majesty or anyone else will note if you're black-and-blue back here; though, of course, if someone would pay for the privilege to get a good look, I'd almost consider it as much as I get from you. No *laissez-faire* for you on these sweet buttocks, my tempting if icy little wife."

To her disgust as well as relief, he dropped the stick beside her on the bed and began to fondle her rounded bottom, squeezing, pinching, even digging his manicured nails into the soft flesh. Pulling her muscles taut, she tried to shift away, but he wrenched her arm along her back again and she lay still.

"All this foolish arguing and this little lesson you're going to learn is making me very late, Susannah, so you'll owe me for that too."

"Please, Theo, just leave," she repeated, hoping she sounded calm. She turned her face away to hide her tears of shame and revulsion. She was meeting Tenn in less than an hour, but this would ruin everything. He'd see these marks; he'd likely go after Theo, and that would be the end of their secret love even as her dear Drury Lane Theater was violated by a paid mob of ruffians.

"Get up on your knees, wife!" The sharp words flicked at her like a whip.

"What? Theo, please—you're hurting me. No!"

He dragged her up with pressure on her imprisoned arm, then shoved her head back down onto the bed so she knelt before him with her bared hips fully exposed.

"Now beg me to perform my husband's duty before I go," his lewd voice ordered. "Say 'It's been long months you haven't touched me, Theo, and I beg you to take me.' Say it like the fine little actress you are, or I'll use this stick so you won't sit down for a week, king's command performance or not."

"Oh," she moaned as he tightened his grip on her and roughly caressed the soft inside of her spread thighs.

"Theo, please don't!"

"Say it then. Beg me as a proper wife should a husband who provides so well for her. A house, career, lovely clothes—say it!"

The cold metal and wooden stick now patted across her buttocks as he talked, the little taps in unison with his chanted words.

"Yes, all right. Please don't—"

"Beg me, I said."

"Theo, I beg you."

"Not enough. Beg you what?" he goaded.

She gasped in a big breath fighting back sobs of humiliation. He had always made her feel this way, even when he didn't touch her, she thought wildly: dirty, shamed, a liar to even pretend to be his wife. How could she have ever been so wretchedly stupid to wed him?

The stick cracked her once. She gasped and tightened her muscles even more. "Yes—I beg you to take me," she gasped out low.

"And you appreciate all I do for you and your damned career," he taunted further.

"Yes, yes—"

He shouted a laugh, loosed her arm, and shoved her down on the bed. She whirled immediately on her haunches to cover herself and scrambled unsteadily off the far side to face him.

He stood to tug his lace-edged cuffs down under his blue brocade sleeves, then retrieved his stick from the bed. He leered at her as she stood defiant-eyed with her arms crossed over her breasts.

"Remember that, wife. I know I shall. For once you were just as you ought to be—offering your sweet body to me with sweet words on your lips, and appropriately humble and grateful. But, unfortunately, my dear, I've more important things to do than tumble an icy little shrew when there are so many willing ladies in the city who will perform any task, and without a stick across their bottoms. Still," he said turning back dramatically at the door, "Since I'm obviously not the beneficiary of all your so blatant charms, we really ought to find someone who could be—and maybe for a price!" He shrieked a laugh and slammed the door behind him.

She hugged herself hard, shuddering as she heard him go out and also slam the back door, an exit he took more and more now to avoid any creditors who might wait in the front street. She sank on the bed and gasped for air as though she were crying, yet no tears came.

She should leave Theo, Susannah told herself, but how could she? She had to work at the Drury, and he'd surely make life more hellish there for her than he already did. She had almost no money of her own, they were terribly in debt, and she could hardly run home to a newly widowed mother who had barely enough to feed herself and Henry Peter. An open liaison with Tenn would prove disastrous for both of their careers. Only last week, she had convinced him they should go on just meeting as they were until she became financially independent. But now, that could never happen. Theo was more and more a lunatic who failed to stop even at the cost of making all their business public in the Fleet Street gossipmonger journals for the whole dratted town to read.

The journals! Poor Kitty Clive had a grand opening tonight and Theo was out to ruin it. That would appear in all the papers too. Kitty would be livid and hate them even more. She had to do something to help Kitty, whatever Theo threatened or did.

She ran out into the parlor and sat at her desk to quickly write:

T.
Kitty Clive needs my help at the Drury so I may

be a little late. Could the coach fetch me at King Street at half past seven instead?

Must hurry.

Yours,

S.

The late December afternoon was mild, but she donned stockings, shoes, and her dark blue velvet cape with the big hood. She didn't have so much as a copper to send this note to Tenn, but when the street boys heard the address was St. James', they'd run it there for promise of reward upon delivery. She had no idea what she intended to do when she got to the theater beyond maybe warning Kitty, but it was so late now that it might even be a hopeless cause. Maybe her brother Tom could help her by directing his orchestra to play until everyone quieted to listen. If news of a disturbance hit the papers, maybe the king would not even come to her command performance tomorrow, and if Theo weren't so obsessed with avenging his own insane pride, he would have thought of that.

Unfortunately, the minute she locked the door behind her and started down the street to find a boy to take the note, she realized she'd made a grave mistake: A little pack of Theo's creditors had evidently come by at the end of their workday and they recognized her instantly.

"Mrs. Cibber, where's that slippery husband of yours? The rascal's late," one sallow-faced man commented and strode along at her side while four others chased after.

"He's at the theater, of course, as it's nearly six. Excuse me, please."

"I told you the weasel has another way out, O'Neal," a man's gruff voice behind her said. "Next time we'll pound on both front and back door 'til we flush him out. Can't see crashing in at the Drury on him at least not 'til payroll day."

Susannah held her letter secreted under her cape and darted across the street. Several of the men fell away. At least, she thought, there was one advantage to married women not legally holding property or money in England. Creditors had business only with the husband—the master, as Theo put it. But the sallow-faced man still brazenly strolled at her side, peering closely at her.

"I'm sorry if we upset you. I've admired your work, Mrs. Cibber. I thought your Zara and Desdemona were wonderful, but isn't it a strain to play all those roles where your husband or lover always kills you in the end?"

Startled by the incisive question, Susannah turned to stare at the man. "No—it's tragedy, you know, and they say I'm better suited for that than comedy. And they are so right," she muttered to herself, and turned away from the watchful, pale blue eyes to nearly run on.

Thank heavens, he let her go, and just a little farther on she found a boy to take the note to St. James'. She hurried even faster now as the theater was another good ten minutes walking and it must be nearly six. A tragedy with a desperately unhappy ending; no, she would never let her life be that! Somehow she would find a way to be her own independent woman, one who could choose the man she truly loved to spend her days with forever—and have her beloved stage career too.

The house numberer who had taken her deceased father's job at the theater's front entrance waved her in when he saw her, though he looked a bit surprised she was coming in with the crowd rather than in the back. But she had no intention of running into Theo backstage before she assessed the tenor of the audience.

Already her heart fell when she saw the crowd. Most came in with previously purchased tickets—in this case, no doubt donated by Theo—and few were women. Even in the foyer and on the steps they were already rowdy and boisterous, and several brazenly sported whistles and catcall noisemakers on chains around their necks. Several even carried in handfuls of rotten apples or orange peels. Her rage at Theo made her blood pound above their racket.

Damn Theo Cibber! He was cruel, malignant, and desperately obsessive to ruin Kitty, and all because she honestly treated him like the bastard he really was. Her stomach churned. Whatever Theo did to her, he was not going to do this to Kitty or this theater or to her own precious career!

Though several fops and rowdies had recognized her, and one had actually thrown an arm around her shoulders, she shoved him away and pushed on. Her hands had just lifted to draw her hood closer when someone behind her yanked it down. "Look," a man's voice shouted, "a real pretty one and all by herself. It usually ain't this early the fancy bawds comes in, is it, Joseph?"

She whirled to hit the man away, but his hands had seized her waist. Several others pressed close. Someone behind her dared to pinch a buttock through her skirts, and she struck back wildly at that. "Let me go. I'm Mrs. Cibber!"

"Hell's bells, doxy, fine with me whoever you are, if you'll jus' sit with us, an' go out after," a rough voice said, and a hand appeared from nowhere to fondle a heaving breast.

"Don't!" she shrieked, even as the little circle of lewd gawkers around her exploded. One man flew backward into a crowd; a fist whooshed by and socked one lout's jaw so hard his head snapped back on his neck. An avenging, copper-headed giant whose tricorn hat fell off turned to shove the last man away from her.

"Tenn!"

He kneed another man who came at him with raised fists, and the crowd melted back.

"Geez, it is Mrs. Cibber, but who's that big brawler?" a voice behind her asked.

"Tenn, how did you get here so fast and find me?"

He pulled her away from the disturbance, toward the exit before she realized it. She was so glad to see him and felt safe and secure to face anything now. "I was just coming in at home with the carriage when the note came," he gasped low and out of breath, "so we raced here. And some of us mortals do tend to use front entrances, Mrs. Cibber, and there you were in a mess, although I was heading backstage as fast as I could. Now, what the hell's going on?"

"Wait, I can't leave, Tenn," she told him as he tried to hurry her outside. "I have to go get help from my brother. Theo's packed the house with the sort you just destroyed to ruin Kitty Clive's performance, and I'm afraid they'll ruin the whole place! If you could just help me get through these rowdy crowds to down front, I've got an idea."

He shook his hatless head. "Too dangerous. I'll go in to your brother and just tell him I'm a friend, while you wait in the carriage."

"No. I've got to try. I need to talk to Kitty too, and stay out of Theo's reach backstage, and I'm not being shuffled off to wait in some carriage!"

She pulled away and started back into the theater with him first behind, then ahead to make a path for her. Near the front seats of the pit, she pushed Tenn into a vacant aisle seat and pulled her wrist free of his grasp. "I'll be all right, and besides, you're right there, Tenn. Please let me. I have to try."

Frowning, he let her go. "But, try what? All right—"she heard him call behind her.

She went two more rows down the center aisle toward the pit as everyone scrambled for seats. Drat, but trying to warn her brother Tom and asking him for help probably wouldn't work now, and perhaps she'd never even reach Kitty in time; the overture to *The Beggar's Opera* had just begun and the big curtain already lifted toward the ceiling.

Still, Susannah pushed around two more men and crouched by the fiddlers at Tom's left as he faced the stage to direct. He glanced down bug-eyed in surprise at her, but went smoothly on. The music rose and cavorted to match her thudding heart, but she felt better with Tenn so close. Then, almost before she could react, a pair of hands from somewhere in the first row of pit benches reached out to pull her onto a lap.

"No, loose me!" she hissed, and slapped at the man's hands. She was desperate to get him off before Tenn exploded at her and the whole place went crazy. Her hood fell off, and the portly fellow gasped and did as she asked.

"Mrs. Cibber? Sorry, thought you was some theater bawd," the man croaked out, blushing purple. She scrambled back to her half-hidden position and sent Tenn a look to stay where he was even as the last loud chords of the overture sounded.

"What the hell are you doing?" her brother whispered down.

"Hush up. Can't you see the theater's packed with hecklers and rowdies?"

"Of course I can tell, but they'll love Clive. She's one of them. Just get away and tell Theo to make a speech or something."

"You idiot! Theo paid them to ruin it all. Do what you can to help, or your precious musicians will get all smashed up, and I need them tomorrow. Wait, Tom! I've got it! Kitty must know the crowd's this way even from backstage. Hold the first song."

It was an insane chance, but she'd dare it. Once the chaos started there would be nothing to halt it, and the crowd was obviously all poised for Kitty's first entrance. Theo would not dare harm her because of the royal performance tomorrow night, and by then he'd be calmed down or so debauched with the London ladies he boasted of that he'd never have the strength. Besides, she could still try to reason with him.

"Susannah!" her brother protested in a shocked whisper as he grasped what she intended when she threw back her hood and quickly climbed the stage steps to stand at the very center where its apron thrust out into the audience. Still, he helped by whispering something to his players who burst into a brief fanfare. Her eyes went to Tenn's serious green gaze. To her utter surprise and delight, he shot her a tense grin.

From backstage, she distinctly heard Kitty's voice hiss, "What the poxy hell?" and Theo's warning for her to "Get clear!" She untied and dropped her cape behind her and curtsied gracefully. Instantly, when the fanfare notes died away, the raucous noise became more muted, though several were so drunk that with the appearance of any woman on the stage, a few stray hoops, whistles, and catcalls for Kitty floated to her and a spiralled orange peel whapped at her feet.

No matter that everyone backstage stared aghast, and Kitty was probably ready to kill her thinking she had come to incite rather than quell a riot; no matter that prologues were always done with the curtain still down and in rhyme, or that a musical like *The Beggar's Opera* had never had a spoken prologue before.

She forced a smile as her topaz eyes swept her theater, the audience, and her beloved Tenn poised for instant battle on the edge of his bench. "Good evening," she began as melodically as she could manage without singing. "As you know, tonight Mr. Cibber and I are proud to invite you all to a wonderful performance of Gay's favorite, *The Beggar's Opera*."

A few more hisses, another orange peel. Her eyes caught Tom's in the musician's pit below and he nodded at her. Her nervous gaze lifted again to Tenn and she felt even stronger. From the wings behind her, she could hear Theo's shrill threats, which she ignored to concentrate on her next words.

"Many of you have had your tickets tonight donated by Mr. Cibber, as his benevolent way of saying that the 'Polly Wars' have been ended in a truce. The part of Polly will be played wonderfully tonight by the inimitable Mrs. Kitty Clive, whom you've adored in many past performances. Mr. Cibber and I hope you will use these donated tickets to sit back and enjoy a fine and rollicking performance—on the stage only." Several laughed and the front row faces smiled.

She dared a sideward glance and caught Kitty's astounded face offstage. She looked livid with fury, or was it shock? "Also," Susannah threw in quickly as the inspiration hit her, "because the king will attend the Drury Theater Royal tomorrow night—"

"German George! German George!" a chant began somewhere in the upper gallery, which she tried to ignore.

"Also, because the king will attend tomorrow, some of his soldiers will be here this evening to oversee the safety of the theater. We believe they will be quite inconspicuous, but we know you will be very polite to them should they be about your seats or the exits at intermission or the play's conclusion."

She curtsied again and gracefully retrieved her cloak from the boards in the same movement. But, when she turned to start off the stage the opposite way she had come, she gasped. Kitty Clive had advanced into full view of the audience, arms akimbo, hips swinging, raven hair loose down her back. Susannah halted unsure whether to defend herself physically or prepare for a public shouting match.

"Your damn prologue didn't rhyme, Cibber, but I thank you for it," Kitty said low out of the side of her mouth as she turned brashly to the audience and curtsied too. "Theo's back there having an apoplectic fit," she whispered, "so let me know if you need a place a sleep. A pox on him, but you've got backbone after all, Cibber." Kitty ended her spiel with a broad smile still plastered on her face. Then, to Susannah's utter amazement, Kitty reached down to grasp her hand and lifted it in hers. A few people clapped, including Tenn, which began a wave of applause that grew and spread, and Tom's orchestra swept into the last few bars of the overture again. Then Kitty unceremoniously pulled Susannah off the stage behind her.

"Quin!" Kitty shouted over the final overture crescendo. "See Mrs. Cibber gets out of here before the little dictator gets his hands on her. I've got a fightin' chance now with this poxy performance, and I'll give them all they can handle!"

The huge Quin bustled Susannah out the side door even as the vibrant, brassy tones of Kitty's first song filled the theater. "I'll walk you home, Susannah," the booming voice told her. "Seems these days I do too much what you used to do, standing about the wings nights I'm not on, but tomorrow, we'll have the king, eh?"

"Yes, James, thank you. And I'll be just fine. It's still light out. You just make certain Theo stays, and I'll be fine alone."

"Stays! I'd like to see the slimy toad try anything else after this wretched trick! Has he no care for the reputation of theater as art? Damn, but it's a lofty esthetic form and not some mercenary, ragtag street show. You go on now. He'll stay all right, maybe all night locked up accidentally somewhere until the king comes tomorrow and he'll have to behave. Go on now, my dear. Maybe this is the first peaceful step between you and Kitty, as you extended the olive branch at great risk and she accepted it in her own way."

Susannah looked up at the massive man at the backstage door. "Yes, she did, didn't she?" she said and smiled broadly as she turned away. Already, out of breath, Tenn was striding toward her from the far end of the alley. She knew James Quin might still be watching, but she threw herself into Tenn's spread arms anyhow, and without another glance, they hurried on their way.

Although Theo was furious with her and hadn't even been home all night or the next day, Susannah's command performance, playing opposite James Quin for the first time in *The Conscious Lovers*, was a rousing success. Not only was the royal box on the left-hand side of the stage filled with King George, Queen Caroline, Prince William, Princess Anne, and the Lord Chamberlain, who had ceremoniously lighted them all to their box, but the next box had also been requisitioned for the Princesses Amelia and Caroline, their music teacher, Maestro Handel, and Tenn Sloper, who had evidently wangled his way by agreeing to sit with the pretty if plump Princess Caroline, whose tinkling laughter came annoyingly to Susannah's ears just late enough after everyone else's to be noticeable all night.

Let Theo glare and fume and sulk; let Tenn be studiously attentive to Princess Caroline as the chubby little giggler hung on his arm, Susannah thought snidely to herself on the stage after the final curtain, while the cast mingled with the royal family and members of the king's government. She knew where Tenn's affections lay and she hardly begrudged the poor double-chinned princess a moment of fantasy gazing up into Tenn's ruggedly striking face with the sea-green eyes. After all, here tonight, the king and queen had come to see her, and had laughed and applauded and smiled: Her lifelong fantasy had at last come triumphantly true.

King George had just said something to Theo, which made him smile, nod, and glance sternly over at Susannah. Then, although she had spoken at some length with the king when the royal visitors had first come backstage, Theo motioned her over with a beckoning, beringed finger. Since the king's pale blue eyes were on her, she went.

"Dear wife, His Majesty informs me he would favor a performance at court of Zara and some other roles you've done in your somewhat brief career."

Susannah's topaz eyes jolted into King George's wide stare, and she inclined her head. "That would be wonderful, sire. Of course, we would be pleased to comply. Would it be to St. James' Palace then? I saw the vast Banqueting Hall there once, and I'm afraid the acoustics would rather do us in, except for someone like Mr. Quin."

King George nodded in a way that all too obviously dismissed Theo, just before he turned his back on him in what his courtiers jokingly called "rumping." Barely touching her elbow, the king moved her four steps away into the wings.

"Shall I be frank, my dear Mrs. Cibber, as kings must be? I was rather hoping to have you do some readings and not all the rest to come also," the king told her, looking somewhat like a schoolboy caught cheating.

The accent was heavily German, the words slow-gaited, but the implication all too clear to a woman who had been forced to put up with backstage dandies for so many years. Only this was King George and, therefore, hardly a man to be handled with clever riposte or icy demeanor.

"How kind of you. I have heard the queen favors drama, and I hope she would be pleased with what I would select to do."

The pale, rounded face under the powdered wig showed surprise, but the large lips pouted in a smile. "The queen, of course, but Her Majesty likes paintings of still life and I favor Greek goddesses. Her Majesty loves London, but next week I go home to Hanover, you see what I mean."

"I hope you will not be gone long, Your Majesty," Susannah told him and fluttered her fan, relieved to have gotten off the subject of private palace readings from the passionate Zara's lines.

"Not long, maybe two or three months, but everyone says I will be missed. The queen frets, Walpole scolds," his heavy voice went on while his eyes all too obviously dropped and lingered on her low-cut bodice, until she fluttered her fan higher between them to distract his blatant thoughts. Her mind raced: She had hoped to be liked and appreciated, but not this way. Everyone whispered he had a young mistress in Hanover he visited, but she had heard that he would never dare to keep one here under the queen's nose. But then, a mistress was hardly what he had been asking for, and she was surely becoming ridiculous. What had that German mistress's name been that Tenn had mentioned? Madame Wallbrook or something or other.

"Ach, here comes trouble. I will send for you to read for me, dear lady, and not forget," the king's words broke into her thoughts, and Susannah turned expecting a cloudy-browed Theo to be standing there. But a piercing giggle greeted her ears—and Tenn's arresting, unmistakable velvet-rough voice.

"The Princess Caroline insisted on having Herr Hendel play and Mrs. Cibber sing a song, sire, and I thought we should ask your kind permission first," Tenn explained with a slight bow.

"Caroline's idea, I believe it," His Majesty groused and glowered at the simpering Caroline. "She never asks the king for nothing on her own. Fine, get the Maestro, since no doubt the Princesses want to sing too with their old music teacher. Just remember the desire to perform after I return from Hanover, dear lady."

He turned his back almost in mid-word, pointed to his daughter, and walked away while Caroline patted Tenn's arm and hurried after her royal sire.

"A *desire* to perform?" Tenn repeated low the moment the royal duo were out of earshot.

"Don't tease," she said. "His desire, not mine."

"A private performance, of course," he observed, and his mouth quirked up in all too obvious amusement that suddenly annoyed her.

"Never mind, Squire Sloper! I believe you've been privately performing for the princess tonight, so just never mind."

"Listen, my sweet. Caroline doesn't have men perform the way this king does women. I even heard him tell Walpole at intermission you reminded him of his dear Madame Sophia Marianne von Walmoden, whom he's going to see in Hanover."

She lifted her fan to hide her surprise. "Really? Walmoden—I couldn't think of her name a moment ago."

Tenn's rakish, russet eyebrows shot up. "He spoke of her to you?"

"Not exactly."

"Exactly what the hell did he say?"

"Tenn! Later please."

"No—now," he told her in an unmistakably undeniable tone.

"Nothing suggestive, not directly. Only that the queen likes still life paintings and he likes Greek goddesses—so there."

"Greek goddesses? He's got two rooms full of detailed portraits of naked nymphs, he means. Damn, I never expected this."

"Expected what, Squire Sloper?" Theo's shrill voice came behind them. Susannah jumped, but Tenn only frowned.

"Good morning, Mr. Cibber," Tenn said calmly and stared down at the much shorter man.

"I hadn't seen you about for ever so long, squire. My wife and I are pleased to see you back to—ah, delight in a career you helped to make."

"If you're referring to my financial investment in *Zara*, I trust Colley Cibber, that's all," Tenn told Theo. "He said the lady was talented and, indeed, I was looking for such an artistic venture at that time."

"Then Susannah fitted your needs *par excellence*, for she's a talent and a venture, that's sure."

"Theo, please—"

"Egads, wife, I'll blow your horn if you won't and now that the squire's dropped back in our lives, why don't you invite him over some day. His Majesty says he wants a song, my dear, so if you'll excuse us, squire. Just have a seat and Susannah will be free in a moment."

Theo pulled her away none too gently while she blushed hot in mingled embarrassment and rage. "Theo, you don't need to throw me at the man."

"Just smile. This royal impromptu gala's going better than I had expected with German George wanting some songs and all. Egads, I warrant he'll be back—the king I mean—as well as avid-eyed Sloper."

Her insides twisted in foreboding. Surely, he couldn't know of her and Tenn. They had been so careful.

"Damn it, Susannah, I swear but I thought our royal old boy was angry with me at first when he turned his back on me so abruptly and took you off," Theo chuckled, "but then I realized I'd been royally rumped. That's what the courtiers call it, you know, as he does it to them all the time—turns his big rump to them and walks away right in the middle of something. They even have a Rumpsteak Club among the most elite at court, *sub rosa*, of course. For love of a bawd, now I'll have a story to fend off all of father's self-serving anecdotes."

"Theo, really, keep your voice down."

"Wife, if I were you I'd be grovelingly grateful I'm even being civil to you after that stupid performance with Kitty Clive last night. But tonight, I'm pleased, pleased *ad infinitum*."

"Pleased about what?" she asked warily as they stood now at center stage while the others grouped about apparently waiting for her to sing.

"Egads, Susannah, use your luscious body if not that vapid little head," he whispered. "The king's entranced, though there may not be much in that. But more importantly," he said and his voice dropped obscenely low as he squinted at her, "I've found how to get some benefit from that pretty little bottom of yours I should have beaten last night. I'd say Sloper's hot for a tumble, dear wife, and I'm going to dedicate myself to seeing you comply fully. I swear, those icy, soft thighs ought to be good for something to me," he hissed.

He shouted a laugh in her shocked face and pranced two quick steps away to clap his hands for silence. Her heart pounding, her throat suddenly dry, she heard his words but hardly grasped them.

"And now, everyone, at His Majesty's request, we shall crown the evening with a few songs from the Princess Caroline and the Princess Amelia with Maestro Handel on the humble clavichord, which is the only one the Drury Lane Theater Royal owns. Someday, we hope to have enough capital to buy an organ worthy of the

Hanoverian master's prowess and our king's discerning ear. But first, at His Gracious Majesty's request, my wife, Mrs. Theo Cibber, will favor us with a song. Are you ready, my darling?"

She stared at Theo, suddenly aware with glittering clarity how much she detested him. She and Tenn had made a terrible mistake to be seen together. She would beg Tenn to say he was busy or go away to deprive Theo of his chance to play panderer, or whatever exquisite, sadistic torment he had in mind to degrade her further.

"I—yes, thank you, Theo. I will sing a song from Maestro Handel's oratorio *Deborah* in which Deborah agrees to go into battle."

Susannah sang for them all, her plaintive voice strong and sure, although she had not sung on this stage for a year and had not sung for Handel for over three years. She angrily shook inside while Theo gloated over her as if he owned her for his personal pleasure and profit. Deborah's lyrics told of ancient battle and prayer for conquest; Susannah's thoughts were of her own coming struggle and hope for sweet triumph.

Chapter Twelve

When spring returned to England, King George did too, and Susannah's social life blossomed anew. Invitations to St. James' and Kensington and Hampton Court rained upon the Cibbers, and ornately worded summonses to elaborate dinners flourished. Susannah's popularity as London's new society actress bloomed brighter than Kew Garden's daffodils. The king acted benignly attentive, Theo seemed appeased by it all, and Tenn was always among those prestigious advisors surrounding the royal Hanovers.

But too soon, such preferments brought storms to cloud the landscape of her life: Theo hovered too close, scrutinizing her every move; he spent money like water to keep up with their new elite crowd; and he constantly tried to flaunt her before Tenn or the king as if she were some sweet spring canary to be bought and caged.

"There it is, everyone, Newmarket Racetrack," Tenn broke her reverie and pointed past her out the window of his carriage. Theo, her brother Tom, and his off and on betrothed, Cecilia Young, all leaned forward to gaze out toward the open stretch of green ground bustling with people, horses, and pennants snapping in the spring breeze.

Susannah looked out too, trying not to lean against Tenn's arm. Theo's narrowed eyes were on her again while he repeatedly jingled, in a muted, unvarying rhythm, a pouch of coins he had obtained from heaven knew where. She smiled at Cecilia's alert face and assiduously avoided Tenn's green eyes where she longed to gaze. Theo made her so nervous she just had to say something.

"It looks wonderful, doesn't it, Cecilia? I just want to watch today; I don't care how much money His Majesty said he'd give us to wager as I don't understand a thing about horse racing anyway."

Theo snorted as he leaned back against the leather seat in the Sloper carriage. Never again, Susannah thought grimly while she kept her smile on her face, would this lovely vehicle of Tenn's seem quite so romantic thanks to Theo's presence in it clear from London yesterday, and now this morning in the king's entourage of courtiers.

"A typical innocent Susannah statement," Theo groused low. "I swear, my dear little wife wouldn't take money or gifts from the king even freely offered, but as for the other, I'll wager this pouch you find someone willing to explain the whole damned racing thing to you."

"Buck up, Theo, and leave off," Tom Arne put in before Tenn could say whatever his annoyed face foreboded. "I'm just poxy glad Fleetwood let us all come, so no arguments."

"Egads, not for me, brother-in-law, as I'm in a smashing mood *par excellence* today. Anyhow, I've got to meet Usher Dangerford down by the finish line with my own unfinished business, so don't any of you think a thing of the fact Theo Cibber's merely along for the ride." He pushed by Tom and Cecilia and climbed quickly down the minute their vehicle halted in the long line of traffic.

"May I trust you'll watch over Susannah, Squire Sloper, at least until the king spots her?" Theo's voice pierced Susannah's hard-won poise. He jauntily doffed his tricorn hat to the four of them and disappeared.

"Are you all right, Susannah?" Tom asked solicitously, more for Cecilia's benefit than hers, Susannah felt, as he was never so civil to her unless his long sought after prize Cecilia Young was nearby.

"Of course, Tom. That's just Theo, you know, only I apologize to Cecilia and Tenn for his brusqueness."

"No need, no need at all for apologies," Cecilia gushed. "Feisty and grumpy he is, but then my father is cut from the same bolt of cloth, now isn't he, Tom?"

"More or less. I'm sure if your father weren't in the next carriage behind us because Maestro Handel asked for his favorite organist from All Hallows to come along, you'd never have been allowed out of the house with me near. This is a poxy lark today all around, isn't it, squire?"

Susannah climbed down behind Cecilia, her mind only half on Tenn's reply and the men's brief discussion of favored horses and jockeys. She was glad to have had Tom and Cecilia along, of course, but Tom had turned as ingratiating and fawning on Tenn lately as Theo had, and it embarrassed her. Then too, she'd had to share Tenn all the way here with the others, and at a huge, crowded dinner table at the inn last night, so she was relieved to see Tom quickly move far ahead with Cecilia.

"He can't wait to get her away from her watchdog," Susannah said low as she accepted Tenn's buff brocade arm, and they strolled up the smooth grass of the gentle rise toward the track where the crowd now hurried like filings pulled to a great magnet.

"I sympathize with him," Tenn replied and shot her a quick, rakish grin. His green eyes, heavily fringed with russet lashes, swept her and warmed her as always, so that the caress of breeze felt suddenly cool on her checks. "You look absolutely lovely today, my Susannah," he murmured as his stare took her in again from plumed hat to brocade toes.

Almost as if she had intended to dress to match the hue of his frock coat, waistcoat, and breeches, she too wore predominantly buff garments. Her full skirts, cuffed jacket, and tilted, low-slung hat were of beige brocade accented by a salmon-pink hat plume, huge upturned cuffs, and figured vest cut in a sporty masculine style. Tiered lace shirt cuffs and ruffled collar with pink bow graced the ensemble, which made her look like a swaying, nodding flower on the crest of a hill in a springtime breeze.

"This place does look exciting," she exclaimed as her eyes drank in the Newmarket scene below as avidly as she knew his jade eyes devoured her.

"Yes, exciting," he echoed and gave her arm tucked next to his lean ribs a quick squeeze. He cleared his throat. "You know, I'd like to put you right back on that coach and spirit you away to West Woodhay, but damn it, duty, career, and king call, so I'll behave. Theo was playing cards until late last night, I know. I hoped it meant he didn't expect to share your room at the inn."

"No," she said and dropped her eyes. "But just to be certain, I slept with Cecilia and told her Theo was with some others. I knew it was hopeless for us," she added.

"Last night, perhaps but that's all. Soon, Susannah, soon. I told you, just give me the word when you're ready and we'll find a way to get away from them all permanently, or at least for a private holiday somewhere."

His voice trailed off as Prime Minister Walpole and his buxom, raven-haired wife strolled by and nodded. Susannah noted only too well how the woman's slit eyes audaciously raked Tenn's athletic body.

"The king's in fine spirits today, Tenn, my man," Walpole chortled. "Damn time too, I'd say," his words floated to them in the increasing hubbub as they moved immediately on.

"His Majesty does need something to help him forget

how poorly his return from Hanover was received by London this time," Tenn observed to Susannah. "I've never seen his critics so brazen. Did I tell you the people chanted 'The king may visit his dominion England someday?' and a few threw mud at his carriage in the Park?"

"No, but I read that scurrilous poem in *The Courier* attacking him for going immediately from his young Hanoverian Walmoden mistress to the queen. It went, I recall,

What, just escaped from Cleopatra's charms,
To souse at once into your Fulvia's arms?
With equal evidence of haste to run
From blooming twenty to fat fifty-one."

She laughed despite herself. "It's terrible how people go to such witty lengths to ridicule His Majesty, Tenn, and the Prince of Wales just gets more popular all the time with his pretending to hate Parliament's intended Gin Act and his drinking with poor people in taverns."

"I know, but let's not cloud the issue—our issue."

"What issue, squire?" she retorted flippantly, suddenly so elated to be here with him even in the midst of many others, almost free from Theo far down in the crowd somewhere.

"I did mean to warn you concerning that vile doggerel attacking the king and what it means, Susannah. Very few realize or believe the king has returned to his 'fat fifty-one' Queen Caroline, but he did catch his 'blooming twenty' Countess Walmoden in a bit of an indiscretion with another man and he's fuming over that, however sunny his mood may look today."

"So, you mean we have to be careful of Theo so we don't get caught like that?"

"I mean, my love," he said low as they joined the fringes of the shifting crowd, "His Majesty is prime to find another young bloomer to heal his hurt heart, and I don't intend for it to be you.'

She pulled back a moment to stare up at him. "But it wouldn't be. He's been a dear."

Tenn's eyes caressed her before he looked away toward the huge grass circle where the horses and jockeys were assembling. His mouth, she noted with a distinct erotic tingle along her thighs, had gone to chiselled stone. "Enough said where everyone can hear, Susannah. I can handle Theo as he's so venal, but perhaps not the king if his flirting turns to pursuit. You'll have to care for that."

She wanted to argue with him, but he led her toward the circle of gawkers around the horse ring. Holding their saddles to be weighed in on the huge balancing scales, or newly perched atop sleek racehorses, were the smallest men Susannah had ever beheld.

"Oh," she whispered to Tenn, "the riders are so tiny, but they're hardly children."

"Dwarves," he mouthed and his hand crept to the small of her back to move her ahead of him into the ring of observers. "Newmarket jockeys are famous," his words came near her ear as he leaned forward, "famous and rich as the king or nobles subsidize most of them. Many are in their sixties. We'd best head down to the track as we're a bit late today. By tradition, the horses have been exercised at nine-thirty, and we've already missed the buffet breakfast and filly sales on the lawn. Actually," his voice teased in a rough whisper, "I have another sort of filly on my mind today. Let's go down by the track so we'll have a good spot when they run."

They strolled the edge of the long racetrack laid out straight, beaten down, and marked by white posts at regular intervals.

"They race exactly at noon," Tenn told her, "and that will be it for the king's race unless there's a tie, and then the whole thing will be run again. We'll get a good seat up here across from the post."

"Which post?" she asked, as it seemed to her identical white poles marched endlessly along toward the swelling crowd ahead.

"The big post in the ground opposite the judge. And if watching the king's pony, Grand Dame, trying to beat out the other horses bores you, you'll find another amusement in seeing everyone under the post trying to get their bets in during the race."

"During? But why don't they bet before?" she asked.

"Tradition, I guess. Some do wager ahead on the sly, but it's all supposed to be aboveboard. The wagering will be a race in itself. You'll see."

The expectant excitement of the jostling crowd thrilled Susannah as much as anything she had glimpsed in this new social whirl entered through her sudden fame in the theater; though, of course, knowing Tenn and the king obviously enhanced her reputation too. How much Tenn knew of Parliament, landowning, government commissions, politics, tennis, horse breeding, and racing, which was another whole world she had only imagined and still could not hope to share openly with him.

"And where have you been keeping our favorite lady actress?" the distinctive Germanic royal voice bellowed from somewhere nearby as soon as they approached the onlookers at the finish post. Everyone in earshot turned toward the king and most swept him low bows or curtsies. "Here, up here, squire, I shall give our Susannah a royal box seat so she can see my Grand Dame come in first!"

"*Our* favorite lady, *our* Susannah," Tenn whispered to her as he complied, of necessity, by escorting her over to the open carriage where the king sat with Prime Minister Walpole and Walpole's sloe-eyed wife.

"But they're all in carriages," Susannah said to Tenn. "There are no royal boxes."

"More tradition," he told her over the crowd noise.

"Just beware, and I'll try to rescue you after the race."

His warnings about the king suddenly piqued her. It amused her if he were jealous, but Susannah had no intention of getting into any situation with stodgy King George where she would be his next little Walmoden. "Really, squire," she only managed as she mounted the steps to take both Walpole and King George's proffered hands. Tenn backed off a little ways and melded into the throng, though it was all too obvious by Lady Walpole's heaved sigh that she too had hoped Squire Sloper would join them.

Susannah's excitement mounted with the heightening buzz of the moving masses. Faces under tricorn hats and bonnets sprouted eyeglasses, opera glasses, even tiny telescopes, to peer down the long, grassy track. Some stared openly at her as she took a seat on the topless, horseless royal carriage drawn up among numerous others at the finish line opposite the judge. Since the men faced the racetrack more directly, the ladies had to crane their necks to look. Across the track, Englishmen of all classes milled about, evidently crowding as closely as they could to the post.

"Many exciting races are being run hereabouts, I'd say," Lady Walpole observed slyly to Susannah behind her lifted fan, her ear bobs jangling.

"Squire Sloper said only one unless there's a tie," Susannah said intentionally ignoring whatever the woman's cryptic comment implied.

"My dear," Lady Walpole said and winked conspiratorially, "I meant *with* Squire Sloper—quite a stallion himself, eh? I'd bet on his victory in any race over any opponent—royal, husband, whatever—" she said and laughed sharply.

"I really don't know what you mean, but I should think it's none of your concern," Susannah shot back low. She felt flustered now, embarrassed and annoyed. If this woman dared say such to her face in the king's carriage, even if in a whisper among all the noise, who knew what everyone else was saying or thinking. And now, the king was leaning forward as if to hear their words.

"Such noise at Newmarket!" he shouted. "My watch says it is almost exact noon. Watch now—they're off!"

Both men stood and produced thin telescopes, which neither offered to the ladies. Susannah intentionally stood in front of the rude Lady Walpole and shaded her eyes to gaze far down the green track dotted with white posts. The flagrant woman wanted Tenn, had been with him or something, Susannah fumed. Not only, she realized helplessly, did she know little of horse racing, but she knew very little of Tenn's past in general, no matter how she had lately accepted his annulled marriage and his glib explanations of Amanda Newbury.

A low beat of thunder arose, rumbling closer down the track in the blur of lightning-fast steeds with diminutive jockeys clinging to their sleek backs. Across the finish line, one hundred paces to the side, bettors of all classes clamored to call out bets to scriveners who somehow made sense out of chaos.

"Royal Grand Dame against the field! . . . Araby and Sultan against the field! . . . A hundred to one on Line Dancer! . . . Ten to four on Brookside!" The raucous babble floated to her ears.

She had no idea how to recognize the king's horse they all screamed for; Tenn hadn't told her. Drat the man, there was entirely too much he hadn't told her!

The brown-black pack was separate horses now; the roll of thunder became thuds of numerous flying hoofs. They blurred across the white post before her: The crowd went wild; a trumpet brayed; the king beamed and grabbed her in a huge, smothering embrace.

"Oh! Your Majesty! Oh!" she protested, squeezed tightly in his bear hug. She blushed as hot pink as her wide cuffs, pressed between her breasts and his huge chest. Theo would gloat and be unsufferable, and Tenn had warned her—

Susannah caught Lady Walpole's slitted stare over the king's deep blue brocade shoulder as he released her. She managed a shaky smile up at the king who still held her by one arm in an amazingly tight grip. "It's wonderful your horse won, sire," her words came low.

"First time since last year. You, dear Susannah, are good king's luck."

"Or perhaps king's good luck," Susannah heard Prime Minister Walpole say almost sarcastically under his breath as he helped his smug-faced wife down the other side of the carriage. Beyond, staring directly at her across the shifting, mingling crowd, Susannah glimpsed Tenn's thundercloud face.

"Such good luck for me, I know it!" the king went on. "You have come to me when I needed you," he said, his blue Hanoverian eyes suddenly intent on her. His voice though lowered, seemed much too loud over the aftermath of the wild race. Everyone would hear.

"Yes, thank you, sire, but I really must go now."

His grip on her elbow tightened. "I shall send a carriage for you to come to Kew soon to be my good luck again."

Her heart fell. The tone and look, if not the somewhat ambiguous words, were unmistakably passionate. "I don't think it would be wise, Your Majesty."

"Very soon, for you alone," he whispered and nodded as if he had not heard her earnest protest at all.

She stared at him dumbfounded a moment as if the setting, the scene, and the royal summons meant nothing at all. This race, Theo, the theater, Tenn—everything whirled distantly in the cacophony of noise while strangers collected on their bets or bemoaned their losses and foolish wagers.

"No, I'm sorry, but that is all impossible, sire," she choked out and pulled firmly away on the little elevated stage of his carriage where all could see and gawk. Hardly the poised actress she had once believed herself, she made an exit so sudden and swift the footman at the carriage steps hardly had time to help her down. The audience, as if at a command performance, pressed inward staring, and she could not see Tenn in the faces anywhere at all.

When Susannah next saw Theo to talk with it was two days after the races at Newmarket. The theater was greatly deserted following a final performance of *Othello*, in which she had played the doomed Desdemona. Theo had not ridden back to London with them in Tenn's carriage; he had not come home the next night; she had barely glimpsed him hovering like some sort of grim harbinger from Hades in the Drury's dim wings during the performance. Now the theater had gone still. She had even sent Anne away to deliver to her widowed mother, who seldom chose to go out anymore, a box of French bonbons and a bouquet from Tenn. Susannah was to meet Tenn around the corner from the theater in less than a quarter hour, when she heard Theo's shouted words outside her tiring room door.

"Wife! I demand to talk with you!"

She gathered a blue velvet robe over the white satin undergown she had worn in the last act. Drat it, she fumed, but she should have changed to street clothes while Anne was still her. She had no wish to face Theo in a state of dishabille; evidently now she had no choice.

She opened the door to the hall and saw, to her great consternation, that her husband was not alone. Two louts she did not recognize lounged partway down the steps. One looked hump-backed; neither glanced her way.

"What is it, Theo?" Her voice was calm. She did not budge at first, as if to block his way, but he motioned her aside to step past her into the crowded little tiring room.

His gaze glinted glassy. He was unshaven, and his usual foppish attire looked unkempt with waistcoat unbuttoned and cravat undone.

"What is it, she asks," he mocked, and shoved her against the door as he stepped inward. He smelled of liquor, and his breath was stale. "Close the door or not, as you wish, wife, as I don't give a rap who hears what I have to say. That's my *modus operandi* from here on out."

For a moment she actually considered leaving the door ajar to not face him alone, but it was best to hear him out and hope he left quickly. Besides, those two in the hall reeked of barely bridled brutality, and she wanted no part of them. Quietly, she closed the door and faced him. He still had not looked directly at her, and now strutted back and forth two steps in the tiny room while running one hand along her double racks of hanging costumes so they swung slightly.

"Theo, please don't bother those. I worked hard to get and keep them up."

"Not hard enough, as it turns out. Your public affront to the king at Newmarket may well have done in our chances to advance ourselves further, wife. Everyone whispers that the little upstart actress Cibber dared to insult the king's goodwill and dart off without a curtsy from his carriage when he touched her. They're all saying that *you* rumped him! And who knows what fancy costumes you might have finagled from the ladies at court if you had been his favorite. But I do believe, in your usual inimitable fashion, ice goddess, you have ruined—ruined it all!"

His voice rose so steeply to a fevered pitch at the end of his tirade that she gasped and pressed back against the wall. He hit at her costumes again so they cavorted crazily, their metallic thread and satin glinting in lantern light.

"Theo, you can't mean that. What did you expect? That your wife would have an affair with the king—and all for a fee or publicity or finagled costumes?"

"That you'd at least be worth something to me—something!" The veins in his neck stood out; he turned blood-red across his nose and cheeks. "You don't love me—give me no comfort as a wife should. Egads, never did!"

"And you, I suppose, have been the model husband and guardian of your home's hearth," she threw at him before she could stop herself. "Lots of willing ladies is what you favor, I believe you put it once. Well, I hardly expect you to earn our bread and board that way, so don't expect I will. You're the man, and heaven knows, all England expects the man to provide for his family since the wife's salary is merely spent at the husband's whims, Theo. Where did all my money go? You've got your ladies, now you provide the money!"

He advanced one step forward, and his finger jabbed the air before her face. "You do not dare to address me thusly! I am master and you—you shall at last bear up with my whims *ad perpetuam* as Queen Caroline does with her wayward king in spite of his Walmodens!"

"Fine, Theo. Let Queen Caroline be a saint! I'll be a saint if you want a thousand bawds a night. You misunderstand. I don't give a thought to your other women, but do not expect me to get up on the barter block to the king or anyone else to fill the coffers you empty through riotous living!"

He laughed so shrilly the sound shredded her rage. "The barter block? That's rare, dear wife, and exactly what you will do for me before I'm done with you. You'll jump as high as I want and lift your skirts at my bidding, those skirts—or these."

He flung his arm back behind him at her rows of carefully hung garments and shrieked another laugh. "Fife!" he called. "Watson! In here, lads!"

She pulled her robe tighter. "Theo. What are you doing? I don't want them in here!"

The door banged open into the wall just missing her.

She pressed back, her mind gone numb with icy fear. Theo wouldn't dare harm her or let these men do such. If only Tenn would come up after her when she was late. If only the theater weren't so deserted, or if she could reach Anne's long scissors in the drawer.

"Theo, I insist you ask these men to leave," she managed.

"They will, they will, my icy little wife, but first, I swear, you'll pay a few bills you've been too stupid to let any of your fond admirers cover for me."

She was relieved to see the brawny men ignored her. They lumbered over to Theo, past Theo. But then to her utter horror, each scooped up huge armfuls of her precious gowns and, heavily laden, started out past her.

"Theo! What? No, you can't! Not my gowns. It's taken me two years to get those. No! Not my gowns!"

She tried to block one giant, but it was like halting a rolling carriage. "Theo, stop it! If I don't have my gowns I'll be ruined."

"Ruined? You? I'm sure your dear friend Bitch Clive will lend you a few, as I recall she owes you a favor, or perhaps you'll wise up enough at last, my dear, to learn to get what you can from your society friends or my father or old Maestro Handel, though I hear the old boy's in debt himself."

One man came back for his second load of gowns and shoved his way past her. Behind Theo, across the tiring room, the double racks stretched suddenly skeletal against the dim wall.

"No, Theo, damn you!" she cried and threw herself at him, kicking and clawing, but huge arms hauled her away and held her still. Tears she had not even sensed coursed down her cheeks while she hung helplessly in the man's iron grasp.

"I do believe, my dear wife, you have finally seen my power, my hold over you," Theo grinned and leered at her.

'You know, I would say my merely selling your baubles, is I have every legal right to do as your husband, is a ather merciful judgment. After all, is not the rape of 'our tiring room an appropriate substitute for your own ape?"

He stepped closer against her while the monster behind inned her arms to her side. "The touted, petted Mrs. Susannah Cibber," Theo mocked. "I declare, my dear, vho would not give a coin for a little tumble with you ately? German George would, Tenn Sloper would, and no loubt half the male theater audience of London. But so 'ou may think all this over and the utmost obedience you owe your husband, I spare you Fife and Watson here, hough I did consider them as a—let us say—a humbling experience for you."

Her entire body felt numb. Fury and outrage made her vant to scream, to claw his eyes out, but even if she had been loosed, she knew she would stand paralyzed by oathing. "Theo, please just go."

"Oh, I will, but you know, I'm suddenly enjoying this. And, I do believe where this robe has slipped open, I see another pretty costume I've missed, the poor strangled Desdemona's nightshift. How wonderfully ironic, Desdemona and you both innocent, but her husband hates her for her chastity and I wish you'd just lean the opposite vay—with the right people, of course. I really had inended to make a clean sweep here, so if you'll just hold he lady, Fife, I'm going to slip this satin gown off her ovely body so we can take it with us."

She gasped. "Theo, please."

"Beg me and I'll consider a little restraint," he told her is he quickly unlaced the white satin bodice in front and peeled it down her shoulders to bare her corset and the creamy tops of her breasts. "Yes, I like this," he breathed heavily as she shrank back from him even though she pressed against the disgusting wretch who held her. "I like the idea of your being willing and still for me once."

"Mr. Cibber, a man's calling downstairs," Watson yelled in from the hall. Fife grunted and Theo's fingers halted as they roughly pinched a nipple through the stiff corset material.

"For love of a bawd!" he hissed, but he snatched back his other hand hooked in her loosened corset as if to pull it down. "Hold her a minute, Fife. Then we've got to get the things away." With a swiftness that denied his usual jerky movements, he pulled off his loose cravat and gagged her. He knotted one of her silk stockings from her dressing table around her wrists and behind her back, to hold her to her chair before the mirror, then tied the other stocking around her ankles.

"Tell them it was unknown thieves, my dear; tell them something to make some of that delicious publicity you so love in the gossip journals. 'Mrs. Cibber robbed and nearly ravished by thieves.' Egads, I like the ring of that. You'll have to tell them, for I know, this one time, I shan't."

Over her bared shoulder, he grinned grotesquely at her wide, stunned stare in the mirror, then hurried out almost jauntily behind his lackeys. Their footsteps whispered away on the stairs taking with them her private, precious store of costumes, her pride, and any hope for inner peace and dignity she had ever held to.

She hadn't heard the voice downstairs: perhaps Tenn, perhaps the night watchman. Her eyes swept the naked room where all the velvet, brocade, silk, and satin bounty of her beloved characters had hung. Gone, raped just as he said; all gone now, like all her joy.

"Susannah?" The deep voice floated to her from a cavernous distance. Tenn. It was Tenn, her perpetual rescuer from all the dreary, empty grief of her life. But he could not help things now: a ruined room, ruined gowns, ruined marriage, ruined life.

"Susannah?"

His footsteps thudded up the narrow stairs. He was running. He turned the landing now. Her wide topaz eyes stared sullenly at her own face with the slash of white gag, then darted to the half-opened door.

"Susannah! What the hell!"

His hands felt good, so warm. The gag was gone, then the constricting stockings binding her wrists to the chair. She couldn't help it: Tears flowed, she gasped for air, and collapsed greatfully in his strong embrace where he knelt beside her chair.

"Love, it's all right. Who did this? You weren't harmed?" he asked.

She shook her head wildly, silently cursing her loss of control. She'd never fallen apart like this, not even when she'd nearly drowned, not with Tenn or anyone. She had held it all in when she used to grieve for never having a career and when she had glimpsed the desperation of her imprisoning marriage. Her tears turned the lapel of his black brocade frock coat to shiny jet and, at last, she pulled away.

"I'm all right. My costumes," she gasped out. "Stolen—Theo."

"Theo? But these are for your career. The bastard's selling them?"

She nodded, furiously wiping the wet away from her slick cheeks. "With two horrible men. He was—almost crazy. I turned down the king, he says. It must be—all over London. Oh, Tenn, what can I do?"

"Come away with me. You said you have a few days Fleetwood owes you. And I'll handle Theo!"

"No. No, you can't. He'll know. Everyone will know. Tenn," she said and her voice quivered, "he actually wants me to lead you on for money, wants me to get money from you or from the king—anyone, I guess."

"Then perhaps we should change our tactics, my love.

Here," he said. In one amazingly graceful move, he lifted her, moved to kick the door shut, then sat down in the chair with her cradled in his arms. Only then did she realize her feet were still tied.

Yes, she was still tied, her numbed brain taunted her, as she reached down to free her own ankles. That was it. She needed to be rid of Theo and his sick, hellish ways at any cost, but while she feared he'd find out about her and Tenn, she was still tied. She knew then, clearly and coldly, what she must do.

"Tenn," she said, her voice more controlled now as she sat up straighter in his arms and blotted her cheeks with his offered handkerchief, "you can't mean to tell him about us?"

"I mean to buy him off to leave you alone, to threaten him if I have to. Pay his debts once and get him to sign an agreement to stay clear of you. Then what you do is your own business."

"He's desperate. You don't know him. It's more than just the debts. He's ravenous for notoriety, anything to sell tickets, to best his father whom he is jealous of."

"And you whom he is jealous of," Tenn put in as his big fingers gently laced up her bodice all pulled awry. Anger flooded him again. He'd give anything to get Susannah away all safe and to himself, but he didn't want her immured away somewhere bitter or unhappy over a shattered marriage or career. His first instinct when Theo abused her was always to kill the bastard, but he wanted more than just her distance from Theo Cibber: He wanted her heart free and clear too.

"Susannah, love, listen," he murmured soothingly. "If he thinks I'm in the picture, he won't pull insane, perverted stunts like this. The bastard didn't harm you, did he? Your bodice—"

"No, not that," she said much too fiercely, he thought, as she wiggled off his lap and stood. "But he's ruined me as best he could. I'll eventually rebuild my collection of gowns and all my cherished things, but—"

He watched her beautiful topaz eyes blur to gold with shiny tears as they swept the barren racks. "Susannah, I promise you, I'll get you some gowns. We'll duplicate the ones from *Zara* and as many of the others as we can. Then I'll get some ladies I know to donate some, as that's the custom anyway—"

"No! No, I thank you, but I have to do this to get control of my life myself."

She began to pace; he watched feeling suddenly helpless to comfort as she straightened her shoulders, clenched her fists at her side, and talked in a restrained, low voice as if she had become a different character from the shattered, tearful woman he'd held only a few moments ago.

"I've got to get some distance from Theo, to think this over, to make him realize he'll never get another pilfered penny from my career if he doesn't stay in line," she said, as though she thought aloud. "I've got to plan this out and not risk your career too, and us, Tenn."

"My love, the only risk I see in all this is if you don't let me help you. I insist you finally agree to take some money from me. It will keep him off. At least, let my pay your personal bills and give you some money for you and Anne to live on, or for the lease on the house so you have a place to live."

"And have him come home to threaten or abuse me when the house is paid for with Sloper money?"

"All right, we'll get you another place, a lovely town house, and I'll hire a guard as I wanted to the first moment I saw you," he heard himself say much louder than he intended. Her wild pacing made him want to seize and hold her, to protect and comfort her, but her rage held his love at bay.

"I can't be your acknowledged mistress, Tenn. My career would suffer. I don't care if they do say I slighted the king at Newmarket. At least refusing him should still make me acceptable on the stage to any patron, high-class or low."

"Now who's worried about selling tickets?" he yelled. This wasn't going as he wanted it to at all. She should be here in his arms, taking his advice, accepting his gifts, and clinging to his offers of love.

"Not the tickets, Tenn—my career. I've fought for it. I love it. God forgive me, I need it."

He stood to tower over her. "And what about me? I've never been so foolish as to ask before, but don't you need me?"

She stopped her pacing and her white skirt belled to a shifting stop around her shapely hips. "Of course I do, but I have to think this through to decide."

His hands grasped her shoulders firmly. "Decide what? If you need to think things over, we'll go away, I said."

"But I can't think with you there sometimes," she murmured low, her eyes luminous as if moonlight gilded them. "With you I always feel first and think second."

He knew he frowned. His mouth went to a hard, pressed line. His heart fell, and fear and fury pounded inside. "And what the hell does that mean? I didn't realize I was such a liability."

She amazed him again by leaning her tousled head on his chest. "A lovely liability, my Tenn. And I do want to go away for a few days, but I need to be alone."

He dropped his hands to her slender waist. "Go where?" he asked, trying to keep his temper in check. "He'll find you at your mother's and you've no money." Damn, but the proud little vixen would have to accept his money at least, if not his presence if she were going away, he thought grimly.

"I have about fifty pounds at my Aunt Emma's in Camden Town. When I discovered Theo had bilked my trust fund out of almost all my money, I managed to salvage that much. I will go to stay with my aunt tonight and then somewhere from there."

"Alone, when we could be together, free of this place!" His voice came as sharp as a saber's edge to his own ears.

"I'll take Anne," she said.

His mind raced. She was distraught, yet so calmly controlled after that hysteria that she must be in shock. She loved him, wanted him, needed him; he knew it. He'd take the line of least resistance now, take her to her aunt's in the carriage, give her a night to calm down—and to miss him. She must! He had never desired her more, wanting to thrust his love deep inside this beautiful, unpredictable, headstrong, and independent woman. He needed her ravishing body and strong spirit more than he had ever needed anything.

"I'll take you to your aunt's," he said. "Then tomorrow, I'll bring Anne to you or whatever things you need. That will give you time to think things over alone."

She looked so immensely relieved, he thought, that she almost cried again. But instead, she kissed his cheek and gathered her street clothes and meager possessions together in the stripped room now shrunk so very small by her proud spirit and indomitable self-control.

But tomorrow, he told himself, when he took her things to her, then he'd see: He'd make certain she felt instead of thought, pressed to him rather than held him off, and admitted that between them love and rage could be passionately one.

Tenn swirled her velvet cloak around her enticingly silken shoulders. He lifted the lantern to light them downstairs and thought again about tomorrow.

Chapter Thirteen

By the next morning at her Aunt Emma's small house in rural Camden Town north of London, Susannah had slept, breakfasted, and dressed. Now she sat by herself over coffee in the parlor window to watch the April sun startle the forsythia bushes to stark lemon on the village green. People had begun to stir outside at daily tasks. The house lay silent but for the cook's occasional clang in the kitchen. This peaceful house and town soothed her troubled heart, and she was momentarily content.

Tenn had brought her here last night, and although she was disappointed to find her aunt had gone to visit one of her children's families for a few days, Susannah had decided to stay. The two servants had made her feel at home, and Tenn had vowed to bring her things the next day after having Anne Hopson take them from the house, so if Theo returned, he would not think Tenn knew where she was.

She sighed and luxuriously stretched her arms over her head. Already hidden away here almost as if she were someone else, she felt the tautness of body and heart unwind. And though she could view things more objectively, she was already lonely for Tenn.

Here at Aunt Emma's house, which had been built in

late Tudor times, she felt almost free. The house stood in a prominent position in Camden Town since Susannah's deceased uncle had once been a prosperous merchant and alderman. As a girl she had cherished rare visits here, and on occasion Tom had come along to further enliven their aunt's already bustling household. Now a clock ticked; that was all. There were no callboys shouting curtain times, no fops or sparks underfoot, no booming Quin or ranting Clive, and—bless the heavens—no vile Theo.

She now knew she had to find a way to free herself from her increasingly dangerous and desperate husband although divorces were an impossibility in England for all but the most noble and wealthy, and those who would face the dreadful notoriety of the London presses she so hated. She could never just accept Tenn's largesse, however fervently he insisted, nor would she drag his name, career, and future down in such a way. Somewhere, out there, if she thought about it long enough here in this sheltered setting, there had to be a reasonable, reachable way to control her own career, salary, and life—and still have Tenn Sloper.

She leaned forward to see what made the approaching rumble on the quiet morning street. It was probably the coach from London or a big market dray. But a huge black carriage with fine equipage and four sleek grays rolled by. She jumped to her feet. Tenn! It was barely midmorn and Tenn was back in Camden Town already!

Her calm exploded to a pulse-pounding excitement. Everything else ebbed to nothing in her instinctive, irrepressible thrill at his approach. He cared, he loved her; his mere presence changed every place she'd ever been.

The carriage had gone on down the street, and she stood breathlessly inside the silent front door waiting for the vehicle to turn around the village green and roll back. She felt as well as heard her heartbeat. She already imagined how his strong arms would feel around her as they had last night when he had left. And if the cook and maid went to Thursday market as they had said they would, she and Tenn could be deliciously alone here in a quiet house they could pretend was their own.

She blushed hot at her brazen fantasy even as the door that she leaned her shoulder against resounded with a trio of firm knocks. She swept it open instantly, and he was there, tall, handsome, and quite casually dressed in fawn-hued breeches, hunt jacket, white shirt, black boots, and hat in his hand.

"Good morning, sir," she told him as lightly as she could manage, "but might you not be lost? I say, but you look garbed for the hunt."

"I am, beautiful lady, and I've just spotted what I've been hunting for. Now, if you'd stop staring with those stunning topaz eyes and let me in a moment so half this town doesn't gawk at us—"

Susannah moved aside and smiled up at him as he entered, and then she closed the door. Neither servant had come to the entry hall so they must be gone already. She had forgotten as always how tall he was, how he made her feel instantly dizzy when he looked her over so thoroughly this way. When he grinned back and indicated the open parlor door, she went ahead of him, vibrantly aware of his magnetic presence close behind her, but wishing he had kissed her wildly at the front door.

"I didn't see the carriage in front," she remarked conversationally as he closed the parlor door quietly behind them.

"It's around in back. Anne sent your things."

"But didn't come herself?" she got out before he stepped warm against her and tipped her chin up with one big hand.

She parted her lips as eagerly as he took them. It seemed at first his mouth merely lingered to taste her, but then the kiss swept her away with powerful intensity. His big hands splayed open on her back to hold her tightly to him; her breasts crushed flat to his hard chest and her soft thighs pressed to rock-thewed muscles. When he set her back a moment later and slipped his hands up to hold her by both shoulders, she almost swayed into him in the desire to throw herself against him for more.

"Now listen to me, Susannah, are you all right?"

Her eyes opened to meet his intense green stare. "Of course—yes."

"I saw Fleetwood late last night, told him you'd left town for somewhere, and quite frankly, I bribed him to keep his mouth shut that I knew you were gone."

"You did?"

"He doesn't expect you back for rehearsals until next Wednesday, five whole days from now, Susannah. I had Anne pack garments for you; all your things are in the carriage."

"Good. Thank you. Aren't your footmen going to bring them in?"

"Listen, I said. I want you to go away with me for those five days. We'll go to Bath as we can hardly head for West Woodhay, even though I should be overseeing spring planting there now. It's a long shot, but if Theo starts beating the countryside for you, we couldn't have him find us there at my estates, at least, not yet."

"Yet, but—"

"It's still off-season at the stylish spa of Bath, sweet, so there won't be crowds or anyone of great importance for another month yet. Who knows, maybe Beau Nash won't even be there and we'll be our own arbiters of manners and fashion. I've a London friend who keeps a town house there on Barton Street we can use."

Her stunned mind raced even as he described the lovely house and delights of the fashionable spa of Bath. The idea of actually immersing oneself in more than a tub of water had terrified her since the night she'd almost drowned in the Thames; but to be away, alone with Tenn for five whole days and nights, where no one would bother them . . .

"But, Tenn, even if there are few there, I have people stop me in the streets now who recognize my face, and if you've been there before, someone could know you and word could get back to London."

"We'll stay in when we can, but I promise to show you everything. Bath isn't London, at least not this time of year. Then too, you are, I believe, a very fine actress who can disguise herself at will, and I must admit I asked Anne to pack that raven wig you've worn on stage."

Despite her surprise at the sudden shift in potential plans, she giggled, then sobered. "Tenn, it's—so tempting."

"So are you, always have been," he murmured in a change of tactics and bent to brush kisses down her temples to her throat. "Say yes, Susannah. You can leave your aunt a note and stop to see her on the way back. I've taken care of all my obligations for the next five days. I've paid Anne a week's wages and she won't tell what she knows anyway. Say yes."

The loosely curled backs of his fingers stroked enticingly up and down her arms, making her skin tingle even through the water-green brocade sleeves as if he touched bare skin. She arched up against him and wrapped her arms around his neck. She could feel the sweet friction of her taut nipples pointing through her corset and gown. He dropped both hands behind her to cuddle and press her soft derriere, and she moaned low in her throat. You fool, she told herself, you want him to seduce you right here in your aunt's parlor while the world goes calmly by outside; but in here, everywhere, there is only him.

"Is this your answer, sweet Susannah?" he rasped hot against the hollow of her cheek where his lips rested. "I'll take good care of you, like this, more than this. Will you come with me to Bath?"

She nodded, but her voice caught in her throat. Yes, the whole world, even her theater world be damned, she would go—go anywhere with him. "Yes," she breathed against his ear, "yes, I will."

The morning blurred by on gilded wings thereafter: a note to her aunt, words to the servants back from market, the shiny carriage waiting out back in the early April sun. Camden Town dropped away, then St. John's Wood and Notting Hill, as they rolled southwestward through the brown and green spring of England toward Bath, almost a hundred miles away. They enjoyed cheese, stew, and ale in a rustic inn called The King's Arms near Maidenhead, and drove on into the early afternoon.

They laughed and teased and kissed and watched the wooded countryside slide by. Repeatedly, the terrible roads yet rutted by spring rains jolted them together on the carriage seat until once they knocked chins hard in a fierce kiss and dissolved to laughter again.

"How about a little stop?" he asked her as they jounced along. "We could stretch our legs, and on these wretched Berkshire roads, I can hardly manage to kiss you, much less what I really want to do."

She poked him playfully in his hard midsection and blushed. "But there have been no inns for miles, and I'm just hoping we're not lost in the forest," she teased.

"And I'm starting to hope we are," he shot back with a grin, and squeezed a thigh through her voluminous green skirts. "George!" he yelled to his driver out the window, "find a good place to pull off for a respite."

It did feel wonderful to stretch the kinks out of jolted muscles, and somehow naughty to hide behind the bushes off the road to relieve herself while Tenn's deep voice speaking to his driver and two footmen by the distant carriage floated to her. When she headed back toward the road in this lovely stretch of tall oaks and chestnut trees, newly budded so the sun still slanted through to light the carpet of forest wildflowers, he met her with a big carriage lap robe over one arm.

He suddenly looked almost sheepish as her eyes met his. "I thought a moment of real rest might do us good as I'm hoping to push clear on at least to Thatcham today," he told her, and gently took her arm to walk her farther away from the roadway.

White and purple violets sprinkled their path and she bent to pick some while he spread the lap robe under an oak so wide that even his long arms could not span its trunk. It was deliciously cool here, yet the sun splotched shifting golden pools on the sweet-scented moss and wildflower carpet.

"Look at how lovely these are, Tenn," she told him as she bent to gather more violets.

"I am looking at my own little wildflower, love. Bring them over here then and let me see."

When she whirled to face him half reclined so casually on one elbow, she felt suddenly shy. His eyes were warmer than the sun, greener than the forest, and more seductive than any sweet-scented fragrance she had ever known. He had removed his coat and waited for her while he rolled up his shirt sleeves with his gaze still on her. She felt her petticoats sway against her silk-stockinged legs. She approached the lap robe as if mesmerized by his magnetic, sensual allure. Each caress of forest breeze made her long for his caress; every touch of sun along her skin made her wild for the merest warm brush of his body against hers.

He reached a big hand up for her, and she went down into his embrace. Violets scattered crazily everywhere as she found herself on her back staring up at his rugged, impassioned face framed by new-budded trees and the blue sweep of distant sky.

"You're like violets, Susannah," he told her, his voice almost a rasping caress. "Beautiful, delicate, yet hardy;

wild, but ethereal somehow. That all sounds inconsistent, I know. Maybe it's that mingling of different qualities that makes you so exciting as a woman and so talented as an actress, this ability to be all things and change your mind and moods so swiftly."

"But not about you, not about us anymore. It's only that, well, like the violets way out here in these lovely woods, we have to stay hidden for a while so there won't be a blowup from Theo or a scandal for our careers."

"I know, damn it!" he said, his voice suddenly gone ragged as he flopped down flat on his back beside her just as she was certain he would kiss her. Impatiently, he brushed several violets off his chest and stomach that had scattered there.

She propped herself up on one elbow facing him. "I didn't mean to upset you," she told him low.

"It's not you, Susannah. I assure you, I do understand your circumstances and desires."

"Do you?" she asked, hoping her voice sounded light. But his finely-chiseled profile frowned and he only put both hands linked together behind his head with a huge sigh. He seemed to be studying the heavily laced branches overhead as an occasional errant sunbeam shifted to gild the coppery highlights of his mussed hair.

"And what am I most like?" he said, but she knew he wasn't really asking her. "Before I met you, I might have said like this oak here—stolid, sturdy, strong, sure of my place in life. But now, maybe I'm more like these moving limbs overhead, attached yet buffeted by winds, hanging on but reaching out. Hell, I don't know. With you I've gone all philosophical, and that's hardly like me either."

He rolled over onto his stomach with his shoulder and long leg nearly touching hers on the lap robe. Still on her elbow, she lifted her free hand to gently stroke his big forearm. "I'm starting to worry that violets and tree limbs don't really match any more than actresses and land owning Whigs," her silky voice murmured to blend with the breeze and forest noises.

He tugged her down in one smooth movement and kissed her fiercely, then tenderly. "I am so completely smitten with you, Susannah. We'll make them match, make the violet and the oak limb fit perfectly," he told her determinedly and a little smile crinkled up the corners of his mouth at last. Then his green eyes glinted at some devilish thought. "I'll prove it to you tonight, my sweetheart, a perfect fit," he added, and again quickly kissed her mouth now pouted to scold him. "Come on now, or I'll be tempted to prove that here since my men would probably like to believe it of us anyway."

He stood and pulled her to her feet. She felt dizzy, happy, tingling all at once. She smiled shakily and gathered violets from the rumpled lap robe, laughing at the one caught in Tenn's russet hair behind his ear. Smitten, that was the word for her too, Susannah thought, as he helped her stand and refolded the big lap robe. She was thoroughly smitten with passion, with an unbridled rage of love for this man above anyone or anything she had ever known.

She held her head high and had eyes only for Tenn, however much his men stared when they went back to their waiting carriage.

The pale marble and ivory stone of the fashionable Georgian spa city of Bath glowed honey-hued in the noonday sun as they drove in the next day. Set in low, rolling hills at the bend of the sparkling River Avon, Bath enchanted Susannah at first glance.

"It's so elegant and that beautiful, old cathedral crowns it all," she told Tenn as her eyes took it all in from the open carriage window.

"That's Bath Abbey," he said, "and over there is the

famous Pump Room where everyone gathers to take three recommended glasses of the egg-smelling, iron mineral waters. I can't abide the stuff, but you'll have to try it."

"If I do, it's the closest I plan to get to the medicinal hot spring water here. I detest the idea of getting all wet in any bath except a tub."

He slipped his arm around her waist and laughed, although she was in deadly earnest. "We'll see, my raven-haired love. You know, I'm insane for you even in that wig."

"And I'm insane to wear it—and to be announced as the fictional Amanda Brompton," she told him. "If I ever thought for one minute you'd been here with any of your other Amandas or rollick in some bath—"

"We can go to Cross Bath," he interrupted, "where men and women can go in the waters together, so I'll be with you. The Queen's Bath allows ladies only, but you'd prefer me with you, I know."

"You blackguard," she told him. "That swim in the Thames was quite enough for this life and I hate playing someone named Amanda even to be with you."

He quickly pointed out libraries where one could read all the London journals, ballrooms where cotillions were held in season, numerous tearooms, card rooms, rows of stylish shops, and stalls from which the famous vermicelli in basins or Bath jelly tarts were sold. "This place is full of cardsharps in season," he told her, "though Beau Nash has repeatedly decreed no heavy gambling along with his other rules he posts all over town."

"Such as what?" she asked, her eyes wide as saucers as she tried to take it all in. "I wish he'd declared ladies who don't like big pools don't have to go in and ones who detest wigs don't need to wear them just to hide their true identities."

He laughed. "Such rules as no dueling, no swords, no cursing, and no private entertainments as everyone goes out and mingles at Bath."

"Do they?" she said and lifted one slightly darkened auburn eyebrow. "Too bad for us then, squire."

His hand lifted smoothly to her low ruffled bodice to merely flick a finger inside the hollow between her breasts before she could react to the sudden ploy. "*That* sort of private entertainment is hardly forbidden, sweet Susannah, as I would wager there's a great deal of *that* in style at Bath in season and out."

When they pulled up at the fine assembly rooms, Harrison's on the left and Lindsey's on the right, bells pealed wildly overhead. "What's all that for, Tenn?"

"More official Bath protocol, as Beau Nash has decreed this welcome for all new carriages. During season everyone turns to gawk to see if they can recognize the carriage and equipage. Everything is proper and controlled here, Susannah, everything, that is, but the—ah—blackguard, I believe you called him whom you are with."

While the footmen went in to sign the city guest book for them and purchase entry tickets to baths and subscription to the assembly rooms, Susannah still scanned the area. Lovely terraced walks with gravel paths and clipped bushes stretched clear to the river from here.

"This whole promenade is called Orange Grove now in honor of the royal visit by William, Prince of Orange, who benefited from treatments here two years ago," Tenn told her. "After some food and a little nap, my raven-haired love and I shall take a long stroll around town."

"Tenn, look at that huge liveried carriage with six grays," she said and leaned out farther. "I thought you said it was off-season and everyone important would be at their country homes."

He pressed close in the window. "I didn't expect this, love. Curtain's up for you, as that's Beau Nash's fancy carriage and he likes to greet one and all who arrive here. Actually, I was hoping he'd be elsewhere until the season started next month."

Susannah gasped as the ornate, almost royal looking vehicle pulled up across from theirs and two white-wigged footmen jumped down to open the door and drop the iron steps. She felt indeed in her element of the theatrical when a short, white-hatted, red-faced man in garments of gold lace, with a huge, glittering diamond buckle in his stock and diamond pin holding back the brim of his tricorn hat, stepped down and strutted toward their carriage. Other liveried servants appeared from somewhere until there were six trailing behind the famous Beau Nash.

She touched her wig to be certain it was straight as Tenn helped her down. Suddenly, the entire scene amused her more than worried her: What a lark this all was to be away with Tenn like this, protocol and Beau Nash notwithstanding. She bit her lower lip to keep from giggling.

"Beau Nash, Master of Ceremonies, 'King of Bath' at your service," one of the liveried servants with Nash clipped out. Tenn and Nash bowed stiffly to each other, and Susannah dropped a half curtsy and kept her eyes low under the steady perusal of the eight gathered men.

"Squire William Sloper, from West Woodhay in Berks, sir," Tenn said, "and may I present my betrothed, the Lady Amanda Brompton."

"Sloper—ah, yes—obviously the younger Sloper, as I recall your father's visit with the king's party several years ago," Nash intoned.

The man's slit eyes scanned Susannah while he smiled rather condescendingly, she thought. "Your first visit here, I deem it," Nash told her with a stylized sweep of gold brocaded arm that reminded her of one of Quin's more grandiose gestures as the Roman general Cato.

"Yes, indeed, my first," she only said, batted her lashes shyly, and took Tenn's arm. It was meekness rather than flamboyance needed here, she told herself. She had no desire to be appealing or remembered, especially not in a place the royal family frequented.

"Residing where?" Nash queried as though ticking off a formal list of questions.

"The Duckett's house uphill on Barton's Street, sir," Tenn put in and swept the man another bow so that Susannah almost burst out laughing. "We shall no doubt see you about, sir, though our stay will be of necessity but a few days."

"Afraid not as I am visiting acquaintances these next three weeks before the proper season," Beau Nash put in, emphasizing the last two words while Susannah resorted to biting her lip again at the man's pomposity. "There are, of course, others at the Duckett's to greet you—ah—to show you about the town?" he inquired, and Susannah read the intended censure beneath the polite words.

"Of course," Tenn assured him, then added hastily even as he pulled Susannah slightly away toward their carriage, "and will Miss Verdun be accompanying you as you leave before the proper season, sir? I recall what a charming hostess she was last time I was here with my father."

Beau Nash startled, half gasped, but recovered his unctuous aplomb, and bid them a lengthy, formal farewell as they parted. "Who's Miss Verdun," Susannah demanded the minute their carriage door closed, "and why did he look like he'd swallowed a canary?"

"He has," Tenn told her. "The proper arbiter of manners has kept a mistress for years, and anyone brave enough has learned to inquire about her to set him back on his pompous, diamond heels when he oversteps as he was about to do by asking if we would be properly chaperoned at the Duckett's."

"You told him there were others at the Duckett's. Are there?"

"Plenty of servants, I'd wager, to fulfill our every whim, love."

"Why does the man have such power here then if he's a

sham?"

Tenn's arm went around her shoulders as the carriage lurched away from the assembly rooms and bells pealed shrilly again. "He's no sham, Susannah. He's made Bath the proper, sociable place it is today where all people mingle and get on and know their limits. He just forgets at times he's human and vulnerable like the rest of us, that's all."

She nodded in total understanding: Human and vulnerable like the rest of us actors and actresses in life, she mused. All tried to project an aura of what they were not at times; to use costumes and clever lines and aids like Nash's carriage or this dratted, tight wig she wore to project the image of what they wanted to be but might never achieve. It was so with poor Theo; her father had certainly been that way; Kitty Clive was sò with men; and to protect her love for Tenn, Susannah Cibber had become an actress of another kind, she admitted. Only Tenn himself seemed real and not at all on stage like the rest of them, but he too must have secrets in his past: his marriage, his Amandas, perhaps even something with Lady Walpole, whose hair was as raven-black as this foolish wig.

"You've become very subdued, love," Tenn's deep voice broke her reverie as her eyes met his stare.

"Just thinking what an interesting place this is," she told him.

"I believe it promises to be a more than merely interesting few days and nights," he told her low and lifted her hand to press it warmly to his lips as their carriage halted before a lovely three-story bow house with pilastered balustrades surmounted by classical urns. With a smile, he helped her down, and they went grandly in.

Although she wanted to sleep late the next morning

after their lengthy walking tour of Bath the afternoon they arrived, Tenn pulled her out of their warm bed with kisses then tiny slaps along her bare flanks and bottom that he had uncovered.

"You brute, stop it! You said you loved me and you don't treat someone you love that way! I have changed my mind about going to the baths today, and I don't see how you have the fortitude after all that lovemaking last night either. Now give me that coverlet!"

"My sweet Susannah, bouts of lovemaking notwithstanding, we've been in bed almost eleven hours."

"Oh. What time is it?" she asked sluggishly, wishing she'd put some sort of garment on before they'd finally drifted off to sleep, so she was not stark naked under his magnetic perusal even now.

"Almost eight."

"Eight? I'll go tomorrow. Give me the coverlet, please."

"No, love. You promised last night you trusted me enough to go with me today."

"But that was in a moment of impassioned weakness," she pouted and sat at last.

"And I'm going to put that lovely bare bottom over my knees in a moment of impassioned weakness," he threatened while his gaze roamed over her nude body. "People go early to the baths or not at all. Now up, because I've sent for the sedan chairs, which should be here soon."

She scrambled up into the loose linen chemise, then the velvet robe he held for her. "But Tenn, I really don't think I'll like it."

He put his arms around her and held her close to his similarly robed body for a moment. "I'll be there all the way when we're at the pool," he told her. "I was there when you fell in the river, and this is nothing like that. I don't want you to be afraid of anything when I'm there to take care of you. Not anything. It's important to me."

She sighed. "All right. Only an hour, you said."

"All five baths are only open daily from six until nine in the morning by tradition, so we won't even be an hour. Put your shoes on and come on down. We'll be all warm and relaxed and delivered back here in blankets before you know it, and then we'll take the ferry to the coffeehouse at Spring Gardens and have a mammoth breakfast. And there's not a thing to worry about as the water won't be over your head."

She trusted Tenn, Susannah lectured herself, as the sedan chair bearers started off with them for Cross Bath; perhaps this would even be fun. But all she could think of was the rushing cold water that night she had fallen in the Thames and the relentless way it had pulled her down. She'd never felt such clammy fear, such hopelessness, except maybe now the way she felt about Theo and her drowning marriage; but there was no way on earth Tenn could ever completely save her from that.

The chairs bounced down the hill from Barton Street and crossed the elegant Queen's Square, which Tenn said had been completed just last year by the famous builder John Wood, the Elder, and dedicated to King George II's Queen Caroline. Tenn was there to take her hand the moment she alighted under the covered portico of Cross Bath. Numerous doctors had stands nearby and hawked various nostrums to those who went in, for the curative power of the mineral waters had brought ailing Britains to bathe here since Roman times.

"You must go in that ladies' line there to the slips to get outfitted, love, and I'll meet you on the other side. The men go over here."

"Tenn," she told him in a jauntier voice than she really felt, "so far the only thing I like about today is we agreed I didn't have to wear that wretched wig."

Brazenly, he gave her bottom a swift pat as she passed under the arched stone door marked "Ladies Slip." She had indeed made a slip to come here, she thought grimly, as a large, dull-faced woman indicated a private cubicle with a canvas door flap, and Susannah entered. The woman was wet from her ample waist down, and her skin was very brown.

"I'm your guide. Been to Cross before?" the woman changed, as her plump hands lifted a capacious dress of brown linen with huge parson's sleeves for Susannah to slip into after she doffed her robe and chemise.

"Cross, no. I've never been to Bath at all," Susannah told her.

"Here's your dish then—nosegay to inhale if you don't like them iron aromas, and put your handkerchief there to keep it dry."

"Oh, I see."

"I take you in until you get your balance, then when you get out a cloth-woman dries and wraps you. Just leave your shoes there."

Barefoot, Susannah padded out behind the big brown woman, down a marble floor pleasantly warm to the touch. They entered a huge, high-ceilinged room decorated with statues of classic figures in alcoves and a massive pool with benches and railings along its sides. Beneath her somewhere she could hear and feel water rushing.

"Don't dawdle then," the woman turned around to call and motioned with an impatiently flicked wrist. "Baths all close at nine."

"I'll just wait here. I'm supposed to meet someone. I'll be fine."

The rounded shoulders shrugged. "You look like a drysop to me."

"Susannah," Tenn called when she halted at the entryway behind the slip woman. "Here I am!"

The woman eyed Ten all encased in his brown canvas drawers and waistcoat, winked at Susannah, and shuffled back the way they had come.

"Are you all right, love?"

"She called me a drysop. What's that, as if I didn't know?"

"I think it's their word for a coward or landlubber at the very least. Hold my hand and we'll go down the steps."

"How deep is it? How much water is this?" she chatted to calm her nervousness.

"About four feet and fifty-two tons of fresh water every morning, so they say. See, it feels good."

"Not to me," she protested as the water lapped up her ankles, then to her knees and thighs. "I don't like it at all, so I'll just watch you."

Swiftly, surely, his hands were on her waist despite the voluminous folds of brown linen gown. He stepped down backward the last few steps into the water, lifting her behind him. She noted for the first time that it was pleasantly warm, and somewhere distant music played.

Her feet touched tiled bottom as they stood together near the side of the pool. His hands still on her waist, he waited, watching her while her floating dish bobbed ludicrously between them. The water moved slightly, circling her legs and shifting her garments into her, but there was no strong current. She finally noticed how firmly she grasped his upper arms.

"Susannah Marie Arne Cibber, what do you think?" he asked. "Not so bad as you thought, I'll wager. As long as this isn't too crowded let's just relax and make some 'wanton dalliance' Beau Nash always worries about at Cross Bath because the bathing's mixed. All right?"

"It isn't too bad, but I don't know about the wanton dalliance part. I think I'll just sit on a bench and dabble my legs."

"Oh no. You're going to learn now, and admit fully later that you were worried over nothing and you were glad once you did it."

He swirled her around him making rushing waves until

she finally laughed and clung to his neck. He carried her effortlessly about all buoyed up in bubbles and mineral water and puffy brown linen. And under the water, he stroked a sleek hip or leg when he could manage, and pinched her derriere once until she splashed him. They chased and laughed and then, exhausted, floated dreamily together until the nine o'clock bell rang, and they climbed out to their separate blanket wrappers and into the bouncing sedan chairs to go back uphill.

Just as he said, she had been worried over nothing, she told herself, and she was glad once she did it. If only deciding to stand up to Theo could be that way, for her fear of scandal and a ruined career was worse than facing tons of rushing water. Perhaps, someday, if only Tenn were there to help as he was today—

"My love, we're here, I said. So relaxed or tired now you've fallen asleep? Here, my pleasure to take you upstairs."

As he carried her all wrapped in her warm blanket, she felt a tremendous sense of peace, well-being, and love. He laid her gently down on the massive canopied bed they had shared so joyously last night, then leaned close over her with his palms down on either side of her tousled head; his own thick blanket pulled away from his heavily muscled shoulders, upper arms, and chest. She put her free hand to his elbow and stroked gently up his warm flesh.

"You look so brown," she said drowsily.

"So do you. It's the warm mineral water, but it will wear off after a few hours. Let me see how the rest of you looks."

She did not protest as he slowly unwrapped her blanket, then boldly parted her robe and lifted her chemise away. She watched mesmerized as his face went taut with passion: A tiny pulse beat at the base of his brown throat, and his jade eyes narrowed as they lowered to study each inch of her while she raised one hand to lightly trace the little hollows under his high cheekbones.

"You're exquisite, Susannah. I can never get enough of you."

"Good. I don't want you to," she began, but two big fingertips touched her lips to still her, so she kissed them and lay quietly.

"Since drinking the spring water here is healthful, I believe I'll try that," he rasped. "Let me see if there's a drop clinging anywhere to this beautiful, satin skin. Let me just taste—"

He did just that, leaning close over the whole length of her to lick and kiss and flick his tongue along her until every nerve was sensuously alive. His warm tongue ran riots of circles around her flat belly to plunge teasingly within her navel; he licked delicious designs up each breast toward the pink-budded tip until she writhed in desire and pulled his russet head down so he would suckle each peak. He took her mouth with driving, demanding kisses she returned until she tugged him down at last onto the bed beside her.

"Tenn, it's so wonderful. Please love me—please take me."

"I will. I will, but I'm not finished with all this yet," he told her and rained kisses and frenzied tongue caresses along her hipbones and even on the soft, inner flesh of her thighs.

"Oh, Tenn. Please—oh!"

She wound herself around him, kissing him back with a wild rage of love unquenched. Her loosened tresses draped a silken curtain along their shoulders; her proud nipples rasped delectably along the crisp, curled russet hair of his chest. His strong hands slid heavily, then darted everywhere over her while her long, tapered fingers entwined in his bronze, loosed hair. She blew into his ear, nibbling on the lobe to fan his passion even hotter as he knelt between her shifting legs at last. He lifted her up to meet his first thrust; he placed her bottom upon a big bed pillow so that she seemed to offer herself to him even more.

The impact of their union jolted her to piercing rapture. She revelled in the fierce pace he set, goading him on with her own frenzied movements. She could not breathe. She could not think. She could only feel and love and desire and fly so far above the threatening flood of waters that fear fell away in the pure ecstasy of transported love. Brazen colors of radiant hues cavorted across her brain as she crashed with him over the perfect edge of oneness, and together they spiralled back down to earth.

He hovered over her lovely, limp body, Tenn mused drowsily, like a protective roof, but shifted to her side to keep from placing too much weight on her. She looked asleep, utterly relaxed and satiated, as he felt with her now and always, when she let him love her and responded so naturally without the slightest hint of actress that clung to her when others were around.

But soon, lying next to her like this, having her all to himself, the demons would beset him again. Once more his ravenous passion for Susannah would arise to drive him on whatever destruction it took to keep her: Again the grim ogre of fear, of somehow losing her that had ever haunted him would ravage him anew.

He pulled the big, mussed Cross Bath blanket over them and cuddled close to her satin warmth underneath. When they went back to London, he couldn't bear for things to just fall back into their regular pattern of stolen moments, while she lived legally as the wife of that deranged and dangerous Theo Cibber—not after all this. Theo was an unpredictable lunatic and had to be kept off. She'd never leave the stage to go away with him to West Woodhay, and she desperately feared any hint of scandal. Yet something had to be done and, if she would conceive his child in all this fierce lovemaking, what then?

What then, his thoughts echoed in the warmth of their blanket cocoon in the middle of the big, dishevelled bed. He had promised her a fancy breakfast; he would like to promise her the world and take her away to see it all. But there were duties in London, crops awaiting at West Woodhay . . . His limbs entwined with hers, he slept.

Chapter Fourteen

"I'm so happy for you, Miss Susannah," Anne Hopson said, and clapped her hands in delight like a small child. "Your face is just beaming with good health and joy after that time away, and I know for a fact Mr. Cibber hasn't been out to your Aunt Emma's to find out whether you were there five days or not as he's been here four, five times a day and sleeping in the bagnios of Covent Garden so's I heard Mrs. Clive say to Mr. Fleetwood when I went to clean your tiring room the other day," Anne finished in one long breath.

"Kitty said that? And how would she know?" Susannah asked, both amused and comforted by Anne's usual cascade of words.

"Can't say 'cept for all the gossip anybody worth his salt at the theater picks up. Then too, if I was Kitty Clive, or Mrs. Theo Cibber for that matter, I'd keep both eyes on everything Theo Cibber did, I would."

Susannah sighed as she watched Anne unpack her things from Bath, which were strewn in piles on the bed. "I know. And if Theo was here four or five times a day while I was away, it was for a great deal more than just pawning some of the silver, china, and furniture to balance out his rampage on my tiring room. He's been waiting for me to come back. I suppose he'll be here soon, and I'll have to face him. I appreciate your not telling him anything you know, about where I've been and with whom, Anne, and I—"

"Hush, now. No need for that worry as I'd have tossed the illustrious Theo Cibber out a good long time ago, I would, even before he started all this thieving with that emerald pendant the squire sent you when *Zara* opened way over a year ago."

Susannah smiled misty-eyed at Anne and hugged her briefly before the sprightly woman bustled out of the room at other tasks. Tossed him out a long time ago: Such things were not done in King George's civilized England where husband's rights ruled house, career, and entire lives, Susannah mused. But despite all that, she still felt dreamy and ecstatic after her blissful journey to Bath with Tenn. If she but closed her eyes, she floated in the warm, shifting buoyant water of Cross Bath in his arms; with but the turn of her imagination, she lay beside him in the soft, deep bed on Barton Street or with him on the forest floor amid strewn violets.

Her eyelids flew open to survey her bedroom at home, and reality crashed in. Now that Tenn must make a hurried, much belated trip tomorrow to oversee spring shearing and planting on the Sloper estates at West Woodhay, she must keep these rich reminiscences safe until they could be together again to create new ones.

"Law's sakes, I told you, Miss Susannah!" Anne's voice shredded her thoughts as she darted back into the bedroom. "He's here already, coming in the alleyway like he does to shake all those creditors, though there's a few out there in back wise to him. I'll stay right here with you, and if he tries to touch so much as a ribbon or stocking of yours in this room, I've got a big iron skillet under the bed all ready as can be for him!"

"It's all right, Anne," Susannah soothed as the woman's

angry words went right by her. "I am ready. I'm fine. You just wait out in the parlor, and I will call if I need you."

Anne shook her head but did as she was bid. "You'd best face him in the parlor, I'd say," she muttered on her way out. Then she hissed, "Remember the skillet," even as she almost smacked into Theo at the door.

"Hello, Theo," Susannah said low and immediately began to put away the few things Anne had not returned to bureau drawers or the cedar chest at the foot of the bed.

"Susannah, you look fine. Very hearty—*par excellence*."

His voice so light and jaunty jarred her so that she shot him a cautious, curious look. He had come no farther in than the doorway, leaning his shoulder on the frame and making no attempt to close the door behind him. He actually smiled in that strange, grimacing mouth movement of his and folded his green brocaded arms casually across his chest.

"Country air does wonders, Theo," she said only, and took a good long time fussing over hair ribbons in a drawer.

"Egads, I came to apologize, my dear," his next words hit her squarely between her shoulder blades, so she turned all too obviously astounded with her hands still in the drawer. "I want us to declare a truce *ad perpetuam* and work together in whatever family trials we may face henceforth."

"Frankly, Theo, that's rather difficult for me to believe after you took all my things from the theater and then I return home to see some plates and furniture missing too."

"I swear, all that's under control now. No more need for such unsettling business anymore."

"You've settled your debts?" she asked warily, wanting to believe him and thankful to face this pleasant fellow rather than the raving fury she'd expected. Then too, she felt a rush of gratitude there were no probings about why she'd been gone so long.

"Do not fret your lovely head about any of that. Of course, it is a *sine qua non* I would have a magnificent plan to refurbish your other costumes, which of necessity had to go. Ah, yes, here we are, my dear."

Still standing her ground at the open bureau drawer, she stared at the white square of paper he produced from his waistcoat pocket and flourished with such a grandiose gesture he suddenly reminded her of the pompous Beau Nash, "King of Bath."

"Well, what is it?" she asked.

"An invitation to the royal water fête at court, Kensington Palace, tomorrow. I swear, Susannah, I was starting to worry you'd not be back from Camden Town in time and I'd have to leave my innumerable tasks at the Drury to go fetch you from your aunt's. For love of a bawd, you don't look very happy about this great honor."

She turned back to laboriously straightening the strewn ribbons in her drawer. "I'm not. And I don't see how that invitation has aught to do with any plans to get my stolen costumes back."

"Now, my dear. Royal favor, of course. It's tradition. Actresses at the Theater Royal have been honored to receive handoffs from queen and court ladies ever since the days of Nell Gwynn."

"Only with some rather sticky strings attached to the king, Theo. I doubt very much if my royal favor with the queen or her court ladies caused that invitation and, I believe, considering the little all too public problem I got into with His Majesty at Newmarket barely over a week ago, we'd do best to turn it down, royal command, favor, or not."

"You're daft, woman! *Non compos mentis!* Handel will be there; do you intend to slight him? The old boy's been in debt lately too, you know, and he's written something called Water Music for this fête, which could help him out financially; but will his old protégé, Susannah Arne Cibber, support him? No—no more than she'd condescend to go help her own husband's cause, or to honor her father-in-law who as poet Laureate is going to be there. He's taking Charlotte, who will probably end up swimming naked in the Serpentine if you're not there to keep a firm hand on her. No, fine, just go on being the royal *personna non grata* to this king whom the theater needs as a patron. Just go on being *personna non grata* to all of us at the Drury Theater Royal!"

"Theo, please, I was only thinking to avoid another scene with the king."

"Scene? Scene, she says. Egads, you're an actress, Susannah, and a clever, witty one at that. So—act! Of course, I don't expect to let you ever get in the slightest compromising situation with His Majesty. You do realize that I must be absolutely sure you don't 'rump' him again, as they say *ad infinitum* at court, so I will keep a good eye out there's no scene, as you put it, where you would even need to snub him. And, my dear, our going there will show everyone publically we're friends, the Cibbers standing united. Susannah, you won't stomp this olive branch the king and I have tendered you under your heel, will you? Can you not forgive?"

She sighed, turned, and pushed the tall bureau drawer closed with her back as she faced him. "You and I—friends only, Theo. And no scenes."

"None we don't rehearse on stage, your *metier*, my dear."

"Tomorrow, is it? And, I daresay, you have already accepted for us."

"Accepted and hired a lovely little cabriolet to drive to Kensington in."

"All right, as long as there will be lots of people there."

He squinted his slightly protruding eyes in a grin. "Lots of people; everyone who's anyone, all elegant, even generous, h'm? Egads, even the Prince of Wales and his pregnant Princess Augusta will be there, and everyone knows the prince and king fight like roosters in the pit. I knew I could depend on you as a real trooper, my dear. Choose something very formal to wear then, and here's some money for new shoes or what you will."

Amazingly, he plopped down some coins on a chair seat, whirled, and was gone. He had never even taken more than one step into the room, as though some invisible barrier protected her now. As for money, Theo Cibber had neither given nor had money for so long she could hardly remember. Susannah picked up the five coins and bit the edge of one to see if it were real, the way she'd seen her father do years ago when times were hard: yes, gold crowns with the profile of the king looking the part of Roman emperor, real as real. But then today, Theo had been full of surprises.

She hid the coins for buying food later in the skillet under the bed, and went to the hall to call Anne.

The sporty black leather cabriolet Theo had hired from a livery stable near their house took them smartly toward the Palace of Kensington. They crossed the great adjoining parklands of Hyde Park and Kensington Gardens after surrendering their invitation at the gate to enter the extensive grounds, since the parks contiguous to the palace were open to the public only when the royal family was not in residence.

The gravel of the long and straight "Route du Roi," which people had already begun to corrupt to "Rotten Row" as its fame spread, crunched under the wheels of their carriage. At nearly three in the afternoon, the sun slanted beautifully across the long, glittering pond called the Serpentine on their right, and reflected in the geometrically shaped Round Pond beyond. They circled the Pond and halted along Broad Walk where liveried royal servants waited to take vehicles away and where grandly garbed guests already strolled before the gentle grass slopes, fringing the many windowed, red-bricked frontage of the palace.

Her eyes scanned the crowd for faces she knew: Handel; her brother Tom, who would play in the large orchestra later; Father Cibber; Charlotte; even Tenn, who had decided to delay his departure for West Woodhay one more day when Susannah had sent a note telling him she had agreed to come to Kensington. Susannah saw a sea of faces in silks, satin, brocades, laces, velvet, and the newly fashionable white-powdered wigs, but no one she recognized immediately.

Theo helped her down and she fluffed out her full, double-tiered satin skirts, which shifted hues from apricot to muted gold when she walked. Frilly lace edged the bodice and layered skirts, dripping heavily from her sleeves gathered tightly to her elbows. A stylish, double white lace ruff graced her slender throat, and her hair was worn in elegant if simple style, both upswept on top and dangled below in tiny auburn ringlets. She had merely tucked tiny clusters of wild pink roses in her hair and a full-blown long-stemmed rose at the left side of her low-cut bodice. Her ivory-ribbed theater fan sported a spray of painted flowers and naked nymphs. Unfortunately, for all her careful selection of the gown, it clashed terribly with the shocking Dutch porcelain-blue of Theo's breeches, frock coat and waistcoat.

"Sometimes, dear wife," Theo told her low as she accepted his arm and they meandered up the clipped sward toward the laden tables being spread near the charming orangery, on the north side of the sprawling palace, "I tend to forget how lovely you are, a rose without equal."

She saw the king ahead in a ring of courtiers, and though Theo seemed not to notice, it did appear they were making directly for him.

"Should we not mingle a little bit, Theo?" she said and pulled back.

"Now, isn't that just like Susannah? I'm complimenting you for how that gown highlights your lovely golden eyes and chestnut hair, and you balk. Come along and we shall mingle later."

An intangible foreboding filled her when Theo so brazenly dared to cut his way through the glittering crowd surrounding the king. To her chagrin, her gaze caught Lady Walpole's slit-eyed stare the same instant she heard the Princess Caroline's piercing giggle. Too late! His Majesty's wide, pale blue gaze took them in, and the royal arm swept some poor soul in half sentence back away.

"My dear friends, my Drury Lane actor-manager and the so lovely Mrs. Cibber," the unmistakably German-tinged voice boomed. Nearby conversations halted to be replaced by the buzz of sibilant whispers.

Theo bowed very low and long with his black velvet hat sweeping the grass, but Susannah was almost immediately plucked up from her curtsy with a plump white hand on her wrist. "So wonderful you came. Your dear friend Herr Handel will be playing after we eat; he will be glad you came too. Come, let me show you part of the palace. Too big to see everything, but still not as grand as our Herrenhausen in Hanover, eh, my dear?"

Theo bowed low again and Susannah blanched. Her Majesty, Queen Caroline, had been sitting in a huge, carved chair a few yards away, and she hadn't even noted her.

"The gardens are lovely," Susannah said, her eyes on the Queen. "All Londoners have heard we owe this great beauty of the gardens open to the public here and at Kew to our queen." Queen Caroline inclined her head, so Susannah dared, "And will Her Majesty walk with us around the palace, sire?"

"No. Too tired, heavy feet," he said curtly and turned them immediately away from the avid crowd.

"Her Majesty has been ill of late, my dear," Theo inserted in a solicitous stage whisper, "so you just go along."

"But the gardens are so lovely," she said to Theo, pretending the words were for his ears only, "and I'd like to see them before it gets dark."

"And, of course, the palace all lighted after dark," the king cajoled, and she tried to appear somewhat surprised he had heard her plea.

Between the king and Theo, whose arm she seized to not go off alone with her royal guide, no matter how many courtiers tagged in their wake, Susannah walked along the endless length of white damask covered buffet tables on the lawn. Stewards and servers fussed over endless platters of haunch of venison, legs of lamb, massive sides of beef, and pyramids of partridge that were delicate by comparison. Almost military rows of silver or gold chafing dishes dazzled in the sun next to huge plates of raw celery, varied cheeses, and geometric piles of fruit from the glasshouses down along the Serpentine. Stacks of dainty dessert plates next to bowls of preserves and comfitures, ringed by compotiers displaying fruit cakes dusted with white sugars, ended the parade of massed delicacies. The tables with the clusters of decanters containing Madeira, sherry, port, and claret crushed their own separate table legs down into the tender spring grass. Beyond the food tables stretched dining tables all set with blinding white damask, silver, and china in the sporadic breeze and lowering sun.

"Something now to drink or eat?" the king asked, leaning close to Susannah as though Theo didn't exist.

"Perhaps a little sherry," she said, deciding it would be something to hold and an excuse not to wander off too far, though she had to loose Theo's arm to manage the crystal goblet as well as the fan.

The king took port, which signalled a general rush to the tables, while they walked on to the crest of the gentle slope overlooking the vast sweep of park and the two artificially shaped ponds below.

"Oh, there's a beautiful, gilded barge in this end of the Serpentine," Susannah exclaimed. "I didn't know you had those here."

The king snorted inelegantly. "First, there were two yachts the queen wished for the children. That silly thing there is the Prince of Wales's idea of entertainments."

"Good evening, sire, and do I hear my princely name taken in vain?" a lively voice chirped behind them, and Susannah and Theo whirled to face the narrow-chinned Frederick, Prince of Wales. Although King George still pointedly stared off over the park, Susannah curtsied carefully with her sherry glass in hand and Theo managed another low sweep of hat.

"I believe I *did* hear my name," Prince Frederick plunged, on ignoring how his royal father fashionably if rudely rumped him. "I've been chasing along at a good clip behind you, sire. Her Majesty wishes you back to greet Herr Handel, your German music maker, so he can begin the violin fireworks or the what-all immediately after we finish gorging ourselves."

Susannah's eyes widened at the not so subtle sarcasm and the crackle of tension between the king and his heir. No one spoke for a moment while the king swivelled slowly back to face them.

"This lady has interest in your fancy boat, Prince of Wales, so tell her of it and come back at once. And do not dart about this way interrupting kings' conversations, if you please. Mr. Cibber, a word with you on the way back to begin this fête, so charming when no rude persons are near."

The king nodded stiffly to Susannah, his blue eyes studying her face for a moment as if he were looking for something he was unsure of. Then he turned abruptly away without so much as a look at Prince Frederick, while Theo sloshed his port on the grass and ran to keep up.

Annoyed at the turn of events and the fact that His Majesty obviously had something to say to Theo in private, Susannah watched them go, then turned to peruse the prince again. His eyes, much his father's, examined her minutely, but the shape of face was entirely different, with no plump jowls.

"Do you think I'm rude, Mrs. Cibber? Faith, perhaps just in my stare. A prerogative of kings and would-be kings, I fear."

His voice bore no heavy clomp of German accent, but she noted it was instantly bitter in tone whatever the words. "A prerogative of most men, Your Grace. Shall we walk back?"

He laughed overlong at her little comment. "The king said you like my barge. He only calls it a boat to pique me as always."

"I'm sure he doesn't mean to. Yes, I like it. It looks very fanciful, like something from an Arabian setting for a play."

"Not a tragedy like *Zara*, I hope."

She smiled at his mention of her beloved premiere performance drama. "Yes, like *Zara*, Your Grace, but it needn't have been a tragedy if people trusted each other more, you know."

"Faith, you are lovely. Best beware his nibs the king, you know, little actress. Forgive me for blunt words, but he's on the utter outs with little Hanoverian Walmoden and you're supposed to look like her."

Susannah gasped, then colored. Sherry sloshed on her

wrist and dripped to the grass.

"Here, I didn't mean it like that," he crooned and wiped her wet wrist with his silk handkerchief, then took her glass from her unresisting fingers, downed the rest of the sherry, and tossed it into a bush a few yards down the slope. "It's only His Majesty and I go at each other a great deal, and I thought to warn you about Walmoden to ruin his fun. He's obviously smitten with you, and, faith, but I really can't blame him."

The words danced through her mind back and forth: Smitten was Tenn's word. That word, all mention of that feeling, belonged to her and Tenn. Drat Theo, she should never have come, and now she stood here like a ninny while the heir to the throne dried off her wrist and warned her about the king just as Tenn had.

"Well, Your Grace, I'm no Walmoden, I tell you that," she said vehemently. "I have a theatrical career I value and I only came because my husband cajoled me. Now I'm very hungry and looking forward to my dear friend Handel's music. I understand you favor only the Italian maestros and give your father's Handel a terrible time." Susannah smiled. She fluttered her fan to regain her poise and moved smoothly away back toward the crowd, very pleased with herself at the deft switch of topics.

"Now you've said it, Mrs. Cibber. Perhaps I favor the Italians *because* the king does not. Perhaps the Londoners favor me because the king does not. It's all intertwined, you see."

"I do see," she said even as her eyes suddenly took in Tenn across the way. He stood so tall, talking to Prime Minister Walpole and his own father, but that raven-haired, cat-eyed Lady Walpole leaned toward him too, as if to seize each word. Prince Frederick's closing comments blurred right past her. What she wouldn't give to be able to walk over there to join Tenn, head held high to protect her claim on him, and converse with his father as if she were someone Tenn could know.

"Until later then, Mrs. Cibber. I shall see if the Princess Augusta is willing to take a little ride on the Serpentine, and I'll show the barge to you then," Prince Frederick told her.

"What, Your Grace? Yes, how lovely. And I do thank you for the conversation and warning," she got out before he nodded curtly and moved back into the crowd.

Theo, she thought, should be ecstatic at tonight's script. The king had walked off with them and had volunteered a private tour of the palace that she was quick enough to squelch. Then the prince had promised a ride in his gilded barge, and there was Tenn whom Theo was always encouraging her to talk to. She wanted to get at least a few words with him as she edged closer through the clusters of people. "Upstart actress . . . Cibber . . . another Walmoden," she heard clearly from someone behind her and she almost turned to stare him or her down. There was something about Theo and the king she sensed tonight—something she didn't like and wanted to tell Tenn if she could ever get him half alone, the way she seemed to get the men she had no desire to be with.

Tenn's green gaze snagged her topaz stare across the bobbing, buzzing heads. He smiled; he gestured. She felt as if she trod the soft grass of dreams. His father's head was white now, but the face echoed Tenn's; the eyes shimmered that same startling green. She cared for the older man instantly, enchanted by the muted mirror of her Tenn, like a reflection in a quiet pond. Tenn and his father smiled. But as she approached, the fantasy shattered: She noted Prime Minister Walpole's grin and his wife's narrow gaze.

"Father, I told you she'd be here this afternoon," Tenn's deep voice was saying as if she were surely someone grand. "Susannah Cibber, my father, Squire William Sloper."

Susannah blushed hot with pleasure and embarrassment under everyone's perusal. Suddenly, here for the first time as she had not with king or prince or queen, she felt utterly awkward and shy.

"She is beautiful at close range as you told me, Tenn." William Sloper bent briefly over, her hand in his. "My dear, I've admired your work both as a singer and actress, and I'm glad to meet anyone who can have a civilizing, cultivating influence on my horse and tennis athlete son here to drag him to the theater."

"No, squire," Lady Walpole interjected silkily as though she had been addressed, "I think we need popular athletes in the powerful landed class of the Whig party. We can hardly leave all the sporting pursuits like the king's horse racing or, on the other end of the scale, low-class boxing matches at Tottenham Fields and such, to the rest of England. Besides, Tenn seems quite civilized and cultured enough to me to have to be dragged anywhere."

"A man after your own heart, in other words, my Catherine?" Sir Robert Walpole's voice sliced through her purred comments, and Susannah took in the obvious double meaning of his words. Drat this raven-haired harpy, Susannah fumed, and the glib prime minister too. Why couldn't they just go about their important business and leave her here with the Slopers, so she had a chance to whisper to Tenn that Theo might have something afoot?

But even as her fervent wish was answered and Sir Robert bowed and nearly dragged his Lady Catherine off, the entire proper gathering seemed to crash out of control. Susannah's wild sister-in-law, Charlotte Cibber Charke, spotted her across the way and waved, shrilling her name even as a pretty blond woman appeared from a cluster of people to drape herself on Tenn's arm.

"Susannah! Theo wants you!" Charlotte called across a length of crowded grass while elegant heads turned to stare. "Something about a song! Are you coming?"

Blushing to the roots of her hair, Susannah waved once to quiet Charlotte and turned to glare at Tenn who was quickly disengaging the blond woman's arm.

"My dear Amanda," the senior Sloper said, obviously recognizing the intruder instantly, "so delighted to see you again. I haven't seen you since you last visited West Woodhay, though I know you've been to our house at St. James' several times to see Tenn."

Blue eyes in the woman's pert, heart-shaped face, framed with ringlets spilling to edge an ivory and pink complexion, bathed Tenn's annoyed face in adoration.

"Amanda Newbury," William Sloper said when Tenn looked at a loss for words, "I'd like you to meet a theater acquaintance of Tenn's, Mrs. Susannah Cibber."

"*The* Mrs. Cibber? Mercy, charmed, I am sure," the woman simpered.

Everything Tenn had told her about his Amanda Newbury or his once fictional betrothed Amanda Brompton merged and mingled with Susannah's angers and fears of his past. This woman had been to West Woodhay. She had come to the house at St. James' once when Susannah had gone there to see Tenn, only to want him to seduce her on the settee where he'd probably enjoyed numerous other willing ladies: this smug blond, Lady Walpole; perhaps even his wife, which she'd never be!

"Susannah, Amanda is only a neighbor, whose family lands are nearby in Berks," Tenn had begun to explain, but Charlotte's calling of her name even closer drowned him out. Drowned—she'd like to do that—Susannah raged silently; drown these snippy, seductive women who wanted Tenn; drown Theo and the king in the Serpentine under Prince Frederick's damned gilded barge!

"Excuse me, please," she interrupted Tenn, looking only into his father's eyes, which merely studied and did not devour, "but my sister-in-law needs me."

She lifted her skirts and turned immediately away, even though Tenn dared to call her first name in that deep, resonating voice. She climbed the slight rise toward the palace, toward Charlotte, while her thoughts cavorted in the cacophony of voices. Charlotte was dressed well for her; Father Cibber had probably insisted when he'd brought her, Susannah observed, trying to control her dark mood. The woman looked almost exotic with her tumbled coal-black hair and green and yellow ribboned gown.

"Char, you look fine today, but I wish you wouldn't yell for me like that," Susannah scolded. "Especially not here."

Charlotte laughed. "Devil take them, they're all yelling to each other, only it's allowed, even proper if you're fancy folk. Frankly, I think the whole thing is one sweet jest—want to see?"

She laughed again and produced three hothouse pears from the folds of her skirts, which she adeptly juggled.

"Char, please, not here," Susannah hissed and started away.

Charlotte was instantly at her side eating the only pear now visible. "Come on, silly goose, laugh a bit. We're all jugglers, you know. Theo juggles his creditors and you. You juggle Theo and, by the way, wasn't that the same handsome rogue who chased you in the wedding parade that day in St. James', the tall, copper-haired, luscious green-eyed one?"

"Did you say that Theo wanted to see me, Char? Where is he?" Susannah clipped out as fast as she walked.

"Don't know now as that was a good half hour ago. Did you see all that poxy fine food? Damn, but I struggle here and there to teach or write or wait tables to put food on my table, and the king dines half the damn town on acres of food for free. I tell you, Susannah, we need a revolution."

"It's tradition—king's entertaining, I mean," Susannah ground out, now feeling more crushed by Tenn's other women than angered by them.

"Piss on tradition. If something's right, I go after it, and I think you do too. But if it's wrong or unjust, we fight to change it. After all, you dared to demand a marital contract with Theo, and are bold enough to tell fat Fleetwood that good actresses deserve the same salary good actors do. And I know you don't cohabit anymore with my snake of a brother because you don't love him. You're brazen at heart like me, Susannah, and you want what's right. A little love, a little rage, all at once. That's why we're friends when the others can't abide me."

Susannah stopped and turned at last under the sweep of endless red brick palace walls to face the impudent, yet serious Charlotte. "That's utter nonsense, Char. If I wanted to say to the devil with society's rules the way you do, I'd hardly be hurrying to find Theo now. Later—I'll see you later—" her voice nearly broke and she hurried away despite the terrifyingly true ring of Char's words in her brain and heart.

Theo was as nervous as a cat on coals at the two-hour dinner, especially when Tenn and his father came over to speak with both of them. Susannah was studiously, coldly polite, although she longed to touch Tenn, to talk with him. And when the Sloper father and son moved off to their seats, she drank entirely too much sherry, ate too little to balance it, and took to casting lightning-quick glances down the table at Tenn, until his ravenous gaze jolted her and she steeled herself to look elsewhere. It was fine with her, she told herself, if he spent all evening with the likes of Amanda Newbury or Brompton or whatever her name really was, or talked intimate Whig politics with Lady Walpole behind bushes on the darkening lawn, even though neither of those ladies was in sight right now.

"Egads, Charlotte's latched onto Tenn Sloper," Theo

complained as the meal ended, and people began to stroll down en masse toward the Serpentine. "Even after the abysmal way you snubbed him tonight, I can't believe crazy Charlotte would be tolerable to him. I swear, if it weren't for the fact I don't want His Majesty getting the wrong idea, I'd have never allowed you to treat Sloper so tonight."

"That's just it, Theo," she told him tapping her now emptied crystal goblet with her fingernail until it rang like a chime, "I don't want His Majesty or these bug-eyed people or the Queen or you to get the wrong idea. And so, I believe we should get our no doubt expensively hired little cabriolet and drive home."

"For love of a bawd, Handel's music is only now starting and there will be fireworks all London will speak of for weeks."

"You stay then. If all London can see it, I'll enjoy it from my own doorstep, or at least halfway across the park without all these peering crowds."

"Actors love crowds, dear wife, love settings *alfresco* or otherwise."

"Yes, Theo, I know. *Ad perpetuam*, as you say. I just don't feel well enough to stay, so don't give me another thought. I'll find the cabriolet and make it home by myself just fine."

"Nonsense. All right, I'll take you. Sit back down here but one moment, and I'll send one of these hovering servants to have it waiting for us. The vehicles are all on the far side along the south terrace. Just a moment."

She sat fanning her flushed face, although the rising evening breeze across the water and sweep of lawns felt cool. Tenn with Charlotte at his side disappeared: just as well. He'd be off to his country duties tomorrow, so perhaps that blond, enticing flesh and blood Amanda would be heading for Berks too. The first strains of beautiful brass and rising strings floated to her where she sat. The music was unmistakably, majestically Handel, but even that was no comfort.

Theo was back. He took her arm. "Charlotte popped back out of nowhere and I just shook her off. The lunatic's been wading in the pond and father will kill her if he sees her, after he put out a pretty penny to make her presentable tonight. Come on then. This way. Since the palace is deserted, we can cut through faster. This man is going to take us," he clipped out jerkily.

Evening muted the lawns to gray, while shadows crept up the tall red brick walls of the palace as they turned into a huge, three sided courtyard and went up a flight of stone stairs.

"Council chamber left," their sober-faced guide said as if he were leading foreign dignitaries on a palace tour. Theo had fallen more quiet than usual, but the size and grandeur of the corridors and rooms awed her too. They turned right again, from a large, elegant wood-panelled room with blue draperies into a vaulted, ornately decorated chamber with gilded, classical statues standing mute in marble alcoves. The overhead blue and gold ceiling studded with flower medallions seemed to reach heavenward, even as Maestro Handel's marvelous melody floated barely in from outside.

"It's so lovely," Susannah breathed. Already she felt spellbound, and her frustration and anger ebbed. Such beauty, such soaring ecstasy of color and form, that was what she felt in those most poignant, intimate moments with Tenn.

"Cupola Room," their guide's voice intoned. "King's Privy Chamber next here."

Susannah's head snapped around to stare at Theo. Their guide had bowed and was walking back the way they had come, leaving only resounding footfalls. "Theo! We're supposed to go through here and out to the carriage!" Her own voice echoed off the vast ceilings and walls.

"Susannah, hush up and listen to me. He wanted just a song, one private song before you went this evening, and that small pittance is hardly to be denied."

"He!" she gasped as the pieces clicked too cleverly into place. "The king is here while everyone's out there? No! You give him a private song, Theo. I'm leaving!"

The door of the room just ahead of them swung open to throw a broad shaft of light nearly to their feet. Theo seized her wrist in a viselike grip and shook her hard once. "Now you listen!" he hissed. "One song and you please him, or I'll see you don't have a house or a theater to go home to. I swear, I'll kill you—"

"Won't you step in, Mrs. Cibber?" a voice asked from the open door.

She yanked her arm free of Theo's grasp. Thank heavens, it was not the king to see Theo threaten her like that. At least there were others here with His Majesty. One song—just one song for them, she reasoned—and then she would find her way out of this maze of magnificent chambers, by herself if she must. She stepped forward to the open, lighted room.

The privy chamber was breathtaking with an airy, painted ceiling, almost Oriental in flavor, over the ornate blue brocade French wallpaper. Massive, gold-rimmed portraits graced the walls, reflecting in the highly polished wood floors that rimmed the floral carpet. The furniture was red velvet and gilt, and there was a clavichord; she took it all in instantly, even though the king's alarming presence made the whole scene shift and fade. There was no one but the man at the door and His Majesty. She felt like a trapped rabbit, utterly betrayed. She half curtsied to the king, yet turned to say something to the other man who had admitted her; she knew not what: perhaps to ask him to stay or invite Theo in.

"My dear, dear Susannah," the king began, even as the

other man swiftly stepped out and closed the door with a hollow reverberation behind him. Annoyed by His Majesty's presumptive, starry-eyed gaze, she rose instantly to the defensive.

"My husband says you favor a brief song, sire. I suggest we have him step in to enjoy it also."

"Such protests, eh, but I do not mind. It is so different to have a lady's protests. Besides, my dear, I doubt your husband is outside that door anymore—or anyone. And then, you cannot tell me you and your Theo really get on."

George, King of England, moved almost warily closer while she held her ground. "I believe we get on as well as you and the queen, sire," she dared.

He looked surprised. His full mouth quirked up, but he stalked her farther to take one of her hands in both of his. "Indeed, the English rose dares to show temper to her king. So challenging, so different—*wunderbar*."

She tried to tug her hand back, but settled instead for flipping her fan between them with her free hand when his grip did not slacken. "Different from your Walmoden, sire? Everyone whispers I look like her."

He actually gasped; his lower lip faltered. "Sophia Marianne, she should be here, but with the queen ill," he mumbled in an accent so heavy she barely caught the words. "*Ja*, Sophia, my Walmoden, but you too are so lovely."

He stepped forward even as his long arms darted to pull her to him. His full lips covered hers in a wet, open-mouthed kiss. He held her pinned to the door that she had retreated toward, his big stomach and chest pressing hard into her softness. She pulled her mouth away, fiercely turning her head to the side.

"No, sire—please! I don't know what Theo told you or what he promised you, but—"

"No fighting! We will go back out soon. We must. Just

let me taste—touch. *Ja*, like this."

One hand crept up to her low-cut, ruffled bodice and fingers dipped deep inside to grasp a nipple, pulling her bodice off one shoulder. "Love your king, little one," he murmured. "Promise to meet me later. Ah, so sweet. *Ach, himmel!*" he cursed and yanked his hand out with the flying rose she had placed in her bosom. A thorn had etched a ragged hairline of blood across his starkly white index finger.

She ignored the thorn's scratch, which so obviously annoyed him. "I can love you only as a loyal subject, sire. Loose me, please. I love elsewhere, even as you."

His great weight pressing into her lessened as he stood back enough to frown at his finger, then down at her. "Cibber said you were hard to handle, but not this lecturing to me like my son. I smile, I command, and Sophia will be mine—you too if I decide so!"

"Perhaps Walmoden can be yours this way, sire, but not I. I swear, if you just let me go, I shall never speak of this to anyone who would tell her."

She stared up unflinching into the astounded blue eyes, which no longer seemed to take her in. Now, she felt the scratch of rose thorn along her own bosom and realized without looking that the breast he had crudely fondled was nearly exposed. She shrugged slightly to return the gown to her shoulder and settled the bodice.

He moved back another step. "The Prince of Wales—he poisoned your mind against me. I shall have him for a lesson he shall never forget—never! If I bring her here from Hanover, the queen and my son would turn the whole damned town against German George. *Ach*, I hate them all!"

He turned away, moved away. She stood frozen a moment, awed by this intimate glimpse into the tormented interior of the stodgy king, only a beset man after all. She waited, wary of another passionate outburst. He lifted a hand, as if for support, to the back of a tall gilt chair and stood so still five feet away from her that he seemed a waxen effigy.

Almost before she knew she would move, her hand darted to the door. She turned the knob, pulled, and ran. His voice echoed behind her, a single word she did not catch nor heed. She tore through a dimly lighted, wood-panelled room heavy with dark tapestries, turned twice through other small, deserted chambers, and raced down a long, resounding gallery lined with windows on her left and ponderous, royal portraits on the right.

Footsteps pounded, echoed behind her! Surely not the king, but someone he had sent—or Theo. She lifted her skirts to run faster despite the fancy, high-heeled shoes. Her fan fell but she went on. Her name, raspy and breathless, echoed off the walls behind to seize at her. She dashed out onto an ornate second-story landing with black wrought-iron balcony and a flight of black marble steps stretching away below. Life-sized paintings of Greek gods and goddesses stared coldly from their shadowy alcoves; the angular sweep of stairs beckoned escape down.

The steps were polished and slick. Near the turn of single landing, her heel twisted. She slipped and fell. Her ankle wrenched. The pursuer thudded closer.

"Susannah!"

"Oh! Oh, Tenn!"

His arms held her, lifted her. "My ankle. Theo ruined everything. The king—"

"It's all right now. I'm going to take you home then come back to settle this with him. Your ankle? Let me see."

"Ouch! Oh, no, you can't."

"Can't what? It's not broken, just a twist. I mean to come back to see Theo, love. This trying to push you on the highest bidder has gone too far. I'm going to carry you. Hold on. These damn steep steps are always deadly and not even used sometimes."

"You can't fight Theo any more than you can the king," she protested, so utterly relieved to see him that all earlier thoughts of his other women mattered not at all. "That will mean everyone will know about us. Tenn, you can't!"

"If he's so desperate he needs a bidder for you, I intend to be that man," he ground out.

"What? You're crazy. And how did you find me?"

"That little butterfly of a sister-in-law of yours told me Theo had sent a message to the king and she pointed out the way the king had hurriedly gone."

Cool night air whispered along her bare forearms and bosom as he strode outside with her. "We'll take my carriage and see to that ankle," he said. "We'll go to St. James' Square."

"No, I couldn't. I've got to hurry home to pack. I'm really leaving Theo this time for good."

"If so, you're leaving him for me," he said curtly. He called out his name in the darkness and someone darted away to fetch his carriage. Her ankle had begun to throb now, and she gripped his neck tighter and inhaled the wonderful masculine aroma of him notwithstanding the pain of ankle and heart.

"I just can't, Tenn, not now. I've so much to think out. I thought perhaps there was a chance for coexistence with him after I returned, but he lied to me and set a trap, and with the King of England. He threatened me with violence tonight if I didn't do as he said, and he's done it before. You have to go to West Woodhay, you said. The estates need you, and your father expects it."

"Fine. You'll go with me."

"You know I can't. Besides, I need to stay in reaching distance of the Drury. Despite the approaching summer recess, I don't intend to have Theo or Fleetwood give my roles away, nor will I be out of commuting distance for

September rehearsals. This time I intend to get at least part of my salary to live on!"

He turned his head which was sculptured by moonlight, mere inches away from her as his carriage rolled up. "It will be a good trick to leave Theo and not the theater he manages, where you're under contract, Susannah. You've got to decide on both things together, I'm afraid. I'm offering you a life with me and the hell with scandal. You must decide."

"I have decided. I want Theo out of my life, but I can never let the theater go."

"And me?" he challenged. "You're going off somewhere by yourself with no money—after what we've shared? Or am I to assume that the elegant cold shoulder I got tonight was no act for Theo or His Majesty or whomever but straight from your confused, spoiled little heart?"

"Sir, your carriage. Squire Sloper," his driver George's voice floated to them from his perch as horses snorted and stomped and footmen stared.

Theo's contorted visage and the king's livid face screamed in her memory as sharply as the pain in her ankle. Charlotte is right, she thought with crystal clarity. I do want what I want and I'm going after all of it. She would be strong. She must, but when Tenn looked at her that way—

"Please take me home, Tenn. Please," she said low, her voice as wan as muted moonlight caressing his bronze head. Stonily, he lifted her into the carriage and silently took her home.

Part Three

LADY BRUTE: Why we may pretend what we will; but 'tis a hard matter to live without the man we love.

BELLINDA: But what think you of the fear of being found out?

LADY BRUTE: I think that never kept a woman virtuous long. We are not such cowards neither.

Susannah's lines as Lady Brute
from *The Provoked Wife*, V. ii.
by Sir John Vanbrugh

Chapter Fifteen

Susannah's first week living with Anne Hopson's parents in Malden, three miles southwest of London, blurred by like the fluttering orange and black monarch butterflies in the tiny Hopson garden where she sat and walked. Each of the seven days and nights seemed endless as she lived them, but now as she looked back, the time merged in one swift fleeting moment. She had spent many hours with Anne and her elderly parents, who still kept a mantua shop in front of the small house, and all of the Hopsons chattered as much as Anne. But it was this silent garden and her own quiet thoughts that she cherished and that made the separation from Tenn, who had gone off angry and hurt to West Woodhay, somehow bearable.

Today was the first of May, she mused, a preciously beautiful day with warm sun on her back and bees buzzing in the tall, nodding pink hollyhocks. So silent here, so peaceful away from theater bustle, the crowded London streets, and Theo's treachery. She had left her husband a curt note that night Tenn's carriage had taken her home from Kensington Palace: She and Anne were leaving for now, but she expected the household on Wild Court would not be sold off, nor her promised roles at the Drury next autumn tampered with. Blessedly, Theo hadn't found her here in Malden—or hadn't looked. Tenn had demanded to know her plans though, and had even delivered her and Anne safely here on his way to West Woodhay. And now, in this quiet week, her twisted ankle had healed, but her heart had not.

She heard Anne's quick footsteps behind her on the gravel of the walk and swivelled about on the wooden bench. The woman's face was crumpled in a huge, uncharacteristic frown, and she wadded handfuls of her skirt in her fists. "Laws, Miss Susannah, this was a good haven while we had it, it was."

Susannah stood and touched Anne's shoulders. "Has he found us then? It's Theo and not Tenn, isn't it? Drat the man! I can tell by your face."

"It's Theo Cibber, all right, Theo *and* your Tenn and looking like old comrades in arms, if you ask me," Anne groused and gave the apron over her grisette skirt a good shake.

"I can't believe it, only perhaps Tenn's decided to take Theo up on his bidding—" her voice drifted off.

"What's that? What bidding?" Anne insisted.

"Never mind. I won't stand for it if that's his plan. I will go willingly to Tenn, but not for some fee like a street strumpet. So, the curtain's up again. Bring them on, Anne."

"Them—together?" Anne faltered.

"Let them decide. I'd rather see Tenn alone, Tenn only, but that's a green girl's dream, and I'm far beyond that now. I'm only sorry I've pulled you and your dear family into all this. I hope there won't be a scene, but I'll have to leave now anyway. My aunt will take me in again, I don't doubt, even though Theo will have easier access to me there."

"I'm glad you came here to Malden, and it's been a wonderful week for me back with my parents. I wanted you to hide here, and somehow, someway, I just know you're going to get rid of that spineless tormentor Theo Cibber, and I'm going to be there to see it!"

Susannah watched Anne go back into the house. She moved out of her favorite, small secluded sanctuary in the garden to wait for her visitors on the back doorstep, almost as if she couldn't bear for Theo to pollute the garden. As for Tenn, anywhere near a garden with him made her want to pick violets and lie beside him on the grass as verdantly emerald as his beguiling eyes.

"Susannah," Theo's shrill voice shattered the sweet sentiment, "as your husband, I told Sloper to wait in the house, and I'd see to you first."

"See to me, Theo?" she replied icily and moved away a few steps to lift her hands to her yellow-gowned hips. "That's just it, you know. I'm asking you not to see me anymore at all. I intend for us to live apart and I shall make my own way."

"Egads, what a lot of silly feminine drivel. I realize you've been upset but, I swear, I have been too *ad perpetuam*. But now with our financial difficulties behind us there will be no more need for bickering, nor do I want to do more than manage your career, I assure you. You do recall you have a rather valuable theatrical career of which I am the sole shareholder, do you not, Mrs. Cibber?" he taunted.

"I recall, Mr. Cibber, that I do hold articles with the Drury Lane Theater Royal, the same theater you manage, but you do not possess my career, nor me, nor are you sole shareholder in aught I have to do with—"

"For love of a bawd, I knew you'd be incorrigible," he screeched, thrusting his hands in his frock coat pockets. "Now you listen to me, because here's the way I say things will be. You will pack your things and come away—"

"No!"

"—and you will do as I say and behave, or I will explode such a scandal in the London papers you'll never have a career left to salvage come autumn!"

Her heart careened down to her feet: Here he was with Tenn so he must know everything now and be planning to expose then with another vile campaign of feeding poison letters to the papers, which waited ravenously for all his scurrilous slander.

"And now, my dear, I leave you only with this," he was saying. "You ruined your chances with the king and made me look the fool. Rumor says he already has crashed with both German hoofs into a quick affair with a sweet-faced Lady Deloraine at court, whom he's nicknamed 'Fly.' She'll reap the bounty of his benefits until he can bring his Walmoden here someday from Hanover, I've no doubt!"

"You disgust me, Theo. I despise you."

"Egads, do you think I don't know it? Listen, you icy little witch, as I'm not finished yet. If you want any shred of your damned, precious career come this autumn, you'd better succeed with Tenn Sloper where you failed with German George. I've known Sloper was enamored of you *ab initio*, but this is a stroke of luck to solve all our problems. He's rented a house for us at Kingston-Upon-Thames for the summer."

"For us—all three?" she gasped unbelieving. "No!"

He seized her arms and shook her hard once. "Yes, and he's paid all our debts just to be allowed to breathe your sweet air, I take it. I'll have your head and your career if you defy me and don't let him in your bed!"

"Theo!" Tenn's voice boomed very close, and Susannah glanced up wide-eyed over Theo's head to see Tenn furiously charging out the back door. His big hand went hard to Theo's shoulder; Theo's grip on her loosened instantly.

She felt dizzy at the mere nearness of Tenn, and her legs felt all wavy like the surface of an agitated pond whose ripples she could feel lapping relentlessly up her thighs, clear over her belly to her breasts. No, she thought, panicking, not this rushing sensual feeling for him the moment he appears, the traitor.

"Theo," Tenn was saying, his deep voice controlled like an angry schoolmaster's, "I believe you told me you wouldn't scold Susannah—or so much as touch her."

"No harm, none at all," Theo clipped out in a stagy singsong voice and forced a grin.

Susannah noted well the raging rate of the pulse at the side of Tenn's brown throat, just above the elegant twist of white cravat, and the way he clenched and unclenched his fists at his side in barely restrained fury.

"Egads, I'm off then," Theo said in the awkward hush. "Busy, so busy, as I'm needed back in London, but it's a *sine qua non* I'll be out to Kingston someday soon to see how things are getting on. And, Susannah, I've given Anne two week's salary as I assume you'll want to keep her with you, and low-class domestic help is so likely to stray these days. I swear, I'm grateful to you for driving Susannah over to Kingston for me, Tenn," he added hastily when he saw Anne Hopson and her elderly, snow-haired mother now stood in the back door. He tipped his tricorn to them all, grimaced a smile, and banged out the wooden gate in the tall garden wall.

"Mrs. Cibber, are you all right or would you wish to come into the house with Anne and me?" Mrs. Hopson's crackly voice floated to Susannah where she stared unmoving into Tenn's fixed green gaze.

"Thank you, Mrs. Hopson. I will be in in just a moment, but I need a word or two with this gentleman."

To break the spell he had so quickly cast over her despite how he'd obviously betrayed her and how he made her want to throw herself brazenly against his powerful chest to cling like a madwoman, she forced herself to turn and walk slowly back to her little wooden bench among the hollyhocks. She sat and deliberately fluffed out her yellow skirts to take up the whole bench so he could not possibly sit beside her. She hadn't learned to simulate certain emotions for nothing, she lectured herself; she could evoke a calm demeanor she did not feel: slow words, deliberate movements, to project a placidity her trembling body and thudding heart could never feel with him nearby like this.

"I see your ankle is well, Susannah."

"Yes. Thank you."

He towered over her, very close, his big form throwing a shadow across her knees. "I don't know what he said to you, Susannah, but this is the only solution I could see for us now. Fleetwood told me yesterday Theo had finally figured out where you were and was coming here to drag you back, so I went to see him to inquire how you were and he thinks he bilked me into this plan. I couldn't allow him to come after you again any more than I could stand being away from you another day."

"How *is* West Woodhay and all the neighbors who like to visit there?" she threw at him, but her voice broke and betrayed her.

"They're right in the midst of planting and sheep shearing and the cherry crop is coming in," he answered somberly as if she had implied naught else. "After we get settled in the house at Kingston, I'll need to ride back and forth all summer to even have a chance to keep up with my usual duties and responsibilities there."

She dared to look up at him, though the sight of his rugged, angular features framed by windblown, sun-gilt copper hair and golden blue sky almost devastated the tattered remnants of her poise.

"You—and Theo—cannot be serious about this plan that the three of us cohabit in one house."

"He won't be there much, if at all. I told you there was no other way to keep you safe and off the streets with your financial situation."

"Off the streets!" she shouted and darted up past the big arm he flung out to halt her. By the sundial she spun to face him, her face furious, her yellow skirts rustled by the breeze and her own movements. He longed to hold her, lift her, carry her away to the lovely little house along the Thames he had leased for the summer; he longed to tell her that Theo, without knowing of their previous liaison, had promised to stay away and not plunge them farther in debt, or else this free Sloper ride out of looming debtors' prison would be swiftly halted.

"Calm down, sweet," he told her and lifted his arms again, as if to hold her or block her in.

"Calm down? You're trying to keep me off the streets, you say? How noble—how very magnanimous of you, Squire Sloper, the Younger. Trying to buy me like a street strumpet, you mean, to make it look to everyone like you're paying for me. I won't have it! Oh, granted I may go with you today because I can hardly impose on these honest, kind, people further, and I do not want to be trouble to my dear aunt or widowed mother indefinitely, but don't expect for one minute I'll do more than stop over at your Kingston-Upon-Thames *ménage à trois* nest. And you may sleep alone, I don't care what you got Theo to threaten me with!"

He wanted to seize her, but he steeled himself to resist the impulse. He could feel his pulse pounding, himself aching to embrace her, seduce her, master her, but he knew that look of fierce fury on her beautiful face. It evoked in him a raging response of domination, but because he loved her as deeply as he desired her, he controlled himself instead. Tonight, he told himself, and then tomorrow, alone with her in the lovely house at Kingston, rage would surely crash to ardent love again.

"Ask Anne to gather your things, Susannah," he said low. "We've only a three-mile ride so you'll be able to see the Hopsons again if you'd like later. And do not mistake the fact I treat you with kid gloves for indecision or weakness on my part. If you are not ready to leave in a half hour, I promise you I will carry you out of here like the wild little hoyden you act at times. There's more of Kitty Clive or your sister-in-law Charlotte in you all the time."

She glared up at him in an alluring defiance so tension-ridden, he almost pulled her back into the bushes to ravish her. He felt his body's usual immediate frenzied response to her almost naive, always devastating sensuality: His palms tingled to touch her, his lower belly muscles tightened; he took a huge breath.

"Fine," she ground out. "I'll be ready. I'll see your house and maybe sing a few songs for pennies to have money to keep me off the streets, and to get away from you and your best boon companion, Theo Cibber, but that's all!"

She swished past him so quickly his nostrils flared with her sweet scent. He whirled to watch her slender waist and shapely hips as she hurried away into the little ivy-cloaked house. Tonight, he assured himself again, she'd be all sweetness and honey in his arms. Never when he had touched her or come to her had she been anything but a wild and wonderful lover. Tonight!

Although the little house on the east bank of the Thames at Kingston was devastatingly charming, Susannah steeled herself not to love it. Two stories of buff stone with a dark slate roof, it lay in the shape of an L sheltering a variegated, rampant English rock garden and fish pond a little way from the main Portsmouth Road. Inside, it boasted a morning and an evening parlor, a fine open dining room overlooking the southward sweep of the Thames, a large back kitchen, and three servants' rooms downstairs. Above, a study, four bedrooms, and a sitting room opened onto a long hall the breezy length of the house. Doves cooed incessantly in the eaves; a family of calico cats bathed themselves in the sun outside: The house was as utterly seductive as Tenn Sloper.

For two days she spoke to him only in polite monosyllables, refusing to join him in the varied activities he proposed like riding horseback or walking along the river. She forced herself neither to look into his green eyes nor to sit with him, except across the dinner table when she had no choice. At night she lay tossing and turning in the room next to his, or staring at the darkened plaster wall that separated them, longing for his touch, tormented by his nearness.

But she'd be damned, she told herself far into the night, if she'd pay for Theo's bounty with her eager body in Tenn's bed, however she ached for him. One foolish look in his eyes and she'd already promised to stay here the summer to keep Theo at bay and protect her career, but she certainly had no intention of rewarding Tenn for playing Theo's game.

On the third day, Theo came and left in an hour's time, with hardly a word to her. She watched him ride jauntily away, and breathed a heartfelt sigh of relief that the lovely little house was free of his presence again.

"He won't be back for a week or so," Tenn said close behind her, and she jumped but did not turn to face him.

"Evidently you told him that everything here is to your liking, that I'm bedding with you," she accused.

"I told him I was pleased and found you everything I'd ever hoped, Susannah. And I told him I couldn't wait until tonight."

"I swear, you've become a fine actor, squire."

He came to stand so close behind her at the window she could feel the power he radiated, feel his deep voice when he spoke. "Not at all, sweet. I *am* looking forward to tonight, as your time is up."

Startled, she whirled, but could not move away as his hands lifted to the window frame behind to block her in. She fixed her gaze at the base of his throat where a little rim of russet hair peeked from his open, cravatless shirt collar. "What?" she faltered.

"Time's up. I've given you two full days of foolish sulking to work this out, but it appears to me you need a little shove. Tomorrow morning early I'm going to have to go to West Woodhay for a day or two, and I'm not leaving without so much as touching you. I don't care if you scream the house down. Now, go up and get a bonnet to keep the sun off your nose, as we're going to ride a little way up the river."

"No thank you!" she dared, even though her heart thrilled at his words. If he forced her, at least she could not blame her own weakness, and the mere thought of his hands and mouth along her skin made her go all hot and shaky. She gasped as he instantly picked her up off his feet.

"No hat. Fine. You can come this way then."

With her belly over his shoulder, the way he might lug a sack of wheat, he carried her squirming out in back past the small stone stables to where the six carriage horses grazed in a buttercup-flecked meadow. He approached one big gray, clucking to the beast over her shrill protests. He sat her up across the horse's broad withers and immediately leapt up astride directly behind her. From the stables, his driver George came running with a bridle and reins.

She balanced precariously, as though she might pitch off backwards, but when she allowed herself to lean into Tenn's arms, she felt safer. She'd never ridden, never had a horse, and had coldly put off his offers the last two days to teach her to ride. Now, in spite of her vow to hold him off, she was forced to accept his embrace as they jogged out of the field and down the grassy bank along the broad Thames.

Warm sun caressed her nose and right cheek, while everywhere her hips and flanks jounced rhythmically against him flamed even hotter. He shifted the reins to his other hand, leaning his wrist and fist casually on her mid-thigh while his upper arm bounced into her breast now and then. His breath stirred her tousled hair even as the gusty river breeze did. All too soon, the old treacherous feeling of rough velvet against her thighs made her blush with a heat that had nothing to do with the sun.

"What does your father think of all this?" she asked him, desperate for some sort of sane conversation to smother the alluring pull the man exerted on her.

"Of my living arrangements for the summer?" he asked, and his voice reverberated to her shoulder and hip when she was pressed into him. "He wants me to be happy but down deep, I suppose he believes this whole thing will explode in our faces."

"He really does know about us!" she gasped. "But he seemed not to at Kensington Palace."

"I've told him since. I believe he was shocked, yet he hid it well. He'll come around to full acceptance as I expect everyone to—including you—sooner or later. You see, my father was a one-woman man and nothing stood in his way once he found her. He adored her, my mother. The only thing he eventually admitted she ever did wrong was on her deathbed when she asked me to marry her friend Catherine."

Susannah stiffened slightly, and to accommodate her, he shifted his legs so tautly covered with tan-hued breeches. "But he did support you when you wanted to annul the marriage, you said. I'm certain it was hard on you all."

He sighed and the deeply poignant sound pierced her. "How sweet and understanding and supportive you can be, Susannah, when you're not fighting me or the dragons inside your head."

She turned to him but his mouth was so close to hers, she squirmed back. "Dragons? Such as what, pray tell."

"Fear of scandal. Of being found out. It took me a while to face that too, love, and I realize I have the advantages of being a character with a disreputable past already, and a man with money and social position to boot. I really believe, Susannah, if you cannot do without the theater, your career would eventually survive any unpleasantness with Theo, and it's obvious the man can easily be bought."

"But you don't know him," she protested, "not really. He does desperate, crazy things, destructive things for revenge and pride, especially when he's crossed. I believe I can keep him out of my bed easily enough, but I may never really force him out of my life."

"We'll find a way. Here, let's get down and walk a little bit."

He tethered the horse to a tree along a grassy bank. Two fishermen in a skiff rowed by and waved. And, although they had meant to walk, they sat instead on rocks at the water's edge while Tenn skipped flat stones and she wove and threw clover boats in to watch them bob away in the sluggish green current.

"Want to wade?" he asked suddenly in the companionable silence.

"I don't think so."

"It's not like you to be a coward, over water at least," he teased, "not since our swim at Bath. You know, if your sister-in-law Charlotte were here, she'd wade or swim. Anyone who will do what she really desires anytime she wishes, even under her father's long nose—and the king's—is a woman after my own heart."

"Her father is part of her trouble," Susannah said and launched another tiny boat of entwined clover. "She says she detests him, but she really doesn't, and she's always trying to please and emulate him though he treats her abysmally. I swear, it's his fault she swaggers about like a man half the time. Actually, as helpful as Father Cibber was in getting my acting career started, I believe he's ruined both Charlotte and Theo in different ways."

"And my mother tried her ignorant, damnedest to ruin my life by having me wed Catherine, and your father half talked you into marrying Theo, I take it."

She stared up, both surprised and enlightened by his sudden flash of insight. "Yes. It was my error in the end, but yes he did. Parents can really harm their children when they try to control their lives—even those as lofty as King George and the Prince of Wales."

"King George never got on with his own father, George I, either, who had locked up his poor mother in Ahlden for over thirty years until the day she died—and all for one brief indiscretion," Tenn added.

Their eyes held and he reached for her hand, crushing the clover she held. "I tell you, Susannah, if we ever have a child, we'll put all this shared knowledge to good use. You have thought of the possibility, I take it."

She blushed hot under the steady perusal of his eyes so green-gold in the sun that they put the buttercup meadows to shame. "I—well, actually after that first year with Theo, and then, the way we've been, I have begun to accept I never will have a child, and I suppose it's for the best the way things are."

He shot her a flash of white teeth in a disarming smile. "We'll see. We'll just see. After all, we're starting over tonight."

She tugged her hand back and stood to brush off her skirts. "You're very certain of yourself, squire. And, I assure you, I could never love or admire a man who would force me."

He stood too, a small frown creasing his brow under his hair all burnished copper in the slant of sun. "Would it really come to that after all we've had, Susannah? I love you and have from the first, and I believe that love will tame your inner rage to willing sweetness."

The almost poetic words stunned her to awkward silence. No more beautiful sentiment had ever graced a lover's lips on stage, she mused, but then there in the wings stood that lurking, ludicrous Theo Cibber to speak to her crudely of her bedding Tenn Sloper and to ruin her career as he had ruined her domestic life.

"I know you do not mean to fulfill your earlier threats of forcing me tonight anyway," she managed in a dazed voice and moved a step away. "Let's walk a ways back. You said we should walk."

Without another word but of the river scenes they saw, they strolled an hour's walk back, leading the big carriage horse.

The hours until supper flew by in time's swift-pulling current, as if the minutes were mere woven clover boats. Although the earlier antagonism she had felt for him had ebbed, the tension of ticking time drove her half mad as daylight fled.

By eight, Anne was out in back and the cook had left until seven the next morning. George and the footmen had gone into a tavern three miles away in town. Susannah had refused a moonlit walk with Tenn in the garden; her hands had begun to tremble and her heart to thud very loudly at his steady perusal of her across the parquet card table between them.

"I do believe that walk and all the sun today tired me," she heard herself say as he won another round of Hazard. "I believe I'll bid you good night and leave you now."

"Fine," his low words floated to her unbelieving ears. "I'll give you twenty minutes."

She knew her mouth dropped open, and she blushed fiercely despite the brazen sun color that had turned her pale skin rosy. She stood, pushing back her chair with her knees.

"No, Tenn. I—I deny you. I will not give into Theo's nefarious plans to rent me to you."

"Nonsense. My arranging this has nothing to do with Theo's damn plans, one way or the other, and everything to do with ours. We've been lovers, and very eager, passionate ones, I might add, for almost two years Susannah, and nothing's changed except we've had to adapt some of our circumstances. Actually, I find my bed upstairs in that windswept country bedroom a more charming setting than a few we've shared, such as my carriage or the settee in the parlor at St. James'—"

"Good night, Tenn." She delivered the lines as emphatically as she could. "I will be up early to bid you farewell in the morning, but please don't do anything you'll regret tonight."

Her exit, she assured herself, was poised and confident. She did not run up the stairs nor slam her bedroom door as she wanted. Something fluttered very low in her stomach and feathered along her thighs at the memory of his intimate touch and words today, but she beat the feelings down. She must not, could not, give in to his desires now, nor her own desperate need for him. As she had done the other two nights, she shot the bolt on her bedroom door.

She glanced at the clock on her bureau as she disrobed, loosed her hair, and bathed. Although Anne helped her dress each morning, she had never summoned her here at night, but now she thought of doing so. But she wore only her thin nightshift, and it would be foolhardy to go downstairs to seek Anne to only appear to be offering herself to Tenn if she should meet him on the stairs. She was certain she hadn't yet heard him come up, so perhaps he had walked outside by himself in his anger.

She stared at herself in the mirror while she brushed the curly auburn tresses that fanned to her shoulder blades in back. The cool wash water had calmed her; she felt better. Perhaps now that she had clearly made her point, when Tenn came back from West Woodhay, she would be ready to be a bit more trusting and friendly to him.

She jumped and dropped her brush into the porcelain bowl of water at his low voice on the other side of her door. "Susannah, may I come in now?"

In the mirror, wide, startled topaz eyes stared from a pinkish face framed by tumbled curls. She darted for her robe. "No, Tenn. Good night, I said."

"And I told you, my sweet, time's up and I meant it."

She gasped soundlessly as she watched the door latch lift, then bounce. "Unlock the door, Susannah, or I'll break it. I meant what I said earlier—all of it."

"I'm not giving in to some plan you and Theo hatched!" she yelled.

"Damn Theo! But you are giving in to *me*!"

She jumped backward against the wall as he obviously crashed his shoulder into her door once, twice. The frame shuddered; the old-fashioned latch jumped.

"Tenn, stop it!"

"Then open it!"

She'd never seen him like this or faced him angry. He had always seemed controlled and alluring, getting his way through his magnetic charm. "No!" she shrieked, as the door cracked wide open and he strode in, slamming it so hard behind him the walls shook.

He wore shirt and breeches, but he was barefooted. His white silk shirt which he had torn along the arm seam, split open in a low V to flaunt coppery chest hair. Immediately, he was across the room, lifting her into his iron arms.

"No, I said! I won't!" She kicked out at him once, but then her legs flailed only air. His hands were hard on her waist and hips as he carried her. A delicious tingle of almost erotic fear raced through every nerve as he deposited her roughly on her back in the middle of her bed. She kicked out at him wildly as he threw himself down beside her, but she only succeeded in opening her robe and lifting the hem of her thin nightshift up above her knees.

She tried to turn her head, but one heavy arm lay across her spread tresses, imprisoning her. She meant to push him away, but one arm was trapped between them and he held the other.

"I like you wild," he rasped as his hard eyes raked her, "but I don't like this shift between me and what you've been wanting me to take all day." His hand cupped a heaving breast through the material, then stroked heavily over taut rib cage and flat belly to tug her lace hem upward while he trailed tantalizing fingers along her bare flesh under the nightshift.

"No, Tenn," she managed, but her voice had gone as silky and shaky as the rest of her. "You won't like it."

He grinned wickedly, then shouted a quick laugh. "My sweet angel, I assure you I'm liking it very well so far, and it's going to get much, much better."

She glared up at him defiantly. Drat the devil! He was actually enjoying this, as sure as he was about the end result. She drew in a quick, involuntary gasp as he bent to cover one bared breast with a wet, flicking tongue.

"Mm, don't," she murmured entirely too breathlessly.

He lifted his copper head. "I'd like to start with your luscious lips, sweet, but I'm afraid my little untamed vixen would bite me. This way, I'll let you worry about that."

His teeth gently teased a peaked nipple, then moved lower. She closed her eyes, desperate against the wild assault on her senses. Now his free hand and mouth roamed her soft, exposed flesh at will. Already she felt the pulling tide of passion that would take her under: Her brain tormented her with lightning quick imagined scenes of her under him, her legs spread wide in blatant invitation. She breathed erratically, moaned incoherently, and opened her thighs mindlessly for him when his bewitching fingers merely stroked her for admission to her waiting, shameless warmth.

"No," she gasped out, startled at her own bitter tone.

"No, you're as bad as Theo!"

His rugged, passion-glazed face, lifted inches to stare down at her. His finely chiselled lower lip set hard; rakish, russet brows crashed to obscure narrowed eyes. His fingers stopped, pulled back.

He was up off the bed instantly, tucking in his rumpled shirt. "I can love an actress and a coward—even a liar, Susannah—but not a hyprocrite who doesn't know what the hell she wants. And don't bother to get up to see me off tomorrow!"

He was across the room and out the door before she could think or react. The door banged behind him, then his own door down the hall. For a moment she just lay still with her robe awry under her and her shift ruffled up around her neck, trying to remember what she had said last. Theo! Oh heavens, she'd actually compared him to Theo!

She covered herself and sat unmoving on her haunches in the middle of her rumpled bed where they had just lain. Slowly, emotion washed into her stunned mind: regret; loss; unfulfilled passion, which lapped higher, threatening to drown her. A jagged tear ran down each sun-blushed cheek and dripped forlornly off her chin. Next door she heard Tenn thudding about, the clink of a glass, the creak of his bed. She stood on quivering legs at last to blow out her two bedside candles, and lean against the window set ajar to catch the sweet, dancing river breezes.

Pale moonlight dusted the scene below with silvered shade, and glittered in the twist of flowing river down the gray sweep of lawn. How otherworldly it all seemed, so ethereal and magic, like a stage backdrop for *A Midsummer Night's Dream*, or some heavenly escape into timeless fantasy.

She gasped one sob, then stopped. Here within her grasp, no matter what mistakes she had ever made, was such a world with Tenn: a dream world, a land where an impossibly beautiful love could all be true if only she would step out onto the stage and let it be. Let Theo grimace and cavort in darkened wings; let the threatening audience shriek catcalls or walk out shocked and angered. The script in her heart said she loved Tenn only, and she knew that better than any pretended passion she had ever mastered.

She dashed water on her teary cheeks and crossed the room in darkness. Her ruined door creaked; the corridor running the length of the house stood dim with but a single lamp on the table farther down. Her heart pounded so terribly hard that it drowned out her timid rapping on his door. Her hand touched the latch and lifted it. Perhaps she had heard wrong and he had gone out, she reasoned. The door swung inward. Moonlight etched the room: table, chairs, bureau, bed. She saw his big head and shoulders lifted against his plumped white pillows with dark oak headboard behind.

She meant to ask if she could enter, but her voice caught in her throat so she stepped in and closed the door quietly behind her. He leaned on one elbow now, naked as far as she could tell, with a white sheet pulled to his waist. His eyes glinted silver for one moment.

She moved barefooted to the rug next to his bed, while his eyes, which she could no longer discern, stared at her. The silence between them shattered her fears. The room seemed very warm, but the breeze from his moonstruck window cooled her.

"I'm sorry for what I said, how I've been," her voice melded with the breeze stirring her bounteous hair and the hem of her shift as she untied and dropped her robe on the floor behind her. "Please forgive me. I love you—I want to love you now—"

He still did not move other than to lift the sheet completely back to uncover his powerful, sprawled body all tantalizingly shadowy. Then he bent one knee upward.

Her hands and legs trembled as she untied the ribbons down the front of her nightshift, then shrugged out of the wispy garment, which clung tauntingly on its way down to a splash of white about her ankles.

Her skin looked purest alabaster as she bent one knee on the edge of his bed and he reached one long arm up for her. Soft flesh pressed to hard; she fell against him with breathtaking impact as he rolled her on him, then over into the depths of the bed.

Her kiss was as hungry, as ravishing, as his. Boldly, her palms stroked and caressed the muscular length of shoulders, back, ribs, and hips, even as he did hers. She fluttered wild kisses down his stretch of throat, nipping at the taut sinew of his neck while his brazen hands roamed her intimately everywhere. She revelled in the soaring passion; she moved enticingly against him; her legs writhed on either side of his flanks silvered by moonlight as he pressed her hips down into the huge, soft bed and entered her.

She could hear her rapid intake of breaths as incoherent thoughts jangled to wild feelings. He leaned a shoulder next to her head to ravish her mouth, then reached down to lift her slender ankles up across his chest to rest on his shoulders. He knelt against her now, thrusting into her until she moaned in a raging rapture she had never known.

He was speaking, saying something to her at last and holding momentarily still, just as she was ready to throw herself over the beckoning cliff; but now he pulled her back to balance on the precipice.

"Never, never do this to us again, my love. Our time together is precious. We can't let my money come between us—or your pride. You're mine. Always will be. Now tell me again why you brought your beautiful ivory body to my bed tonight. Tell me—" he crooned while he set up a rocking movement that shoved her toward the thrilling brink.

"I love you. Tenn, I belong to you. I—I want you so."

"To do this?"

"Yes. Yes!"

"Love me, Susannah. I belong to you and you to me—"

The delicious torment went on and on as he pushed, then pulled her back from the edge with verbal and physical demands she revelled in. Finally, finally when she could bear no more, he forced a demanding pace that swept them both entwined over the edge of love's sweet rage, which she had never fathomed could exist in any distant dreamworld or this one of moonlit flesh.

Chapter Sixteen

Susannah's halcyon summer of 1737 living with Tenn in the river house at Kingston-Upon-Thames drifted by them until there was no more of it to cherish. Theater rehearsals began; the high and mighty of the land returned to the city from country estates or European jaunts. Parliamentary commissions reassembled, and fashionable carriages with liveried drivers and footmen crammed the streets of Georgian London once again. In just three days Susannah and Tenn would leave their rural haven behind to plunge again into their hectic, public city lives, but today they had only come into town for varied businesses, shopping, and a visit to her sister-in-law Charlotte, whom Susannah had heard was ill.

"You'd think it was the height of the season already," Tenn groused as he stuck his copper head out the window of their carriage to survey the jam of carriages, barouches, cabriolets, and even a mail coach, in and along the crowded shopping area of the Strand. "Londoners' manners are abysmal! There's a damned woman ahead who's just traipsing from shop to shop while her carriage crawls along beside her!" he added and sat back so hard onto the leather seat beside her that she bounced.

"Now, my love," Susannah soothed and leaned over to

kiss his cheek, "you're only being a bear today because you're used to riding clear along the Thames bank without another soul in sight."

His green eyes snagged with hers in the dimness of the carriage, and he flashed her a guilty smile while he lifted a long arm around her shoulders to pull her against his side. "And the fact I can't stand for our lovely sabbatical to be over," he said, and his other big hand squeezed her knee through her sky-blue brocade gown. She swayed across his chest as the carriage jolted off again. Their lips met lingeringly as though the rampant love that had consumed them all summer were tended and new again.

"Bow Street, squire!" George's voice boomed down to them. "Shall we go north to the Drury then?"

"I'll get out and walk," Susannah put in quickly to Tenn. "It's only two blocks, and then you won't be late for your meeting with Walpole. Besides, it's lovely weather."

"All right, but I want Frederick to tag along. I'll fetch you from the theater at noon. And don't take any guff from Fleetwood or Theo. You know, I really don't like this plan of yours at all."

"My love, I can hardly avoid them as I am going into rehearsal next week anyway, and would have been already at it if Theo had had his way with his foul attempt to steal another of Kitty Clive's parts again. He promised me once he'd never repeat that earlier fiasco, but when he scents free publicity, however damaging, he's a lunatic."

"George! Pull up here!" Tenn called out the window, then held her wrist a moment. "Still, my sweet, be careful. I approve of your ideas of independence and equality, but others may not."

She laughed musically and darted another quick kiss on his cheek before he could react. "Don't think for a moment I believe that, Tenn Sloper," she chided gently. "You may believe in my equality in your bed, but you'd like to hide me away in the country under your lock and key without my taking up my career again, and don't I know it!"

He grinned, then brazenly pinched her bottom, despite her full skirts, as Frederick opened the door and she alighted near the brick curb of bustling Bow Street off the Strand. She waved her gloved hand at Tenn as the big carriage rolled away.

She felt almost the elegant lady as she set off northward toward the theater at a leisurely pace with Tenn's young footman Frederick several steps behind. After all, most fashionable women shoppers trailed lackeys or servants of some sort: maids, footmen, carriers, even a turbanned or white-wigged blackamoor or two for show. Today, Susannah wore a new, stylish blue gown with buff-hued mantua Tenn had purchased for her at Anne's parents' shop in Malden, and her purse was no doubt as heavy with coins as most ladies here. She had come around to accepting his gifts and his money without quite so much guilt or protest; indeed, she had come around at last to totally trusting him as much as she loved him.

Besides, she told herself as she walked around a beggar with a monkey on his shoulder, through her advice, Tenn had begun to make some worthwhile investments in the arts in London: He subsidized a young painter they had found at Vauxhall in July, and they had made several anonymous contributions to Maestro Handel, whose debts and misfortunes, notwithstanding royal favor, had been a great burden lately. The dear old genius would never have accepted their charity outright, and besides, Theo would have thrown a raving fit had he found out. Still, she planned to go home to Little Wild Court to live and support herself on her own salary this autumn, despite the offer of Tenn's bounty. That salary was one of the reasons she had to see Charles Fleetwood today.

She read the painted, dangling shop signs and perused symmetrical displays of goods in windows as she went along: a Drapery that sold bolts of rich materials and men's cravats; aromatic snuff shops; Chair and Cabinet Makers; Dealers in Spirituous Liquors; and numerous Bauble Shops. In the bow window of a Men's Furnishing Shop, a jaunty peacock-blue velvet tricorn edged with lace caught her eye, and she went in to buy it for her irrepressible sister-in-law Charlotte, whom they were calling on later today.

She could tell Frederick felt better carrying something, and she chatted happily away to him about how she and Squire Sloper would redecorate the house at Kingston if it were really theirs. But when she entered the theater through the familiar back actors' door, a rush of poignant memories assailed her and she fell silent. She sent Frederick out into the pit to watch the rehearsal and stood backstage soaking it all in, awestruck anew. Her love for Tenn and her love for the theater were the only true passions she had ever known, she mused. The clatter of carpenters putting up a scaffold, the brushing scuffle of dancers' feet from a practice room overhead, the lingering smell of brimstone and resin someone had lit for a fire and lightning scene. It was all magic!

The familiar voices of James Quin and Kitty Clive in rehearsal on the stage floated to her: lines from *Hamlet*, the play with the part of Ophelia that Theo had recently tried to publically wrest from Clive's possession. Susannah passed the now empty Green Room where "Black Mac" Macklin had fatally stabbed poor Thomas Hallam over two years ago. She would not even go upstairs to her locked tiring room today, as it would make her miss all her costumes she would have to work so hard to replace this year. Hoping to find Fleetwood without Theo this time of day, she stopped at the door of the Manager's Office and lifted her hand to knock. Inside, voices were raised in anger: Fleetwood's and an unknown, strident man's voice.

"Be damned to you and Cibber then, sir," the voice

yelled. "First you advertise for properties of new playwrights in *The Courant*, but when a man of genius falls on your front door, you rip his dramatic creations to shreds and cast aspersions to boot. Damn the Drury, sir, and may you and Theo Cibber both go to—to your debtors!"

The door yanked open and a rail-thin man with peruke askew shot out, nearly toppling her. As if cradling a babe, he held to himself the shuffled, rumpled pages of a script. He thudded off down the hall screeching more muffled imprecations and disappeared.

She glanced through the still open door into the familiar Manager-Treasurer's Office with its distinctive red leather walls and red leather armchairs studded with brass nails, storage cabinets for scripts, and worn, woven Dutch mat on the floor. Fleetwood, looking fatter than ever, produced a silver flask from a table drawer and tilted his head back to drink. Instead, his eyes widened, and he choked, coughed, then sputtered at the sight of her.

"Damn, Sus—annah!" he hacked as she stepped in.

"Are you all right? I didn't mean to startle you after that disgruntled playwright flew out of here."

"They're a penny a hundred," he coughed out. "Damn, for a moment there, I thought you'd materialized like that silly backstage—ghost."

"The man in gray?" Susannah asked as she stepped even farther in. "Has he been seen again clanking his sword about to ruin rehearsals?"

"Never mind," he rasped out more quietly at last. "I see—you're flesh and blood well enough, as always. I take it you're not looking for your husband."

"No. I assume he's at the rehearsal with a prompter's book or some such."

"He and Clive are cats and dogs again over the latest fight in the press. Damn glad you refrained from getting into the fray."

"Then if you're glad, perhaps I don't have to pay this silly five-pound fine for refusing to show up at rehearsals for a role that rightfully belongs to Kitty," she inserted adroitly.

"Rules are rules, and I'll not have any of my articled actors or actresses willfully breaking them. Willful about rules, that's been you from the start, my girl—a female iconoclast if I ever saw one."

"Because I feel the theater is an art form and deserves to be treated as such, instead of as just another cheap moment's amusement like rope dancing or fire swallowing, you mean?" she challenged.

Fleetwood wiped his wet mouth with the back of his plump hand and stood behind his desk. "Now, isn't that just like a woman—inconsistent as hell," he accused. "If the theater's to be worshipped as some ethereal art form, why should you be paid one groat for serving at the shrine, madam? Tell me that!"

Susannah was instantly angry. She had come to speak reasonably; to merely ask for a fairer salary for herself and for all actresses who were grossly underpaid, compared to what even some of the minor male actors earned; and that she be allowed to draw at least part of her salary herself, however meager it was. But now Fleetwood was insulting her as vilely as Theo had.

"Now that's typical male inconsistency," she shot back. "An art form needs to be fully supported, and actors and actresses who promote its cause should be fairly compensated. If we expect thespians to be respected in this society, their salaries should reflect that respect. I daresay, hack doctors at Bath probably earn more and are, therefore, more believable!"

She could tell he was furious. His round face flushed pink; his jowls actually quivered. "Mrs. Cibber, you *will* pay your fine for insubordination, and quickly too, before I assess another for your female rebelliousness! And you will *not* take on the duties of a man to preach to me salaries or policy—or respect! However much a blackguard Theo Cibber may be, you are in his charge. I believe we have had this discussion previously, madam, but I tell you this is the last time for it."

He flopped back down in his seat, puffing at his outburst while she stared contemptuously at him. She placed her gloved hands on the tall table and leaned slightly forward. "Mr. Fleetwood, I came here today to pay my fine—for doing something you just said you're very glad I did in not agreeing to take Kitty's part away from her. If that doesn't illustrate masculine inconsistency, even illogic, I don't know what does. Therefore, I see it is futile to pursue my fair and logical female cause here."

She darted her hand into her drawstring silk purse and grandly flourished a handful of gold coins, which she counted out noisily on the table.

"Sweet heaven, but Tenn Sloper has his hands full with you in more ways than one!" Fleetwood yelled after her as she moved dramatically to the door. "No doubt that's his money now, as it could never be Theo's," he sneered as he saw her startled face. "Ah, surprised are we, Mrs. Cibber? Don't fear; I'd say the news of your—ah—partnership with my old racetrack comrade Tenn Sloper has not yet hit the London papers at least. Not yet, though I daresay every theater rumor mill is churning with the titillating news that your husband's turned you over to him."

"Every rumor mill," she repeated, so stunned and furious she could hardly get the words out. Then people knew all about her and Tenn! She'd never imagined that, never once thought that people, even those as snide and illogical as Fleetwood, could know. Enraged, she stepped out and slammed the door.

Susannah stood breathing hard in the corridor. She'd made a terrible mess of what she had meant to be a civil, fair request to Fleetwood as legal patentee of the theater.

She only hoped that she hadn't made a terrible mess of her career, as well as Tenn's, by their happy summer liaison. And now, if everyone knew. . . . Her jaw set hard, she hurried down the hall past the Green Room to fetch Frederick and be gone before she ran into Theo.

"Cibber!" an unmistakable voice clipped out from the Green Room. It was Kitty Clive, but Susannah hardly needed her taunting after what she'd just been through. "A truce for a minute. Hell, come back here, as I'm waving the white flag, Cibber!"

Susannah walked slowly back to lean her shoulder on the Green Room door frame and glance in. Only Kitty, sitting with her feet up on the andiron of the cold hearth, was in the room.

"So—the mad Ophelia unless I'm mistaken," Susannah said quietly, and Kitty flashed her a quick smile, which flaunted her distinctive front chipped tooth.

"Mad—and supposedly passionately in love with Prince Hamlet, the stupid fool. Pox on Ophelia, as I don't plan to drown myself over any man ever."

Susannah smiled tautly, despite herself. The little, awkward silence between them lengthened.

"So, Cibber, I hear you've found a prince of your own to love passionately."

"Do you mean to taunt me for it, Kitty? If so, I'll be off as I'm already fed up with innuendos."

"Hell, Cibber," Kitty insisted and sat up straight to swing her feet to the floor. "I'd say you finally wised up on that poxy son of a bitch you were daft enough to marry. He ruined his first wife Janey's life, so maybe, just maybe now, he won't ruin yours. Only, don't sell the slippery bastard short. He thrives on scandal, upheaval, and sports a yellow streak clear up his back that makes him love to torture others."

Susannah realized she was actually nodding vehemently as Kitty spoke. Suddenly, both appreciative and appalled, she turned away from Kitty's burning stare.

"You and me agreeing on anything—a devil of a good joke, Cibber—but I'm out and out beholding to you for keeping off my Ophelia role, that's all."

"Ophelia's yours, Kitty. I've got to go now. I've just got to go."

But she was not to be spared what she dreaded most. Her failure to succeed with Fleetwood and the fact that everyone seemed to know about her affair with Tenn all paled when she stepped outside with Frederick on her heels to see Theo and Tenn standing by the waiting carriage in a loud, heated discussion. She halted so abruptly that Frederick hit into her before she pushed him back into the alleyway as Theo's shrill words pierced the air.

"But I hardly thought some sort of extended arrangement was part of our *ex officio* agreement, Tenn. Needless to say, privileged, well-heeled gentlemen of your class usually tire of a lady in question once they've sampled her sweet wares, but not with you, eh? I really must tell you, I need my dear wife back as a comfort at my side and in my bed *ad perpetuam*."

"I would suggest you dispense with the lies and histrionics, Theo," Tenn's deep voice rumbled to her where she stared at the two men's profiles. Tenn towered over Theo so that it looked to her that he could easily crush him in one blow. "You and I both know your liaison with Susannah is over *ad perpetuam*, Theo, and you're just lucky I have stayed willing this long to put up with your machinations. It's no secret to anyone who's been one hour in London lately that you've been spending money way over your head again in the brothels and bagnios of Covent Garden, when part of our original agreement was you'd do nothing to endanger the meager holdings I got out of debt for you and Susannah last spring."

"Egads, how dare you lecture me thusly after your

morally reprehensible behavior all summer, Squire Sloper! Either you will apologize forthwith and increase my benefits as I just requested or, *ipso facto*, I am insisting Susannah be delivered to my home and my bed at once!"

To her dismay, Susannah noted a crowd gathering. Despite her first impulse to hide herself, so no one would know she had overheard, she stepped forward. Susannah heard her own sharp voice before she knew she would speak; she saw her fist raised to shake at Theo's face just before Tenn lifted him by his natty yellow brocade coat lapels and strode toward the brick wall of the theater to pin him aloft against it.

"Susannah! He's a madman!" Theo yelled as soon as he saw her. "Tell him to loose me! Fetch help!"

Tenn's big head snapped around. Instinctively, she jumped a step back at the fury that blazed on his face. "Susannah! What the hell . . . get in the carriage and wait for me!"

"Tenn, you wait. I know he's low and infuriating, but you can't just do it this way in the public street with people watching."

"Can't I?" he roared. "I should have long ago!"

She seized Tenn's arm even as he pulled it back to pummel Theo, who seemed to shrivel against the wall. His buckled feet dangled; his expensive wig twisted awry; he writhed like the flopping fish Susannah had seen pulled from the shallow Thames at Kingston all summer.

Tenn's bent arm hesitated, and he let Theo slide down the rough wall. "Now you listen to me, Cibber," he threatened low. "You suggested, you abetted my relationship with Susannah, and you've profited prettily from it. Our mutual benefits will continue as long as she wishes it so. You're just damned lucky I don't treat you the way you deserve, or cut you adrift to your creditors either. So stay clear of Susannah as you promised before or, I swear, you won't be in one piece to rot away in debtors' prison.

Do you understand?"

"Please Tenn, let's just go," she interrupted. "The crowd . . . people are staring."

"I told you to get in the carriage, Susannah. This is between Theo and me," he growled at her, then turned back to Theo.

Furious at them both, she shoved her way through the small crowd, which unfortunately included several people from the theater, flounced around the far side of the carriage, and crossed the street before glancing back. Frederick had evidently stayed behind to help guard his master, and George and the other footman leaned away from her, watching the fray from their perches on the driver's seat. Just as well. She was sick of dratted men ordering her around, thinking they owned her or her career: Fleetwood, Theo, Tenn, father years ago, King George—all of them. Let them argue over who possessed her and be damned to them all. She was her own woman and next week she had a career to care for again, the career that would eventually make her famous and financially self-sufficient enough to be completely independent. It was Tenn she wanted eternally, of course, but she'd meet him as an equal in all ways and never let him think she needed him because she was too poor or weak or frightened.

She hurried north toward High Holborn, where Charlotte now lived at a new address that Susannah had never visited. Let Tenn and Theo brawl in a public street; she'd not lend her presence to such a scene. Charlotte always made her feel better, and afterward she would hire a sedan chair and return to her house on Little Wild Court until Tenn came to apologize; or since Tenn knew Charlotte's location, perhaps he'd come directly there after her, much chastened that she had just left him behind.

As soon as she turned right down Newton Street, the houses seemed to lean inward, all dingy and tattered. The shallow drainage ditch in the center of the street stank where ragged children splashed about in it. Women called obscenities from protruding stories overhead, and no proper vehicles rumbled along with passengers or wares.

Susannah halted and looked swiftly about. This was the street her brother Tom had written that Charlotte had moved to, but she was appalled by how wretched the neighborhood had instantly become, as if stepping into another time or place from the elegant shopping and theater area several blocks over. Perhaps she should never have come without Tenn, and she should head back home until he joined her. But no. She was not some weak, helpless woman who needed the so-called, self-dubbed logical, strong men about before she could make a move.

"Excuse me," she called to a slovenly, frazzled appearing woman who leaned passively against a wattle and wood building, "but I'm searching for Newton Close just off Newton Street. I'm certain this is Newton Street."

"Got a copper for a poor widow?" the woman drawled. Huge dark circles reverberated from vacant brown eyes. The smell of stale gin and sweat nearly choked Susannah even at this distance.

"Tell me where Newton Close is, then," Susannah insisted and lifted a gloved hand to her nose.

"Down there—on th' left."

Susannah threw a coin at the woman's feet and hurried on as the swarm of gutter urchins rushed the woman, then pounded after Susannah screeching for coins. On the left, as the woman had said, a narrow close twisted away between two filthy walls. Gathering her blue skirts tightly, Susannah darted in.

The children did not pursue her down the crooked close, and soon her thudding heart drowned out their cries. She should go back to find Tenn, her inner voice told her, but after all, she could handle this. Newton Close off Newton Street, her brother had written, so surely that was here. And if Charlotte were really ill in a place like this, she would need her. It was a warm day, and windows above gaped open to spill out a mingled cacophony of babies' cries and arguments, smells of onions and fish, and a slop pail that barely missed her gathered skirts.

"Charlotte! Charlotte Charke, are you there? It's Susannah!" she called upward in a shaky voice.

An old hag as thin as porcelain appeared above. Lank gray hair dangled around a toothless face as she leaned out. "Susannah is it, dearie?" she wheezed, then hacked into her hand. "You lookin' for that saucy baggage what dresses like a man? That one?"

"Yes, that one. Could you please tell me where to find her? I'd like her to come out."

"Used to live in the garret, used to even sit on the roof, she did," the old woman managed and pointed skyward before her frail frame shuddered with coughing again. "She's my daughter now. Up the stairs from that door," she added and disappeared.

Susannah stared up where the woman had been. It could be a trap, and she was here with a purse of Tenn's money for the mere picking in this vile neighborhood. Memories of being trapped, abused, and nearly prostituted in Covent Garden by the infamous Moll King assailed her and she hesitated with one foot in the open doorway. She had better leave: This was no wiser than arguing with Fleetwood today, or ever trusting Theo, or loving Tenn so completely.

"Susannah, is it really you?"

She stepped back out to look up. Charlotte's chalk-white face framed by coal-black hair had joined the old woman's at the window. As ludicrous as it looked, it was obvious the bone-thin old woman supported the girl.

"Char! I'll be right up."

She tried not to breathe in the fetid air as she dashed up

the creaking, narrow stairs. Three crooked doors opened from the first landing, three from the second. She had stood there only a moment breathing hard when the skinny old woman opened a door and a clawlike hand motioned her in. At the threshold, she saw Charlotte sitting up on a sort of pallet under the window across the tiny room.

"Char! Char, you look awful!" Susannah knelt at the edge of the straw mattress, took Charlotte's hands, then pulled the frail body against her to cradle the shoulders. The usually snappy, dark eyes looked glazed; the saucy face was stark white and very still for one always so animated.

"Devil take you for that sweet compliment, sister-in-law," Char's wan voice retorted, and her upper lip lifted in an attempt at a smile. "Devil—you know, I was thinking to be handed over to old Satan if I died, but you look like an angel."

"Char, I didn't know you were so ill. Does Father Cibber know?"

"Him—he doesn't give a damn, hasn't since I shot up the neighbors' chimneys dressed in his clothes when I was young. Girls aren't allowed to be like their fathers, you know."

"You have a fever. I'm going to take you with me."

"I'm too weak to walk. The money's gone from my gown I sold from the river fête at the palace. Father would kill me for that too."

"But how long have you been sick—and here? Have you been fed?"

"Old Bess here thinks she's my mother, so what she begs she gives me some of. I had fish and biscuits yesterday, I think."

"Bess," Susannah addressed the old woman, "could you please send a boy on the street or someone for a hackney or a sedan chair? I'm going to take Charlotte away with me, and I'll give you some coins for caring for her."

"No, she can't go. She's sick. She's my daughter—my son too."

"Heavens, Char, I can't believe this," she whispered down at the girl. "I swear, but it's a miracle you've survived your crazy antics this long, and now this!"

"Don't scold me, Susannah, please," the raspy voice whispered. "You're the only one who cares. I can't help it how I am; I always loved you so for letting me be me and still being my friend."

Tears blurred Susannah's eyes. "I know Char. I—I bought you a fine peacock-blue tricorn today—lace and all—but Tenn's footman has it," she said in a rush before she stopped and bit her lip.

"Oh, Tenn's footman, is it? Pox on it, I knew you loved the handsome devil that night at Kensington, Susannah. I could just tell what people said was true."

"People said? I'm sorry, Char."

Charlotte tugged back from Susannah's supportive embrace and struggled to sit up straighter against the dirty wall. The delicate raven brows crashed down over dark eyes. "You silly, stupid, cowardly goose! Be glad! Be happy, Susannah! I told you to do what you knew was right, Theo be damned! Go after what you want, I told you—"

"Char!" Susannah caught the frail body to her as she slumped forward. "Please Bess, please, go on down to the street and send someone for a sedan chair!" Susannah begged the hovering woman. "Please, if Char is your daughter, she needs you to do that. I'll pay you. Go on now."

When the woman just retreated to a rickety chair in the corner and glared at her, Susannah laid Charlotte back on the pallet and stood. The girl's eyes flickered open. "I just get dizzy, Susannah," she whispered. "You've got to do what you've got to do, just like me, devil take them all."

"I'll be right back, Char. I'm going for help."

She ran down the steps and out into the narrow close. She lifted her skirts to run; her heeled shoes rattled strangely on the cobbles. The rabble of street urchins still clustered at the mouth of the alley as though its inner precincts were forbidden to them.

"Get away! Let me through," she ordered.

But several grabbed at her skirts and one yanked her silk purse strings. "No! Don't! Find me a sedan chair and then I'll give you a coin. No!"

She tripped into one small grubby boy with sticklike arms upstretched. The gin-sodden woman from down the street staggered up, screeching for another copper. Someone from a window above shouted an obscenity, and then a tall, bearded man blocked her path.

"A fine lady come a callin'," he sneered, his long arms spread to block her in against the building. "Back, back, whelps! This fine lady's lookin' for the Raven and no other, right, you fancy slattern? Here, gimme that!"

He ripped her purse from her grasp even as the crowd of urchins scattered. One huge, dirty hand pressed Susannah back into the wall while the other dared to instantly yank her skirts up as he pressed hard against her.

"No! No!" she screamed even as the woman beat feebly on the man's big back from behind. He reeked of garlic; she couldn't move or breathe.

"Gotta give you your money's worth," he told her, then leered down at her even as the fierce rumbling shook the world and the scarlet scene that whirled her down into its vortex exploded.

Thundering horses, heavy wheels, and a massive carriage crowded very close. The man assaulting her flew back; a fast fist cracked into the lout's jaw to throw him away. Tenn! Tenn and George and Frederick, fists flying as they hit the man and the crowd screamed away and coins spewed everywhere until only the carriage and Tenn loomed over her still. Finally, silence reigned.

"Susannah, damn it! Did he hurt you?"

"No—I—just a little. He took my money and then tried—tried—"

"All right. This time you are getting in my carriage when I tell you to!" He picked her up. His iron embrace felt so good. She clung to him.

"Tenn, you have to go back for Char. She's in that little close on the third floor with some crazy old woman. She's penniless and sick. I went to get help."

"I will. Frederick! You and George stay here with Mrs. Cibber and beat off anyone who tries the carriage—and tie Mrs. Cibber if she attempts to get out!"

She leaned back against the padded black leather seat and closed her eyes to stop the dizziness and the rage—not at Tenn but at herself for allowing such a sordid scene, much worse than what she had blamed him for earlier today. Always, he had rescued her from others and from her own foolish steps to destruction. In a very real way she did not want to admit, she was every bit as willful and foolish as poor Charlotte.

Her eyes shot open to see both George and Frederick standing guard by the open carriage door, but no one was visible up and down the street. It was a cruel world, this purportedly refined and civilized society of King George where one could take but a few steps and go from propriety to depravity on London's streets; where both harlots and wives could be bought and sold and owned; where scandal was more revered than art or honor. But now that she knew the way of the world and knew her own weaknesses and strengths, she was more convinced than ever she could conquer it despite the pitfalls, snares, and traps it offered.

Footsteps, Tenn's voice. Charlotte looked so fragile in his arms as he placed her on the seat across from Susannah and climbed in.

"The scene back there was pure theater," he said low. "That old crone screeched I was abducting her only son, no less."

Susannah leaned forward to chafe Charlotte's wrists as the door slammed and they pulled away. "Tenn, I cannot thank you enough for everything," she said, her eyes on the girl's bluish, flickering lids. "She's always been so strong. Thank heavens we came today, and you to rescue us both."

"A hero," Charlotte said so low they hardly caught her words. "A rogue of a green-eyed, damn Sir Lancelot hero. Look out, Susannah—I already love him too!"

"Hush, Char. Just sleep."

"You told her you love me?" Tenn asked.

"She's wiser than I am, Tenn. She's known for ages."

"She's asleep, Susannah. Sit back over here and we'll cover her with my coat. We'll take her to Kingston with us and you and Anne can nurse her for a few days, as we can hardly trust her brother or father to care for her." He spread his mussed and torn frock coat over the girl, chin to knees, while tears blurred Susannah's gaze in her gratitude.

"Tenn, I decided something just now, or maybe back there when I first found Charlotte."

"If it's something about trying to get along with Theo, forget it," he ordered curtly.

"No—except I want to have a good season at the Drury so I can move on to another theater as soon as my articles are up, and then I will ask him for a legal, permanent separation."

The green-gold eyes startled, then narrowed between thick, russet lashes. "If you're so sure, why wait? Rumors about us are out, so what's the point of waiting?"

"I believe we must be very careful not to be seen together until I have put in this year and really leave Theo for good. Rumors can be put to rest. By then, my career will belong to me even if my salary does not, and your reputation will be intact."

"My love, I don't give a damn for my reputation if we can be together, and I detest the sneaking about you're suggesting. I think I settled Theo down today, but he's not to be trusted at close range or far, anymore than the King of England—or that bastard in the street back there. You're a fine actress. It may take your audiences a while to accept a married woman who openly chooses a man to love who is not her husband, but we and your career will weather it eventually."

"I will—after this season when I can have it all."

"Have it all? You sound like some child surfeited on fantasy. This is not the theater, love, where you can control the script or endings—"

"I can! I say I can if I want to badly enough!"

"Susannah," Charlotte's voice floated to them.

"Char, I'm sorry I yelled. I woke you."

"Susannah." She bent closer over Charlotte while Tenn's big hand rested comfortably on the small of her back.

"What Char? Are you thirsty?"

"Yes, but listen," she whispered so low that Susannah bent even closer to catch the words. "Don't you remember those lines of Lady Brute you liked; you know, ' 'tis a hard matter to live without the man we love'?"

"Yes, I remember. Sleep now. We're taking you to Kingston with us."

"But, listen. It's true as true. Say the rest!"

"All right. 'But what think you of the fear of being found out? I think that never kept a woman virtuous long. We are not such cowards neither.' "

"Yes, that's it, that's it. I only spent the night with Richard Charke because father made me marry him, and in one night I knew it was wrong, so I have been brave to never need a man since. You have to be brave to need this one. It's all the same—"

"What's she whispering?" Tenn asked. "She's not delirious?"

"No, not at all. She liked some lines from a play, that's all."

Tenn pulled her hard into his arms and tipped her head back so she looked up so close into his intense stare. "I ought to thrash you for that stupid move of running off to such a dangerous area by yourself today, but somehow you're never stupid, and together we always manage to get out of danger unscathed."

"Except," she told him breathlessly, "the danger I always face in giving myself so completely in this raging love I have for you."

"I'll give your career this year, Susannah, but then I publicly claim what is mine. Like this—"

His hard mouth softened in a kiss to entice, seduce, and possess her heart as completely as ever. Susannah molded her soft body to his angular, powerful frame as unashamed and passionate as if all scandalized London could dare to watch her with a flick of eyelid, rather than just dear Char.

Chapter Seventeen

While a wet February snow fell heavily outside, Tenn Sloper paced the parlor of the two adjoining rooms he and Susannah had leased through Anne Hopson five months ago, on Blue Cross Street in the Leicester Fields neighborhood of London. Dusk had already come, and Susannah was uncharacteristically late after her appearance as Isabella in *Measure for Measure* at the Drury. By now he had seen this play four times, as well as the numerous others she'd triumphed in during the 1737-1738 season: tragedies like *Agamemnon* and *Othello*; revivals of comedies such as *Love's Last Shift* or *The Careless Husband*, a play in which a libertine husband was brought to contrition when he discovered his wife's unfaithfulness.

"Damn it all to hell!" Tenn cursed vehemently to the empty room and paced faster at the thought of husbands getting back unfaithful wives.

Tenn hated all the underhanded machinations he and Susannah had gone through to meet clandestinely this past year. They knew Theo was aware of their continued liaison, but he assiduously left them alone and had avoided Tenn ever since that day last autumn when he'd thrown him against a brick wall.

A brick wall, Tenn mused, as thought linked to

thought. That was exactly the way he would characterize Susannah's attitude about the necessity of leaving Theo without worrying first about her career—a brick wall. But she'd always pleased him so, driven him so wild with unreasoning passion for her that he had steeled himself to give her this chance for pride and independence. Still, she'd never been late like this and with Theo and the fops who hung about the theater on the loose, anything could have happened. He should never have let her talk him into staying away from the Drury tonight and just meeting him here after.

His stomach knotted at the mere thought she might be in danger. Memories taunted him: Susannah in Moll King's clutches; Susannah devastated when Theo and hired thugs ravaged her precious costumes; Susannah drowning in the Thames; Susannah being assaulted by that crude bastard when she went to find Charlotte last autumn.

He yanked open the door to the large back kitchen of the Hayes house and nearly fell over John Hayes, the owner. The swarthy man looked startled and jumped back.

"I see it's still snowing," Tenn said gruffly. "My friend is late, so perhaps the snow has delayed her. Anne Hopson hasn't been here either, I take it."

John Hayes shrugged and lifted his hands and eyes in his usual annoying gesture even if he would answer. The man was an Italian immigrant despite his British name, and Tenn believed he really knew much more of the king's English than he admitted. Across the room his mousy wife looked up from peeling potatoes into a wooden bowl on her lap.

"Not here yet," the man intoned in his singsong voice. "Both ladies late, and I hears you walking, walking, *si*."

Without more than a glare at the man, Tenn wheeled around, went back inside, and closed the door.

He'd give her ten minutes and then go out looking for her. And he'd be damned if he was going to let such covert arrangements in such a sordid setting continue. The place was in Anne Hopson's name, but the Hayeses, whom he trusted not at all lately, surely knew what was going on. He hated living like this away from his estates when, if Susannah really loved him just a little more than she did her damned career, she'd be willing to go with him anywhere, face anything to be free with him.

He swept aside the heavy brocade drapery to stare out at the thick falling snow through his own reflection in the glass. Behind him, the coal fire burned merrily in the small grate to illumine the little parlor, and in the bedroom beyond two lanterns glowed. But without her here, it was all as cold and lonely as outside. When his marriage to one woman that had nearly ruined his life had ended, he'd vowed never to let another one control him, but here he was. Somewhere—perhaps the first moment he had seen Susannah with those gilded eyes and that lovely face—he had lost control of his life by losing himself in her. Time was fleeting, falling, melting, like these snowflakes. Soon, very soon, he must find the strength to make her choose, because deep inside he couldn't fathom how in King George's England even a determined, talented woman like Susannah could, as she phrased it, have it all.

The dark box of a sedan chair between two burly carriers emerged from the curtain of snow, and a woman alighted. His heart raced: Safe and here, she had come at last. He let the drapery fall into place, silently chiding himself that his hands shook in anger and relief—and fervid anticipation.

He heard her come in through the Hayeses' kitchen entrance. Her musical voice greeted them. Anne had evidently not accompanied her, but it was just as well as it was always too blatantly obvious when she stepped out to leave them alone for hours while she shopped or helped

Mrs. Hayes prepare supper or dinner. He couldn't tell what she was saying now. Good, he thought, for that meant their voices in here did not carry outside either, however close that Italian eavesdropper hovered by the door.

She came in, still speckled with flakes on her dark blue cape. Her auburn curls in front were damp, and her thick eyelashes glittered as she blinked away melting flakes. She closed the door behind her.

"My love, I'm sorry I'm late, but I just couldn't help it."

"What the hell happened? I was starting to worry."

"Cecilia has left my brother Tom in a tiff. Tenn, they've only been married a year, and it was a mammoth thing to her."

He strode over to her and latched the door behind her, not touching her yet. Cold emanated from her cloak but he resisted the fierce urge to crush her to him. "I see," he clipped out more harshly than he intended. "Always rescuing sisters-in-law or on some angel's errand of mercy to old Handel or starving artist or musician. Tenn will wait—he'll keep until I get there."

"That's not fair. Tom evidently stayed out all night last night, came home reeking perfume, and she was distraught!"

"Not fair? Hell, I'm distraught. You should have at least sent Anne to tell me you'd be late!"

"My love, I apologize, but don't carry on like I do this all the time. I feel sorry for Cecilia as I think Tom married her for her voice and what fortune it would bring—about the way Theo did me. And I know how important it is to her to have someone to rely on when a marriage goes sour."

"Fine, just fine. Did you counsel Cecilia to find a lover—someone who's so crazy about her he'll wait until all hours until she can drop in?"

"Of course not! I sent her in a sedan chair to my

mother's in St. Giles as her father won't take her back after she married Tom against his wishes, and I wasn't going home myself! I said I'm sorry, Tenn."

He leaned his hands against the door on either side of her head. Her sweet scent assaulted his flared nostrils at this intimate distance; she smelled like lavender lilacs in May. "It's just I can't stand the secrets, the sneaking about sometimes, the hellish waiting for us to be together permanently—if we can ever live openly."

She lifted her hood back slowly while he stared down at her lovely face so close. Already he could feel the all too familiar tightening in his loins for her. He knew he loved her too much to force her to choose him or her career—at least not yet.

"We are going away this summer," she soothed. "You said we might even go to visit your sister in Italy." He could see his own silhouette in her wide, dark pupils framed by the golden irises of her eyes.

"Take me away now," he rasped low. "Take me away now and make it warmest summertime here, so I'll find the strength to wait until I can really have you away and all to myself."

Her soft lips parted in shy surprise as she stared up at him as if mesmerized. She nodded almost imperceptibly at the gentle challenge and one wayward curl bounced across her flawless forehead. His pulse pounded: He loved her, needed her, even as she did him.

Susannah's heart thudded to warm her chilled body under his fierce gaze. She felt deliciously disrobed already. The little stage in her brain paraded scenes of her under him in the soft bed in the next room, moaning, writhing, loving. Her knees went weak even as she lifted her arms around his strong neck and stretched up on tiptoe to kiss him. Her wet blue cloak split away as she pressed to his warmth.

The kiss was deep, powerful, and robbed her of breath

and strength. Still, she fluttered tiny kisses along the russet hair of his rakish eyebrows and down the bridge of his nose. Her knees pressed into his legs for stability, even though he had a firm hold on her waist.

"I've been selfish and nasty," he was murmuring as his big hands lifted to the braided frogs fastening her cloak. "You're cold. Let me warm you by the fire."

"It's summer already just as you said," she whispered as her cloak fell away to the floor. "It's warm in here, it's going to be so very warm."

He lifted her and strode a few steps to the small brick hearth boasting its footed iron grate with the glowing pile of cherry-red coals he had purchased from the Hayeses. He sat on the edge of the tall chair with her in his lap. Even as they kissed fervently again, she felt the spreading boldness born of her passion for him. Her tongue darted to challenge his, and he moaned deep in his throat as he searched out the sweetest recesses of her willing mouth.

She could feel his building desire for her and marvelled how her desire for him sprang always wild and new to match his, however many times or ways or places they had bedded. With him only, she felt passionate, independent, natural, and in command of her life, only to dedicate it to him in the same flow of ravishing exaltation she experienced only on the stage.

"You make me so hot, love," he said as his big hand slid heavily up her leg under her heavy skirts, and over her bent knee and the top of silk stocking to the bare, warm flesh of thigh.

"Yes, yes! Here, wait. You asked me to make it hot summer here tonight. Just wait."

She scrambled off his lap while he watched surprised. She stood before him on the hearth and swiftly pulled out her ivory-headed bodkins until her tresses gilded gold by firelight spilled free in all their bounty.

"Susannah, I didn't mean to be angry tonight, but you

drive me completely mad sometimes."

"Good," she brazened as her fingers lifted to her front bodice ties. "I want you mad for me. Now just wait a minute," she scolded as he reached for her.

He leaned back then with a deep sigh, long arms sprawled on arms of chair; muscled, booted legs extended on the hearth on either side of her skirts as if to block her in. His rugged, handsome head leaned on the high carved chair back; his green eyes lit by darting golden fire glow gleamed devilishly as he watched her continue to undress.

She unlaced her heavy velvet skirts and her voluminous petticoats, dropping them to the small braided rug under his chair. She trembled now, nervous and shy as his devouring gaze raked each soft, alabaster limb she exposed. His firm mouth quirked up in obvious, blatant appreciation and anticipation. Slowly, she pulled off her unlaced bodice with attached sleeves and heavy lace cuffs. The fire warmed her legs and back through the thin linen and lace chemise as his eyes warmed her breasts, which pointed pertly beneath the gauzy garment.

"You're so beautiful, my love," he rasped, "so utterly beautiful."

Before she could go further, if indeed she dared, he scooted his chair closer until she stood completely between his spread legs backed nearly to the hearth. Their eyes locked as he lifted one hand to caress her hip, waist, rib cage, then cup a full breast. "You've made it July, my sweetheart," he whispered. "The sunniest, hottest, fiercest day in July—"

He moved toward her and tugged her slightly down to him to kiss a pointed nipple through the linen and lace. He moaned, suckling on it, moving his big head in slow circles while she cradled its back with her fingers entwined in his mussed, copper hair.

The feel of warm, wet lace pressed by lips and tongue against her nipple excited her so wildly her knees buckled.

Instantly, he lifted her, settled her facing him on his lap, her knees spread on either side of his hips still covered by soft, taut breeches. She gasped as her chemise ruffled up to her hips so she sat naked and open against him while he still looked so impeccably attired in silk shirt, cravat, waistcoat, breeches, and boots.

"Suddenly shy, my sweet?" he teased and grinned. "But you can't expect to uncover this stunning, seductive body for me and have me keep control, now can you? Such a wonderful performance needs an appreciative audience."

His mouth and hands were suddenly everywhere, kissing, caressing, commanding compliance. The flames behind her heated her skin even as his touch branded her body and her heart. The crackle of the fire, a whirlwind of sweeping sound, blue and violet and red-gold flashing lights, enveloped her in a shatteringly beautiful embrace as she merged with her beloved Tenn. Dazzled by his flaming touch, she lost awareness of her separate self and became one with him in the sparkling heat of their blazing union.

They clung together after, limbs entwined. "The fire's not so warm now," she mumbled against his warm neck where she pressed her face.

"I know. We'll get into bed to keep warm."

She jerked fully awake. "Right now?"

"Indeed, my love. All this was merely to warm you after your jaunt in the snow and to get your attention."

He looked so sleepy, yet so serious, she giggled. "Tenn, you tease," she chided gently.

But he carried her to the chill bed and they soon had the sheets warm as they pressed sweetly together. And, as always, when they were as one, time flamed, then was no more.

When the sedan chair delivered her home to Twelve

Little Wild Court at nearly midnight, she knew immediately something was wrong. Her drowsy, heavy limbs sated with Tenn's lovemaking turned tense; her lulled brain snapped alert. Lights illuminated the house from every window. People's forms flitted by behind drawn curtains. Strangers stood on the curb. Theo—surely he would not ask his bagnio cronies here for a party—surely, he wouldn't dare to invite strangers in!

"Men! Here, over here," a voice exploded at her. "Mrs. Cibber's here at last, men!"

Strangers emerged from the gloom, several asking questions she did not grasp. One man had a pen poised over a sort of ledger book. Panicked, she hurried to the front door and lifted the latch. Tenn, if only Tenn had seen her home, but she had convinced him it was better this way. She swept the door open. Furniture was piled in the small foyer, entirely out of place.

"Anne! Anne!"

She moved quickly in to gape at chaos. Men she did not recognize carried furniture, searched drawers. Two big louts carried a rolled rug past her, and then she saw Anne.

"What is it? Theo?" Susannah shrieked, the memory of the rape of her tiring room all too vivid. A group of people began to chatter at her even as Anne answered.

"No, no, he didn't call them in this time. He's gone lock, stock, and barrel bankrupt! One of his creditors got a court order they can claim his goods and sell the house, and he's threatened with debtors' prison if the constable can find him, he is!"

"No. No!" Susannah heard herself screech.

"Mrs. Cibber, we haven't touched your garments in the clothes press, ma'am," someone said. "And I told them you're a fine, fine actress so they just dumped the things in your desk over there and didn't touch a one of them."

"Oh, yes," she said inanely, not even looking at the man. Tenn had made Theo promise not to endanger their property; Tenn had paid over seven hundred pounds to assume their financial safety just since last summer, and now this!

"Miss Susannah," Anne was bending low and whispering to her where she had slumped on the rolled bedroom carpet set diagonally across the parlor in the chaos, "I can hurry to St. James' Square to fetch the squire."

"No. No, enough is enough. Theo—we both deserve this."

"I was packing your things in the bedroom but some blackguard took the tablecloth I was wrapping them in. Where will we go?"

Susannah's dazed eyes lifted to Anne's distraught face at last. "Go? To my mother's in St. Giles for now. She only took in poor Cecilia tonight and now she'll have me—" Soundlessly, without moving, she began to cry.

A vase with dried flowers went by in some stranger's arms; the new brocade draperies she'd wheedled from Theo, but probably were from Tenn's money, came down and disappeared. People kept asking her questions and finally it dented her stunned brain that there were journal reporters here as well as Theo's rapacious creditors.

"Mrs. Cibber, do you believe the constable will find your husband? He's to be incarcerated in the Fleet Debtors' Prison, you know. Is it true a wealthy admirer has been supporting you, and you've been living apart from your husband?" a man's voice rattled on.

She turned her wet face to the man. "I live here where these men are destroying everything. Vultures! Get out!" she said so loudly that several bustling by turned or halted.

"Your husband's profligacy is public record now, Mrs. Cibber, so why not make a statement? I'm from *The Courant*, and our readers would be entirely sympathetic as you're a popular actress. Only last issue, *The Courant* printed a glowing review of your Isabella in

Shakespeare's—"

"Get out of here. Get out!" she shrieked. Everything halted. Someone coughed. She stood and pointed to the door. Her voice was steady now, her clearest projecting stage voice. "I understand some of you have a legal document to take Mr. Cibber's goods, but it is past midnight, and I insist you return tomorrow. Leave me your documents to study and depart. I need to see my attorney. If you will not comply, I assure you the press will raise a hue and cry against you by name, and—and you shall never be welcomed in the theaters of London again. Get out and return tomorrow after I have consulted my attorney. Go now, please. All of you."

She stared at the reporter from *The Courant* who shrugged and turned away. Two men set a table down they had held through her entire speech. She faced down a frowning man holding a sheaf of papers. Under her fierce gaze, he dropped them to the settee in the middle of the floor. "We'll be back," he said low and stalked out. That signalled a general exit to the door until she and Anne stood alone in the clutter.

"Oh, Miss Susannah, that was wonderful. Now I can slip out in back and go for the squire."

"No. We'll not be involving Squire Sloper further in the Cibbers' financial ruin. It's all on Theo now. I swear, I could kill him!"

She dropped her cloak where she stood and sank on the settee to pick up the sheaf of legal documents, all lettered beautifully in flowing scrivener's calligraphy and stamped with a wax seal. Then she merely shoved them to the floor and lay down sideways on the settee, curling her legs up and wrapping her arms around herself.

"I'm exhausted, Anne. Theo's finally done me in—bereft of everything I've worked for, any security at age twenty-four to beg bread from my widowed mother. I can't touch my salary, I have a pitiful collection of costumes to show for my theater work, I'll probably never be able to live openly with the man I love, and now this house—"

A sob racked her as Anne bent close over her to touch her shoulder. "Laws, I never should have opened the door to the wretches, I shouldn't, but I didn't know. I didn't know!"

"It's all right. I just need to rest a few minutes, to think. When it gets light, we'll go to my mother's. If you're not too tired, gather my things: the clothes and papers, my scripts, and any personal items. Hide a few pieces of my French porcelain in the garments too."

"That's the first thing they took when they swooped in here like so many locusts. The porcelain's gone, it is."

Susannah sighed and felt a warm tear trace a jagged path down her cheek to plop onto the settee. "It doesn't matter. I've got to rest. I'll find an attorney in the morning, maybe swear the peace against Theo so he can't get near me to involve me anymore. I'm on stage tomorrow as Desdemona, and I can't look a fright—not until my husband Othello kills me," her voice drifted off.

She felt so drained she almost floated. Tenn's heavenly lovemaking and then this hellish nightmare: too much emotion, too much upheaval for one night, and Theo had made too much chaos for one lifetime. She was done with him—finished. Let him do his worst, for her career was hers alone and not his to plunder anymore as he had her costumes.

She drifted off, away, around. Tenn's handsome, green-eyed face swam at her through the dappled mist, and she kissed him. His arms held her afloat in the warm, buoyant waters, but then she was tugged away from his embrace by quickening currents. Her father's pinched face rushed at her mouthing words that she must marry Theo. Her brother Tom nodded and played even shriller sounds on his fiddle while Theo's sharp voice shrieked at her: Beg me. Beg me! Beg me, Susannah, to never, never let you go—go—go.

His hand was on her. She jumped and screamed. "Oh, Anne. It's you. I was dreaming."

"It's Mr. Cibber, upstairs on the back steps big as life, I said. He's going to go, but he wants to see you."

"Go? Go where? He's where?" Susannah floundered, trying to clear her muddled mind.

"He says he's fleeing to France, to Calais. He's waiting on the back steps outside, clear up under the eaves. He came over the rooftops and says he's leaving the same way."

Susannah sat up on the settee, cradling her aching head in her hands. "To Calais. I ought to turn him in, but that wouldn't help in the end. My cloak. Is it still snowing? I'll speak to him."

Anne wrapped the cloak around Susannah from the end of the settee where it had evidently fallen and lighted their way up the backstairs toward the servants' cramped quarters above. Susannah noticed that Anne had on her own cloak too, and something she carried glinted in the lantern light.

"What's that?" she asked, and seized Anne's wrist to make the swinging lantern dart crazy shadows on the walls.

"I'm going up with you. Him all desperate and sneaking about like this, he's not to be trusted a whit. It's a butcher knife, it is, one the greedy wretches overlooked downstairs when they ransacked the kitchen."

The two women stared at each other in wan lantern glow. No doubt many would like to kill Theo Cibber, Susannah thought wildly: disgruntled playwrights, Kitty Clive, his debtors, perhaps Tenn—and his own wife.

"No, I—we can't take a knife out there," Susannah whispered. "If he's leaving for France, that has to be enough for now. I swear, if I had it, I'm terrified I'd use it.

I should never have said earlier I wanted to kill him. Here, give me the lantern and you wait right here. You won't be afraid?"

"No, but you can't face that blackguard alone. I can't let you."

"I have to, Anne. I'll call out if I need you, I promise. It's best, really. After all, he's leaving, and I couldn't ask for more now. All will be well."

Anne nodded reluctantly, and their cold fingers touched as Susannah took the small lantern and moved up the last stairs to the servants' quarters. Here, one door led to the garret bedchambers for servants, long unused but by Anne, and one to a small deck just below rooftop level overlooking the back alley.

The door creaked piteously, and cold air smacked her face. The lantern wavered as she stepped out. No Theo. Then the door slammed shut and hands pushed her back against the wall on the narrow landing.

"Egads, are you crazy? Douse that lantern. They're down in the street!"

Theo's form bent to scoop wet snow from the landing, and the lantern hissed to blackness. It had stopped snowing. He stood near her, his dark outline now silhouetted against a spatter of diamond-point stars in blackest sky.

"I can't believe you dared to come back to show your face," she began.

"Quiet. Voices carry on such a night, and I have no intention of spending the next few years as prisoner in The Fleet. I swear, I'll go the way Black Mac did first!"

"And murder some poor innocent?" she heard herself mutter before she could seize the words back. Her breath frosted the air between them in a smoky cloud, and she shuddered from the chill.

"I meant, my dear, that's how Mac escaped imprisonment at first. He went over the rooftops to the harbor and escaped to Calais as I shall."

"Good riddance, Theo. I'm going in now."

He leapt at her, shoving her back hard into the wall of the house where her head just missed the heavy, overhanging eaves.

"You icy little bitch! In your element out here in this snow, aren't you? But not for Tenn Sloper, no. At least you've been some use to me as he paid my debts last time, and I expect him to now, but it's too hot for me to stay about here. I'll have to wait in Calais until you write me you have the money from him."

"Never! You've bilked him long enough."

"Bilked him? My dear, I'd say he hasn't paid me half enough for the willing way you whore for him, strip for him on the hearth, give your hot little body to his lusts any way he wants in your little love nest on Blue Cross Street."

She gaped at him even as he loosed her wrist now gone numb. Strip for him on the hearth—Blue Cross Fields—love nest—the familiar scene just earlier tonight taunted her.

"What do you imply?" she asked shakily.

"For love of a bawd, I see I have your attention now, dear wife. I wish I could have seen it all. There you were, enjoying every minute of it, so I hear. Egads, you've become skilled with the Sloper stud, *par excellence*."

She hit out at him so hard he nearly fell, but he clung to her until they both fell to their knees on the narrow, snow-covered landing. "You've—you've spied on us! You've—even tonight," she gasped, desperate to have his restraining hands off her.

"You didn't listen, my dear. I didn't see you, though I planned to stop by for a little theater performance soon. But, I daresay, John Hayes—who knows perhaps half the neighborhood at Leicester Field—has enjoyed your talents with Sloper, and that is precisely why you will ask Square Stud for the money I need to pay off these damned creditors. Let them have the house in the process; I don't care."

She stared at his grotesque grin and the wildly sparkling whites of his eyes. Her stomach churned at the thought of anyone watching her lovemaking with Tenn to defile its precious, intimate beauty. There must be peepholes somewhere in the rooms. Tenn had been right: The secrecy, the setting, was all wrong. She gasped, pressing her hand to her mouth to keep from retching into the snow.

Theo stood and brushed the snow from his knees. "I'm glad to see you understand me at last, Susannah. Tell Mr. Benefit Sloper I expect two thousand pounds in my name sent to the *Deux Hommes* Tavern on the Calais waterfront within a fortnight."

"He won't do it," she managed low.

"He'll do it posthaste or, I swear, the London presses will have a field day with the letters they receive from Calais about his athletic exploits with a certain married actress—or a certain married ex-actress, as the case will be at that point."

"I've never been married to you, Theo Cibber," she said, sitting back on her haunches despite the cold snow and the twisting pains in her head and stomach. "You broke the premarital agreement you signed, you terrorized me, you cheapened me, you lied, you used and sold me first to the king and then to Tenn—"

"Enough!" he shrilled entirely too loud. A man's voice somewhere below; then another sounded. She longed to cry down to the men that Theo was here for the mere taking, but fear and loathing held her tongue.

"Quick," he hissed, "boost me up and I'll be gone. And if you fail me in any way, I swear, all London will read about the illustrious Mrs. Cibber's greatest performance—in a rich, supposedly reputable gentleman's bed!"

She stood wearily and, despite her nausea at the thought of even touching him again, forced herself to boost him up the extra height he needed to scramble clumsily onto the gently slanted roof.

"You're wrong, Theo," she whispered up to him. "My greatest performance was in ever letting you touch me or call me wife. I swear—I swear to you, you shall never do so again without being denounced, and in your vile, scurrilous London presses if necessary. Get out of my life."

He turned back; his black form hunched above her. A voice, a dog's bark, resounded from the street below. "You'll never, never be rid of me, wife, *ad perpetuam*," he spit down at her, then turned and disappeared. She heard him scramble off, slipping once, heard him drop heavily to the next contiguous rooftop, and then there was nothing but black, chill air and stars.

She leaned back under the eaves where they had stood. The rooftops of London looked stacked one upon the other from here. Distantly, church bells chimed three o'clock. The night reached out as vast and dark as her heart.

Ruined, she thought; one love, one life, all shattered by the eternal, demonic presence of Theo Cibber. She wished for one careening moment that she'd brought the knife up here or dared to shove him off, but then there would be scandal and guilt even as now, and she was no murderer at heart however much she hated.

She stood breathing in the cold, crisp air she knew not how long. Her nose went numb, her fingers. She jolted from a near trance as Anne opened the door.

"Thank heavens, you're in one piece. I hadn't heard voices for so long I just had to look despite my promise. He's gone at last, is he? Get in here now, or you'll catch your death of cold."

Death. She wouldn't mind, but for Tenn and her career. But now with Theo gone, she could perhaps breathe easier if just for a while. And she had no intention of telling

Tenn that Theo had demanded money to keep from spilling his poison to the presses. They'd merely change places, and give that foul spy John Hayes the slip. If she told Tenn of that, he would probably kill Hayes; besides, Theo would be cutting his own throat if he ever admitted setting up the liaison that he had then observed and yet did nothing but demand more money.

Anne stepped out and pulled her by her arm toward the door. "The lantern's gone out, I see. Come on now, we'll go down carefully in the dark and then to your mother's in the morning before the locusts swarm back. Come in here with Anne now where it's warm," the soothing voice comforted.

Susannah let herself be led like a child. With Anne, the warmth of friendship; with Tenn, the heat of love. The devil's own goblin had danced off across the cold rooftops into blackest night, and somehow, tomorrow would come. She held tightly to Anne's hand as they went down together.

Chapter Eighteen

All that winter and early spring while Theo spewed out a stream of suddenly contrite, nearly groveling letters from Calais to her—but none, as she had gambled, to the London papers—Susannah and Tenn Sloper dared to enjoy themselves in London. Sometimes they rode out in the suburbs to inns or taverns wagering they would not be recognized; other times they both went in disguise to fashionable city spots like Will Urwin's Coffee House on Russell Street or even riding on Rotten Row. Susannah would wear the too-tight wig she had used in Bath, and Tenn looked entirely elegant in powdered and curled white peruke. She went almost daily and sat in the back row to see him play tennis, and he came late and stood far at the rear of the theater to miss scarcely a performance of hers.

They gambled more literally to be seen at the same carefully selected private dinner parties given by Tenn's political Whig cronies. Occasionally they spent charming evenings with Tenn's father at the St. James' mansion or, now that Theo's creditors had taken her house and goods, with her mother in plebeian St. Giles' where Tenn was well liked and amazingly accepted by her mother, who had always detested Theo.

Tenn and Susannah played for other sorts of stakes

when he took her gambling in disguise either to the traditional Groom Porter's Lodge or the new Brooke's Club in St. James', so very late at night that even the most fashionable fops had gone home to breakfast. He taught her to wager, and they made teasing, whispered erotic bets with each other they paid off later. Soon, just like any stylish London lady, Susannah could pick out the puffs and squibs seeded about the gaming tables with coins donated by the management to lure others to play; she could also tell the planted flashers who assured the potential victims that the house lost heavily; and she could tell which peevish, out-of-humor customers the captains would bounce from the room for misbehavior.

They had spent one wonderful winter evening at a Frost Fair on the frozen Thames with half the populace of London: Tented booths made from quilts, winnowing sheets, and even old petticoats dotted the ice to display goods, food, or entertainment. Turf fires heated kettles of cider and roasted sides of beef rotated by turnboys. Music laced the frosted air with country dance tunes, and children darted everywhere with muslin kites or the latest novelties of popguns and noisemakers.

Susannah enjoyed and cherished it all, though as Theo's letters to her increased, she sometimes felt she too was a dancer on ice or a kite flyer in a stiff, threatening cross-channel breeze. She knew Fleetwood sent all of her salary to Theo and probably a little more besides; although she had spoken with Fleetwood again, none of it was yet hers to claim. But her career seemed increasingly secure. She gained further confidence and poise with Theo absent from the Drury, and her popularity with London's audiences burgeoned. She and Tenn were very happy: It was almost possible to pretend at times they were really free to be seen together, to laugh, to share, and to love. Even tonight at an elegant political gathering Tenn's father was hosting at the Sloper's St. James' mansion, she could almost imagine she was Lady Sloper here across the white damask tablecloth all aglitter with silver, porcelain, crystal, and sparkling candelabra. Even the company totally suited her this evening, as Prime Minister Walpole had not brought his catty wife, Lady Catherine.

"I declare, I must really be in favor with the father-son Sloper team if they entrust me to sit next to the most beautiful and highly touted actress in London this evening," the hefty Robert Walpole told her. He leaned slightly toward her, one arm extended on the table to twirl his iced champagne goblet by its slender stem. "I do hope all this political jabber of possible war with Spain hasn't been a bore to you, Susannah."

"Not at all, Prime Minister Walpole—"

"Robert, please."

"Robert, then. You see, since I've known the Slopers, I have learned to think more politically, and I take it all the rabble rousing by people like this Jenkins character everyone speaks of is meant to be an embarrassment to you since you oppose a possible war with Spain and such stories of atrocities as he tells incite everyone."

"Ah, astute as well as lovely, Susannah. But to tell you bluntly, idiots like this Captain Jenkins, who probably had that ear he totes around in a bottle cut off in a drunken tavern brawl and not by some sadistic Spaniard, are out to do more than embarrass me; actually, they want my head cut off and on display in some Tory bottle. They mean to literally cut me off from the king's good graces, you see."

"But surely Parliament and the people should be able to understand that you're hardly sending these renegade British smuggling ships into ports on the Spanish Main in violation of treaties. The ships the Spaniards have captured are obviously privateers commanded by wretches like this Jenkins."

"True, but some damned Tory politicians who are evidently writing dramatic lines for this Jenkins like, 'I command my soul to God and my cause to my country,' have such a script for a national tragedy written that I must be more than wary. The common and rich folk of England made a potentially explosive audience for any popular figure, Susannah. You note, do you not, you have even me thinking in terms of grand drama, my dear?"

She laughed low, and there was a moment's lull as the first course of fish, beefsteak, and veal was paraded to the table by numerous bewigged Sloper servants. "But Tenn—well, I mean everyone—says His Majesty relies so heavily on you," she told him above silver clinking to porcelain as people began to eat.

"Indeed, but frankly, Susannah, much of my popularity with King George initially stemmed from my popularity with our recently deceased Queen Charlotte. Poor woman, dead but five months, and the king has already shut off half of her beloved Kensington Palace and imported his little German Walmoden mistress and ensconced her in the other half. German George, they brazenly call him in the streets. I only hope to hell that German George will see me through as I try to buck this war fever."

"I heard a wretched story last week about some doggerel verse someone dared to post on the Royal Exchange about Queen Charlotte's death," she said low.

"True, very true. I take it Tenn told you that too as he's the one who had the backbone to tear it down in front of that rowdy crowd and bring it to me. 'Oh death,' it read, 'where is thy sting to take the queen, and leave the king?' And now that German mistress is another albatross around the royal neck. Forgive me for asking a rather personal guestion, Susannah, but—"

She braced herself as a butler dipped between them to offer grilled or pickled salmon set in beds of peas and mushrooms alternating with potatoes in their shells. Robert Walpole would ask her about her close relationship with Tenn, she was certain. He'd hinted at it. Too often, astute folk did, but she had learned to ignore it and merely plunge ahead. A huge tray of crab arranged symmetrically with cheesecakes delayed the guestion a moment longer. She glanced down the table, caught Tenn's green gaze, and smiled undaunted.

"It is only, my dear Susannah," the Prime Minister resumed, "that I have thought once, indeed it appeared, that His Majesty did favor you and that he might forget his Walmoden, as she evidently had insulted him. Forgive me, but how I have longed for a—well—intimate contact with him who had Whig sympathies and friends, one who could help bond him to the people and not alienate him so as Walmoden does and will."

"No, I—well—of course, I believe His Majesty was taken with my acting, my singing also."

"Quite, quite," he agreed so quickly, she could tell she had done a terrible job of glossing over the truth. She stared down at her crab and delicate button mushrooms. If she were so transparent here, how easily had many guessed her real relationship with Tenn, and not such clever politicians as Sir Robert Walpole either.

Heavily laden dessert trays eventually made their rounds: cherry blancmange, Dutch cheese, raspberries in cream, currant bread with orange butter. The talk leapt from jokes about Tory foes to the new, fervent London itinerant evangelist John Wesley, who had recently returned from trying to Christianize the savages from Georgia in North America to the increasingly popular style of powdered wigs for men, rather than ones of their own natural hair color. Later, Susannah regaled everyone with stories of eccentric stage personalities like Quin and Clive, but when someone asked her how and where her husband was, the dinner seemed to end with a crash.

"He writes from France that he is as well as can be expected," she heard herself say to a suddenly hushed table.

"Time for one more taking of the wine, and then the gentlemen must be off to their pipes and claret," Tenn's father chimed in immediately as if to rescue her.

Again, she was paired with Robert Walpole next to her in the traditional toast as, down the vast length of table, each couple lifted their glasses simultaneously, linked arms with goblets, and drank together. "To the king, wisdom, long life," Squire Sloper intoned, and everyone echoed the sentiment.

Heavy with food as they were light with the endless flow of champagne, the dinner guests filed out of the huge, formal dining room, the men turning left to the study, the women right to the parlor.

Tenn's hand touched the back of her waist briefly in the nearly empty dining room; his warm breath stirred her hair. "I'm sorry that last question happened," he said low.

"I should expect it. It's only I have had such a natural time lately, I can almost forget he exists in France or anywhere else."

"I know. And then the world crashes in. I hope Walpole behaved himself."

"He was charming and informative. And he knows about us."

"I suppose so. Did he ask directly?"

"No. Tenn, I believe I'll excuse myself early and leave. It takes you men so long to be done with claret, pipes, and talk anyway."

"I'll get away as soon as I can. Let me order the carriage to take you to Chelsea when you leave, and I'll join you as soon as possible. Don't protest. You've no performance tomorrow."

"Over there. I think your father wants you," she told

him while trying to look merely conversational in case anyone else noted.

"Promise me, then. I'll see everyone gets out of here at a reasonable hour. Promise me."

"Yes, all right. We need to talk."

His voice went hard and crisp. "About what? Is aught amiss?"

"Of course not," she lied. "I will be there." She walked away to mingle with the other lady guests, and within an hour was in Tenn's coach, which her sedan chair had delivered her to, and halfway on the familiar route to their dear Blue Rose Inn near Ranelagh Gardens in Chelsea.

She took her last letter from Theo out of her purse and fingered it nervously, though she could not read it in the dim carriage. It was cloyingly, ludicrously sweet—and such a sham. She could not quite grasp why he had switched tactics from the cruel threats he used since parting from her four months ago.

"My dearest, best of women, my angel," she recalled this last letter had begun. "Where are words to express my fondness! My high opinion of you!"

Surely, he did not think to win her back after all that had passed between them, she reasoned.

"Yes, you shall be mistress of yourself. Your dear heart shall feel no pang," he had promised, yet she believed not one word of it. "Let me but live once more to breathe my native air with liberty, and to convince you how much I love you, how highly I esteem you, how tenderly I feel for you," it had gone on and on. Surely it was Theo's standard treachery of some sort, but what? She had considered showing the letter to Tenn, but it would make him furious that she hadn't shared the earlier ones with him, even though they were not as maudlin as this one. Had Theo taken leave of his senses, or worse, did he later hope to use these contrite letters as proof he was the wronged party when she asked for a permanent separation?

And ask she must. Insist she must, for her world of love to protect at all costs had suddenly grown larger than just her and Tenn. After over four years of passionately loving Tenn, she was certain she was with child.

Susannah sat later in the plain, familiar room at the Inn with her feet up, listening to June crickets, listening for a single, fast-ridden horse. Tonight she would tell him of the child and they would plan together, but in the few days she had been certain she was pregnant, she had made many decisions on her own.

At any cost, the child must be declared Tenn Sloper's, whatever ruin ensured to reputation or career, because of the child's illegitimacy. Theo must never, never be able to claim the babe, either publicly or privately. But, however more complicated this now made her already chaotic life, she still dared hope to have it all. Once she had longed desperately to become an actress when it seemed out of reach, and that had come true. Now her career was admired, her talents esteemed, herself accepted by society as one of the premiere actresses of the land.

The child was due in February, as close as she could reason it out, so that meant she must retire for the next season, but that would be all. She would need to rely financially on Tenn for the child's sake in that year of seclusion, but the next year she could leave the Drury to strike out on her own at another theater like Covent Garden. She prayed so fervently that Tenn would be as thrilled as she and see all this so calmly and logically.

He came even as she had begun to doze. Even in the short span that she had been pregnant, her body was clearly not her own: Drowsiness assailed her; too often the smell or thought of certain foods she had once favored made her queasy; already certain gowns no longer fit very well. He knocked once on the door even as she unlatched it. Their embrace was warm; how enticingly he smelled of fresh river air.

When he sat, she stood behind him as she often did to knead his neck and shoulder muscles tired from the swift hour's ride. They did not speak for a moment, content in each other's presence and touch as if, Susannah mused, they were old married folks.

"Aren't you going to tell me? I was worried all the way out," he spoke at last and gently seized both her wrists to pull them to the base of his neck in front. He tilted his big russet head, all mussed from the wind, back against her breasts and stared up at her. "Did someone say something tonight besides the usual? Has Theo made a move?"

"Yes, well, Theo has. I've received a few letters lately."

"Lately? When? You didn't say a thing."

"I don't like to worry you."

He jumped up to face her, one hand on the chair back, the other uncharacteristically flailing the air as he spoke. "I can't believe you'd say something like that at this point in our relationship, Susannah. Damn it, let's have all of it! What is the bastard threatening now?"

"Please calm down. He isn't really threatening anything right now. He's being ludicrously contrite and friendly."

Tenn frowned so fiercely, his emerald eyes looked shadowy black beneath the screen of thick brows. "Friendly! Then he's probably laying the groundwork to get you back or make a public case of it. How friendly? I can't believe you wouldn't tell me this unless you're enjoying it."

"That's unfair! It was only a relief to be out from under the harangues and latest threats, that's all."

"Latest threats? Such as what?"

She paced away so he would not see her face. She'd never told him of Theo's departing demands for two thousand pounds sent to Calais, never told him most of what Theo had ranted and raved that night before he'd escaped like a criminal over the snowy rooftops of London more than three months ago.

"Susannah. I'm in this to the end with you, but not with

my eyes closed. Now what the hell is going on? I haven't seen you so jumpy or weepy for months—years."

She turned to face him and carefully brushed the wetness away from under each eye. "I know. I'll just explain everything."

She pulled Theo's last rambling letter from her silk purse and extended it to him. She sat in his vacated chair and watched him read it. She felt tired; her knees were weak.

"This goes in circles for four pages," he observed as he skimmed it. " 'And believe me, my angel. I am most cordially your fond, affectionate husband,' it closes. You don't believe all this?"

"No. I guess he must be planning something, but you see, he wanted a great deal of money—your money, of course—sent to him in Calais, and I refused. I thought the letters would be abusive and threatening, but this—"

"You haven't written him?"

"No. I told him when he left he was out of my life permanently and that as far as I was concerned, whatever it took, I was not his property anymore. And now, it's more important than ever that he never comes near me again."

When he saw tears well up in her eyes, he tossed the letter on the table and knelt before her chair. "Summer's almost here, my sweetheart," his voice soothed. "We'll get a lovely house or maybe even go to Italy. I'd love to take you home to West Woodhay, but he could track us there and that would be open admission of our affair if he does intend some sort of public trial."

"Trial! Oh, he couldn't. Not a trial with those terrible vulture journalists hanging on! Our careers! Our—our future!"

His long arms rested on either side of her thighs and hips along the chair seat, his hands lifted to hold her waist. His thumbs tenderly, almost unconsciously, stroked her belly as if he knew a child grew there; yet his face now so calm showed he could not.

"Our future, my dearest love, is to be together whatever befalls," he comforted. "These last few months when we've thrown caution to the wind to be together, don't think I didn't realize it could come to a public fight for your freedom. Only, you see, I would be content to have our London world fall down about our ears. My father's old and will retire to West Woodhay soon, and I can happily forgo my rounds of the stylish tennis courts, the Commission meetings, the Whig political intrigue, and the Prime Minister's flattering interest in my advice. I'd gladly give it up to be Squire Sloper in Berks. The estates, manor, the model village, and people need me there, and I have at times sorely neglected them these past few years."

"I know. I'm sorry."

"No, I did it all of my own free will to please myself. I simply needed you more than anything could have possibly needed me."

She began to cry: His big image blurred, then doubled as twin tears raced down her cheeks.

"I only speak, Susannah, of this right now when I can tell you're tired and distraught because it worries me—it frightens me, that you cannot say the same. It has always been evident to me, however much you love me and need me, that you have a passion for the theater too, and you may have to leave it, at least for a while, until we see our way through this mess."

"I can. I will."

"What?" His brows lifted in blatant surprise. "Look, love, I don't just mean for the summer."

"I believe it will have to be longer," she said low, her limpid eyes intent on his greener than forests or wild emerald seas. "At least until after next February, my dear love Tenn."

He startled. His hands stopped their gentle stroking and

froze along her belly. He opened his mouth to speak, but when she smiled through her tears and nodded wildly, he whooped with joy and lifted her into a high embrace.

"With child? You're carrying a child? Are you certain?" He looked so suddenly serious she almost laughed.

"Of course, I'm certain, you big lout. Did you really think tennis was the only physical endeavor you could win at?"

He threw back his head and roared with laughter while she clung to him halfway between tears and giggles. He spun them once, then carried her quickly to the bed to place her carefully on her back. He leaned over her now, holding just one of her hands in both of his.

"I'm so happy, my sweetheart," he told her. "Nothing else matters now by comparison. We can face anything to be together now."

She nodded fiercely up at him. "I thought exactly that, and I prayed you would too. I thought I never, never would have a child. I couldn't believe it at first—a child. And, I swear, Theo Cibber will never, never have claim to him or come within a mile of him while there's breath in my body."

"A him, is it? You're carrying a him? And what if she's a ravishingly beautiful and talented wench like her mother? And what—heaven help me—if she's as saucy and stubborn and then I'm stuck with two of them?"

Giggling through her poor attempt at mock anger, she reached over and flung a feather pillow at him. It whapped into his arm lifted to protect himself and dusted puffs of fine goose down over both of them.

He pinned one arm over her head when she tried to swing the pillow again. He flopped down beside her, tickled her briefly until she shrieked and begged, then sat upright.

"My love, I don't know what possessed me," he gasped. "Settle down, please, we could have hurt you. I—we've got to take care of you."

"Mm," she murmured and tugged him down beside her again, "take care of me like this." She cuddled to him, oblivious of her wrinkled satin gown and dishevelled tresses Anne had so carefully arranged.

His arms enveloped her; his lips sought hers in a tender possession that smote her soul so deeply she almost cried out in utter longing. "Love me, love me, please, now and always," she whispered against his firm, chiselled mouth now gone so beseechingly soft against her bare throat.

"Yes, I will, my love. And nothing can ever harm us now."

The first month of summer sped by in a charming house they leased in Burnham, Buckinghamshire twenty miles west of London, from which Tenn commuted back and forth to oversee the operations of his own four-thousand acre estate in Berkshire. When he was gone, Susannah slept a great deal, walked the gardens, chatted with Anne, or occasionally went in Tenn's big carriage to visit her mother and brothers in London. Tom's wife Cecilia had gone back to him, so her mother was now living alone except for Susannah's younger brother, Henry Peter, who turned eighteen this summer and usually worked as a minor actor or singer at the Drury. Unlike his two elder siblings, the youngest Arne had not yet found his niche in the world of London theater.

Today, Anne had draped the laundry out in back on hedges and had gone off to market in Burnham while Susannah read two-day-old newspapers from London. War fever with the Spanish was still heating up. The full story had finally come out, evidently through pure gossip, of how the Prince of Wales and the king had actually been heard calling each other names and wishing each other dead; and how last July when Augusta, the Princess of

Wales, had gone into childbirth labor at Hampton Court where the king and queen were residing, the prince had hauled the poor woman in great agony to St. James' Palace to be delivered so that the child would not be born in the same palace where his detested royal grandsire lay his head. Since then, the prince's entire family had been expelled from St. James' to rural Kew and generally ostracized.

"How terrible for the royal family to set such a precedent," Susannah whispered aloud to the small, sunny garden overlooking beige-green fields of rye. Yet her own situation was just as sad, for she and Theo were now permanently estranged, he was ostracized, and she would die before she let him get a hand on her child. Only with someone all propriety forbid her to have—like the king with his flagrant Walmoden—had she found love and true fulfillment.

From the back garden where she sat, she saw the distant blur of a single rider coming fast down the private road. Tenn! Tenn back a day early! She stood, spilling the newspapers off her lap. She smoothed her skirts carefully over her now barely rounded belly. Every time Tenn was even briefly away, he said he could see more changes in her, including a new radiance and deeper, calmer joy. She ran around the brownstone house waving, but then she froze to feel her heart's own thudding beat mingle with the horse's flying hoofs.

The man was not Tenn: too small and not a good rider; even the horse was dappled gray and not sleek midnight-black as Tenn's mount, Ebony. No! It could not be. Back from France and to have found her here! Instinctively, she pressed back against the cool stone of the house and crossed her arms in front of her belly as Theo Cibber pulled the snorting horse to a halt by the front gate.

But he had already seen her. "Susannah! Surprised to see me, I know," he called even as he dismounted. He tied the lathered horse to the gate and came in. The little gate bell rang crazily, then silenced. He stopped halfway up the walk, hat in hand. Her feet leaden, she walked slowly to meet him.

"I had no idea you were back, Theo."

"Obviously, and neither do the authorities. Unlike you at this posh little *alfresco pied-à-terre*, I have been forced to slip back into my native land, a *persona non grata* to hide with friends in Goodman Fields until I could wheedle from your mother where you were. Egads, where's your wealthy keeper? I had expected to have to ward him off to even get the briefest of interviews with my legal wife."

Her heart fell. Desperately, she had hoped that getting her back would not be his plan of action. Anger, hatred, violence—anything but that.

"I am sorry for your financial problems, Theo, but what I told you when you left in February is still the case. I would ask that you return to your friends in London and in a few days I can send a lawyer to see you." Her mind raced even as she spoke so calmly: She needed to summon a servant but she wasn't even sure where they were. Anne had gone to market, Tenn would not return until tomorrow, and if he noticed she was pregnant, who knew what he might do.

"Send a lawyer?" he shrilled and came several quick steps closer. "For love of a bawd, no lawyers unless they're Sloper's solicitors come to pay me overdue wife-rent! No, my dear, I want my wife herself—you—returned to my waiting arms. Now, wait before you reply! I've been lonely for you in Calais—yes, even before. I've seen the error of my ways as my letters to you have clearly stated, and I will have you come home."

"Home?" she challenged. "Home to where, Theo? Some bagnio in Goodman Fields or a waterfront tavern in Calais? Or maybe we could live on the London rooftops to escape debtors' prison."

"Obviously, I am recouping my losses, Susannah, or I would hardly be out here on a new horse or elegantly garbed; but of course, you didn't notice that."

Her mouth dropped open slightly as her eyes went over him. It was true: Under the short riding cloak, he wore hunter's green breeches and frock coat over a canary waistcoat and natty silk shirt.

"You've seen Fleetwood?" she asked, unable to think where else he could find a penny in London and still not be arrested. "Besides, I was thinking that brindled gray horse looks like his."

"Egads, he did loan me the mount, but I'll probably buy it from him. But my financial windfall is hardly loaned. Another reason you must come home with me, my dear, is to be a mother as well as a wife."

She gasped, and his eyes dropped to skim her head to toes at last. But she hadn't told anyone, not ever her mother yet, of this child. He stared at her face strangely now with that peculiar, cockeyed squint of his, and she dared to hope that despite his thorough perusal he hadn't guessed.

"I—why do you say that, Theo?"

"Egads, if we're not to have our own brood—and I admit that would be a drain on our rebuilding finances at this point—I intend to rear poor dead Janey's and my two daughters from here on out."

"Your first wife's girls? But, Theo, you've wanted nothing to do with them since Janey died. Everytime I asked you to bring them to our home even to visit, you refused. Your sister Catherine Brown's love is all they've ever known, and if it weren't for the money your father has paid for their upbringing, they'd have starved years ago!"

"Don't you dare to lecture me on them. Wives! Wives, ungrateful, shrewish wives *ad nauseam*! Betty and Jenny are six and seven now, and old enough to go on the stage or sing bit parts. If you don't have it in your hard little heart to mother and teach them what they need to know to succeed, I assure you my sister Charlotte will!"

"Char! She can't love and care for those little girls anymore than you could! She's been even stranger since she was so ill, and she's still living a split life in unspeakable dives here and there."

"How dare you criticize others when you refuse to mother these dear daughters of my body and of the poor woman who bore them and died so sadly—"

"Cease the melodrama, Theo. You haven't supported, loved, or seen them in years. I take it you do so now only to get what pitifully meager salaries you can from their forced labors in a harsh world they are probably too young and innocent to survive. The thought of you and poor Char in charge of two naive children around all those lewd fops and mincing sparks backstage sickens me."

"Afraid they'll turn out like you, my dear?" his shrill voice sliced like a knife. "Married to one, whoring for another, maybe several since you've been loose and easy these last years, as a husband's always the last to know. I swear, you could have even warmed the king's bed if you'd but dispensed with that dramatic virginal icy demeanor."

"I'm going to ask you to leave now, Theo," she said calmly and pointed toward the road. "As I said, now that you're back, in a few days I'll have someone come to see you about a legal separation."

"Legal? Separation? Egads, there's no such thing for us! Never! Fleetwood says you're convinced to take a year off and now I see why. When he told me, I couldn't fathom you giving up your precious theater career, but I've reasoned it out now. I see why!" he screamed and pointed at her midsection as if in blatant challenge to her gesture of pointing toward the road.

She took a step back as he advanced. His face alternated between stark white and livid pink as he berated her.

"No wonder there will be no return to the domestic fold, not even when two dear little stepdaughters need a mother's love. I swear, you're breeding Sloper's brat, aren't you?"

He lunged at her even as she both darted back and swung her open hand wildly. Her palm smacked his cheek; two nails raked under his eye. He shrieked and fell back cursing. "You icy bitch! You cold little whore! All those letters I sent groveling at your feet—this kind offer to take you back after a flagrant *affaire d'amour*—how do you think that will all look to London papers? Ruination! And now a bastard child to boot! Egads, *The Courant* will love all this. Why, I won't need Betty or Jenny to turn a single brass farthing after all this!"

"I dare you, Theo! It will be your final ruin too, and there's no way you'd be able to get or keep a penny of that scandal money once the journalists and your creditors scent you're back in London. I believe the arrest and incarceration of the once grand actor-manager of the Drury Lane Theater Royal, son of the illustrious poet laureate of King George II might just vie for columns on page one."

His fierce gaze wavered. He actually looked beaten. A defiant speech to culminate a tragedy on stage had never filled her with more poignant joy or pride. She almost felt her baby leap and stir within her. But his voice, when he spoke, was like a snarled whip waiting to cut her to shreds.

"We'll see! We shall see, Mrs. Theophilus Cibber, who has the victory at last! Law and right are on my side. Lost wives are viewed as lost servants or chattel in the courts of King George's England, Mrs. Cibber. Send no lawyers. And enjoy these last few days here stewed in illicit lusts, for they shall not be long to survive."

He whirled away, one hand still covering the cheek she had slapped and scratched. He untied the horse and mounted clumsily. Glaring down at her, he hesitated as if he would speak another exit line.

"Until you return to me, bastard babe and all, Susannah. Until then!"

He spurred the tired horse away in a streaming cloud of road dust. Her knees suddenly weak, she sank into the grass. Her mind went blank: It was as if she could not recall a separate, single thing he had said; only that she had faced up to him, he'd gone away, and Tenn was coming back tomorrow.

She stroked the tender grass next to her crumpled skirts and inhaled the June day. How sweet smelling the rising breeze; how warm the afternoon; how deliciously drowsy she felt sitting here by the house that was hers and Tenn's for a while. This baby which grew right here, the product of their love, would always be safe and would set the world aright like this with no clouds or storms or Theo Cibbers on the horizon.

She stood and went out in back where the breeze had blown her discarded London newspapers about the garden. But behind the house, the sky was gray, the wind was stiffer, and the air smelled of rain. She wondered if Anne would be caught in a squall and be late for supper.

She gathered armfuls of now dry laundry from the hedges. Then she bent slowly to retrieve the papers all full of war news and illicit court gossip. Even as she went dreamily inside, thunder split the air and the rain came.

Chapter Nineteen

The last days of summer stretched out into gold September. Three months with child now, Susannah bloomed with radiance and love. Tenn had been with her at their summer house in Burnham for a whole week this time, but tomorrow he would be heading back to oversee the early harvest on his estate for several weeks. Loathe to be parted again, she was going with him, not all the way to the Sloper mansion house called "The Belvidere" at West Woodhay, but to a friend's house a mere four miles away where Tenn could come every night.

Blessedly, they had heard no more from Theo, though Tenn's London contacts said he was still hiding out in the city, no doubt continuing to live well enough on Susannah's summer salary. Colleagues of Tenn's lawyers were covertly preparing a request on behalf of Susannah for a legal separation and, if that went awry, a document to swear the peace against Theo, to at least keep him away from her. The coming months with the eventual birth of their child had never looked more wonderful.

Susannah stirred lazily against Tenn in their big bed and listened to the cooing doves in the ivy-laced eaves. Someday perhaps, she mused drowsily, when all this dratted, precarious balancing of career and scandal and Theo was over, she and Tenn could have a house like this or the one last summer, somewhere outside of London. That way, she could reach the theaters easily enough on the nights she performed; they could be in West Woodhay as often as possible; and the child would not grow up in London fraught with the pitfalls, dangers and eccentric and menacing characters of that city.

Tenn's warm breath stirred her hair along the nape of her neck; the deep tone of his words caressed her even as his hands did. "Are you awake, my love? I couldn't tell. I think we've slept late, and I'm starved."

She rolled over to face him and stretched luxuriously. "Mm, you would be. But I'm the one eating for two, you know, not you."

He grinned at her and moved a hand to stroke, then squeeze a pliant, rounded buttock through her sheer nightshift. "But I didn't say what I was starved for, did I? Did you really think I could be lying like this next to you and be referring to food?"

She giggled and poked him playfully in his hard, flat midsection. "You tease. After last night, I would assume you do mean food and not me."

He leaned up on one elbow to push her down, then deftly skimmed the sleeve of her nightshift until he bared a full breast. "But I love sweets, delicious woman. Damn, but you're so beautiful all tousled like this."

She intended to toss back another clever line of repartee, but his treacherous mouth had already dipped to cover the exposed pink tip of breast. The stubble from his night's beard growth grazed enticingly around the aureole of breast where he moved his head.

His free hand roved the length of her warm, smooth body first along the sliding satin shift and then under it. His softly whispered words came as if from a great distance. "You know, in a few months we'll have to stop this until after the child."

"But not kisses," she told him, "not kisses."

His lips covered hers gently, then with an increasing possessive passion that ignited every nerve and yet made her feel so soft and floaty. Her arms encircled his neck as she held him to her locked in a vibrating, sweeping kiss.

He was always so careful to keep his weight off her now, but she cuddled against him lifting a silken thigh to caress the outside of his muscular, hairy leg while her shift rode up even higher. The bed cover pulled awry, and she felt the cool morning air on her bare bottom. His hand stroked her there even as they both heard a loud noise outside. They lifted their heads and froze.

"Whatever was that?" she whispered.

His muscles had tensed so that he looked suddenly like a carved statue. "I don't know. Almost a shot, I guess. Stay here."

She gave a little sigh of disappointment as he got up, turned away, and hastily pulled on breeches and a shirt. He parted the draperies to glance out the window, throwing a bright slash of sunlight across the bed.

"Nothing by the stables," he said. "Maybe George or someone was cleaning a hunting gun and it went off. I'll just check," he told her and went out in the hall, closing the door behind him without looking back.

Tenn seemed obviously worried, Susannah mused as she sat up to straighten the nightshift he'd pulled clear up above her breasts. Her body ached for him still, and her skin tingled everywhere that he had rubbed his lips and beard: How erotic it was to tingle with Tenn's touch even when he was not here.

Susannah got up to brush the tangles from her hair and wash her face. She really was hungry and couldn't fathom what was keeping him so long. She could summon Anne to help her dress, but she had no intention of not being ready for him if he did come back intending to resume where they had left off.

She stared at the wild woman, in the oval-framed mirror on her tall bureau, who dared think such things. Her topaz eyes looked dazed; her mouth pouted. "Susannah, I can't believe you love and want him so—almost enough to say good riddance to everything in London," the mouth in the mirror spoke aloud.

The woman with the rampant auburn tresses frowned. Almost enough: but not to give up the stage, for that was a passionate love all its own, a separate thing also so integral to her being. In acting, when she became those different people and the audience approved, she was so alive, so very much Susannah. In loving Tenn, she had also found that depth of self, in giving herself to him as the most intimate of audiences.

Tenn's open pocketwatch ticking beside the mirror tiptoed into her contemplation. She lifted it to see the face better. Nine o'clock. Why hadn't he come back up? Perhaps George or someone in the stables had been injured.

She wrapped a blue silk robe around her and stuck her feet into satin mules with wooden heels. From the hall at the top of the stairs she heard nothing below: not Anne, not clattering breakfast dishes, not Tenn.

Holding onto the bannister, she went partway down. "Anne? Tenn?"

Something had happened outside, Susannah thought, and she went down and out toward the back of the house through the kitchen. She fumed at the sight of half prepared breakfast trays and Anne's discarded apron on a stool. Drat everybody for just going out without telling her!

She glanced out toward the stables even as Tenn had. Nothing amiss, though the wide stable door stood ajar. She really should go up and put more clothes on before venturing out. She stepped onto the flat stone back entryway. The morning sun warmed the crisp September breeze. Her first instinct was to call for Tenn or Anne again, but something held her back. She took two steps out and halted aghast as the stable door swung wider at her and Theo emerged with a pistol in each hand. Two huge men followed also with guns, and between them they dragged the trussed, unconscious body of Tenn Sloper!

"No!" she heard herself scream. "No! Oh, Theo, what have you done?"

Insanely, she ran toward them, toward Tenn. Both high-heeled shoes almost tripped her as they flew off. She darted on, barefoot. The breeze flapped her robe away from her legs as she ran. She ignored the guns, the men, Theo. "Tenn! Tenn!"

As she tried to kneel by Tenn, Theo grabbed her by one elbow so hard that she flew in a half circle to face him. "Take your hands off me! What have you done?" she shrieked.

"He's not dead, dear wife, though *de facto*, the bastard should be. Traitors! You're both traitors, and I swear it took all three of us to surround him and knock him unconscious. The others are tied in the stables, and the one called George had to be shot. Now, egads, you behave or it's your precious Tenn who will be our target next!"

She pulled free of Theo and knelt by Tenn's big crumpled form, only to be yanked up again so hard by Theo that her silk robe ripped. "He's only beaten and unconscious right now, Susannah. Stop all this hysterical fussing and perhaps I can be persuaded to leave him merely that, though I swear, justice dictates he pay. And by all that's holy, pay he will!"

"I don't wonder it took you and both of these hired bullies to knock him unconscious. No doubt you even jumped him from behind. I'm going to see to his head wound and bring him around, and then take care of George," she dared, her voice as calm as she could manage through her fear and rage.

"You'll give your lawful husband no more orders ever,

woman! Fife, bring Mrs. Cibber in the house. Watson, see to the squire here, and we'll get on with our delightful little drama."

"No, Theo!" she protested as one huge lout seized her arm and literally dragged her along toward the house to match his huge strides. Then she recognized both ruffians: the same two Theo had hired to ravish her costumes from her tiring room that night at the Drury almost two years ago. This thug's face looked brutish; his eyes leered at her. Susannah's stomach churned. The baby and Tenn! She had to find a way to stop whatever was going to happen here.

"Theo, please. What is it you really came for? More money? If you'll just loose Tenn, I'm certain he'll—"

"No money! I came for justice, wife, justice and my husband's rights long, long overdue. Here, Watson, tie Sloper in that chair. Tie him down well, as he's a raving lunatic even with three men on him."

"Please, Theo, just take what you want and get out," she pleaded, trying to wrap her torn robe back around her. Her knees felt weak, and she fought back the urge to be sick.

"Egads, I will take what I want, my dear, and make no mistake about that, but justice is justice and cannot be purchased at any price!"

"Theo, any concept of justice has been long dead in our marriage. Granted, I have been unfaithful, but in the beginning it was at your express desire and behest. You tried to sell me to the king and then Tenn. You have killed any respect I ever had for you. You took my pride. You not only ignored the legal premarital agreement you signed, but the moral agreement to protect and love a wife. I'm going to see if Tenn is all right now."

"Hold the little chit, Watson, as we planned. Fife, get water to douse our audience with here. Of course, his hands will have to remain tied so we'll simply do without applause, dear wife."

Watson brutally pulled her arms behind her. She cried out once in shock and pain. Theo strutted closer to her, his beady eyes raking her. "Just warm out of bed, I see. May I compliment you on being suitably dressed for this scene you're going to play for us all, Mrs. Cibber."

"Theo, please! I don't know what you're intending, but—"

"Intending. Egads, what you've been best at *ab initio*, my dear actress wife, is what I'm intending. Grand tragedy and farce all combined. Poor Theo Cibber, everyone whispers. His father a great comic genius on the stage, his wife Susannah the new reigning queen of Post-Restoration actresses. I've always wanted to manage your career for you, but no. 'Father' Cibber and Handel advised you; even Tenn Sloper, and his world is the tennis courts of the rich and fashionable, Whig parties at the palace, his vast country estates—and my wife's all too willing thighs. You know what I've thought of, Susannah? Once—once I told you I'd shoot you if you didn't cooperate with Sloper, but now I'd like to shoot you that you have."

His voice rose to fevered pitch; both pistols jerked and wavered in his hands throughout the tirade. She stared aghast, her mouth dry, cold fear making her skin go clammy. Tenn; the baby; her own life threatened by this madman she had never really loved, never known.

Theo's eyes darted away from her as Fife lumbered back into the room with a wooden bowl full of water. He smacked Tenn's face with a slap of the water, then tossed the bowl aside. Tenn sputtered, moved, coughed. His green eyes slit open; he jerked fully awake so hard at the sight of Theo, guns, and Susannah held by an ugly lummox, that he had half lifted the chair off the floor before he realized he was tied to it. "Theo, put those guns away and let her go," he roared. His head ached so fiercely for a moment he wasn't sure if they had shot him or merely hit him.

"Glad you're back with us, squire. Egads, a command performance for a royal audience of one, king of Susannah's love, His Majesty, Tenn Sloper."

"Theo if you harm her, I swear I'll kill you!" Blood pounded through Tenn's veins; he fought so hard against his bonds he was certain they had to burst asunder.

"Fife, gag our audience please," Theo clipped out with a grotesque grin while he ludicrously spun one dueling pistol on his trigger finger. "We have the eminent Mrs. Cibber here on stage today and we simply mustn't have her performance interrupted by fops or rowdies in the pit."

"Theo, I swear to you—" Tenn got out as the huge man called Fife brutally grabbed a handful of copper hair from behind to jam a handkerchief in his mouth. He nearly dry heaved, but then his eyes sought Susannah's: He took in the proud carriage, despite her fear; her regal bearing, however dishevelled and tattered she looked; her trembling lower lip below the fierce, topaz gaze; the slightly rounded belly and full breasts all there for Theo's mere touch. Tenn sat still breathing hard while he furiously twisted his wrists in their bonds behind the chair.

Susannah tried to smile at Tenn, but her lips felt frozen. She nodded stiffly, not sure what message that sent even as Theo's form blocked her view of Tenn. "As actor-manager here, let me explain, my dear wife. The scene: a country *pied-à-terre* where you live with your husband: that's I. The situation: you are passionately in love with and pregnant by said husband—I."

"Theo, please, I beg you—"

"Save it, though, I swear, I do love it when you beg. My angel, I'll let you beg me in this scene a little later. Now, it seems your husband—that's I—has been too busy for you lately, but you're all brazenly desirous for a hot tumble here on the floor of your summer house. So, in this scene, you undress, you seduce me, and I take you here all spread and writhing and begging on the carpet for me."

"Theo! Never, I—" she shrieked, but Watson pulled her arms back so tightly she gasped.

Theo gave a gruff laugh. "No scene? Then no audience will be needed, my dear. In other words, I want that very scene and very prettily too, right here before our watchful audience, or Fife and I here dispense with our audience of one. These pistols are loaded, you know."

He lifted one gun toward the ceiling and shot. She jumped. Her heart thundered. A sifting of plaster spewed down to the carpet. "Egads, let her loose, Watson, as I'm certain Mrs. Cibber is ready to honor us with the scene. She is such a quick study, Father Cibber and Fleetwood always said. Come on now, my dear."

When Watson loosed her, she almost fell. But Theo's other pistol wavered in her direction, and Fife held two guns very close to Tenn's mussed, russet head. Her mind raced as she rubbed her bruised arms to restore circulation.

"Get that torn robe off, my dear," Theo goaded. "We'll begin with that silk nightshift you've been flaunting for Sloper here, and then you can take it off to play the last part stark naked until I decide to favor you with the final—ah—climax."

"Theo, please don't shame me like this."

"Shame you? You, who chooses to desire a man not your lawful husband? Get it off, I said!"

He stuck the gun he had shot off into his belt, then with the other gun in hand, darted forward in one quick motion to strip her torn robe away.

"Let's hear your first line, great actress! A rounded belly to match those full breasts and sweet bottom now, I see. You have ten minutes to seduce me and get flat on your back on the floor with your legs spread for me!"

Great actress, the eminent tragical actress: The words

taunted her, words which had recently been spoken of her or written in the London papers. And now, whatever the cost, she had to try to stop this dreadful, dangerous charade, to protect Tenn and the baby at possible great agony to herself.

"Theo," she said as silkily and calmly as she could, "I'd like to go back to London with you now. I see the error of my ways. I'm ready to go home."

His pistol wavered. His mouth dropped open. Across the room Tenn shouted an incomprehensible warning through his gag and struggled so hard Fife clamped huge hands down on his shoulders.

"You said you'd never live with me again," Theo objected, but his tone was at a new, low pitch. "I'm still living in a tavern on Bow Street."

"It's been a long time, but we can start over. After the baby comes, I plan to return to the stage. Perhaps Tenn will pay us for the child as it would be better if he reared it anyway."

"You're lying, of course, dear little wife, but as you've declared these things openly in front of witnesses and intend to go with me willingly—you do, of course?" he paused.

"Yes. If you leave everyone here further unharmed, I will go with you."

"Egads, I'll take you up on it, although you've absolutely ruined my mood for the lovely little drama I had planned here for the squire. No matter. Justice and revenge shall be as sweet *ad perpetuam* while he thinks of you in my arms every night, spreading those naughty soft thighs and begging to be used as any good wife does. Watson, take her out to the carriage."

"Please, Theo, I'm hardly dressed. I need some garments, and I'd like you to untie Anne in the stables so I can take her along. And please, can we send help back for the man you shot?"

"No! No! Always trying to take over, give orders, have your own way! I'll bring out a gown or two, but we're off now for—parts unknown. Take her out, Watson."

She tried to look back at Tenn, but Theo blocked her view. Thank heavens, she breathed, as Watson hustled her outside, they had a carriage and not just horses, or she'd never have survived the ride. Barefooted, she was forced to let Watson lift her up into the tall carriage. He smacked her bottom through her thin silk shift as she scrambled in away from him.

She felt numb all over, bereft, beaten. But she had stopped Theo's insane plan; she had kept herself from having to submit to his loathsome body, to be publicly defiled before Tenn, and she almost had Theo off the premises. Blessedly, there were no sounds from the house, no shots as she feared at the last moment. Theo clambered in beside her, several wadded gowns in his arms. He tossed them, then his hat, on the opposite seat. He slammed the door behind him, but the carriage didn't move.

"I had a good nerve to castrate the rich bastard, but I thought it might be nice over the years for you to think of him studding other ladies while he thinks of us much the same."

She shuddered as Theo's hand dropped to squeeze a knee. "Egads, my dear, we can't really be off until you show me you're sincere, you know."

"What?"

"I spared you the public scene back there, but I'll not spare you private ones. Just slip that tantalizing silk thing off for me and we'll be on our way. Come on now, just a sign of good faith, or I'll go back in to visit your lover."

Trembling, she closed her eyes to shut out his leering face with the dear stone house in the background that she could see out the carriage window. She slid the nightshift slowly off one shoulder, then the other as the chill September air nipped at her flesh to make her breasts bud. Tears trembled on her lashes but did not fall. If it was the last thing she ever did, she vowed silently, she would be rid of Theo Cibber, as soon as she could escape him here or somewhere!

She darted her eyes wide open even as he reached out to fondle a breast. Then she turned away to be very sick out the coach window even as they pulled away.

The ride back to London was one eternal jolting torment, except for the fact he dared not touch her as she huddled on the seat across from him and moaned occasionally even between the wrenching grips of nausea. By the time they had reached the town of Slough, she was ill enough that Theo decided to stop for the night. Afraid she might try to escape, he sat by her bed all night while Fife and Watson, pistols on their laps, waited just outside the door. She refused to eat as she was afraid she'd never keep it down and hoped Theo would be too frightened to go on with her. Yet the next morning at dawn, he forced her to the carriage and they were off again, driving a roundabout way to London despite her discomfort, since Theo seemed terrified Tenn could be ready to jump out from behind every bush or tree.

Her heart soared as the carriage rattled into familiar London, for if Theo was stupid enough to take her to the Bow Street address he had mentioned, Tenn would have a hint where to look for her. But he was not so foolish: He took her instead to a garret above a tavern called the Bull's Head near Clare Market, where evidently, before his foray to Burnham, he had leased a room and arranged for a guard.

"Get in, in there, my dear," Theo ordered imperiously, gun still in his hand as he pushed her into the dim attic. The wooden ceiling slanted crazily over a dusty floor. The room felt chilled. Immediately, she sneezed.

"There are quilts over there on the big double bed," Theo told her. "Food will be brought to you. Sleep well tonight, for when I return it will be entirely up to you how long you're my guest here. When you've convinced me through deeds, not words, in that bed that you deserve to be my wife, you may emerge into the world again to be delivered of your little bastard and then resume your work on the stage guided by me."

"Where are you going?"

"My dearest—no scolding and no questions. You see, I've read the law. *Flagellis et fustibus uxorem* it is called, and it will be upheld in any court in the land; to wit, 'husbands may give their wives proper correction, a larger control than that by which they are allowed to correct their apprentices or children.' You see, my dear, I have you now, for it's entirely illegal for a lover to attempt to wrest a wife from her husband. So, quite plainly, stud Sloper's choice is to leave you to your husband's proper and legal correction, or to break the law—and then I'll have him too. Egads, sweet, sweet justice."

"Revenge, you mean," she heard herself accuse before she could seize the words back. "Revenge, not even for the fact I love Tenn Sloper as I never could you, but for the fact you're an amoral wretch at heart—if you have a heart at all."

"Don't provoke me, Susannah! I swear, I have nothing to keep me back from tying and beating you, from showing you very graphically on that bed to whom that lush body of yours belongs!"

She turned away to lean on the ledge of a small shuttered window. "Please leave, Theo," she said, suddenly aware her voice sounded very, very sad. "Go to your brothels or bagnios or wherever you seek a haven of your own kind, but leave me alone."

She heard him breathing hard. She could feel he was

searching for some appropriately scathing, scurrilous retort. To her great relief, he spun sharply about, strode to the door, knocked, and went out. Even as the door slammed, her shoulders crumpled and she began to cry.

By the time Tenn had managed to shove his chair across the room to the desk and awkwardly saw through his bonds with a letter knife, the carriage had a huge headstart. He darted to the stables, freed the servants, and sent Anne on a horse to the village to bring back a doctor for George's shoulder wound. He was on his horse Ebony pounding for London in a little over an hour.

But they had evidently not taken the direct route. Desperate, he doubled back and rode another way on his exhausted mount. Finally, of necessity from his pounding head and blurred vision as well as the horse's weakened state, he slowed to a canter to ride into London.

At the Sloper mansion in St. James', closed up and shuttered now for summer with a mere skeletal staff of servants, he cleaned and bandaged his head, forced some food and whiskey down, took a new horse, and was off. It was evening and darkening fast as he rode the length of Bow Street, which Theo had inadvertently mentioned, looking for them or a hired carriage.

It was possible, he reasoned, they had stopped somewhere outside the city and he had actually beaten them back. Hell, he fumed, it was possible Theo wasn't even bringing her back to London at all.

His head throbbed rhythmically with his horse's hoofbeats as he scoured the length of Bow Street clear from Long Acre to Russell Street again, then rode from Gray's Inn Field to his lawyer's house. He knew the law already from lengthy meetings with more than one of the Sloper attorneys: Susannah was little better than legal chattel, like a servant or child under Theo's control, if it came to a court fight. At least, he prayed foggily through his blinding head pain, if it did come to a legal battle, Susannah's servile status, as antiquated as medieval torture instruments, could stir English hearts even as she did on stage—if he could only find and rescue her.

For two days Susannah staged the command performance of her life: She acted meek and contrite when Theo came to visit, but she claimed to be ill and asked him sweetly for more time before they bedded. He fumed and blustered, but evidently awed by her apparent compliance, he did not force the issue. In the long hours he left her alone in the wretched garret, she forced herself to rest, to eat for the child's sake, and to plan. The moment the guards went away, the moment she saw one clear step toward freedom, she would be gone from him for good.

She gazed out the four-inch crack in her window for hours, and even had considered screaming down to the street. But Fire or Watson in the hall would no doubt get to her before help would come—if it would come at all in this vile section of town.

She scoured the room through old storage chests for pen and paper to drop a note, but there was none. So she dreamed of Tenn and wiled away dragging minutes by walking and talking her way through entire scenes of various dramas she had done, playing all the parts to calm her frenzied, growing panic. None of the comedies were humorous now, and to suit her own mood, she became only the doomed Desdemona and Juliet over and over.

It was getting dark but the guard had just brought her a light, she mused drowsily, as she lay on the bed, one arm thrown up over her eyes. The September night was chilly; she wished she had a fire. Fife! Her eyes shot open and she jerked upright. A little fire: The guard would rush in to put it out! She could dash away. Others would surely come.

She strode to the lantern the guard had left just inside her door near a tankard of ale and plate of biscuits. It was imperative she act quickly, as Theo came about this time between his daily rounds and his nighttime bagnio haunts. Each night he had been more adamant about Susannah surrendering her body. She must have this burning before he came to stop her—or to demand she stop holding him off.

Her hands shook as she took the brass and glass lamp across the room. The fire would have to be here so the guard would run clear over to put it out. For lack of anything better, she grabbed a quilt from the bed. Yes, perfect irony, she mused, to burn any bed where Theo Cibber thought to claim her.

She bit her lower lip as she lifted the warm glass chimney from its brass base. The flame was low and sluggish above its little pool of oil. She turned up the wick, then lit one corner of the thin, soiled quilt. It flared lazily, smoked, then spread.

She held it for a moment, then arranged it in a little pile on the floor beneath the edge of the bed where it would leap up to other bedclothes. She crossed quickly to the door and watched it flame brighter. Already she could smell the burned char of material and batting. She hadn't thought about the danger of inhaling smoke in this closed-up place.

Susannah stepped back a little ways from the door. She pictured how she must look, as if she were awaiting the curtain's rise on stage: dishevelled, her hair loose about her shoulders, appropriately and honestly distraught.

"Fire! Fire—a fire! Help me!"

There was nothing from the hall for a moment, and she feared the guard might have actually stepped away. She pounded on the door. "Fire! Fire! Help!"

Voices at last. Running feet in the hall. Voices: Horribly, one of the voices was Theo's!

The door opened, blessedly whisking in some better air. Fife came in, Theo behind. Her timing had been bad; two of them to handle.

"The fire! Oh, Theo, it's spreading to the bed," she wailed and darted into his arms as he blocked the doorway, then just as quickly, when he moved to embrace her, out of them. "Please, Theo, it smells so awful. Please put it out!"

Blessedly, the flames now licked up onto the other bedclothes, and Fife across the way halted, momentarily stymied. "Not enough water," he grunted.

"Egads, beat it out, man!" Theo shouted and took several strides away from her into the room.

Instantly, she darted out into the dim hall, then toward the narrow landing edged with a bannister.

"Susannah!" she heard Theo screech behind her, then his footsteps pounded after her.

She flew down the narrow stairs, one small flight of steps ahead of him at each turn. She forced herself to grasp the rickety bannister at each step down: Too vividly, she recalled the night she'd fled King George at the palace and fallen down the steps. But then Tenn had been there to rescue her, and there had been no unborn child to protect.

"Fire! Help! Help me!" she screamed, praying to draw a crowd and allay Theo's fears she was really trying to escape. On the street, if she could only get to the street before Theo could seize her, perhaps someone would at least recognize her. Someone!

Theo grabbed her arm on the last turn of the stairs even as a crowd of men surged up at them from the ground floor. "Theo, no. No! We've got to get help for the fire," she managed, but she stood frozen in fear, pressed to the wall as Theo's drawn pistol lifted toward her.

"Please—" she gasped out even as the gun went off with

a deafening roar in her ears. She waited for the pain, for something. Two, three, four men crowded close on the narrow steps. She opened her eyes. Her brother Tom had come from nowhere and stood over Theo pressed down on the steps under his spread legs. The smoke of the fire and the gun seared her nostrils. Her eyes darted from face to face. Her younger brother Henry Peter touched her hand to pull her away.

A miracle! Both her brothers! Gratefully, she leaned against him, quite dazed as he helped her down the rest of the steps. Two other men below backed down the stairs ahead of them, pushing the crowd away: young Frederick, one of Tenn's footmen, a tall man behind Frederick with a huge brown beard and mustache, whom she didn't know. Strangely, that man lifted her in iron arms. She was so tired that it felt good. Anyone but Theo—

"My love, we have a carriage down the street," the unmistakably deep, resonating voice whispered.

Her eyes flew open even as he carried her out through a crowd of cavorting people pressing inward. Disjointed voices rattled at her as she stared, shocked at Tenn's familiar green eyes over the beard and mustache disguise.

"See, there is a fire, Jamie, a real one. Told ya!" someone shrieked.

"The rumors are true as true," another voice bombarded her stunned brain. "See, that's the actress Mrs. Cibber, what people heard was being kept here somewheres."

As Tenn lifted her into a carriage and onto his lap, she began to laugh and cry at once. People peered into the carriage like a grotesque audience gone mad. The air was laced with that same awful smell of burning quilt: a marriage gone up in smoke.

"You found me, you found me," she heard herself say over and over as she clung to Tenn against the theater beard. Her shoulders shook with either laughter or hysteria as Tom and Henry Peter clambered into the carriage and they jolted off. The crowd noise roared, then diminished. She was certain amidst the crackle of flames and cacophony of calls she heard Theo's shrill commands.

"I started that fire," she murmured against Tenn's warm neck.

"Yes, my love, you always, always have," Tenn comforted low even as Tom and Henry Peter congratulated each other raucously.

"You're done for good with that bastard now, sister," Tom told her. "When I took his gun away and shoved him down on the steps, he nearly got trampled by the crowd. Pox on him! If you ever face him again, it will be only in court!"

"Which will mean about as much chaos and confusion as tonight, Tom," Tenn put in. "Men, I can't thank you enough. Susannah, the minute I finally found out where you were and asked them to help so it would just look like your family taking you back, they dropped everything. Henry Peter even borrowed this terrible hairy stuff from the theater, which I believe I'll take off," he said, but she only nodded and cuddled against him while he peeled it away and threw it down.

The men's excited voices flew past her understanding. Safe again in Tenn's arms, now she would sleep. Murmured endearments sprang to her lips, but inside her like a boiling cauldron mingled the seething love she felt toward Tenn and only rage toward Theo.

The carriage halted. Tom and Henry Peter patted her back as they climbed out. Still, she sat cradled in Tenn's arms in the dim carriage. It was a little glimpse of heaven.

"You've got to go in, my love," he whispered at last.

"Do I? Where are we?"

"Your mother's in St. Giles. Listen to me, as it has come to this, Susannah. Theo will have no choice now but to raise some public hue and cry to get you back, and we must face up to it."

She sat up and faced him, her hands pressed to his powerful chest. "Hue and cry? In those terrible London scandal sheets he loves to write for? He'll be arrested and imprisoned for debts if he goes public."

"Someone's evidently paid them or he couldn't be seen about untouched as he had been lately. His father, Fleetwood—I'm not sure who."

"You didn't—to bring him out in the open to trace me?"

He actually threw back his big head and shouted a laugh. "No, but it was my next desperate move. It seems Theo talks when he drinks and he boasted to some doxy in Covent Garden that he had you imprisoned above the Bull's Head in Clare Market, and she told someone who told someone who told Kitty Clive who told me."

"Bless Kitty!"

"Indeed, but there's more to tell. Since we may have to construct our own court case and since we're both guilty as hell in the eyes of England's wife-ownership laws, we're going to have to depend partly on the public's aversion to Theo, and bank that our own propriety from here on out will help. So you're staying here at your mother's and I'm going to St. James' and then to West Woodhay, to be seen very publicly there for a day or two."

"But Theo will know I'm here!"

"But we have the guards now, three of them, and they'll be living covertly in your mother's parlor. No, he won't dare abduction again, probably not even a visit."

"Tenn, I can't involve my mother."

"It's too late, love. If it hits the papers or courts, everyone will be involved—everyone, damn it."

His big hand rested gently on her rounded belly, even as his lips took hers. She savored the sweet, possessive caress a moment, then pulled away.

"Tenn, I'm afraid. In court, or in the rabid presses of

London, we could lose everything—our right to be together."

The high brow covered by tousled russet hair crashed over emerald eyes. "Money, power, influence, what is really right about what the cruel law says: We have all those things to bolster us, Susannah."

"And our love for each other and this child," she breathed low.

His voice caught. He sounded as if he could hardly speak. "I've waited so very long to hear you say that, my beautiful love," he whispered. "And—your career?"

Her heart careened to her feet. Energy she had thought sapped from the ordeal with Theo coursed through her. "I'll still have it. I'll protect it, demand it. This year I've been flying so high. Even the papers have extolled me. Surely, in the long run, it won't damage that."

He heaved a deep sigh, kissed her forehead. Then he handed her down into the waiting arms of her mother, who had come out to the street to see why they tarried so long.

Chapter Twenty

In the many weekly or daily papers of London, on the lips of highborn and lowborn alike, the name of the illustrious and beautiful actress, Mrs. Susannah Arne Cibber, became public property and pastime as Theo's law suit against Tenn Sloper approached. The first act of this unfolding drama had begun when Susannah had sworn the peace against Theo shortly after being rescued from abduction and imprisonment. Since the reign of Charles II in the last century, the English courts of law had ruled "a wife might have the security of peace against her husband." But Theo went to the papers with his first flagrant salvo: English law also permitted a husband to restrain a wife of her liberty in case of any gross misbehavior, proof of which, he vowed, would be publicly forthcoming.

The drama stretched out over the autumn months of 1738. Susannah, more heavily pregnant with the child due in February, even dared to go with Anne Hopson for a visit to Reading, the market town closest to the Sloper estates in Berkshire, where Tenn had gone now that the late harvest was in full swing. But when Susannah saw a week-old copy of the *London Daily Post*, which claimed she had left London for a rendezvous to continue her "slide down the Slope of pleasure," on the first of December she went back ahead of Tenn to her mother's house to prepare for the approaching December trial that all London awaited.

To her dismay, as she and Anne alighted from their sedan chairs in front of her mother's house, a gaggle of people stood in the street gawking.

"There she is at last! Mrs. Cibber, is it true you've been living at the Sloper mansion in Berks? A friend of the squire there, a Lady Amanda Newbury, says you probably have. Your mother wouldn't even give us a statement, Mrs. Cibber."

"Please get away from the front door," her voice rang out to temporarily quiet the crush of people, some evidently journalists with pens poised, others merely onlookers. "And I would greatly appreciate it if you would leave my mother alone."

"The child you're expecting, is Mr. Cibber going to publicly claim it when the trial starts in five days?" someone dared to ask.

Gathering her cloak close, she ignored the question, even as rage pounded inside her. "Come in, Anne. We'll send Henry Peter out for our things."

Suddenly a young man from the crowd darted forward with both their parcels and the portmanteau. "Here you are, Mrs. Cibber. I think you're just wonderful on the stage."

"The stage," she murmured half to herself, startled to remember that other precious world in the middle of all this. "I—thank you. Just set them down."

"Mrs. Cibber," someone else asked, "before you go in, do you have any comment on Mr. Cibber's touching new memorial to his dead wife."

Her head swivelled back around even as she stepped up on the threshold of the house and knocked. How could her mother not know she was here and come to open the door, if half the rabble of London did, she fumed silently. Then the words hit her full force. "His dead wife? What monument?" she faltered.

Several people pressed so close she could hardly breathe. One thrust a copy of the infamous *London Daily Post* before her face. Stretched down the top column was a poem in Latin and above it the dark-printed heading of three lines: "Theo Cibber, Gent. Plaintiff, Honors a Faithful Wife—his dear, departed."

"Oh, drat him," she let slip as she stared wide-eyed at it. Several pens instantly scratched away on parchment. The door swept open. Her mother was there with Henry Peter behind. "May I borrow that?" Susannah said. Without looking at any of the vultures, she snatched the paper, and darted in with Anne in her wake.

She fled past the family greetings and Anne's scoldings into the small kitchen at the back, as far away from the curious mob as she could get. The room was warm and smelled wonderfully of something with onions and garlic her mother must have been making. Still in her cloak she had once foolishly thought would hide her pregnancy from prying public eyes, she leaned her elbow on the single window ledge in the room and skimmed the *Post*'s latest reaction to Theo's most recent journalistic endeavor:

> We hear Theo Cibber, plaintiff in the approaching law suit against the well-known Whig Commission member, tennis athlete, and landowner from Berks, Squire William 'Tenn' Sloper, to be heard before the Court of the King's Bench, will be erecting a monument to his deceased first wife, Mrs. Janey (née Johnson) Cibber. His first wife being dead six years now, Mr. Cibber told us he had been lately moved to spend a good fortune on the stone marker in the Church Yard of St. Paul's, Covent Garden, in honor of 'one obedient and faithful wife.' In lieu of Cib-

ber's complaint against Squire Sloper stating that the well-known confidant of Prime Minister Walpole did 'assault, ravish, and carnally know' his second and current wife (damages asked, five thousand pounds), the timing of this touching tribute by Mr. Cibber to his first wife must be admired. His present wife, the famous and esteemed tragical actress, Mrs. Susannah (née Arne) Cibber, is, of course, well known to all London theatergoers.

"Damn the low, vile wretch," Susannah clipped out even as she accepted her mother's embrace and kissed her cheek. "Do you see what he's done now?" she asked them, waving the paper. "It's his old stupidity in public again. He thinks he's admired, but all London is merely amused and titillated!"

"But it will surely help you and the squire if they are all onto his bluster, Miss Susannah," Anne Hopson put in. "Here, let's take off that cloak, shall we?"

"Wait. This terrible memorial poem is in Latin, but I think I can get it. Listen to this, and poor Janey's been dead six years without even a wooden marker to tell the place and her two daughters shifted off and abused by their dear father. I could just kill him sometimes! Kitty Clive will throw as much of a fit over this as I!"

" 'Beneath this stone lies the remains of Janey Cibber'," she translated haltingly, " 'the famous actress; her friends mourn her death. Her virtue was proven and she clung to her faith. In her most sweet memory, Theophilus Cibber, her husband and sad survivor.' "

"James Quin used to call Theo a low toad, and he was right, he was!" Anne put in vehemently.

Susannah sank into a chair and dropped the paper to the floor. "This whole thing is one endless nightmare. Those men out there on the street hanging on my every word just to print more vile lies like these; it's like the night Macklin killed Hallam or the night debtors took the house at Little Wild Court all over again. The trial—I thank God it will be tried without my being called to testify, but it's a living hell anyway. If Tenn were only here, if we were only able to be together."

Her mother's frail arm around her shoulder, she bowed her head as two huge tears plopped onto her hands clasped in her lap. She stared at her knees and her rounded stomach: the baby, Tenn, her whole future on the stage, endangered and attacked. Rage suddenly filled her at the inequity of it all: a world where husbands owned wives and could crush from them all the pride and love they held dear.

She stood as her mother's arm dropped slowly away. "I'll fight him. I swear I will. I don't care if I have to get into the witness box myself, where I'm not bidden. I'm going to win this for the child and Tenn and me—for other women King George's civilized land says can be owned like slaves," she said, and swept out to go upstairs to unpack.

The day of the now infamous Cibber-Sloper so-called "wife suit" dawned dreary and rainy. Since the whole thing was to be handled by teams of lawyers, who would call a string of both upper-class and lower-class witnesses before the Lord Chief Justice, Sir William Lee, in the court of the King's Bench, neither the two principals nor Susannah would be in court. As the papers had been reporting for weeks, "Theophilus Cibber, Gentleman, was suing William 'Tenn' Sloper, Esquire, for 'assaulting, ravishing, and carnally knowing Susannah Maria Cibber, whereby the plaintiff lost the company, comfort, society, and assistance of his wife to his damage of five thousand pounds.' "

Susannah, who had not slept well ever since she'd come back to London and discovered the crowd of ravenous journalists and curious voyeurs on her doorstep, got up at six in the morning, had tea, and paced the small bedroom she slept in next to her mother's. The witnesses' testimonies were bound to riddle her life with grapeshot—even cannonballs: Fleetwood was to be called as well as that scum John Hayes, who had spied on her and Tenn's secret meetings through holes he had bored in their bedroom and sitting room last year. She and Tenn could always go to West Woodhay or take the baby when he was born and live away, but her career was here and she meant to have and preserve and build what she had desired so desperately all those lonely years of dreaming.

As the morning wore on toward nine, when the trial would begin, she still sat alone in her room. Anne had helped her dress, but she had now gone to testify at court, nervous as she was about the whole ordeal. Susannah stood by the window washed gray with running rain. She felt entirely helpless, even though she had seen Tenn at a mutual friend's house last night. He had written that he was back in London, and had sent flowers and a lovely emerald ring. Still, she felt so separated from him by this looming destruction of the trial. If only she could do something but pace and stand about like some weak lamb waiting for slaughter!

She jumped as someone knocked on her chamber door. "Susannah, it's Henry Peter. Would you believe it? Mrs. Clive downstairs to see you."

She opened the door instantly. "Kitty's here in this rain? Today? Downstairs?"

Her brother laughed sharply. "Have I been on stage for four years and can't even make a little speech understood, Susannah? Yes, Kitty Clive—downstairs, rain and all—and to see you. Kitty Clive in the flesh. Now, isn't that a kick?"

"Oh, thank you. I just hope she's not here to argue today, but I am dying to take someone on!"

In the narrow, dim parlor downstairs, Kitty waited where Henry Peter had evidently put her. Susannah could hear Tenn's footman Frederick's voice from the back of the house, but it was really just her and the vibrant, brazen woman she had fought with so over these last few years.

"Kitty, I am pleased to see you. I feel so separated from everyone at the Drury now that I'm taking a year's leave of absence."

Kitty's sharp eyes in the florid face assessed Susannah, lingering without accusation on her rounded belly. Her foot bobbed nervously where she sat in her chair, and Susannah took the one across the low burning hearth from her.

"Cibber, I mean, Susannah—you've never been a real Cibber—I came to wish you poxy good luck today, especially after that low-assed cheap trick Theo pulled last week with that pious piece about poor Janey's maudlin tombstone," Kitty told her in a rush. "I swear, anyone in town with brains saw through it, and Janey's grave will stay as bare as bare in old St. Paul's until I put up a marker there for her myself someday."

"Kitty, you've been a true and faithful friend to Janey, as much after her death as you surely were before, and I'm certain, somehow, she knows it."

Kitty's fierce gaze misted and wavered before their eyes locked again. "I used to detest your snotty blue-blooded accent, your looks, education, and all, Susannah. I guess I just had to tell you before this stinking trial throws dung all over the place that I'm sorry for some things I said."

"Thank you, Kitty, but I've been pretty bitter too. You know, in the beginning I used to watch you all the time before I got my own chance, loving your work on stage, so magical, so way beyond my fondest dreams."

"Dreams. Pox on it, don't go by dreams. You have a real career now, every bit as magic when you're out there in your tragic roles as I am in my comic ones. I'm only sorry for you that it will probably end like this with this bastard trial."

"No! No, I won't let it. Hannah Pritchard told me once how you—you and Janey—fought and clawed your way up to get a chance, and I did too. And nothing on this green earth is going to make me lose what I have—not even Theo Cibber will ruin my career!"

Kitty looked surprised, then she grinned broadly to flaunt her chipped front tooth. She nodded and hit her knee. "I'll tell you what, Susannah. I was going shopping—you know, on a rainy day to cheer myself up and all, as I'm not on tonight—but if you want, I can go to that poxy court, hear what that snake Theo's paid lackeys are saying, and let you know the lay of the land, as the papers will just pervert the whole damned thing."

Now Susannah looked surprised. "You would? I mean, I'm sure I'd hear later how it came out, but I've felt so helpless not being there to really know," she faltered. "None of the three of us is expected to go, of course, as it would make a shambles of everything and, besides, crowds dog me whenever I step out now, and for all the wrong reasons."

"Done, then. I'm off for King's Bench. I wish they'd have called me to testify, as I'd give the bastards a good earful of the truth about Theo Cibber."

She rose immediately while Susannah fetched her damp cape for her. Awkwardly, they walked to the door together. The rain had slackened slightly. For once, there were no people in front of the house gawking; they were no doubt all at the trial.

"Thank you, Kitty, for everything. I hope we'll work again together soon."

Kitty looked as if she would speak, but only patted Susannah's shoulder, flipped her hood over her head, and started off. Then, instantly, an idea hit Susannah like a shot. Anne was at court; her mother was out. She and Kitty were actresses; masters of assumed roles, accents, disguises.

"Kitty, wait!"

She ran after her in the light rain and seized the woman's arm. "Please. Wait down at the corner for me, just down there. I've got a wig. We can stop at the Drury on the way and get milkmaids' costumes or some such. Please, Kitty, I've got to go with you!"

"What a poxy lark! I'll wait. I've got a red wig I can wear," she called after Susannah who hurried back inside. She left a scribbled note to her mother saying she had gone shopping with Kitty Clive. She grabbed the wig, whirled a cloak around her shoulders, and went out, carefully avoiding both Frederick and Henry Peter. True to her word, Kitty stood in the rain on the corner.

By ten, dressed as frowsy Irish street vendors in shapeless theater garments, the redhead and the raven-haired woman, both with their faces hidden by hoods and one obviously with child, tried to enter the Court of the King's Bench through a side door.

"Absolutely no admittance," a plain-faced man rattled his usual lines at them. "There's plenty wanted in didn't get in, journalists and onlookers and such, but they are all waiting the verdict in the front street where the likes of you can too."

"The verdict, man?" Susannah asked in her best Irish brogue. "But it canna be even near over yet."

"Of course not, but with a famous trial like this, they'll wait all day. It's only an hour underway. And you two best hie yourselves back to hawking whatever you sell in the streets," he scolded and slammed the door on them in the rain.

"Drat him!" Susannah shot out. "So close and yet so far."

"Come on back here. Just stick with Kit Clive and

you'll soon learn every place has a back way in and it leads to the same poxy end. Well, come on!"

They darted around to the back alley, and Susannah followed Kitty down a few steps below ground level to a cellar door. "We do look like street strumpets with these wigs and cosmetics and clothes, Kitty. Maybe we'll get tossed out anyway."

"Piss on it! Men seldom toss tarts out however shabbily dressed, the bastards. You'll see."

Susannah had no choice but to follow Kitty through what appeared to be a nondescript storage room stacked with barrels and crates. Brazenly, they went out into a dim corridor, up some stone steps, then up marble stairs with an iron bannister.

They could hear distant voices ringing, declaiming, faintly echoing from somewhere nearby. Susannah's heart pounded; she kept close to Kitty as they opened one door a crack to peek in and then tried another.

"Psst!" Kitty hissed and gestured. "Down here!"

They squeezed onto a narrow balcony overlooking the crowded courtroom below. A man's voice rang out questioning Father Cibber. They could see the scene well from here. Stunned at the reality of what she was viewing when she should not even be here, Susannah froze until Kitty reached back to drag her on. They slid carefully along, backs to the wall, behind an avid crowd of people until they were in a good position to see the elevated witness box below, fenced in by its polished wooden bannister just under the judge's lofty stand. Off to the side, the jury of twelve men sat as if entranced.

"Now, Colley Cibber, as the plaintiff's barrister, I must ask you plainly, sir, what do you know of the plaintiff, your son Theophilus, being married to his present wife?" Theo's lawyer asked grandly.

"I was not at the marriage, but married they were. At the time, I was against the match," Colley Cibber's words carried clearly in the hushed court, only to be followed by buzzing like a thousand bees at that disclosure.

"Why were you against the match, sir?"

"Because she had no fortune, though I must admit when I met and saw her read a part for a play, I knew she would have enough fortune someday through a theatrical career."

"Aha, exactly the heart of the matter we are here to try today, I must say. Then this fortune, which she would earn someday through her skill as an actress or any other, must rightly belong to her husband and her husband only according to English law," Theo's long-faced lawyer, his face nearly hidden in the barrister's traditional curled white peruke intoned.

"Let me say only that one with my background, my knowledge, my varied abilities in the theater, could tell easily she had the looks, the carriage, the voice, the talent, the desire to—"

"Indeed, yes, Mr. Cibber. And is it not her husband who has greatly overseen the ascendancy of her career and ought indeed to triumph from it?"

Kitty elbowed Susannah. "I'd like to have ten minutes alone with that idiot," she whispered. "Nobody, Theo Cibber especially, deserves a damn farthing from any woman's career."

Susannah nodded fiercely, her attentions on the exchange at the front of the courtroom. "Did not her husband take pains to instruct her?" Theo's lawyer was prodding.

"When they married she was a singer, and she was that before she met my son. As to her acting career, I believe I was the person who chiefly instructed her. In forty years experience that I have known the stage, I never saw a woman so capable of the business at the beginning."

Susannah and Kitty grinned at each other like street urchins. Despite the circumstances and the ravenous crowd hanging on every word, Colley Cibber's compliment thrilled Susannah, even as he had that first day he had let her read a part over Theo's peevish protests.

The buzzing arose again and only quieted when Lord Chief Justice William Lee banged his gavel and called for order. Charles Fleetwood was sworn in next. Susannah's legs were tired; she could feel her ankles swelling, but she leaned forward to hear the questioning as avidly as everyone else.

"Fleetwood detests me almost as much as he used to hate Theo," Susannah whispered to Kitty, "ever since I dared to first ask him for my own salary and for a raise for his actresses."

"You've got to learn to be poxy docile with Fleetwood—docile, just like me," Kitty shot back and grinned.

"Mr. Fleetwood, sir, is the plaintiff's wife a good player at your Drury Theater Royal then?" Theo's lawyer was at his carefully worded harangues again.

"Yes, sir. I think her a good player. Our audiences and the town critics certainly do, as anyone who attends the Drury or reads a London paper well knows."

"What advantages of salary did she legally bring her husband?"

"She played three seasons, made approximately one hundred fifty pounds her first year and over three hundred her third; an excellent salary, may I say, for such a young woman."

"Sir, how comes it then that Mrs. Cibber does not play this season?" Theo's lawyer asked while the bees buzzed and someone near them tittered. Susannah flushed hot; her hands dropped protectively to her belly. She should not have come. She held her breath.

"First of all, Mrs. Cibber has oddly radical notions of salary payments."

"Such as, sir?"

"Women's salaries should match those of the male

actors, she has told me on more than one occasion, and she was forever being difficult over her desires to have her salary paid directly to her and not her husband."

"And besides—"

"Besides what, sir?" Fleetwood asked testily.

"Why else is she not performing at the Drury this year?"

"Whatever else is hearsay, since I haven't seen the woman for months!" Fleetwood exploded.

The crowd moaned. Susannah breathed. Kitty whispered something to a man on the bench in front of them and wedged Susanah in so she could sit against the wall.

"One more question, then, Mr. Fleetwood, if you please. Perhaps Mrs. Cibber and thus her husband deserves a high salary if she is as good at her craft as everyone says. Is she not as good a player as any in the house?"

"H'm—well, I can't say that. I can't pretend to determine that. I must say, I have gotten more money so far by Mrs. Clive."

Susannah darted a grin behind her up at Kitty who thumped her shoulder. Whatever comes of this wretched mess, Susannah told herself, she had a friend in the incorrigible Kitty Clive.

The next two witnesses jolted everyone wide awake. First Mrs. Hayes, then her foreign husband, John Hayes, testified about what they knew of the assignations of Susannah Cibber and Tenn Sloper in their house on Blue Cross Street, Leicester Fields last winter. Susannah gripped her hands so hard her fingers went numb as the couple told of their numerous private meetings, of Anne Hopson leaving them alone, of spying on them at Theo Cibber's request through holes John Hayes bored in the wainscotting of the walls of his house.

Kitty's hand was on her shoulder again as she leaned down. "Want to go now? Anytime you say?"

"I—no, I want to know."

The man beside her turned to eye her curiously. "Sh! We all want to hear," he hissed with a fat finger to his lips.

"I have a closet on the same floor, next to the room where they used to sit," John Hayes began slowly in his halting accent. "I bored holes through the wainscot, I could see them very plain. He used to kiss her, take her on his lap. On the twelfth of January, he very angry because she so late, but when she arrived, they make up for it, *si*, practically standing on the hearth, *si*, and then—"

The whole room exploded in sibilant whispers as His Lordship rapped for silence. "Quiet in the court, quiet! There is no occasion to be more particular, Mr. Hayes, as we are not trying a rape here. Proceed with your questions for the plaintiff, Barrister Strange."

"Very well, Your Lordship. Mr. Hayes, are you absolutely certain the man Mrs. Cibber spent all this—ah—privy time with was indeed William 'Tenn' Sloper, Esquire, the defendant in question?"

"Oh, *si*, yes. I dogged them both home in their chairs different days. Her chair take her to Number Twelve, in Little Wild Court, and his chair to St. James' Place. Besides, I did see him at the tennis courts. He so good there too, everyone bets on him."

The crowd roared with laughter, and it took another five minutes for the Chief Justice and bailiffs to restore order, after which an hour intermission was declared. Susannah and Kitty bought gingerbread and milk on the street, though Susannah could eat none of it and ended up giving it to a ragged boy in the alleyway. They reentered through the cellar door to watch the long procession of witnesses continue: Servants from their lovely summer home at Kingston testified Susannah and Tenn Sloper cohabited in house, chamber, and bed; servants from Burnham said the same. But when Tenn's chief counsel, Mr. Sergeant Eyre, with his team of four laywers began to make an opening statement, the entire courtroom shifted to the edges of their seats; Susannah, as exhausted as she was, nearly leapt up with excitement.

"We have heard here testimonies on behalf of the plaintiff, Theophilus Cibber, which have indeed established the following: Firstly, Theophilus Cibber is not responsible for his wife's successful theatrical career, although he was actor-manager of the theater where she acted. Rather, her father-in-law's guidance, her raw talent, and her own sheer will to succeed brought her success. Secondly, we grant Mrs. Cibber and Mr. Sloper were intimate. Are we here to pretend the liaison of a married woman with another man shocks us—that it is rare in any stratum of Mother England? Or, indeed, if it is deemed a punishable crime? No, for the Puritan ghosts have been laid to rest a good century ago. Now, let us look more deeply at this particular case."

He's good, Susannah thought, and breathed a sigh of relief. His voice rose and fell like Tenn's: a deep, believable voice, no doubt the best London barrister Sloper money and Whig influence could buy. A voice resonant, reassuring, like Tenn's—

"The Hayeses and these other domestic servants of various leased households have proved here not so much that there was indeed a liaison between my client and Mrs. Cibber. The defendant admits this and bids me say he loves the lady dearly and their as yet unborn child, which my illustrious opponent tried so hard to have Mr. Fleetwood announce here earlier."

Susannah gasped so loud that the man beside her stared again. The room went wild; the gavel pounded, pounded.

"Again, let us be realistic Englishmen here," Barrister Eyre's voice commanded them to silence. "I say we are trying not Squire William Sloper here, but Theophilus Cibber as a dissolute, neglectful husband, as promoter of his wife's unfaithfulness in any way that would get him money to squander—"

"Objection, Your Lordship," Theo's lawyer, John Strange, bellowed over the chaos. "The trial is clearly against William Sloper, the so-named defendant!"

"Order! Order!" bailiffs intoned repeatedly, while Chief Justice Lee nearly coughed himself off his lofty perch and the crowd quieted.

The man beside her leaned closer, his eyes wide. "I—I've seen you on the stage. I loved your Desdemona," he whispered. "Is it really you?"

"I don't know what you mean," Susannah challenged. Then she added in a beseeching tone, "Please don't say a word."

He nodded, but his eyes annoyingly seldom left her face afterwards. At least with him turned to her like this, she knew he wasn't spreading his discovery, Susannah thought as she concentrated on Tenn's barrister's words.

"But I am merely drawing logical assumptions from the plaintiff's witnesses, Your Lordship, though I do intend to call them back to further corroborate my claims," Mr. Eyre insisted. "Surely, my honorable adversary, Barrister Strange, did not expect us to understand otherwise than that his client, Theophilus Cibber, was not only privy to what went on between Sloper and Mrs. Cibber, but indeed he promoted it for his own financial welfare long after he arranged for informants to keep him fully informed. I call Anne Hopson to the box."

Susannah's heart flowed out to Anne. Her voice broke repeatedly as she answered Mr. Eyre's preliminary questions. But as he led her skillfully into comments about Theo, Anne's voice strengthened with resolve. Kitty leaned forward once again. "I swear, I'd give a year's salary however much Fleetwood thinks he pays me to be standing in the witness box right now. I'd fry Theo for everything he did to you—and to Janey!"

"Yes, sir," Anne was saying. "Mr. Cibber used to refer

to Squire Sloper as moneybags and Mr. Benefit, more than once, he did. Mr. Cibber was then very bare of money as usual—"

"Objection, Your Lordship," Theo's barrister cut in. "The witness is neither to assume nor generalize."

"Objection sustained. Lead on, Mr. Eyre," Chief Justice Lee pronounced.

"Laws, anyway, Mr. Cibber was afraid of his creditors," Anne resumed pluckily. "We would have lost the house and everything much earlier if Mr. Cibber wouldn't have had large loans from Squire Sloper."

"Loans?" Mr. Eyre queried and turned dramatically to face the jury as if, Susannah thought, he were a consummate actor ready to speak his exit line. "And what, pray tell, was the collateral for such loans to help Mr. Cibber hold off his creditors?"

"Why from the beginning, Mr. Cibber forced Mrs. Cibber to be kind to any man from whom he could benefit. It serves him right she actually fell in love with one of them, though she had consented to none of the others, she hadn't!"

Susannah bit her lower lip. The king! Surely, neither Anne nor Tenn's lawyers would dare to bring up the king!

"And so, you've been privy to this liasion from the beginning?" Mr. Eyre prodded Anne.

"I am loyal to Mrs. Cibber, I admit it, sir. But just like all the other servants said, it's no business of ours, since her husband not only consented to it but was satisfied."

Again gavel, voices, and shouting bailiffs created a cacophony that rose and swelled and crashed. Cross examinations and concluding arguments stretched out after that, but repeatedly, Barrister Sergeant Eyre drove home his point: Whatever had been the wrong, Theo Cibber himself had authored and promoted it for his own ends.

At nearly four in the afternoon, the case rested. His Lordship Chief Justice Lee droned on summing up the evidence on both sides, then cautioned the jury to be fair and just. The twelve men withdrew. Apparently oblivious to the two frowsy Irish servant women, people in the balcony mingled and chatted. Kitty wedged in next to Susannah to keep the portly, staring man from being such an embarrassment. Annoyed, the man moved away into the noisy crowd.

"He'll probably tell someone and we'll get trapped up here with curious crowds or journalists," Susannah said listlessly. She felt exhausted now after being tensed up for hours. "We'd better go. We can stand across the street or something to hear the verdict."

"What do you think?" Kitty asked with one dark brow lifted under the flagrant red wig.

"I'm afraid you might be right. Even if Tenn and I should win a victory here, so much has come out that—that, damn it, at least the middle and upper-class theatergoers will be so scandalized I'll never be acceptable again as anything but a novelty in their houses or on their stage! Whatever happens, I'm afraid Theo might have won anyway. Tenn and the babe I may keep, but only because Tenn Sloper's too much of a strong, independent man to care what they say. But my career—"

"Come on, then. Let's go out and wait across the way if it's stopped raining," Kitty whispered, and pulled Susannah to her feet.

But they were barely to the balcony door when the pitch of the crowd noise rose feverishly. People shoved rudely by scrambling for their seats.

"But it's only been a half hour or so, Kitty," Susannah whispered and seized her arm in an iron grip. "A verdict so soon. What would it mean?"

They stood at the very zenith of the courtroom balcony, pressed back against the wall as the jury filed in stone-faced. Everyone stood noisily, then benches creaked again as Chief Justice Lee lumbered in and sat.

"Does the jury have a duly decided verdict to announce?" the Chief Justice asked grandly.

"Yes, Your Lordship."

Susannah closed her eyes so tightly that tears squeezed from between her thick lashes. She clasped her fingers together as if she were praying. Her wig hurt terribly, but she hadn't noticed until now.

"Is there an award to be made to the plaintiff, Theophilus Cibber, gentlemen of the jury, by the defendant, William Sloper, Esquire, of the five thousand pounds damages asked?" the Chief Justice intoned.

"Yes, Your Lordship. We, the king's lawfully appointed jury, do hereby solemnly award for damages rendered—ten pounds."

The courtroom exploded in cheers and hoots, roars and catcalls, and applause worse than any theater first night fun Susannah had ever heard. Stunned with joy and shock, she gaped at Kitty's beaming face, then hugged her. Ten pounds awarded of five thousand sued for: a victory for Tenn and her and for a woman's financial independence from her husband, however they worded it.

"Come on, or we'll get trampled," Kitty's words came to her above the hubbub, and they started away as quickly as they could.

Emotions bombarded Susannah: She felt ecstatic, numb, yet strangely bereft. Her love for Tenn, public; her baby, scandalous; her career, ruined.

Tenn had been right that she would have to face going away, Susannah thought, and suddenly resented him for that. He was leaving nothing behind in London he could not do without. He'd admitted that. He had never desperately wanted something he'd never had, and when he got his chance at last, he had not had to fight to keep it. Sloper money and influence—that wily, brilliant lawyer back there had said it all in more ways than one. He had even sounded like Tenn, reasoned like Tenn. Surely, Tenn had told him what to say knowing her career would be in shambles and she would have to go away with him and leave the stage at last.

She nearly tripped, bumping hard into Kitty's shoulder. "Susannah, pox on it, you're crying."

"Am I? I didn't mean to, only I'm so tired." Outside the rain had begun again.

"Here. Stand right here next to this wall. I'll fetch you a chair somewhere to go on home," Kitty said. She patted her arm and darted off. Susannah, wrapping her cloak about her full midriff, wearily leaned a shoulder on the glazed brick wall of a shop. Across the street, people poured from the courthouse, talking, laughing, and dashing for carriages, horses, or chairs. As someone rushed by, she caught disjointed snatches of conversation.

"—Theo Cibber reaped what he sowed again—scandal—love affairs made fashionable."

"—brazen notions of women's salaries—"

"London's stylish Queen of Tragedy no more—"

In the falling rain, Susannah sobbed aloud. One man stopped to stare, but went on when she turned her back on him.

"—maybe now other women won't live with the fear of being found out," she heard a woman's voice at last as it hurried by in the patter of raindrops.

She sniffed hard and straightened her shoulder. Yes, that was it, just as Bellinda's lines in *The Provoked Wife*, she thought distractedly. And that is my cue as I show my mettle on stage. Aloud she recited Lady Brute's proud lines: "I think fear never kept a woman virtuous long. We are not such cowards neither!"

Kitty's florid face pressed close in the rain jarred her reverie. "A pox on it, Susannah. You're talking to yourself and some are staring. You're getting all wet. Come on!"

Susannah let Kitty help her into a sedan chair. She heard her tell the carriers her mother's street in St. Giles.

The chair lifted.

"Damn. You all right, Susannah? Maybe we shouldn't have come."

Susannah's glazed eyes snagged with Kitty's worried stare. "No, it's fine, dear Kitty. 'Pretend what we will, but 'tis a hard matter to live without the man we love'—or the career we love. And I intend to have both."

Kitty frowned at the recited lines Susannah had made famous.

"Of course," she agreed quickly. "Of course, that's right. And I'll come see you someday soon or see you somewhere." Kitty's voice was swallowed by the noise of the courthouse crowd, then the babble of London street sounds as the carriers moved the chair swiftly away in the rain.

She wouldn't tell Tenn she'd gone to see his clever lawyer dressed like some low-class huckster hussy, Susannah thought. And she wouldn't tell him she could never do without her beloved theater and that she meant to earn it back. For now, this life of public shame and scandal was to be boldly faced and overcome. Still, she bid her sedan chair carriers take her around in back of her mother's house and hurried in the servants' entrance.

Part Four

'Tis madness! and I were unworthy power,
To suffer longer, the capricious insult!
I have distrusted her—and, still she loves.
Gen'rous atonement, that! and 'tis my duty
To expiate, by a length of soft indulgence,
The transports of a rage, which, still, was love.

Osman's words of Zara (Susannah)
in *Zara,* IV. i.
by Aaron Hill

Chapter Twenty-One

For her mother's sake as well as for their own sanity, Susannah moved away to live quietly under an assumed name in a charming old house across the Thames in secluded Kennington Lane. Crowds of journalists, theater *afficionados,* and the merely curious had gawked in windows and knocked on doors of her mother's house until Tenn had managed to spirit her away at night to this lovely sanctuary in the home of a kindly Smith family.

In their rural home, Susannah enjoyed a commodious bedroom and sunny sitting room overlooking a secluded garden with a summer house and grape arbor and a huge apple tree nearly pressed to her bedroom window. There were several adjoining rooms: one for Mrs. Allen, Susannah's temporary lady's maid now that poor Anne Hopson was too easily recognized and often followed; a lovely room for the baby and nurse; and an airy dining room.

As the end of April neared, Susannah knew she had much to look back on with gratitude despite all the tumult. Once she had thought she would never bear a child, yet the birth of her child, a beautiful daughter born on the twenty-sixth of February, had gone smoothly; and she had both her privacy and Tenn's company living here with the Smiths, where she was known as Mrs. Archer.

Yet her heart all too frequently mourned her great loss of reputation and career—her other precious love besides Tenn and her infant daughter.

Bathed in a dappled square of sunlight, which filtered through the apple tree at the south window set ajar to catch the spring breeze, Susannah held her two-month-old namesake, Susannah Maria, whom they had nicknamed Molly. She frequently sang to the child, mournful tunes as often as not, but today she had been silent for the longest time.

"Yes, there, my little love," she crooned. "Daddy's coming and bringing Uncle Henry Peter. My sweet, sweet Molly, mother's pretty girl, I love you so."

It was seven weeks since the child's birth and munificent if private, christening, Susannah mused; time enough that she and Tenn could share their love again every way. The mere thought of that shook her to her very core; despite the fact he'd been so patient and protective their long months, she knew he thought of it too. He wanted her to go away to Naples, Italy, where his sister lived, to have a honeymoon. She knew, of course, there could never be a honeymoon at all as long as there was Theo out there somewhere, full of demonic, threatening hate festering until he exploded in some bizarre attempt at periodic revenge, which now if he ever found Susannah would have a target more vulnerable than just her or Tenn.

Cradling the baby against her shoulder, she stood and paced in little circles around the table in the center of her sitting room. The April breeze sighed through the open window and bounced the huge, blossomed apple tree limb against the sill.

Susannah had dressed and arranged her hair more carefully today than she would like to admit. She had piled her long, burnished auburn tresses in gentle, tumbled curls in the French style of practice *negligence*. The gown was new, a gift from Tenn to celebrate the return of the famous slender Cibber shape. Lilac satin bodice, sleeves, and puffed skirt accented a draped creamy underskirt over paniers all fringed with ruffles of a deeper purple. Heavy, layered lace dripped from tight elbow-length sleeves and edged the squared, low-cut bodice. The shoes were lilac too, with very fashionable long, narrow toes she knew would take some mastering if she were to wear them on the stage.

On the stage, she thought, and sighed as she rhythmically patted Molly's back. The mere thought of her carefully tended lead roles at the Drury going to other actresses pierced her with a raging pain that made her eyes sting with tears. Quickly, she blinked them back as she heard men's voices and heavy feet on the stairs.

Henry Peter, a huge grin on his face, even beat the long-legged Tenn in the door. "Susannah, you look wonderful," her impetuous younger brother shouted halfway across the room, and the baby jerked at the sudden sound.

"Sh, you big lout. Your niece is—was sleeping. Here, you hold her then. Carefully, my doting uncle."

Over Henry Peter's shoulder, Susannah's topaz eyes snagged with Tenn's green-gold stare. As Henry Peter stepped away with Molly held gingerly in his arms, Tenn's gaze went quickly, thoroughly over her, from fashionably toused head to lilac satin toes.

"You look absolutely stunning, my love," he told her in a slow voice so intimate with longing, even Henry Peter looked up and Molly quieted at the familiar voice. Tenn went over to kiss the babe and little Molly gazed up trustingly to seize his big finger in her tiny hand.

"Thank you, Tenn. And may I return the compliment," she smiled, hoping her voice sounded light and breezy. "You're looking fine yourself—for a man who has a daughter this old already."

It was as true as ever. Whatever the man wore, the impact of the powerful physique and magnetic personality was overwhelming. The sensation of swimming in a relentless, pulling undertow Susannah had tried to hard to suppress for months lapped up her thighs and tugged at her self-control.

She kissed Tenn's warm mouth with a mere tantalizing peck, then, still leaning lightly on his blue brocade arm, turned back to Henry Peter. "Let's hear it brother dear. You're the best one I know to tell news from mother and all the rest of it."

"The rest of it?" Henry Peter echoed as he rocked the baby a bit harder than necessary. "Mother's coming to see you Wednesday as usual. Tenn took me to Parliament yesterday and I saw Walpole give a rousing speech against the mounting Spanish War fever. Pox on it, I almost forgot too, James Quin is so distraught without you at the Drury he says he's likely to quit and hie himself for Dublin's stages."

"Dublin?" she said. "Does he have some sort of offer to act in Dublin then?" Her mind raced. If James Quin went to Dublin and wanted her for a leading lady. . . . Drat it, but maybe the Irish did not act like lunatics over fallen actresses, and maybe there they still appreciated 'raw talent' as Tenn's clever lawyer had put it in court that day.

Tenn's big hand on her waist jolted her back to reality. "I see the stars in your eyes, my Susannah, but for a while at least, Naples, Italy will suit you better than Dublin among the wild Irish. I guarantee it," he said, his voice suddenly edged with sternness.

Their gazes locked again, and she drifted in a sun-speckled pool. "Yes, I suppose," she faltered. She wanted desperately to embrace him, to feel his hard chest muscles and angular hips pressed to her, to feel the firm possessive touch of his lips against hers.

"Ah, Susannah," Henry Peter stammered. "Look, the little moppet Molly's gone to sleep. I can take her out to the nurse or something if you want a word with Tenn."

"I'll hold her. She likes for me to," Tenn said and pulled his engulfing gaze guiltily away from Susannah.

"Let's just put her right down here on the settee with this bolster beside her and then have our tea sent up," Susannah put in. "You two just sit over there and Tenn can hold her when she wakes. I'm sure there's plenty of time."

"Plenty of time tonight," Tenn said smoothly, "as I've had an emergency Commission Meeting called."

"Yes, and it takes a while after we get off the ferry from Whitehall Stairs to dodge around and lose any journalists or Theo's spies in the throngs heading for Vauxhall Pleasure Gardens—" Henry Peter chattered on before he caught Susannah's stricken face and halted. "Pox on me, sister. I didn't mean to bring Theo up and all."

She bent over to stare down at the sleeping baby much longer than she meant to. "It's all right," she said low. "He's a fact of life, I suppose. His ludicrous benefit performance at the Covent Garden Theater, supposedly for upkeep of his two poor little daughters he's letting his wild sister Charlotte rear, has made the newspapers again. Isn't it just brazen like Theo to perform each night at Covent Garden after Fleetwood sacked him from the Drury? He'll do anything for laughs and money even when it's all the rage to pelt him with garbage they need to sweep up every night. He never did care a tinker's damn for respectability for the theater if he could earn a penny from it. You know, it's ironic," she mused as both Tenn and Henry Peter stared grimly at her, "but he abuses what I'd like most to be doing."

Susannah halted, stunned she'd spoken the words. Her eyes darted to Tenn; his rugged, handsome face crushed in a frown.

"I think I'll just take my tea and pop out to wait for Tenn in the garden," Henry Peter said in a rush. She knew she had annoyed Tenn, probably hurt him too, but her brother's words, whatever they were, buzzed by her.

"Oh, yes, fine," she murmured as Henry Peter beat a quick retreat.

"I had hoped you were happy—under the circumstances," Tenn said the minute the door closed.

"I have been, of course. Molly's all I hoped for, despite the fact you tease me that I was convinced she would be a son," she said, hoping her voice sounded amused, but his gaze was still fierce.

"I meant in being resigned to not being on the stage," he said, his tone like deepest thunder. "I was hoping you had really accepted the fact I had to publicly declare our love at the trial to defeat Theo and get him out of our lives. But deep down, you would always choose secrecy at any cost if it preserved your career, wouldn't you?"

"That's not a fair statement," she said, her words louder to match his challenge.

"Wouldn't you, my love?" he repeated and was out of his stiff position next to Molly on the settee and at her in one smooth, pantherlike movement.

"Tell me, tell me what you want," he said as he pulled her to him, tipping her head back so she seemed to offer him her lips to kiss. "Tell me the truth!"

His kiss was devastating, sweeping her mind clear of confession or protest alike. She went rigid in surprise at the stunning tactic of possession, then returned the powerful kiss with a fervor she was certain she had forgotten. The kiss deepened, shifting as he slanted his lips hard across hers to plunder her willing mouth with his insistent tongue.

"Tenn, it's been . . . so long . . . quite like this I'd nearly forgotten," she moaned, her face pressed against the side of his sinewy neck when at last he loosed her mouth. She was like a smitten virgin, she chided herself, but nothing could allay the trembling in her legs. His hands roved her derriere through her carefully draped gown, but she didn't care. A wanton curl bounced loose on her forehead, but she revelled in his fierce caress.

"Tonight, Susannah, I'll be back about seven—by seven, I swear it. We'll have a light supper, play with Molly, and put her to bed early, then an early bed for us too."

She feathered little nips and kisses up his throat and along his angular jawline until he moaned deep in his throat and crushed her harder to his hips as if to flaunt his obviously blatant desire for her.

"Tenn, my love, if there were only time now, but Henry Peter—"

"And your maid with that blasted tea. I hope she knows to knock," his words came to her as if he joked, but his face was taut with barely leashed passion.

He tipped her back in one iron arm and dipped a warm, skilled hand into her low bodice to sweetly caress a budded nipple. "I've been so damned hungry for you," he rasped. "I want tonight to be perfect, but just another little taste before I go."

She barely gasped as his mouth covered her again to ravish her mind and senses. His hands cupped her bottom through rustling satin and lifted her up against him. Her arms wrapped around his neck crushed them together in sheer desire. His tongue invaded, plundered, and retreated at last to leave only their mutually intertwined breaths. Reluctantly, he set her back on her feet, then steadied her until she opened her eyes, gilded by the slant of window sunlight.

"Oh, Tenn. I'm going to be begging you to stay."

"Tonight," he said only, but he reached for her again. Even then they heard the obvious rattle of tea tray and Mrs. Allen's distinctive, heavy tread. When she knocked and was bidden enter, all she saw was two doting parents standing over their sleeping infant, but the lovely, young mother had a rosier glow to her fair cheeks than Mrs. Allen had seen in weeks.

The hours of that afternoon dragged for Susannah while she awaited Tenn's return at seven. By five she had changed to a thin green silk summer dress without corset or petticoats or wide-hipped paniers. She had eaten and fed the baby; she felt so invigorated in fierce anticipation that she had run through several scenes from *Othello* while Molly's wide green eyes curiously followed her movements and voice. She felt alert, so alive: If the London public disowned her, they were fickle and not worthy of all she had given them. There was always somewhere to perform like the rural English shires, or Dublin, or maybe even the amateur theatricals among the expatriate elite in Italy that Tenn had told her of. She could feel it. She just knew it. Somehow, somewhere she would again become her most beloved, suffering tragic women who rose above it all!

" 'That I did love the Moor to live with him my downright violence and storm of fortunes may trumpet to the world,' " Desdemona's lines came easily to her from Act I of *Othello*. " 'My heart's subdued even to the very quality of my lord. I saw Othello's visage in his mind, and to his honors and his valiant parts did I my soul and fortunes consecrate.' "

She whirled and postured; the innocent, gurgling Molly was the grandest audience of the century. Rapt in the role, Susannah barely heard the door of the room open, though deep in her mind's eye she pictured Tenn at the threshold. " 'And I a heavy interim shall support by his dear absence. Let me go with him.' "

She spun and crashed from the fantasy of poor, doomed Desdemona to the stark world of shocked reality. Not Tenn, but Theo stood in the gaping doorway, his face contorted in grim smile, his hands clapping, clapping in bitter derision at her performance.

"Theo!" She darted back to stand between him and the

baby lying on the settee. He stood casually, even slovenly dressed before her, with two pistols in his belt. His hair was mussed, his stocking awry, his face mocking.

"Bravo! Egads, bravo! Keeping all your parts alive *par excellence* in exile, are you, my dear little wife whore, Susannah?"

"How did you find me here? How dare you come here after everything!"

He slammed the door behind him and stepped in to pollute her precious sanctuary with his pernicious presence. "It took me weeks—weeks, whore—but last Wednesday your mother was hardly as skilled at darting through the Vauxhall Pleasure Garden crowds as your beloved Tenn is. Speaking of Tenn, I swear, ten pounds is all you brought me, and you owe me thousands, sweet slut. For love of a bawd, ten pounds in court was an obscene pittance of what you owe me for the fact I own you still."

He advanced several strides into the room, his hands resting nervously on the pistols in his belt. Instinctively, she stepped back to lift the baby into her protective embrace.

"Ah, our first born little Cibber," he crooned and leered squint-eyed at the child. "My dear little daughter, so cruelly and unfairly kept from me as were dear, dead Janey's two. But I've come to claim this one at last. And what a little beauty like her mother, but more malleable in my hands over the years *ad perpetuam,* I have no doubt."

"No!" Susannah heard herself shriek. "She's Tenn Sloper's and you know it! All of pious, proper London knows it after that scandalous trial you caused! No, you'll never touch her to ruin her the way you have your other two, poor Janey's little orphans, the way you've ruined my life!" Molly began to cry shrilly at Susannah's raised voice.

"Egads. Of course, if you choose to continue to play harlot for Sloper, that's your business *de facto,"* Theo's voice lifted over Molly's wails, "but I'll claim publicly I've bedded you—before I went to Calais, numerous other times—and that this child is mine. I'm here with my man Fife and you, Mrs. Theo Cibber, may follow me and that child and act like a wife at last, or stay here to rot!"

He reached for Molly even as Susannah dashed back. "No! No, Theo. Help! Help!" she shrilled although she knew the Smiths had gone out. A servant somewhere in the house—there must be someone. The window stood ajar, but the house was set off a good distance from its neighbors' down a quiet lane.

Theo yanked Susannah around so hard she almost dropped Molly. His eyes were glazed, his mouth grotesquely contorted; he smelled of acrid tobacco and gin. "We watched the family leave, Fife and I. We've been so clever, you see. You will come now if you have any wish to accompany this child. If not, I take her only—"

The baby squawled, pressed between their bodies where Theo roughly held Susannah to him. Her thoughts darted, raced, leapt for a stalling tactic until the hour Tenn would come, any fathomable escape to rescue Molly from this demon-possessed Satan and the relentless reaches of his eternal hell.

"All right. All right, Theo. Let loose. You're hurting her!"

"Scaring her a bit perhaps, as her mother never really was. For love of a bawd, *she* at least knows whom to fear, Susannah. And what, pray tell, does 'all right' mean?"

"It means I'll go with you," she brazened, "if you promise not to lock us in some garret and if you promise to get me back on the stage as soon as possible."

She stared unflinchingly at him, level-eyed, to see if he'd take the bluff. He looked at first surprised, then he grinned and shrugged. "Gather your things then and quickly. We'll send Fife back for what we can't carry and sell it all after you and I and our child are safely away."

"Sell it all?"

His narrowed eyes raked her contemptuously. "Surely, you have heard, Susannah," he mocked with a flourish and a swagger of one now drawn pistol. "There's a warrant out for my arrest as of today. My letters to the newspapers have been refused, my rightful profits from the benefit performance of *The Relapse* for little Janey and Betty confiscated, garbage and slime tossed on the stage each time I act, thanks to you and that bastard, Tenn Sloper. Even that fat relic, James Quin, has been challenging me to dangerous duels. Egads, my dear, pack well, for we're off for France 'til things cool down again," he raved on while she stared wide-eyed with her mouth open.

"Your debts?" she asked in an unbelieving whisper. "Debts—again?"

"Again? They haven't been settled by Sloper as they should have been if his Whig money hadn't rigged that trial! His fancy lawyers promise much, but only if I'll sign a document of permanent, legal separation from my lawful wife, you see. I swear, you look surprised, my dear. Did he not tell you? Ah indeed, his clever trial lawyer Eyre has been trying to bribe me to that for weeks, but I won't sign. I prefer to have Sloper's woman—and his bastard daughter—as my own forever. Egads, won't that child stop screeching?"

The thought of desperate escape came to Susannah then; a full-blown plan, the only way perhaps. Theo would never wait an hour here until Tenn arrived, and then there could be gunplay. If there was no one in the house, at least she could run down the servants' back staircase with Molly and down the lane to busy public Vauxhall Gardens to get help—if she could only get Theo out of the room for a moment.

"Theo, the baby's crying because she's hungry. It's time to feed her. She'll wail all the way if I don't."

"On with it then, but quickly."

"I—I'm nursing her," she lied, "and I really need a moment's privacy. It won't take long."

He grinned crookedly, and his eyes raked her so obscenely her stomach nearly heaved. "The lucky little chit to have those lovely bosoms of yours for the mere taking, but soon, in Calais, it will be my turn on every inch of that lovely, ice-hewn body you've never really given me."

"Please, Theo, I don't think I could feed her if you're here now. Only ten minutes. You could go into my room and get some things together."

He looked shaky for the first time, even though his breath reeked heavily of gin. He nodded. "But only ten minutes and the door stays open to the other room. I have pistols, Susannah, and I'm sick to death of your tricks and protests. Quiet that child and hurry. And, my dear, by the way, Fife is on the back stairs, so don't try anything foolish."

He swaggered out and left the door ajar. She heard him immediately rummaging in her room. She stood stunned while the baby cried brokenly. Fife on the steps. But there had to be a way!

She considered barricading herself in the room, but Fife was a giant and stray bullets could be as lethal as aimed ones. Her eyes lifted longingly to the window. The evening sun still faintly gilded the big apple tree, and the breeze rustled the new leaves and white blossoms.

She moved forward instantly, jogging Molly to shush her. She yanked the lace cover so hard off the central table that the bowl of tulips dropped, then spilled on the carpet. She did not wait to see if Theo had heard. There was enough noise coming from ransacked drawers in her bedroom. She pulled the tablecloth around her back like a shawl and knotted its four corners together in front of her chest. Then she lifted the still whimpering Molly into the makeshift sling and retied the knots to pull the child tightly to her, cradled on her bosom.

The window shoved the rest of the way open quietly enough, and the sweet breeze of freedom caressed her feverish face. The tree limb across the window almost touching the house was so huge it would hold her easily. Her thoughts darted ludicrously back to watching her brother Tom climb the apple tree in their backyard on King Street years ago. The one time she'd gone up it, father had punished her and delivered a lengthy sermon on ladylike behavior, but she was done with lectures and punishments now at all costs.

Molly had gone blessedly silent, but Susannah prayed Theo wouldn't come back in the room or call to Fife. She realized too late she would have strapped the baby to her back: The child was as great a hindrance as her dratted long skirt when she sat on the limb to scoot toward the tree trunk. She scraped her hands, hit her head. Her shoes fell off even before she clung to the trunk to start awkwardly down limb by limb. She almost pitched backwards in her haste. Her heart pounded and her arms shook, but she felt invincible and brave in the raging fury of her love for the child and her hatred of Theo Cibber.

One hand still clinging to a limb, holding Molly to her with the other, she dropped to soft grass. Not waiting to retrieve her shoes, she tore out to the front lane praying that Fife really was on the back steps. Barefooted, her hair wild, she lifted her skirts knee-high with her free hand and ran down the lane lined with newly leafed trees.

Amazingly, for when she turned her head to glance back he looked a long ways off, she had heard Theo's shout clearly behind her. He and Fife pounded after her. She could hear them, feel them, sense the cold threat of guns in their hands.

She dashed off the lane through willow trees by the riverbank. Already she could hear the music from the nearby Pleasure Gardens of Vauxhall over her own thudding heart and ragged breathing. Willow leaves whipped her face. She nearly threw herself to the ground as early fireworks exploded overhead like a hundred sparkling gunshots in the darkening sky.

The ferry landing was farther, clear on the other side of the gardens where Tenn would disembark thinking to find her waiting for his love. His love—

They had already lit the colorful Oriental paper lanterns in the trees at Vauxhall to illuminate the fountains and artificial cascades set among the small summer houses, the ornate Baroque, Gothic, and Chinese lovers' bowers, but the grounds looked nearly deserted. Surely, there would be a constable here somewhere among the puppet shows or the displays of waterworks and fireworks; just someone to stand up to Theo if he caught her.

Gasping for air, she darted inside a fancifully gilded Chinese pagoda nearly surrounded by a shallow lily pond. Molly was quiet as if actually lulled by the pounding run or her mother's heaving body. Why were there no people yet, Susannah wondered, as a new wave of panic washed over her. It was late enough for large crowds, and stirring martial music floated from the direction of the main pavilion.

She peeked out and saw neither Theo nor Fife amidst the gentle scene of man-made walks, bridges, and bowers. She started off again moving quickly around the shallow pond where big orange carp glided under water lily pads. But on the tiny Oriental arched bridge, she saw her mistake.

Theo and the quicker Fife rushed toward her from a little copse of trees beyond the pagoda, guns raised. "Stop, or I swear, I'll shoot!" Theo shrieked, but she tore onward into a far cluster of trees on the edge of a gentle valley.

She picked her way down the slope and then went directly upward toward the main pavilion and all the noise. Yes, people's voices, crowd noise like an excited audience; she heard it clearly now. Her feet hurt, bruised by little stones and twigs. Handel's music—she recognized it now! If only the old master could be here, but she had read he'd gone to Ireland.

She heard Theo and Fife thrashing along somewhere close behind her. She slipped to her knees but scrambled on up the embankment. The scene before the elegant stone pavilion exploded at her as she ran headlong from the trees: a huge, fashionable crowd all in a vast semicircle pressing toward an ornately gilded, massive carriage with eight plumed, matched white stallions, four liveried footmen, and two drivers. Behind her, Theo shrilled something even as she recognized the royal insignia painted on the door of the carriage: Frederick, Prince of Wales, had been here, but he was leaving now while all the people crowded and stared.

"Wait! Wait, Your Grace!" she shouted and ran, shoving her way through the outskirts of the crowd as the carriage moved slowly off. Fireworks and shouts drowned her words. Her hair streamed completely wild over her shoulders as she tore on.

A sharp pain sliced through her side; she could no longer feel her legs as she put one foot ahead of the other. She cut across the grass and closed her distance to the carriage as it neared the gates leading to the great Lambeth Palace Road. Others ran too, shouting good wishes and huzzahs to their prince. Like a terrible dream the scene revolved around her: Her feet leaden, her body floating in sheer exhaustion, were not her own. And like avenging demons of blackest nightmare, Theo and Fife were so close behind they could almost seize her!

The prince, smiling under powdered wig, leaned out to wave from the carriage window, his elegant lace cuff under blue brocade gleaming stark white in the growing dusk. Nearly to the carriage, she screamed his name in the exact moment an open hand smacked hard across he face. She fell backward, cradling Molly to her while th baby's shrieks created crazy cacophony amidst all the wil tumult.

"Get up, damn you, get up!" Theo hissed and dragge her to her knees. "It's all right," he told someone. "It' only that she drinks. I'm her husband."

"No, no, you're not!" she sobbed hysterically holdin the shrieking Molly to her. She wanted to explain to th suddenly hushed crowd; to tell them that she'd sworn th peace against Theo; to tell them it had been proved in trial, which had cost her her beloved career, that a woma could not be so enslaved by a man. She gasped for breath shook Theo's touch off violently, and stood. But there behind Theo, loomed the impeccably attired Prince o Wales alighting from his coach with two huge liverie footmen at his side.

"Faith, it really is you, Mrs. Cibber—Susannah?" th prince half asserted, half asked. The crowd melted bac away in hushed murmurs while Theo stood dumbfounded When his hands with the pistols slowly lifted, one of th prince's footmen lunged and knocked him down to spraw flat on his face.

Susannah curtsied with a funny wobble, her achin arms holding the crying baby to her. Only then did sh realize how wretched she must look, all dirty, torn bruised, and dishevelled.

She took a deep breath and chose her lines carefully. "I is I, Your Grace, and in dire need of your assistance, a this man, Theo Cibber, here with the pistols and hi henchman Fife, that tall one over there, meant to do m and my baby great harm."

Theo croaked out a garbled protest, but the prince' footman kicked him once and he went silent.

"And you've obviously been fleeing them here at Vaux hall?" the prince said low and moved a step closer to stud her with eager, blue eyes.

"Yes, but he came to my house to abduct me to France where he is fleeing since there is a warrant sworn for him."

The crowd's murmurings turned to gasps. "Mrs. Cibber, it's that actress, Susannah Cibber," she heard whispered, while several men grabbed the protesting Fife and dragged him forward.

"Then, by all means, let me offer you a ride with me and send my men back across the Thames to London with the—ah—these criminals to Newgate Prison," the prince proclaimed.

She turned away instantly on the prince's proffered arm while Theo screamed muffled invectives, protests, and vile threats. It was like the grandest drama of her life, she mused through the blurred haze of her exhaustion: an audience jolted alive by human conflict; a heroine rescued from a terrible fate with a villain. But when she glanced out the carriage window as Theo was dragged roughly away, her hatred muted to pity for his wasted life, for her own warped, inescapable ambition that had caused her to marry him, and for a career now as shamed and torn as she felt this very minute. The love and rage so mingled throughout her life nearly drowned her in suffocating grief.

"Mrs. Cibber—Susannah," Prince Frederick was saying as his narrow face pressed close. "I can offer you a shelter at Kew House with my family, if you would like. The Princess Augusta and my heir are there as the king has exiled us from his palaces, you know." The prince's imperious, often bitter tone had gone strangely gentle and his blue eyes in the dim carriage were obviously sincere.

"I would appreciate it greatly, Your Grace," she managed low, "if you would bid your driver take me back to the Smith's home down the lane near the ferry landing—Kennington Lane."

While she cuddled the now silent baby to her, he patted

her hand awkwardly and gave his footmen above orders that they were repeated to the drivers.

"That trial last December," he began, then hesitated. "Faith, my dear, are you and Tenn Sloper still together then if you don't mind my impertinence? That is the child?"

"Yes, Your Grace, our child Molly. Yes, we're still together, though Theo Cibber has refused to free me. I tied Molly to me and climbed out the window," she said sounding suddenly silly in her own ears.

"Damn that runty bastard Cibber! Let's face it, English laws or no, there is a point at which one needs to stand up and refuse to take hellish orders. And I ought to know at the price of my father, our sovereign king's continued royal displeasure. Then too, it galls him so now that I am beloved by the masses while he sits behind palace walls with his Hanoverian mistress Walmoden and hears chants of 'German George, German George.' I swear, but the English populace can be cruel to reputations royal or otherwise."

She nodded vehemently, but did not answer. At the foot of the rural lane as the long team of horses and carriage swung around, she saw the house she had only recently fled with Theo at her heels. It looked somehow lonely now, ruined, and faintly foreboding.

"Horseman behind on the lane coming fast, Your Grace," one of the prince's men shouted down to him.

"Tenn," she said, "perhaps it's Tenn. It must be nearly seven."

With Molly still tied against her in the crude lace sling she stepped down from the carriage with the prince's help Tenn! It must be Tenn, a dark form so tall in the saddle so sure and swift above the silhouette of the huge, thundering animal. He was off and she flung herself into his wide arms.

"Susannah! What the hell is all this and Molly—you're

all so—Your Grace!" he shot out and crushed her sideways to him with one iron arm while his other big hand lifted to help her support the baby. "I've been to the theater to have Theo arrested when I heard a warrant had been sworn for him, but he wasn't there, and I hurried out here so afraid—"

"He's been here, Sloper," the prince interrupted, "but Susannah proved tonight she can do a good deal more than act so grandly. She climbed out some window, I take it, then ran with the child over to Vauxhall to ask me to arrest him. He's on his way to Newgate where I hope he rots. Faith, I love to see the underling rise up and claim what's his—or hers!"

"We can never thank you enough, Your Grace," Tenn managed, despite the fact his voice wavered with wasted rage and spent emotion. "Will you not come in to accept our meager hospitality before you set off?"

"No, I've a child of my own to see and a wife—" he said, before he caught his words. "Forgive me, Susannah, but I must be off. Will you two not accept an invitation to visit me at the Dutch House at Kew soon? Rebels and exiles from king's theater or king's family should have a lot in common, I believe."

"How kind of you, Your Grace," Susannah replied before Tenn could answer. "But the squire and I are off for Italy soon to visit his sister, enjoy our daughter, and see the world."

Tenn's green eyes glinted misty in the reflection of the lanterns the prince's footmen were lighting. "Yes," Tenn said low, "we're leaving, but we will be back someday, as I have the estates and Susannah, of course, has her career to rebuild."

"Here?" Prince Frederick questioned. "With the self-righteous, fickle Londoners after all that's passed? Faith, it's a grand goal, I swear, but at what cost?"

Tears she had held back blurred Susannah's vision at

the truth so blatantly spoken. The lanterns now dangling from the carriage hooks darted and doubled. Leaning against Tenn's strong side, she dipped a ragged curtsy to the prince even as Tenn's arms picked her up with Molly held warm against her and carried them into the dark house.

Chapter Twenty-Two

The blue Bay of Naples, Italy glinted crystalline in the autumn sun above the orange tile roof of the villa on the hill. Below her balcony in the enclosed, sunny patio Susannah could see Tenn's sister Margaret Lethieullier read ing a book under a parasol, while one of the Italian housemaids embroidered nearby. Tenn had evidently left their bed before Susannah had awakened to have an early walk with his brother-in-law, the wealthy Smart Lethieullier, as he sometimes did when she slept late. After all, she told herself still languorous with sleep, they had played at amateur theatricals last night where she had presented the Lethieulliers' local English friends with whole scenes from *The Provoked Wife*, and then Tenn had made love to her until long after midnight; therefore, he could hardly expect her to rise at the first blush of dawn.

She tossed her thick chestnut tresses in the sweet breeze from the Bay of Naples where she, Tenn, little Molly, and her beloved maid Anne Hopson had stayed in the gracious home of Tenn's sister for seven weeks after a leisurely jaunt through France and then a voyage south to spend a month in ancient Rome. It was stunningly healthful and beautiful here: Molly flourished; Tenn seemed relaxed, although she knew he longed to go home to oversee West

Woodhay. She understood that well enough, for sometimes she actually ached with an unnameable malady, not for home but for the theaters of home. And so now, as happy as she was from time to time, her greatest amateur theatrical was pretending to be always content.

She leaned over the wrought-iron balcony and waved to Margaret, who had glanced up from her book. Tenn's sister was a dear: passive whereas her younger brother Tenn was impetuous, serious whereas he could be teasing, but as beautifully copper-haired and green-eyed as Tenn.

"Good morning, Susannah. You were wonderful last night. Everyone loved your Lady Brute," Margaret called up to her.

"Your friends are wonderful too, Margaret. They make me feel so at home."

"Shall I have breakfast sent up? Tenn and Smart went out to the carriage house. Remember, we're going to Herculaneum to see the archeological diggings."

"I think I'll just look in on Molly in the nursery and be down shortly."

With a wave and a smile, Margaret went back to her book, and Susannah stepped into her spacious, airy bedchamber off the balcony. Tenn's room was next door, but their balconies adjoined and they spent their nights here in Susannah's bed. That lovely balcony was a perfect setting for Act II, scene ii of *Romeo and Juliet*, she mused before catching herself. Too often lately her mind wandered to the Drury, the stage, her precious roles. She feared she would forget them, that her vast repertoire would dwindle away to nothing. She'd lose how to memorize as Father Cibber had taught her, forget how to invoke the ten expressible passions as Aaron Hill had instructed. Too often, her mind darted off in reverie when others were talking, even talking to her.

She brushed her long, loose hair and discarded her silk robe in the rising heart of the warm Italian mid-morning.

Her nightshift of thinnest gossamer, which was nearly transparent, fluttered about her bare legs and thighs in the breeze from the bay. She opened her leather jewelry case and stared down at the letter again, her hand with hair-brush aloft stopped in midair.

The letter was from James Quin in London, and she'd had it over a week. After months of dissatisfaction without her at the Drury, he was going to Dublin to try his fortunes where her old mentor, George Frederick Handel, had already gone to recoup his. She touched the parchment that she had long ago committed to memory: The Duke of Devonshire, Lord Lieutenant of Ireland, patron of both music and the stage, had invited Quin to Dublin. "The elite of Irish society," James Quin had written, "are starved for culture and have recently constructed several fine facilities to house opera, concerts, and plays." Repeatedly, she had rehearsed the written words in her mind, though she had only dared to discuss them once with Tenn: "Dublin is certain to appreciate you and Ireland is far from your husband's reach, whether he is in debtors' prison or not. The proprietors of the theater royal on Aungier Street would pay you three hundred pounds, and Handel wants you for several parts, including the contralto lead in a new oratorio he has written called *The Messiah*."

She stood like a frozen statue in the sunlit, airy room. Appreciation, patronage, music, drama, her own salary at last—the stage. She jumped as if startled from a dream at Tenn's voice suddenly so close.

"Molly's fine and Anne's taken her out for a bit of air before we leave for Herculaneum," he said.

"Oh, good. I was just ready to get dressed and go down to see her. How long before we go? Margaret said you and Smart were out in the carriage house."

His gaze glowed a shattering green in the sun-laced room as he studied her. "At least two hours or so before we leave, I'd say. You were marvelous last night, and I was so proud. Has it made you sad to act again and so far from home? You know, I feel as if I'm losing you sometimes, just when I really have you safe and to myself at last."

She darted him a quick smile and resumed brushing her hair, deliciously aware that despite his serious tone, he could not stop his eyes from dropping to her body barely hidden by the gauzy nightshift. "Of course I'm not sad," she told him. "I loved acting here for them all last night. There's nothing like an appreciative audience."

"And you're not putting on a little act for me now?" he asked carefully and took a step closer. His voice was that intimate, sensual rasp that stirred her blood so, the blackguard. He knew he could coax any confession, any promise from her, when he looked and talked that way. Icy fingers raced along her spine, and she felt her nipples burst taut to flaunt themselves at him through the thin bodice of the gown before he even touched her.

"Entrancing," he whispered. "You're making me forget what I asked. Let's see, I believe I was wondering if you'd act the part of Siren for me."

"Siren?" She laughed, hoping he would not know how easily he made her legs go all watery like this. "You never did really know your Shakespeare, my love," she teased lightly. "Who, pray tell, is Siren?"

One big hand took her hairbrush from her unresisting fingers and placed it on the dressing table behind her. The reach of his hands nearly spanned her small waist. "Siren, sweetheart, from the story of Ulysses. You never did really know your Homer, my dear. The Sirens were beautiful, naked women who lured sailors to their doom."

She smiled tremulously up at him and lifted her arms to link them behind his neck. "But my love," she said silkily, "you're hardly a sailor and I'm certainly not naked."

"Almost," he said low. "And going to be very soon."

His mouth took hers so gently while he moved his head in little tantalizing circles that the sweet friction on her lips drove her nearly mad. On tiptoe, she pressed up against him, the pert nubs of her breasts grazing his white shirt and, beneath that, the resilient mat of his copper chest hair. His hand dropped from her waist to caress, then cup a soft buttock. She stepped against him harder, full-length, and his kiss deepened to a quest for driving possession.

She raced her open palms along the molded muscles of his back through his thin linen shirt; she moved her hips in mindless, teasing circles against his lean, angular frame. Powerful thighs pressed her soft ones back. His obvious desire for her rubbed fiercely against her soft lower belly, while his roving hands stroked, grasped, and plundered her quaking flesh through the gentle rasp of gossamer gown.

"Oh—oh," she breathed out in a helpless moan as one hand tipped her back and the other fondled a heaving breast. "And what—what about sailors luring Sirens?" she stammered.

"It's not allowed today," he told her low, his handsome face glazed with passion gone darkly serious. "Last night I was, shall we say, rather forceful and brazenly demanding. Today, I'll not force a thing my beautiful, naked Siren doesn't ask for or want to give me."

Her full lower lip pouted, then trembled under his steady gaze. Those eyes greener than spring fields or wild, churning seas beckoned her to their most unfathomable depths. She bit her lower lip and slowly pulled his white shirt up and out of his dark brown breeches.

Susannah unfastened and brushed the shirt back off his big shoulders while Tenn's gaze devoured her. She entwined her long, tapered fingers in his curly chest hair and ran her fingertips down his flat midsection and back up again until he moaned deep in his throat.

"Did the Sirens lure men in broad daylight like this?" she whispered. "And did they kiss them all over to make them beg?"

"You little witch," he moaned. "I adore you. You've already lured me, caught me. Anything you want—"

In a daring move that left them both breathless in the rage of wild anticipation, she skimmed her ribboned straps off both shoulders and pulled the gown slowly down over her full breasts to let it drop about her ankles on the carpet. She unhooked the waistline of his breeches, then stroked his long back, dipping her tingling palms down inside to caress his firm, bare buttocks.

She nibbled on his earlobe, then whispered, "You always touch me here and it drives me wild."

"I too," he groaned. "You know, if you continue all this sweet torture much longer, I'm not responsible for any promises of restraint I break."

In one fluid motion he stepped away to strip off his breeches, stockings, and shoes. At the gaping distance of three feet away, he faced her, legs planted slightly apart with his arms down at his sides in open challenge.

Again, as always since the very first time she'd beheld him in the wavering lantern light at Moll King's in Covent Garden five years ago, she felt transported, wildly swept away into some whirling vortex that had no end.

"Tenn. Tenn, I love you so, whatever happens," she breathed and pressed hard against his iron length to wrap her arms around him. Her open mouth lifted for the kiss; her tongue darted to entice him further. She moved closer, closer between his powerful thighs.

His skilled tongue skimmed the slick inner side of her lips, then flicked over her tongue. She responded fervently in a sort of growing, fiery rage she could not control: She entwined her arms and legs around him and nipped his lower lip in gentle bites.

He laughed once gruffly, then strode to the big canopied feather bed with her still clinging to him. He stretched her out with her hips on the edge of the bed and lifted her shapely legs on either side of his waist. Instantly, he leaned close, driving deeply into her ready warmth.

He rocked against her; she thought she would scream with pure rapture. He held still, rakishly grinning down at her while he felt her wild crest and pull of passion. He lifted one russet eyebrow, the joy of both giving and receiving lighting his rugged features. Again, he set up a fierce pace that exploded vibrant lights before her eyes and swift, soaring ecstasy that pulled her higher, higher into the azure sky over the sunny Bay of Naples out their open window.

He rolled her under him in the middle of the bed. She stared upward at his taut, high-cheeked face framed by loose wild hair all dishevelled. His gaze devoured her as she blushed hot under his thorough perusal. "I love you too, sweetheart, and I have shouted it to the world before myself."

"Oh, did I shout? I don't remember."

He grinned down at her. "Susannah, I'd like nothing more for us to have another child—a son you thought that sweet Molly would be. I know it's early yet, but someday soon. And I want for you very much to be happy and fulfilled."

"A son, yes, to be a Whig landowner like his father," she tried the feeble tease. Still he pressed close, nestled deep within her. She was trying to concentrate, but she could not think.

"A world of landowning Whigs—it seems so far away, so far away, but we're here together now and always, my love," he said.

She gasped and held to him as he moved in her again. More tender, more deliciously sensitive at each plundering thrust, she moved and shifted her hips to meet the brazen challenge of his raging love. She lost control of her thoughts, her fears, her longing, her breathing. For now, nothing else mattered but Molly and Tenn and this sweet, piercing union that could make such joy—that could make a son. Again, she lost herself in Tenn and he in her as they flew aloft to spiral down into the softest sleep of spent exhaustion.

Later, leaden-limbed, she shifted a leg drowsily and grazed a bare hairy leg. "Are you awake, my love—at last?" his deep voice came to her. "They'll be sending up a search party for us if we don't go down."

"Mm, I know. I told Margaret I'd be right down ages ago."

"Everyone believes actresses always sleep late anyway," he murmured, but his voice drifted off as though he wished he hadn't said it.

By early afternoon, they gazed from their open carriage over the small Italian city of Ercolano set like a stark ivory carving on the azure Bay of Naples. Above them to the southeast loomed the twin peaks of Mount Vesuvius all blue-gray in the sun.

"It almost seems too far off to have buried entire cities," Susannah observed.

"They say it literally blew its top off," Tenn's middle-aged, slightly stern looking brother-in-law Smart told them. "It rained down not only gas, pumice, lava, and ashes, but the top part of the mountain itself to bury ancient Pompeii to the south and Herculaneum that's been covered by modern Ercolano. It was only by accident, thirty-years ago in 1709, that a well digger looking for water sank a shaft that struck the ancient Roman stage of Herculaneum nearly one hundred feet underground. That's why I thought you'd like to see it, Susannah. Imagine, a whole theater world buried deep and never to be used again."

She nodded as their driver moved their landau down the gentle slope toward the town, but Smart's last words struck her so she could not find her voice. A whole theater world buried deep and never to be used again, he's said. She knew Tenn was watching her, studying her, but she only shifted her parasol as they turned and did not look his way.

Holding onto the rough board rails, they walked down into the steep tunnel. They were awed to silence at first. Lanterns hanging on iron hooks along the walls cast eerie shadows on faces. Finally, Margaret spoke in the dim crudely excavated room they first entered, her voice echoing strangely hollow.

"They say, Susannah, this was the costume depository. I'm sure it's hard for you to imagine compared to the lovely tiring rooms you're no doubt used to."

"It is really about the same dimensions as the common storage room in the cellar of the Drury. You remember, Tenn, all dusty with rows of gowns, armor, and wigs," Susannah prompted.

He nodded. "It's all so sad, isn't it, my love?" he asked her in a sort of quiet challenge, as if Smart and Margaret were not here at all. "Not only the volcano, but the fact the rich ruling nobility of Naples have plundered this buried theater of all its wealth or marble facing, its statues, and other treasures, yet the skeleton of the structure remains and will not be denied."

Susannah swivelled her head to face Tenn at last; she admitted to herself she had actually been avoiding his probing gaze, his desire to discuss her future, even his protective possession of her for weeks now.

"Yes, it's sad," she said rather loudly, and her voice jumped back at her from volcanic walls. "But someday, maybe soon Margaret said, the Italian government might dig it all out and restore it." Let him think whatever he wanted from that reply, she thought, and turned away.

They moved onward as ghostly voices of other visitors approached behind them. Amidst the forlorn drip of water, despite the numerous defacements and graffiti of the theater's looters on the walls, Susannah's mind repeopled the huge, crumpled, barren stage before them. The roar of the audience across this stretch of broken tiles, the applause and music, echoed yet to her mind down through twenty buried centuries. Masked actors shouted their tragic or bawdy lines to carry through the once vast, open-aired theater. Little Roman girls in the audience, or slave maidens standing backstage with cup or tambourine, dreamed of stepping out to act in the most wonderful and very real fantasy for an approving crowd.

She jerked alert. Margaret and Smart had walked on. Tenn stood close to her, his big hand gently on the small of her back.

"Oh, Tenn. I was just thinking."

"I believe I know about what. Susannah, at this point at least, it would be foolish and downright dangerous to go back. Here in Italy, with my family appreciating and caring for you so, with all the ready acceptance and even adoration by the English people here, I believe you have forgotten how it was."

"I have not. Besides, if I can get back on stage—Oh, I assure you, I wouldn't try to get back at the dratted Drury with Fleetwood there, or if Theo would get out of prison—"

"Drury, Covent Garden, Inns of Court Theaters—what's the difference? Susannah, it's all London with the gawkers, those damned vile newspapers, their ghoulish journalists—and Theo Cibber."

"I can't—I won't run from or hide from him all my life."

"Hell, woman," his deep voice rumbled off the ancient volcanic walls, "he's harmed your career more than once, abducted you, pointed guns at you, and threatened Molly! There is Molly to consider now too, or have you just looked past her as you have me?"

"You? I've never looked past you! Besides, I could go to Dublin to act with Quin and test the waters before I go back home."

"While I stand about backstage like some bodyguard or lackey afraid Theo or his hired henchmen will show up with guns? While I continually desert my aged father and estates? I won't have it. I've rescued you, stood by you all too patiently in your quest to make the stage your life with precious little else getting in the way. Damn it, now there's Molly and maybe a son I pray you have conceived—"

"You mean, all this blaze of passion lately to get me with child so I can't possibly go back?"

"Lower your voice. I hear others coming," he said and seized her satin shoulders in a hard grip. "That's not what I meant at all. Our loving gets more fervent all the time, that's all, and it's nothing else."

"I swear it is. You know, something like that almost makes you sound like Theo!"

"Theo!" he roared. "After all we've been through, all I've done, you dare compare me to that lunatic bastard!"

He loosed her so swiftly she fell back against the wall. His russet brows nearly obscured his dark gaze; his fists were clenched at his sides in a rage she had never beheld from him.

"Go back then, Susannah. Go to Dublin, London, wherever they will have you. Go back to the fickle crowds and prying eyes, to all your beloved roles you evidently take more seriously than those of being my beloved or of being Molly's mother. But I'll take the child and be at West Woodhay, and not only for brief holiday or summer visits from you!"

A small group of curious visitors stepped onto the ruined stage behind them. But Tenn was already stalking away, his broad shoulders and back so stonelike as she stood there stunned. Whispers of the four strangers floated to her, and she quickly turned away to follow down the dim tunnel through which Tenn had exited.

Dazed, she halted, suddenly staring up at the haunted face of a man pressed into the hardened volcanic flow overhead. A statue of some ancient tragedian had once leaned here, or perhaps some fallen god. She trembled. Tears blurred her eyes.

Those harsh, bitter words Tenn had said so long buried inside: Surely, when she spoke with him again, when she explained once more how much she loved him and Molly, he would understand. Tenn had always understood, or else he had bided his time well to get her permanently away.

Her gasped sob echoed in he ears. She must go back. She had to try to recover, to build again what she had fought for so long. Tenn and Molly—he would understand. There had to be a way for her to have it all!

Ruins like this permanently shut away to darken and decay all dead with distant memory: No, no, she would go back and not let it happen to her whatever anyone believed!

Susannah Marie Cibber sat months later in her lovely tiring room at the Aungier Theater in springtime Dublin while her Irish maid Colleen fussed over her expensive new costumes. In the hall outside she could hear the noise of patrons and well-wishers, the elite of Irish nobility, and the crowds of the hearty, sociable Dubliners waiting to see her. And yet she felt so empty.

"Ye're still lookin' a bit peaked, ma'am," Colleen observed. "Shall I fetch a carriage home for ye and help ye change and shoo all the folk away too?"

"I'm just going to sit a few more minutes, first, Colleen. Never mind the carriage. Maestro Handel's promised to stop for me on his way back from his performance to drop me home."

"Such a pace, I say, ma'am. Fifteen roles in but two

months and now this singing role in *The Messiah* next week. I say! Ye must be so proud. If I could only do half of that someday, I'll swear I've died and gone to heaven to see St. Pat!"

Despite her heaviness of heart, Susannah smiled tautly in the mirror at the red-haired, freckled girl. "It's been a long road for me, Colleen, a long road that began way before Dublin."

"And then that first night ye and Mr. Quin opened here as Bevil and Indiana in *The Conscious Lovers*, who'd have thought it!"

"Yes," Susannah mused aloud, "a terrible first night with all those empty seats and barely ten pounds taken in. I was so afraid it was over here for me too."

"But then the Irish, full of blarney maybe, but they know brilliant talent like the papers say, ma'am. So word of mouth just spread and they keep comin' back and comin' back to see Mrs. Cibber, and goin' on in such a rage for you, I say!"

"Yes, it's wonderful how the Dubliners have taken me to their hearts—in such a rage, as you say."

Her voice trailed off and she stared down at Anne Hopson's last letter from West Woodhay, in her characteristic childish scrawl. Molly was walking, Tenn was busy, ever furiously so, at overseeing and local government work, with occasional quick trips to London.

He'd come here to Dublin for a week with Molly, but they'd had the same arguments, and when he had heard his father was ill again, he had gone home. She missed him desperately, missed them all, but as to Molly, he had been right: Daily performances, rehearsals, parties among the adoring nobility of Dublin, was no setting for a toddling daughter. It had been only for a little while, she'd told herself: a few weeks; maybe one short month. Before she realized it, she had sobbed aloud.

"Oh, for the love of St. Pat, what is it, ma'am. I say, ye

gonna be sick?"

Susannah shook her head, tried to smile, then collapsed in shuddering sobs on her folded arms amidst the cut glass bottles and gifts of flowers atop her dressing table.

Commitments, demands—now she had to stay: Calesta to Quin's Horatio; Monimia to his Chamont; the Lady to his Comus; and now a singing role with Handel for at least another month while Molly grew and Tenn raged about West Woodhay, the next estate to where that vapid, rapacious blonde, Lady Amanda Newbury, lived!

She lifted her head to stare at a face ludicrously streaked with tears and blue eye colors. Stolidly, she seized hold of herself and wiped the smears away with a lace handkerchief.

"Colleen," she said steady-voiced to her distraught maid, "fetch me a pen and parchment please."

The girl rummaged in the wooden chest with costume jewelry, then darted back to produce the items. "What is it, ma'am? Ye for a certain be all right?"

"I'm not now, but I'm going to be. I've decided I've got to go home to London to act as soon as possible, but you mustn't tell anyone yet. I love the Irish, but it's too far from my family, you see."

She addressed the top of the paper carefully: To John Rich, Manager of the Covent Garden Theater, London, England.

"Yer family, ma'am. I know ye said yer mother misses ye and is getting on and then that lovely lass of a baby girl and such a handsome admirer, Squire Sloper."

"Yes. I'd be going home to them all, but to act too. In London, I can obviously do both."

"Oh, yes, ma'am, but we'd miss you so. I would for a certain, 'cause I'm always standin' in the wings and watchin' every move ye make out there, every beautiful word ye say to those audiences what love ye so."

Susannah's still teary eyes lifted to Colleen, then she

dropped her pen to reach up to give her a quick hug. "Listen carefully to me, Colleen," she told the wide-eyed girl and took her hands. "You keep your dreams and cherish them. If anyone tries to take them away, you hang on harder and believe in yourself. I believe—I am certain—it is possible for a woman to have it all!"

Colleen looked moved, but puzzled. "All, ma'am? A fine theater career and the singing too like ye do? But I can hardly sing a note, me brother says—"

Susannah loosed the girl's thin hands, surprised she still clasped them and glanced back down at her note to John Rich. "I meant, Colleen, if you ever find a man to really love—" she said, her voice now gone very faint and shaky before the words trailed off. "Look," she said, "I'll ask the theater manager here to give you a reading when you think you're ready, because I don't want you or anyone else falling prey to some theater fop who declares he can get you a chance. You do understand what I mean? Just don't trust anyone who hangs about backstage making promises. You've got to learn to rely on yourself—like I do."

"Oh, yes, ma'am. I say, just like ye do," the girl echoed, her voice awestruck.

Bent over her letter, Susannah wrote the words she was certain could earn her the love of London again—and, hopefully, Tenn Sloper too.

Chapter Twenty-Three

On a sunny knoll overlooking the vast panorama of the fourteen thousand acres of his West Woodhay estate, Tenn Sloper reined in his mammoth black stallion, Ebony. The crisp September day was no doubt like many others that had gilded the rolling hills and wooded dells: Midday sun bathed the seventeenth century stone manor house called "The Belvidere," as well as the barns, stables, gardens, and orchards all set in a half circle of russet and gold trees. In the distance, he could see the model village of houses, school, new church, and almshouse he had overseen so assiduously these months since he had returned from Italy. But today was different; Susannah was a mere sixty miles away in London opening in a Shakespearean tragedy at the Covent Garden Theater tonight.

He spurred Ebony downward past the orchards and onto the gravel road, which led tantalizingly eastward toward London. He ached to wheel the horse about and ride like the wind all the way to tell her he loved her still, wanted her, desired her; but his raging pride held him back. Yet, he'd been much too solitary lately and he knew it: a sort of hard driving, work-obsessed despot sharp to his servants, his aged father, even to precious little Molly. "Damn you, Susannah, but I love you so," his deep voice carried to his ears over the pounding of Ebony's flying hoofs.

Tenn left his horse at the stables and stalked into the big, steep-roofed graystone house he'd once planned to renovate when he had thought Susannah would come to live here. In the next room he heard Molly's sweet chatter with the housemaid Sally, but he didn't go in yet. Besides, it was only about two o'clock and he was back earlier than usual to play with his lovely moppet, so hauntingly a blend of Susannah's face with his green eyes.

He'd sent Anne to be with Susannah for her premiere night, as a sort of futile love gift. Surely Susannah had been back from Dublin several days for rehearsals with a new cast, no matter how many times before she'd reigned as Desdemona in *The Tragedy of Othello*. Surely she'd write soon or come herself, for he had no intentions of breaking down and going to her to agree to be only the second passion of her life. Rage at her, at himself, nearly drowned his desperate, frustrated love.

"Excuse me, squire," his house butler Milward interrupted his thoughts, and Tenn looked up startled to see he'd sat in a chair clear across the room from where he remembered being last.

"What is it? My father's well?"

"Yes, squire, he's just arisen from his midday nap. It's only you've a visitor, a lady who wanted, she says, to surprise you so—"

He leapt up, vaulting past the startled Milward. "Here? She's here?" he shouted as he rushed out into the entry hall heavy with old oil portraits of past generations of Slopers. He neared the big, open front door even as it swung inward—and as blond, buxom Amanda Newbury all in pink satin and lace stood there smiling.

"Oh, dearest Tenn, I startled you, I'm sorry. I told Milward I wanted to surprise you, as I'm sure you needed cheering, and you've been such a reclusive old bear lately."

Her coral lips pouted, and prettily she smiled at him despite his grim visage.

"You did surprise me, I assure you. It doesn't matter," he said half to himself and shrugged. What the hell was wrong with him, he told himself, mooning like some starry-eyed rural lout over a woman: a city actress, the type he'd used to detest, who had snubbed him, defied him, rejected him. Slowly, he lifted a hand to indicate to Amanda she should walk ahead of him into the parlor.

"You see, you do need cheering," she chattered on while he let his eyes roam her back and swinging hips under the swishing pink satin skirt. Hell's gates, he told himself, it had been months he'd denied himself a woman after almost five years of fiercely beautiful lovemaking with Susannah. He'd been certain he should swear off females in general, no matter how the local matrons flaunted their nubile daughters at him; but now, he was not so sure.

"And just how do you propose to cheer this reclusive old bear, as you put it, Amanda?" he challenged low, and studied her flushed face in brazen perusal.

"It's just obvious to me—to all of us hereabouts—that you're free again," she said and smiled, nervously shifting her knees to scoot her rounded hips back on the deep leather wing chair directly across from him.

"Free, Amanda? Free to do what?"

"Don't play games, Tenn Sloper. I know you take my meaning."

"Do I?"

"I swear, you rogue, I hardly came here to spar with you! Free of your—your association with that actress, I mean. Now, don't get all huffy. I've just received *The Courant* by coach from London. You've seen it, of course, and you're obviously still here."

Unaware of the fierce frown that crushed his russet brows down over his eyes, Tenn leaned back in his chair and crossed one booted leg over his knee. "I don't wish to speak of it, Amanda, but if you mean do I know 'that actress' is premiering at the Covent Garden Theater tonight 'after a triumphal reign in adoring Dublin,' yes, I've read that."

"And you're obviously not going."

"Obviously," he drawled, his eyes lowered to her clinging décolletage.

"Then, I'm merely volunteering to be completely—ah—available to cheer you whether she's out of your system or not. After all, now that her husband's being released from debtors' prison, you'd be a fool to get involved in all that scandal again and I just thought—"

His head cleared. His eyes focused. "Released? When?"

"My dear Tenn, you said you read *The Courant*."

"Last week's. I've only read last week's," he said. He leapt to his feet. Theo, loose just when she returned to the London stage—crazed, perverted Theo.

He was halfway up the stairs to the second story, taking them two at a time in huge leaps before he even remembered Amanda. "Milward! Milward!" he bellowed.

He threw on a riding jacket over his work clothes and grabbed his moneybelt and a hat as Milward came tearing in.

"Yes, squire! Squire, what is it?"

"I have to go to London immediately. Go out to the stables. Find George. I need him and two horses saddled. I'll ride Ebony. Tell my father after you get George. Go on!"

He clattered down the stairs two at a time and almost beat Milward to the stables. Amanda had followed him outside, but he barely saw her. Sixty miles: a six or seven-hour ride at a white-heat pace, he calculated. The performance was no doubt at six. As is, he'd barely make it halfway through.

George ran out the door pulling their two saddled mounts. "To London, squire? I swear, I've longed for some sort of adventure. What is it?"

"Later, on the road. Milward, be sure Lady Newbury gets off the grounds and tell Molly I love her—love her," he repeated back over his shoulder as he and George spurred their horses away westward down the gravel road.

For the first time in years, Susannah trembled as Anne Hopson dressed her for the final act. The audience of the beautiful, five-year-old Covent Garden Opera House and Theater had been entirely gracious and warm for the first four acts. So far, her triumphal return to London theater as their once deposed queen should have been pure exaltation. Faces she recognized, some she could link to names, others not, crowded the front seats where she had glimpsed them beyond the row of lighted floats that edged the stage. Prince Frederick and his Princess Augusta were in the house; and the greatest miracle of all, King George II and his German mistress, Sophia Von Walmoden, graced the royal box.

The pure white, almost bridal silken gown and attached train slipped past her head while she stood stock-still to protect her piled, auburn curls. "Laws, Miss Susannah," Anne told her as she fussed over the few tumbled tendrils pulled loose, "this will knock that fine audience wild in your death scene. I never saw such a fine collection of folk: your mother, King George and his lady, the Prince and Princess of Wales—"

"Though still, unfortunately, not speaking a word to his royal father and vice versa," Susannah put in as her mind darted again to Tenn as it had these few busy days she'd been back from Dublin. Though still, unfortunately, not speaking a word, her mind echoed her own words. She was going to West Woodhay to see them, she told herself;

to see Molly; to speak important words whether he wanted her or not after all this raging silence—after she'd failed him so.

"Miss Susannah! I swear, you're crying," Anne's alarmed voice jolted her back to reality. A callboy's shout sounded in the bustling hall outside her spacious tiring room. She could hear even now the distant music from the auditorium between acts four and five of the tragedy.

"I'm all right. I usually have such iron control of my emotions," she said firmly.

"Humph! On the stage maybe. But I've been watching you, I have," Anne put boldly in as she carefully blotted the wet from under Susannah's eyes.

"I've told you, Anne, no talk of real life outside between acts. I've got to get Desdemona ready to be murdered by her husband, Othello, and that's why I'm weepy-eyed," she scolded, cursing herself even then for the lie.

The callboy yelled her name through the door, and she went out into the noisy corridor with Anne two steps behind holding up her white satin train. It was wonderful here at Covent Garden, she assured herself: The management and staff treated her like a queen, and she'd been promised a veritable flow of great roles with Quin and that young, talented actor, David Garrick, whom she had only met once. Still, still, if only Tenn would send word or come to see her; but she knew that he would not.

She halted in the wings, hushed now with anticipation, and surveyed the great sweep of stage. This bright new edifice with its pillared, Doric portico and plush seats was no buried, ruined Herculaneum, she reassured herself. And yet, now that she had this all the way she had always wanted, she knew the cost had been too great.

"Cost—great cost," she heard two green-coated stage attendants whispering about the elaborate, expensive new set the manager John Rich had lavished on the production. He had spared no cost, so unlike Theo who had been so niggardly in everything she'd ever done at the Drury. Poor Theo: His future was a shambles too, for he had ruined his life as surely as she had ruined her own by not choosing Tenn, even at the cost of all this.

A strong arm darted around her waist to give her a lightning quick hug. She turned expecting to see Anne trying to mother her again.

Kitty Clive grinned at her, pressed close between the two flats as everyone waited until the between-act entertainment of singers and jugglers ended. "Bet you didn't think to see old Kit Clive backstage at her rival theater, Susannah," Kitty whispered.

"I'm so glad to see you, Kitty. You know you're welcome here. I was going to call on you, but rehearsals have been a complete rush."

"You're wonderful tonight," Kitty mouthed back. "I swear, I couldn't even get a poxy seat, so I sneaked in the back door to watch from here."

"Back doors—you're marvelous at that," Susannah told her with a wan smile at the memory of Kitty's brazen help at the trial.

"Best of luck, my dear," Kitty said and grasped her hand. "And just remember to give that husband what-for before he kills you!"

Susannah startled until she realized Kitty referred to Othello. What was wrong with her tonight, all caught up in the outside world she had so exactingly shut out in performances before?

Kitty stepped back away and the wings and reliefs were rolled onstage in their grooves to make the doomed Desdemona's bedchamber. I am Desdemona, innocent and tragic, murdered by my husband Othello because he believes I have been unfaithful, Susannah recited to herself to recapture that fantasy world.

The cue of the orchestra's low strains floated to her and

she watched seemingly impassive as the first short scene in which she had no part blurred by. From here she could see Maestro Handel seated in the royal box with His Majesty. Her beloved mentor, Handel, who usually slept through theater was at least awake for her; and His Majesty, evidently pleased enough with his Walmoden, had forgiven her at last.

She could see Theo's roguish sister Char too, all elaborately decked in foppish men's garb in the second row. Poor Char, striving to be what she never could be; but then had not she herself, the illustrious Susannah Cibber, ruined her chances with the man she should have left everything to follow?

Immediately on her cue she moved onstage, as if in a dream, to take her place as the sleeping Desdemona; but her concentration on her character kept wavering to Tenn. And when James Quin as Othello woke Desdemona, Susannah could tell he was stunned that her face glistened with silent tears.

She heard herself speak Desdemona's startled words, but her tears would not stop. Tenn. That sunny day in Italy, that day he'd left her in Dublin, their stolen days in Bath, that very first day so long ago she had known she loved him: she had lost Tenn and killed their love!

"Talk you of killing?" her line flowed instinctively from her lips.

"Aye I do," Othello threatened, and Quin's darkened visage frowned.

"Then Heaven have mercy on me!" she cried.

"Amen with all my heart!"

The audience murmured approval. A few applauded. The lines rushed by. She spoke, she moved not missing a cue, but she was not Desdemona. With all her heart she needed Tenn. Tomorrow at dawn, she'd go to West Woodhay to beg him for a chance. She had wanted desperately to have it all; but Tenn was all, and she had not realized that until now when it could be much too late.

Sitting up on Desdemona's bed, she faced the furious Othello in the blaze of chandelier lights overhead. Her melancholy voice lifted to grace the heights and crannies of the hushed theater.

"And yet I fear you, for you are fatal then when your eyes roll so. Why I should fear I know not since guiltiness I know not—" she got out before the theater exploded with wild applause.

She halted the rest of the speech as the roar of approval went on and on. She and Quin froze like statues, their wide, surprised eyes on each other as the stage nearly reverberated.

"What is it?" she mouthed.

Close up, with his back to the audience, he winked despite his stern stance as the grim Othello. "You just said you're not guilty, and they're telling you they agree. Damn, fickle-hearted crowds content enough to have you driven off once. They've missed you."

She blushed hot as the realization hit her: Tonight, when she so struggled to be Desdemona but could only think as Susannah, the crowd had seen her as herself—a woman greatly harmed and slandered by a trial, a town, and a tyrant husband.

The wild display subsided. She resisted the temptation to rise and stride forward as Susannah to thank them all; for then, she told herself, she would dare to keep walking off the stage, out the door, out of London, to Tenn. Instead, she went on with her following lines.

And then, in the next shattering instant as she faced Othello boldly, the way she had so many other times, she saw and heard it. In the dim wings, a movement, a glint of metal barrel caught in candlelight: Theo's distorted face above a lifted, flaring gun and Tenn behind him lunging forward.

The gun cracked. The shot roared past her, and the acrid smell of smoke drifted. The audience silenced. Othello, his back to the offstage ruckus lifted a pillow to smother Desdemona. She lay back, pressed down for the death scene as Quin's resonant, booming voice rolled over her: "It is too late."

Her mind raced to take it in. Tenn, Tenn here. That was all that mattered whatever the demon Theo had tried to do. Tenn here so close and surely it was not too late!

Desdemona's serving woman, Emilia, berated the cruel Othello for his murderous deed: "Do thy worst. This deed of thine is no more worthy Heaven than thou wast worthy her."

As the wild scene continued over Desdemona's corpse, Susannah Cibber's thoughts rushed on: To have it all, she could renounce this. Molly, Tenn, a life with them; that was the only chance to conquer this consuming rage for love.

Unmoving as Emilia and Othello died upon the green carpet and foot of her bed, she slit her eyes carefully to not be seen even from the royal boxes. Theo and gun were gone as if they had never been and there, tall and russet-haired in the dim wings, Tenn waited. His dark silhouette with big shoulders and dishevelled head blocked out the whole world for her as the final, deafening applause rocked the rafters.

She was offstage into Tenn's arms before the first curtain call, her tears blinding her, her usually melodious voice gone raspy. "I love you, love you so. Please take me away with you forever, Tenn."

"Yes, my love, yes. But we can be both here and there—"

The cast tore her away to make her belated curtain call as the huge curtain rang down behind them. Through glistening tears she took her bows and smiled in purest joy not at their adulation and forgiveness, but at what Tenn had bestowed.

Wherever they were in the theater, people stood. Charlotte sailed her plumed tricorn hat across the stage and screeched for joy. Petite Walmoden tossed a bouquet at Susannah's feet while the king and Maestro Handel beamed, and her mother leaned on her brothers' arms crying. In the wings, Susannah heard Kitty Clive and Anne Hopson cheering raucously.

But she darted back, ran off to Tenn again. His green eyes lit by rampant candlelight glowed to crystalline emerald with his own unshed tears of pride and love.

"I've been so wrong, so selfish," she began as he seized her hands to kiss them adoringly.

"No—I too. A treasure like you is meant to be shared with all England if you'll only be mine at night and all your days you're not on the stage."

"I want to live at West Woodhay, my love."

"We will. West Woodhay and Molly await your—your premiere appearance. And we'll live in London when we need to be here now that Theo's gone."

"Gone?"

"Back to prison—deported. I'll see to that after this murder attempt tonight. We'll hush it up, but he's done at last."

Her slender white arms lifted to link around his neck. "Please, please take me away. I can leave all this if you but ask. Please love me—"

He swept her high into his arms even as James Quin bellowed her name and other cast members called for her to join them on the stage again.

"The king's coming back. The king! The king!" the theater manager, John Rich, was shouting excitedly in the backstage tumult. "Everyone line up on stage now!"

But with his green gaze straight ahead, Tenn Sloper lifted Susannah Cibber in his iron embrace, and strode with her from the theater to the sweet caress of evening air beyond.

Author's Note:

With the exception of such minor servants as Sloper's driver George, every character in this book was a real person who is known about today because his or her life became involved either with the famous actress, Susannah Arne Cibber, or her eminent father-in-law, Colley Cibber.

Susannah was one of the first women in England to, as she put it, "have it all": career, family, and the man *she* loved, a man society said she could not have. Today, fortunately, the Susannah Cibbers of the world are more in evidence.

Over the next quarter century after her glorious return to the London stage, Susannah Cibber reigned as queen of the Georgian theater, specializing appropriately in tragic heroines and strong, long-suffering ladies. David Garrick, one of the great actors of the English stage, was frequently her leading man. When she died, her reputation was so great that London theaters were closed for the night in an unprecedented move, and she was buried in the North Cloister of Westminster Abbey, the church of geniuses and royalty.

Beyond the world of her career, Susannah deemed herself entirely happy also. She and Tenn spent the social-theater season in London and their summers at West Woodhay where Tenn renovated Belvidere Mansion for her. She bore him a son, Charles, in 1750.

From West Woodhay, she wrote her brother Tom: "I am in charming health and spirits and as full of fun as I can hold. Therefore, if you have a mood to be very agreeable with life, wit, and good humor, this is your place!" In London, the Sloper-Cibber town house in Old Scotland Yard was filled with wits and geniuses of the musical, theatrical, and political worlds under both George II and George III.

Although she was never able to divorce Theo, Susannah lived ostensibly as Tenn's wife until her death. Theo spent much of his life in debtors' prison or scraping out a living in foreign theaters. Years later, he drowned off the coast of Ireland in a great storm.

Over the years, Susannah remained close to her family. Although her younger brother, Henry Peter, died at an early age, she and Tom remained great friends as Tom's career also reached the heights: He eventually composed the famous song "Rule Britannia" and the British national anthem, "God Save the King." When Tom deserted his wife and children, Susannah supported them as well as giving continued financial aid to her eccentric sister-in-law, Charlotte Cibber Charke, for the rest of her life.

Susannah, beloved by the English who had turned their backs on her once until they missed her great talents, survived all her trials. During her long stage career, she earned greater respectability for actresses, helped to elevate the stage as a cultural rather than strictly mercantile institution, and promoted important trends such as a more natural, less declamatory acting style. One memorial to her, written by an often critical satirist and political writer, perhaps recalls her personal and professional life of love and rage the best:

Form'd for the tragic scene,
To grace the stage;
With rival excellence
Of love and rage;
Mistress of each soft art,
With matchless skill,
To turn and wind the passions
As she will.

Charles Churchill in *The Rosciad*

CONTEMPORARY ROMANCE FROM ZEBRA

ASK FOR NOTHING MORE (1643, $3.95)

Mary Conroy lived her life as daughter and wife in the safest way possible—always playing by the rules. But this didn't guard her from cruelty and pain. Mary found a new way of experiencing the world as mistress to a very attractive, but married, man. A world where desires and betrayal were separated only by a plain band of gold.

WINTER JASMINE (1658, $3.50)

The beautiful Beth wanted Danny and longed to be a part of his exciting life style, but Danny was tired of the fast lane and yearned for stability. Together they shared a searing passion and searched for a world in between.

SOMEBODY PLEASE LOVE ME (1604, $3.95)

Cat Willingham was every woman's ideal of success. She was smart, wealthy, and strong. But it took Wall Street millionaire Clay Whitfield to bring out the sensuous woman trapped deep inside her, and to teach her the passions that love can bring.

Available wherever paperbacks are sold, or order direct from the Publisher. Send cover price plus 50¢ per copy for mailing and handling to Zebra Books, Dept. 1717, 475 Park Avenue South, New York, N.Y. 10016. DO NOT SEND CASH.

BESTSELLERS BY SYLVIE F. SOMMERFIELD
ARE BACK IN STOCK!

TAZIA'S TORMENT	(1705, $3.95)
REBEL PRIDE	(1706, $3.95)
ERIN'S ECSTASY	(1704, $3.50)
DEANNA'S DESIRE	(1707, $3.95)
TAMARA'S ECSTASY	(1708, $3.95)
SAVAGE RAPTURE	(1709, $3.95)
KRISTEN'S PASSION	(1710, $3.95)
CHERISH ME, EMBRACE ME	(1711, $3.95)
RAPTURE'S ANGEL	(1712, $3.95)
TAME MY WILD HEART	(1351, $3.95)
BETRAY NOT MY PASSION	(1466, $3.95)

Available wherever paperbacks are sold, or order direct from the Publisher. Send cover price plus 50¢ per copy for mailing and handling to Zebra Books, Dept. 1717, 475 Park Avenue South, New York, N.Y. 10016. DO NOT SEND CASH.

THE SAVAGE DESTINY SERIES
by F. Rosanne Bittner

#1: SWEET PRAIRIE PASSION (1251, $3.50)
The moment the spirited Abbie set eyes on the handsome Cheyenne brave, she knew that no life was worth living if it wasn't by his side. Through America's endless forests and fertile acres, their awakened desire ripened into the deepest love. . . .

#2: RIDE THE FREE WIND (1311, $3.50)
Choosing love over loyalty, Abbie can never return to the people of her birth. Even if it means warfare and death, she belongs only to her Cheyenne brave—and will forever share his SAVAGE DESTINY.

#3: RIVER OF LOVE (1373, $3.50)
Through the many summers of their love, railroads are invading Lone Eagle's and Abbie's range, and buffalo are disappearing from their prairie. But nothing can diminish their passion. Together, they will fight the onrush of fate to build their own empire in the wilderness and fulfill their dreams.

#4: EMBRACE THE WILD LAND (1490, $3.50)
The chaotic world breaks in upon Lone Eagle and Abbie on their ranch by the Arkansas River. The horror of the white man's Civil War separates them, but believing in their love they will again share their passionate SAVAGE DESTINY.

Available wherever paperbacks are sold, or order direct from the Publisher. Send cover price plus 50¢ per copy for mailing and handling to Zebra Books, Dept. 1717, 475 Park Avenue South, New York, N.Y. 10016. DO NOT SEND CASH.